PRAISE FOR **THE WR**

'Bump it to the top of your must-read

ᴬᴺᴺᴬ DOWNES

'The pay-off is criminally good . . . As always, Pomare keeps the best surprises until last. Prepare for a late night'

SYDNEY MORNING HERALD

'An expertly plotted mystery with echoes of Lee Child. I raced through it and missed it once I finished'

ALLIE REYNOLDS

'Deftly plotted, pacy and sharply written. Twists come out of nowhere and the high drama of the final few chapters is edge-of-the-seat stuff'

NEW ZEALAND WOMEN'S WEEKLY

'J.P. Pomare has given us another juicy small-town read . . . Expect plenty of twists and turns in this thriller'

WOMAN'S DAY

'Fresh and complex . . . Delivers on every front'

ARTSHUB

'An engrossing tale of investigation and discovery, which will keep the reader fascinated to the end'

CANBERRA TIMES

'The definitive J.P. Pomare whodunnit . . . rich with red herrings and clues alike, drip-fed to the reader, enticing them to unravel the mystery. Pomare is, in every definition, a masterful page-turner'

GOOD READING

PRAISE FOR *THE LAST GUESTS*

'Carefully constructed, chilling and compelling, Pomare's latest creation will keep you guessing right up to the last page'

ROSE CARLYLE

'A twisty thriller with an ending I didn't see coming'

MEGAN GOLDIN

'*The Last Guests* is a brilliantly executed siege set-piece that keeps readers guessing until the final few pages'

GREG FLEMING, stuff.co.nz

'A twisty thriller . . . Possibly not one to read in your rented holiday cottage. I'll certainly be checking the light fittings at my next beach holiday rental'

THE AGE

'This is a rip-snorting read that burbles along on fine prose, from a novelist who while still early in his career has already stamped his mark as a masterful storyteller. An excellent read from a must-read author'

GOOD READING

'Chilling . . . Should keep readers up at night. Pomare knows how to keep the pages turning'

PUBLISHERS WEEKLY

'An emerging master of the taut and fast-flowing psychological thriller'

ARTSHUB

PRAISE FOR *TELL ME LIES*

'Some startling surprises towards the end and a dark, thoughtful conclusion will keep you frantically turning the pages'

CANBERRA WEEKLY

'A thrilling story about a celebrated psychologist who gets too close to a patient'

WHO MAGAZINE

'J.P. Pomare spins another intriguing tale in his latest thriller'

READER'S DIGEST

'A deliciously tight and twisty tale that is guaranteed to keep you turning the pages into the wee hours. If you enjoy your psychological thrillers at a breakneck pace . . . then add this to your wish list'

GOOD READING

'A twisty tale full of suspense and mystery'

NEW IDEA

'*Tell Me Lies* is a fast-paced mystery thriller'

SYDNEY MORNING HERALD

'A whodunnit with a limited number of possibilities that encourages the reader to guess between them'

HERALD SUN

PRAISE FOR *IN THE CLEARING*

'Pomare's books are testament to the fact that he could be one of the most exciting literary thriller authors to come out of the country'

SATURDAY PAPER

'*In the Clearing* is written with a technical aplomb that proves *Call Me Evie* was no fluke'

THE AUSTRALIAN

'Will keep you on the edge of your seat and wide awake until you've raced to the end. A true psychological thriller that is totally believable and which will stay with you long after you've finished'

HERALD SUN

'There are lots of premium crime-fiction offerings this summer, but this bloodcurdling exploration of the asphyxiating grip of a cult on its followers deserves to be at the top of your pile'

NEW DAILY

'A very fine thriller from a very fine author'

NEW ZEALAND LISTENER

'If J.P. Pomare's *Call Me Evie* was a slow-burner of a psychological thriller, his follow-up, *In the Clearing*, is a pared-back firecracker'

BOOKS+PUBLISHING

PRAISE FOR *CALL ME EVIE*

'A whip smart debut from our newest thriller star'

NEW ZEALAND HERALD

'Almost nothing will turn out as it initially appears in this devastating novel of psychological suspense'.

PUBLISHERS WEEKLY (starred review)

'Read this one with the lights on, and keep Pomare on your radar'

KIRKUS REVIEWS

'I felt pure dread reading this book. Enjoyable, exquisite dread'

SARAH BAILEY

'It's a tight, compulsive, beautifully written thriller with echoes of Gillian Flynn, with characters that keep you guessing and a plot that keeps you turning the page'

CHRISTIAN WHITE

'A striking and suspenseful read'

SYDNEY MORNING HERALD

'Will have you guessing and second-guessing until the very end'

HERALD SUN

'A one-sitting kind of book, ideal for readers who enjoy fast-paced thrillers that keep them guessing'

BOOKS+PUBLISHING

'Pick this one up when you have plenty of time as you're unlikely to put it down after a few pages'

DAILY TELEGRAPH

J.P. POMARE
17 YEARS LATER

Who *really* killed the
Primrose family?

hachette
AUSTRALIA

Published in Australia and New Zealand in 2024
by Hachette Australia
(an imprint of Hachette Australia Pty Limited)
Gadigal Country, Level 17, 207 Kent Street, Sydney, NSW 2000
www.hachette.com.au

Hachette Australia acknowledges and pays our respects to the past, present and
future Traditional Owners and Custodians of Country throughout Australia
and recognises the continuation of cultural, spiritual and educational practices
of Aboriginal and Torres Strait Islander peoples. Our head office is located on
the lands of the Gadigal people of the Eora Nation.

 A catalogue record for this
book is available from the
National Library of Australia

ISBN: 978 0 7336 4964 6 (paperback)

Cover design by Alex Ross Creative
All cover images courtesy of Alex Ross, except texture image courtesy of Shutterstock
Author photograph by Leah Jing McIntosh
Typeset in 12.1/16.5 pt Adobe Garamond Pro by Bookhouse, Sydney
Printed and bound in Australia by McPherson's Printing Group

 The paper this book is printed on is certified against the
Forest Stewardship Council® Standards. McPherson's Printing
Group holds FSC® chain of custody certification SA-COC-005379.
FSC® promotes environmentally responsible, socially beneficial
and economically viable management of the world's forests.

For my brothers, Ben, Kent and Leon

There are those who believe in my innocence
and those who believe in my guilt. There is no
in-between.

AMANDA KNOX

I believe that, by and large, New Zealanders enjoy
a fair and effective criminal justice system. However
mistakes are possible in any system that relies on
human judgement.

STATEMENT OF INNOCENCE AND APOLOGY
FOR WRONGFUL CONVICTION OF TEINA PORA
THE HONOURABLE AMY ADAMS
MINISTER OF JUSTICE

PART ONE

Detective Marsden: Can you describe to us what happened this morning?

Jo Blackwell: Well, I woke up suddenly. I don't know how long I was asleep for but it was late.

Detective Marsden: And what woke you?

Jo Blackwell: Well, umm. I heard screams, these animal screams, you know. Like nothing I've ever heard before. I knew someone was in trouble so I sat up and shook my husband, Paul. I figured there was a fight at the house. I didn't want to interfere but the screams were so loud and so desperate that I thought I better call the police.

Detective Marsden: You called the police as soon as you heard the screams?

Jo Blackwell: Well, maybe I waited a minute or two. Paul thought I might have been hearing things, then he heard them too.

I called the Primrose house but no one answered, then I tried Gwen's mobile but she didn't pick up. By that stage, the screams had stopped. But then I heard them again.

Detective Marsden: Okay. And were these screams also animalistic? Or different?

Jo Blackwell: A bit different, just this long, winding scream. I put my dressing gown on and we wandered down the driveway. We can see their house from there, we're directly across, you see. We thought we'd wait for the police because we didn't know what was happening — we didn't want to be seen. After a few minutes, we heard sirens. The fog was really thick but then we saw a man come out of the property. We could sense something was wrong. He didn't seem to notice us but he came out of the gate and went off down the road.

Detective Marsden: Can you describe the man you saw?

Jo Blackwell: We both recognised him. He used to live there — we'd see him on his skateboard some days. He was Māori. He was their chef. Maybe Paul's height.

Detective Marsden: Did you see anyone else? Or any vehicles?

Jo Blackwell: No, just him. Just that man. He was stumbling. Dark patches on his clothes. It looked like he had blood on him. We sort of froze. We didn't know what to do. Then you all turned up and Paul ran over to tell you but by then the chef was long gone.

TK

HUMILIATION: THAT WAS one motivation offered by the prosecution. The shame of rejection drove Bill to stab each member of the Primrose family with his chef's knife. Or *wrath*: he did it in a fit of rage because Simon and Gwen Primrose fired him and withheld his final paycheque. *Lust*: Bill's infatuation with their teenaged daughter grew to an obsession. He'd sent her lewd notes and couldn't live knowing he would never have her. Or a sort of *psychosis*: Bill was drunk, unstable.

Endless possible motives, that's what the prosecution had – and circumstantial evidence for every one of them.

But if you believe Bill's version of events, he simply found the bodies, heard the sirens and panicked, fleeing from the crime scene. Wrong place, wrong time.

I spent three years of my life trying to figure out what really happened and concluded that two facts should have created reasonable doubt:

One, Bill Kareama has experienced lifelong severe asthma.

Two, Bill Kareama did not have an inhaler on the night of the murders.

But the jury did not agree: when he was on trial, they decided the second fact was a lie, or seemed to believe a young man with severe asthma was capable of running three kilometres in twelve minutes *without* an inhaler.

It's true that Bill did not do himself any favours the morning of the murders: at approximately 6 am, he walked 900 metres from his flat, past The Pope sports bar, past the strip of shops and the service station, to the Morning Star bakery on the corner of Pope Terrace. As he made his way there, he placed a shopping bag full of ashes into the skip beside the BP. The ashes were once the clothes he'd worn the night before, when he was at the Primrose house. At the bakery, he sat and ate a mince and cheese pie, staring out into the quiet street. It also didn't help that he'd cut his nails to the quick, shaved his head, bleach-cleaned the flat he'd recently started renting and destroyed his mobile phone.

These acts alone do not make him a murderer but they sure as shit didn't help his defence. Because most people don't really understand what trauma, fatigue and drug-induced chemical imbalances in the brain can do to someone's behaviour. Behaving strangely after exposure to death and extreme violence should not automatically get a man locked up for twenty-five years.

There were other issues with the original trial too, and if Bill ever got his retrial, it's likely he'd win for a number of reasons. First, the question of procedural fairness and sub judice. Second, the police failed to consider, let alone investigate, any other potential suspects. Third, the coercive interview techniques used on Bill.

But there would be no retrial. Today I read that he's now been in prison for seventeen years – it was reported in the Sunday paper, his face on page three, a recent shot from inside. It sucker-punched me, and for a moment, I was back there, meeting Bill. The first thing I noticed about him that day was his size – the photos in the press didn't seem to capture it. He was big but lean. The second thing I noticed about Bill Kareama was his unusual calmness.

As I drive from my parent's place in Rotorua back home to Auckland, I feel the pull of Cambridge. Just like before. I can't shake it. So I take the familiar turn-off and head out toward the house. I park outside a pair of iron gates set within a stone wall bordering the property – the sort you might find in the British countryside. I get out and approach the gates, and feel a funny sort of nostalgia as I look through. I hadn't exactly forgotten, but it had been a while.

A wide driveway splits the generous garden, leading to the expansive frontage of a stately home that looks more country manor than New Zealand farmhouse. The surrounding grounds have long since been sliced and diced, each portion auctioned off, built on. The density of suburbia has closed in on what was once a small number of properties with serious acreage, the surrounding landscape now blighted with townhouses. All that remains of the Primrose estate is that grand old house. Last time I was here, you could barely see the house through the tall grass and unruly hedges. Now it's tidy, well maintained, with hedges trimmed tight and lawns buzzed close. The new owners have done a good job.

I promised myself I'd move on, put this place behind me. So why am I here? Promises are funny like that – once you break one, the rest don't seem to matter.

Tyres on gravel. I turn to see a Mitsubishi Pajero slowing, turning into the driveway. I step away as the gates begin to open and the vehicle pulls in and then stops.

I look in and smile, but the woman behind the wheel isn't smiling back. The window lowers.

'Leave us alone.'

Each syllable is bitten off with such rage I'm struck silent for a moment.

'Sorry?'

'You heard.'

'I was just admiring the ho—'

'I know what you're doing,' the woman says. I see the tiny spider veins in her cheeks, she can barely meet my eye. 'Go on, clear off or I *will* call the police.'

'Sure, sorry,' I say, exhaling. I take one more look up at the house. It's perfect – you could almost believe nothing bad ever happened here. I take my keys from my pocket and walk back to my car. Why did I come here? I shake my head. I remind myself that I don't owe Bill Kareama anything. Not a bloody thing.

SLOANE

ONE ALWAYS REACHES a moment during any good hangover when the only thing you feel like doing is eating a plate of greasy carbs: carbonara, French toast, hot chips and gravy, the greasier the better. I think back over the night, count the drinks off. Four champagnes, at least two chardonnays, one end-of-night Ardbeg with the editor of the *Sydney Morning Herald*, a friend. Then two self-flagellating glasses of water before bed, as if that was going to prevent the inevitable. It did not. As soon as I'd opened my eyes: a strobe-light, throbbing headache, sawdust throat, nausea.

I reach the greasy carb stage of my hangover around ten. I send a silent thank you to Tara, who booked me a late check-out. She's a gem. Last night was the first big night I've had in God knows how long, probably since we wrapped the last season of *Legacy*. I never expected to drink so much but, then again, I never expected to win – only once has the Gold Walkley gone to a podcaster.

I was already a couple of glasses deep when the host, firebrand journalist Des Holder, read out my name. I looked around, checking the grinning faces at my table to confirm I'd heard correctly. They rose, clapping at me like trained seals.

'Me . . . I won?'

I managed to get through my acceptance speech without tears, thanking my producer, Esteban, my assistant Tara, and expressing my deep sadness for the victims of the case. I only hoped that my podcast, my book and my work had helped to shine a light on domestic violence, I said. After that, the real celebrations commenced. Things get a little fuzzy from there.

I hate that feeling of waking with an undercurrent of anxiety accompanied by an enduring queasiness. Now that I think back over the night, I'm worried that the bright lights only served to highlight the platitudes in my speech, that I spoke too quickly or sounded drunk, that I was incoherent or offensively chatty at the afterparty, still running high on the win. Worried that I'd gaffed and said the wrong thing to the wrong person, burnt a bridge, maybe even burnt a few.

I roll over and stretch my limbs in the hotel sheets, my hand finding my phone. I still have the itch to get straight on the social media treadmill: Instagram, Facebook, X, refresh each, do it all over again, but I've been off social media for a few months. We're all addicts of some sort these days but I've managed to kick this particular habit. I have other good old-fashioned vices instead.

But email is harder to avoid – my work depends on it, after all. I open my inbox, contemplating ordering room-service – *do they even do breakfast this late?* I find a stream of messages: lots of well-wishers, though Tara has likely already filtered out today's batch of crazies spewing their hate. Who would have thought domestic violence was such a combustible subject in this country? I guess our role in bringing charges to a former rugby league star over the disappearance of his wife didn't help.

A journalist friend has emailed me, with the subject line, 'Remember this case?' There's a link to an article in the body of the email. I scan the article – it's familiar. In fact, I remember the crime from when it happened. It was in the media in Australia too.

A private chef stabbed each member of the family he had worked for. Now, the article says, seventeen years of the chef's prison sentence have been served and there have been calls over the years for a retrial. He's not once acknowledged his guilt and the kicker is: if he had, he would be eligible for parole and probably be a free man now.

This could be something. But not for us. There's a lot of story here, lots to investigate, but it doesn't have the feel of a *Legacy* case. I close the window and open another email, this time from my producer. He wants me to look at the case of a family who disappeared without a trace in Adelaide in the late nineties. After reading for five minutes, I put my phone down, reminding myself that today is not a work day. Today is a recovery day, a day of gratitude. Which is hard when your brain is in a bench vice as it slowly tightens. The next project can wait.

'Room service,' the voice comes down the phone line.

'Hi, yes, can I get the eggs benedict and a double espresso to room 903?'

'Sure. It won't be too long.'

'And can I add a hash brown and a Bloody Mary?' Somewhere in Melbourne my PT is cringing.

'Of course.'

I drag myself to the bathroom, where the mirror kindly reminds me I forgot to remove my make-up before I fell asleep. I slurp a few mouthfuls of water straight from the tap and splash my face, before grabbing my laptop from the chair, and falling back between the sheets.

I pick up where I left off, partway through a trashy dating show, ice-cream for the brain, on Netflix. Only half-watching, I grab my phone, and begin to double-screen, vanity-searching my own name on Google. Call me a masochist but I can't help seeking out the worst things people have said about me online. I am not disappointed.

For instance, did you know that *Sloane Abbott is the rancid afterbirth stain of gender studies bullshit and millennial self-obsession?* Did you also know that *Sloane Abbott reeks of low IQ Reddit leftard hypocrisy?* Did you know that, despite assorted MRA rape fantasies, I'm *actually mid, a low-quality woman, without make-up a five at best?* I'm a *grifter who appeals only to middle-class white feminist guilt,* but another poster insists I'm *not evil, actually cute despite the woke posturing.* What a charmer.

No one took issue with my podcasts until I made the fatal error of pointing out the domestic abuse rates in this country, until I pointed out the failure of police to protect women from ex-partners – that was the catalyst for the violent sexual fantasies and harassment. It didn't help when I spoke out against rape culture in Canberra, our nation's proud capital.

One hit a bit further down the list is a link to a popular feminist forum. My people, I think, at least some have positive things to say about me.

SLOANE ABBOTT, THE QUEEN OF PERFORMATIVE WHITE FEMINISM

Shit. Don't click, don't click, don't click. I click, of course I click, despite the acid filling my chest.

So here's why we need to stop supporting this 'trojan horse' feminist:

1. She has recorded four of the biggest podcast series in Australia's history, has won journalism awards and written countless articles commenting on criminal cases. How many of these various journalistic endeavours have focused on a crime with a non-white victim? You guessed it: 0. Google: Missing White Woman Syndrome.

A pang of anger. Who the fuck is this person?

2. She is the definition of privilege. Her father was a famous photojournalist (nepo baby), she grew up in Kew (white, privileged, elite), attended private school and received a scholarship (that could have gone to a more needy/disadvantaged/marginalised student) to Monash University. She is white, able-bodied, conventionally attractive, wealthy and does nothing to lift up less advantaged people.

3. Look at the company she keeps. See links for photos with any number of prominent right-wing voices. Extra points for spotting the anti-trans activist.

4. Dating history. I couldn't find much, but on her socials and anecdotally, she has only ever dated white men. No women, no BIPOC. It's fine to be straight, babe, but try harder next time to hide your racial bias. She probably believes she's a good little intersectional feminist because the cognitive dissonance would be crushing, but the fact is she doesn't find black or brown men attractive enough to date.

Bile builds in my gut. This is not how feminism works. You shouldn't need to be perfect to help. I hate this person, their all-or-nothing view of the world. Combing through my entire life, dating history and career for imperfections. They're painting me to be something I'm not – frankly, the diversity of my dating history would put the UN general assembly to shame.

I let my breath out, close my eyes for a moment and force big gulps of air into my lungs.

This is, in the face of some stiff competition, the most crushing thing I've ever read about myself. Not because it's all true – it's not – but because it has revealed a blind spot that's so obvious now. Point number 1: I've never written about or investigated any crimes against non-white victims. But I have a producer and editors, and we have a media company funding our endeavours. I'm directed by other people. I've never chosen my subjects in isolation, it's a collective decision . . . but there's still a nagging voice inside. I can't ignore it. Plugging my eye sockets with the heels of my palms, I let the thought emerge: *White crime sells, you've always known that.*

Ambition, I think. That's my sin here. Knowing it would help my career, my subconscious has leaned toward the stories that are 'podworthy'; a tidy euphemism, I suppose, for 'white'. It's never been about justice or feminism – it's always been about me.

I close my laptop. The anxiety rolls me back into a ball on the bed. It warms my eyes, closes my throat. The anger cools, sharpens, cuts open a cold cavity in my gut. I do what I always do when I have strong feelings: I welcome the anaesthetic distraction of work. I reopen my emails, go into the folder named 'Leads'. Time to block out the noise and find the next project.

BILL

EVERYONE KNOWS HOW it ends: my chef's knife snapped in Simon's chest. Each member of the family stabbed. The police had an eyewitness who saw me departing the house. My bloody boot prints led between the rooms then out the back door, over the pavers and down to the gates. I was arrested within hours and haven't been free since. That is where the story most people know ends, but few people know where it truly begins.

All I ever really wanted to do was cook. There is something about the fizz of salt in hot oil, the moment when you press a knife into a ripe peach and it weeps over the blade. Something about the crackle of breaking open the perfect meringue, the hiss of a lamb chop hitting a smoking grill.

At the time, cooking for the Primrose family felt like my destiny, but it started with a simple phone call. I wish I hadn't bothered getting up to take that call. I could have stayed in bed, called back later. By then, my uncle might have already passed and maybe I'd have decided to stay in Australia. But that's not how life is. There are no do-overs in history. There only is what was.

The call came at five in the morning and I'd arrived home from work at one. The landline never rang that early, especially on a Saturday. So I knew it was something serious. My housemate banged on my door. I forget his name but he didn't get much sleep either. A DJ and club rat who wore sprayed-on black jeans and believed all the world's problems could be solved with MDMA.

'Someone's on the phone,' he said.

'Who?'

'Your aunt or someone. Reckons it's important.'

And it turned out it was. My uncle, the man who'd raised me after my mother died, had collapsed from a heart attack in the night. He was on the third step of the staircase at the time and he'd clutched his chest as he fell back, hitting his head on the tiles. Now he was on life support.

The news shook the sleep from my mind. I made a coffee with trembling hands then walked to the travel agent on Chapel Street and waited until it opened at 9 am. I booked a flight for that afternoon. I called my boss, who told me to take all the time that I needed. I wept on the plane and drank four tiny bottles of Jim Beam with Diet Coke. I must have known in my bones I wouldn't be returning to Melbourne. Why else did I book only one way? Why else did I pack my chef's knives?

My uncle died while I was soaring over the unbroken blue of the Tasman Sea. The funeral was to be held three days later, but I knew I'd be needed there longer. I was back where I started, sleeping on a single bed in my aunty and uncle's flat in Rotorua. There were bills to pay for the funeral, my aunty needed support. I helped with what little money I had saved and tried to do what I could. Family gathered around, and while it was good to see them all, the sadness of my uncle's death overshadowed that first week. I was just taking it one day at a time.

I saw Maia at the funeral, and the week after texted her. Grief is more potent than Cupid's arrow. I wanted company and Maia wanted me. We picked up where we'd left off, before I moved to Australia, spending all our time together, mostly at her place. We lay in bed for hours, just talking, just being.

'Tell me your biggest fear,' I said one night a few weeks after I'd got back.

She looked up, surprised. 'Where's this come from?'

'I don't know,' I said. 'What are you most afraid of?'

'Probably dying. Or something happening to people I love,' she said. 'Whenever Teimana gets in a fight or disappears for days, I get anxious something really bad has happened to him.'

Her brother had been arrested a dozen times – nothing serious, not at that stage anyway.

'What about me?' I asked her. 'Ever worry something might happen to me?'

'Nah,' she said, with laughter in her voice. She placed her hand on my cheek. 'You? Not scared of dying, eh? Too tough for that?'

I shrugged. 'I guess so,' I said. 'But right now I'm more scared of not ever really living than of dying. Scared of always being stuck in this place,' I said. 'In this town, forever.'

'Too good for your home, eh?'

'No,' I said. 'I don't mean that.'

'Is that why you up and left me the first time? Off to the big smoke in Aussie.'

I shook my head, my nose rubbing hers. She was still sore about it, even after all this time. 'I just want more.'

'Yeah, me too. I've always known you'd get out of here . . . and actually *do* something with your life. You were never that much of a talker, but even back at school you were saying that. Do you remember we used to talk about it?' she said.

'I remember the other stuff more than the talking.'

She play-punched me in the chest. 'It's weird to think about now. Pashing at the back of the rugby field.'

I laughed, pulling her body closer, soft against mine.

If I'd known what was to come, I would have never let go.

BILL

ABOUT A MONTH after the funeral, my aunty was doing a lot better, but I knew I wouldn't be going back to Melbourne. Things with Maia were serious, I was even starting to think about a future together. But I'd burnt through my savings and was back where I started. I needed to get a job. That's when Uncle Mooks called me. Mooks had been in Rotorua for the funeral and stayed a week or so before he returned to Cambridge where he was living then.

'I was gardening for this family. They've got a bloody mansion, boy, out there in Cambridge. They're looking for a chef.'

'I'm not a private chef,' I told him.

'They don't know that. Worth a try. They've had trouble finding someone.'

'Won't they want a resumé or CV or something?'

'I'm tossing you a big juicy bone here, Bill. You decide if you want to chew it.'

I'd already dropped into a few restaurants in Rotorua to see if I could pick up any shifts, but work was thin on the ground. And even if an opening did come up, I'd be starting on half of what I'd been making at Noir.

I asked Mooks how I should apply.

'Email a CV – just tell them you saw the job in the paper.' He texted me the email address,

I sent through my CV and before long I was on the bus to Cambridge for an interview. Mooks met me at the bus stop. It was good to see him, he was a mess at the funeral but now he was back in high spirits.

'I think it's best they don't know we're related,' he said as we drove off.

'What? Why not?'

'I don't work there anymore, nephew. They didn't like how I tended the plants. British. They're all funny about their gardens, you know. I'm only good for mowing lawns, pulling weeds, bit of maintenance. I don't know how to prune a rose bush properly.'

'They fired you?'

He just smiled. 'Don't worry about that. I got plenty of work, starting at the high school next week.'

'Jeez, Mooks, I wish you'd said that. Now I feel like I'm lying from the start.'

'Nah, it'll be fine, trust me. They're going to like you and it's a good job. Sort of money that could really set you up.'

'I don't know—'

'Go on, just have a chat. See what they're offering and then decide. No harm in having an interview.'

Eventually I agreed. But still, it felt a bit dishonest.

About twenty minutes later, Mooks pulled the car up across the road from a set of ornate iron gates set into high stone walls. Looking through the gates, I could see a driveway and manicured garden. The house brought goosebumps out on my arms – it was huge, and old-fashioned looking. I'd never been inside a place like that. And now maybe I was going to live there, cook there.

I looked back at Mooks and let out a low whistle.

'Not bad, eh, neph?' he said. 'See you in a bit.'

I stepped out of the car and watched Mooks drive off before I crossed the road. I took a breath and pressed the intercom button at the gate.

'Yes, hello? May I help you?'

It was not the British I was expecting, but the long throaty consonants and puckered vowels of French.

'Hi, I'm, ah, here for the interview.'

'The chef, yes?'

'Ah, yeah, for the private chef role.'

'Okay, one moment please. I'll get the gate.'

The gears ground as the huge gates began to swing inward.

I walked through and up the wide driveway to the front of the house. A great wooden door with a brass knocker swung in as I raised my hand. A woman, standing barely five feet tall, had opened it. She was older than me – late twenties, with very dark hair, pale skin and fire-hydrant-red lips.

'So,' she said, looking past me and out to the street. 'No car?'

'Ah, no,' I said. 'I got a ride with a friend.'

She arched a manicured eyebrow. 'Well, you better come in.'

I couldn't keep my eyes off her as she led me through the oversized foyer. She was exotic, sophisticated, like someone out of a foreign film. I followed her to a loungeroom and lowered myself into the leather chesterfield that she gestured to. She gave me a bit of a once over and then left, without saying anything more.

As I waited, I looked around and recognised something on the mantel in a glass box. A white comb with three prongs, intricately designed and patterned, made of bone. I noticed other things too: art, hardwood furniture, other markers of wealth. And weird taste, too – like the taxidermy fox mounted and hung on one of the walls. *That's something you don't see every day*, I remember thinking.

Ten minutes later, the door from the foyer opened and an elegant older woman with a chestnut bob came in.

'Bill?' she said.

'That's me.' I stood up.

She reached out her hand. 'Pleasure to meet you. I'm Gwen. Gwen Primrose.' She gave a tiny nose-wrinkle smile. 'Come on through.'

I followed her into an expansive office overlooking the garden. The walls were lined with books. She sat down behind the desk.

'Take a seat,' she said. 'This is my husband's office but I thought it's the best place to talk. Official business, this.' She smiled again but, despite the warmth of it, her gaze seemed to trap me. 'So,' she said, without glancing down at my CV. 'You've never worked as a private chef?'

I swallowed. 'Umm. No. Most of my work has been for one of the top chefs in Melbourne. Noir is the only Australian restaurant ranked in the top one hundred in the world. It has three chef's ha—'

'Is that so?' she said, cutting me off. 'Impressive.'

'Yes. And I've also helped a catering company to cater events.' I don't mention it was for a marae up north, and the 'events' were tangi. I also don't mention it was unpaid and that I was a teenager making sandwiches. 'I can cook anything you like.'

'Anything?' she said.

I wanted to say that I'd cooked for my family for years even before I became a chef. Would it be clichéd or silly to tell her I've always been a student of the kitchen, endlessly seeking new recipes, trying new combinations of ingredients, new techniques?

The words wouldn't leave my mouth, trapped by nerves. I just nodded instead. 'Yeah, I think so.'

'And, you are, ah . . .' She moved her hand in front of her face. 'What's your heritage, Bill?'

'My heritage?'

'You're not white, are you. So, what's your ethnicity?'

Heat at the back of my neck. 'Oh.' From the moment I saw the house, I knew I wanted the job. Maybe if I hadn't wanted it so badly I would have asked why it was important to know my ethnicity. Her gaze narrowed. 'My mum, she was Māori. And apparently my dad was or is Pākehā, or European.'

'*Apparently?* You didn't know your father?'

I shook my head. The corners of her mouth lifted and her head tilted. There was something a bit like joy in her eyes.

'Nah, I don't know him. I've not had anything to do with him.'

'How terrible. That must have been hard?'

'It wasn't so bad.'

'So you must be very good with the local cuisine?'

'We don't have too much of our own cuisine, really. We mostly inherited the British diet, I think.'

'Well, we love traditional British fare in this household, there's no doubt about that. But there must be some local specialities as well?'

Pork bones and pūhā, fry bread, hāngi. 'Yeah, I suppose there are a few things.'

'Well, I'd be eager to learn more.'

The interview continued on. I tried my best to answer her questions and to make a good impression but it felt like she was going through the motions. It was as though she had already decided I wasn't going to get the job.

'And you could live on site?' she asked. 'It's important that you are available twenty-four hours. We've found it difficult to find someone who could commit to this but we think the compensation is fair.'

I hadn't asked and was almost afraid to mention it.

'Yeah,' I say. 'That would work. I could live on site. And the compensation . . .'

'Ninety thousand dollars,' she said. 'Plus a room here, bills covered, and food. We know that's well above the industry average.'

I couldn't help it, my jaw dropped.

She laughed, just a huff of air really.

I knew this opportunity wouldn't come around again. Surely Maia would understand. Private chef experience would be great for future work – plus the money was almost three times what I'd be able to get in Rotorua. The house and the luxury lifestyle I'd have here was tempting too. Plush beds, soft sheets and a spacious room with views over the garden were already running through my mind. I could show Maia around, introduce her to this lady, this new world.

'Is that okay?' she said, clearly amused.

'Umm, yeah, yeah, definitely,' I said. 'I can live here and make myself available twenty-four hours, you know, for whatever was wante—'

'Great, so when could you start?'

'Well, if I got the job, I'd be free now.'

She rose, stretched her hand out.

'Why don't we start tomorrow?'

Was this a test?

'This tomorrow?' I said, and she laughed.

'You're funny, Bill. Yes, *this* tomorrow.'

Maybe it was too good to be true, but I was filled head to toe with bubbles of excitement. I could barely keep them contained. I would have to learn the kitchen, sharpen my knives, buy food. I would be making more money than I could have dreamed of and it was all starting the next day.

'Of course. Yes. What time? I can come whenever.'

'Nine am,' she said. 'Don't be late. First thing we can do is run through your menu plan.'

Menu plan? I'd have to knock something up that night. A lump grew in my throat. The excitement was hardening to nerves. I'd have to check the morning bus schedule from Rotorua. Or maybe Mooks could pick me up. I'd work it out. For ninety grand, I'd walk back if I had to.

'Nine am. Sure, thank you,' I said, standing to leave.

On my way out, I glanced over the back lawn to the pine forest and my eyes snagged on something. A young woman – a girl, really – with her feet up on the outdoor table. She wore glasses and held a book in her hand.

'That's Elle, our daughter,' Gwen said, noticing me look. 'I hope you can make a decent salad. She's just decided she's a vegetarian now.' She rolled her eyes.

In the garden, Elle turned, lowered her glasses with her index finger and stared in at me. For the second time that day, I felt snared by the gaze of a Primrose woman.

SLOANE

IT'S BEEN DAYS but still I feel a hum of anxiety. It's the forum, I think. It's those people, *my* people talking about *me*. Talking about how much of a bad feminist I am. I can't stop thinking about it. My next chat with my therapist is tomorrow – she'll help, but for now I keep my head on my work. I message Tara.

Brunch?

Sleepy's Cafe? she responds.

See you there.

On my walk through Princess Park, I listen to another podcast episode on the Primrose murders. I learn something new about Bill Kareama every day – this episode mentions that he was accused of stealing from the house. I google how to pronounce 'Kareama' and realise the host of this particular podcast is mispronouncing it. I repeat the right pronunciation a few times to myself – it's the minimum effort, frankly.

Tara is there at the cafe, effervescent as always. With her smooth amber complexion, soft eyes and Pilates-instructor physique, she manages to be beautiful at any hour of any day. My long black is set on the table across from her.

'Tara,' I say, smiling despite the recent stress. I hang my bag off the back of the chair. Tara pushes her laptop aside.

'Hello Miss Gold Walkley.' She stands to hug me and I feel like a toddler. 'What's so urgent that you can't just relax for a few days?'

We both sit. 'It's already been a few days. And I'm thinking about the next case,' I say. 'I've found it. Or rather, you found it.'

'Me?'

I open my laptop, turn it toward her. She sees the story about the mass murder in New Zealand.

'Bill Kareama,' she says, surprise in her voice. 'You want to look into his case?'

I nod. 'It's *fascinating*.'

'This is different.'

'I know,' I say, watching the uncertainty settle over her face.

'Umm, have you spoken to Esteban? I'm for it, I just don't know—'

'—if it's our kind of story?'

'Yeah,' she says. 'Will it connect with our listeners?'

This is it. The bias we have developed, to connect with 'our' listeners. We know the demographics. Female, white, twenty to fifty.

'We're journalists,' I remind myself as much as her. 'We go where the story goes and hope our audience comes with us.'

'Yeah,' she says. Her mouth smiles but her eyes remain unconvinced.

'You know the case well?'

'Of course, everyone back home does. It was a huge story. It's still a huge story.'

I bring the coffee to my lips, take a sip. 'I'm more energised by this story than anything else we've looked at lately. I know, I *sense*, he shouldn't be in prison, based on everything I've read. Guilty or not, the defence sounds incompetent, and he was arrested and charged the day of the murders. That doesn't strike me as a comprehensive investigation.'

'No,' she says. 'I've always thought about this case. There are so many angles we could come at it from and they really did zero in on him. But why this one? Why now?'

I shrug.

'It just came to you?'

'Look, I think it's time we looked at different crimes. We've looked exclusively at dead white women.'

'The victims here are white, Sloane,' she says.

'I know . . . but Bill Kareama.' I find myself stumbling. I can't put it into words, not in a way that represents the complex feelings I have. 'I sense a race and class element to this story. If Bill Kareama is innocent, then he's a victim too, right?'

She nods.

'It just feels like the deck was stacked against him. Maybe he did it, who knows, but it feels like there's a lot more here. It's worth scouting out, looking into. You know about the inhaler, right?'

'Yeah, I agree. The inhaler and running thing never made sense and it was mostly glossed over in the trial. It's just I don't know if Esteban will be on board, but that's a knot you can massage out.'

'I can handle Est.'

'I am sure you can,' she says with a wry smile. 'I'll send some emails and we can start planning.'

'I'll let Esteban know. Let's start tracking down the major players here. Lawyers, police, friends and family. And of course Kareama himself. The prison will need a bit of notice and we will have to apply to visit.'

'He doesn't speak to anyone,' she says. 'He's never acknowledged guilt. He hasn't given an interview in years. If we're doing this, it will probably be without his cooperation.'

'Public opinion in New Zealand?'

She shrugs. 'It's overall negative. People think if he's not guilty of murder, he's guilty of something.' A waiter approaches, takes our empty coffee cups.

'Eating today, ladies?' he says.

'A croissant would be great,' I say.

'The grain salad, please,' Tara says.

Grain salad, I think. *Of course.*

Tara turns back to me. 'I'll do what I can to help before the baby comes, then I'm in aunty mode.' Tara's sister is expecting this week.

'Of course, aunty duty comes first,' I say, smiling. 'So he won't speak to anyone, even if it could help get a retrial?'

Tara opens her laptop and punches away while continuing to speak. 'I remember there was someone, years ago. He was leading the charge for a retrial.'

'Who?'

She leans a little closer to her screen. 'Te Kuru Phillips, his name is. He was Bill Kareama's psychologist in prison. He did some media interviews, quit his job to help the cause, but they never got the retrial. If Kareama talked to anyone, it was him.'

I nod. 'Okay, can you get in touch with both the psychologist and the prison? I've got a flight booked early next week.'

'Sloane,' she says. 'Are you joking?'

'I'll head over, check it out,' I say. 'No harm in that.'

'As your assistant, friend, mentee, fan – please just take a break. Go drink some cocktails in Bali for a couple of weeks, I could find you a villa in Ubud. You've earned it. This case can wait. I'll get the preliminary stuff sorted for you to dig in when you're back, then we can both head over.'

I exhale. 'It's just a recce, Tara. I'll go over there, ask a few questions. If it's a non-starter, I'll go to Queenstown and spend some time skiing. Okay? But for now, please help me get everything ready for next week. Oh, another thing: the people now living in the murder house, contact them too. I want to see it.'

She rolls her eyes. 'Alright,' she finally says. 'I'll send some emails, make some calls. Et cetera, et cetera.'

'What would I do without you?' I say, as my croissant is placed in front of me. Good, I'm starving.

T K

MY DAY STARTS when the sky is pink, before the birds have even rolled out of bed. A three-minute cold shower. Then a hot black coffee. By 5 am, I'm in the garage of my townhouse. This morning, I do five sets of deadlifts, five sets of chin-ups and bent-over rows, then fifteen minutes of skipping, all while the dulcet tones of Neil deGrasse Tyson's *StarTalk* podcast comes through my earbuds.

I have a second shower before breakfast, this one hot. Overnight oats with Greek yoghurt and a smoothie, out on my terrace watching the dawn glow drain from the morning sky. Then I'm on my bike heading to my office in the city. When I arrive, I check today's appointments and start reviewing my notes for my first patient.

My space is small but smart, a modest office and a single-toilet bathroom above a convenience store in a beautifully restored heritage building near the CBD. I do not have a receptionist or an assistant. It has taken me three years to build this practice up and I have fifteen or so appointments each week, which keeps the lights on, pays the mortgage. This has been my routine, more or less, in the years that have passed since I gave up on Bill. Routine keeps me focused.

I'm reading through my emails when I see something that makes me pause.

Email subject: Bill Kareama. And the email address: Tara@legacy-podcast.com.au. It can't be – *Legacy* podcast is huge, a powerhouse in true crime. Each season is a deep dive on a cold case, and I've listened to every episode – they've had results too. Evidence uncovered in the last season prompted the police to relaunch investigations into a decades-old case. They've always investigated Australian cases but now they're interested in Bill Kareama. I drag the email and let it linger over *Trash*. I stare at it for a moment. I can't help. I won't help. It's a dead-end for them and me. But curiosity is a relentless itch and dropping this in the trash folder won't scratch it.

The message is what I was imagining. They're interested in the case, they want to interview me and for me to help connect them with Bill. The answer is no. I don't even need to think about it.

I'm sorry, I can't help with this.
All the best.

My last appointment finishes around seven in the evening and, despite how much I focus on my clients, the email has been niggling away at my consciousness. I lock up my office and ride my bike home.

In bed that night, I take my laptop out. I've got to pick up Amelia from school tomorrow. I check my calendar, then my emails. A follow-up from *Legacy* podcast; this time I don't read it. The laptop issues a sound of paper scrunching in a ball as I drop the email in the trash. It's the only thing I can do. Bill Kareama is in my past. His case is an old house full of ghosts and obsession, a place I don't want to visit again.

BILL

'SO YOU'RE JUST going to stay there with them? Live in Cambridge?'
Maia said. She was hopeless at hiding her feelings, disappointment
all over her face, but her voice almost sounded happy for me.

'It's part of the job and there's free rent,' I said. 'I will save up
for a couple of weeks and get a cheap car so I can come and go.'

'Ninety grand? You definitely heard her right?'

'I've got the offer in writing. It's all there. This is life-changing. This
could set us up. After a year or two, I could have saved enough for a
deposit for a house. We just need to get through a couple of years.'

She thought for a few moments, those big brown eyes searching
around the bedroom before coming to rest on my face. 'Well, I could
borrow Teimana's car and visit you there too.'

'Yeah, that should be fine. I'll check.'

'What do you mean?'

'I don't know their rules. I don't think it will matter.'

When I went to Melbourne, she stayed back to finish her last
year of high school. She wanted to be on TV, a news presenter, but
I'd told her they never let people like us on the news, not reporting
it anyway.

As I packed the last of my things into my bag, Maia rose from the bed. She strode past me, out of the room. I exhaled and followed her. She wasn't in the loungeroom. I walked past Teimana's room and opened the door to the garage. Teimana was there, and two others, big guys I didn't recognise. Their eyes all hit me.

'Close that door!' Teimana said. He stepped toward me but by that stage I'd backed up, closed the door. I didn't have a chance to take in what it was he didn't want me to see. Drugs, or weapons, or something else. I found Maia outside on the lawn. She didn't often smoke cigarettes but she had one between her lips, the end glowing. A deep inhale, a long slow exhale.

'Maia,' I said.

She turned back. 'Yeah?' Tired eyes and a sour mouth.

'It won't be for that long and it's not so far.'

'Yeah,' she said. 'I know. Just like last time.'

On the bus, I read through Gwen's email again. The job responsibilities were clear: cook every meal for every member of the family, buy all the groceries. A bank card would be provided to use for purchases. The pantry and fridge were always to be kept well stocked. They had been paying the house cleaner, Shirley, to collect the groceries for them until I started. Gwen liked to cook occasionally – she wasn't bad either – but most nights it was my job. I'd written up a menu plan for the first two weeks, and had emailed it to Gwen in advance.

That first day, they were all gathered in the living room when I arrived at the door with my tattered suitcase and backpack. I'd worn the same clothes again, trying to look the part. I'd be back in my chef's whites once I started working.

'Bill, hello,' Gwen said. 'Put your bags down here, we can sort that out after. Come and meet the family.'

A gust of wind at my back gave me the impression the house was inhaling, sucking me in. I pulled the door shut and left my bags there in the foyer.

When I walked into the loungeroom, it felt staged, like a photoshoot. Simon, well dressed in shirt and slacks, sat in the deep chesterfield armchair. Elle and Chet sat with a wide gap between them on the three-seater, Chet deep against the leather back of the seat, legs straight so his feet were off the floor. He had fine, blond, corn-silk hair and the sort of green eyes that could have broken hearts if he'd lived long enough.

'Hi,' I said. Simon rose, came over. He stretched out his hand. I was expecting a plummy, posh accent like Gwen's but his was different. Harsher, thicker somehow.

'Alright, Bill. Pleasure to meet you. I hear you know your way around a kitchen.'

I smiled. 'I like to think so.'

'Well, you charmed my wife, no mean feat. Took me a number of years, in fact.' A soft jab on my arm. 'This is Chester, my son.'

The boy stared at my shoes for a moment, before pulling himself up and offering his hand.

'Hey Chester,' I said, giving him a smile.

'Hello,' he said, barely meeting my eye, his cheeks coloured like apricots. 'You can call me Chet.'

'Shy,' Simon said. 'And my daughter.'

'Elle,' she said. She was liquid, rising with grace and finding me with disinterested, almost weary blue eyes. 'It's nice to meet you, Bill.'

Simon blinked, the sharp corners of his grin softened. Gwen sat with her legs crossed on the arm of the couch.

'Well, I'm just looking forward to cooking you folks some good food,' I said, looking down to avoid Elle's eyes.

'*You folks* – I like him already.' Simon laughed. 'Such a strong, working-class vernacular the Kiwis have, don't they?'

'So Bill is going to be living in the cottage with Fleur and cooking for us, just how Marlon did back home. You can ask him to make you anything,' Gwen said.

'Can he make Marlon's poutine?' Chet asked, turning to his mum.

'Well, you may need to ask Bill that. He's right there.'

'I can do that,' I said. 'I don't know who Marlon is but I can make anything you like.'

'Cool,' he said.

Gwen turned her beatific expression toward me. 'Cool. Alright,' she said. 'Well, let me show you where you'll be staying. Then I'll run you through everything in the kitchen and we can look at your menu plan.'

I'd hoped for a cushy, spacious room but instead I got a cottage that might have fallen over in a storm – and I was sharing it with Fleur, the au pair. The only thing it had in common with the house was the sense it had been there a long time, but where the house had heritage features – pressed-tin ceilings, hardwood floors – the cottage had spiderwebs, threadbare carpet and draughty sash windows. It had apparently once been the milker's cottage, and was hardly bigger than the pool house beside it. The kitchenette was small, even for my standards, with an old oven, a toaster, a kettle and a microwave, and that looked to be it. I sighed. It was small quarters, tighter than I expected. And there were two of us in here.

'I'll let you unpack. Come to the house when you're ready to complete the tour,' Gwen said.

I put my bags down in my room and came out into the shared area, with its tiny box TV and old leather couch.

'This is our little honeymoon suite,' Fleur said, her French accent soured with sarcasm. Turning, I found her standing in the doorway of her room. 'So, do you have a girlfriend?'

Heat flushed my cheeks. 'Yeah,' I say. 'Sort of.'

'Well, they don't like us to bring guests to the house. So perhaps it's best you don't bring her here.'

'Oh, uh, thanks for the heads-up.'

'They are funny like that. But you get used to it. I think it's the British. They have their little habits – prudish. Is that the right word?'

'It depends what you mean.'

She ignored me, turning back into her room. 'It gets cold out here. I have a heater in my room. You should get one too,' she called.

Then she closed the door.

I sent Maia a text message but the reception out there wasn't great. I went into the backyard and held my phone up until it went through.

All moved in. The family are nice. Miss you so much already.

I waited a moment to see if a reply might come back. With my eyes looking up at the phone in my hand, I felt her gaze before I saw it. From upstairs, through a window. Elle. She just stood, motionless, watching me. She could have been a ghost. I dropped my arm, jammed my phone into my pocket and went back inside, wondering why my heart was beating so fast.

SLOANE

I LOVE FLYING. I feel guilty given the carbon toll but it's one of those rare and perhaps slightly odd joys – being trapped in a steel bullet over a body of water. Maybe it's the quietude I like, maybe it's the fact strangers bring me food and drink for hours on end. On this particular flight, I read more of the trial notes and court transcripts. I discover new aspects of the case, things that muddy the water even more. The whole thing is practically a swamp.

Bill got skewered by the prosecution on the stand – how much prep did his lawyers do with him? Right now, I am thinking that the central premise of the podcast will be about the failures of the justice system. Guilty or innocent, Bill Kareama did not have a fair trial. The centrepiece of the defence was the implausibility of the timing – the first scream was heard less than twelve minutes after Bill Kareama was captured on CCTV at an ATM three kilometres away.

It's not uncommon in a legal defence to present a number of alternative theories to put doubt in the jury's mind, but it was a bold gambit for the prosecution to present so many possible explanations for this most important fact of the case. To explain how Bill managed to get all the way from the ATM to the Primrose property, through the gate and up to the bedrooms by the time of the first scream, they asked the jury to consider a number of possibilities. Some seemed plausible: the timestamp on the CCTV or phone records was wrong; the first scream was unrelated or misheard; there was an accomplice who drove Bill, or he stole a bike or skateboard that was never found by police in their subsequent searches. Other theories were decidedly less plausible: Bill was faking his asthma, despite extensive medical records; Bill 'planted' himself at the ATM, then set off at an Olympic sprint.

None of these theories were ever put forward as the single source of truth – rather, the point was to prove each was technically possible, and that therefore the inhaler defence did not amount to reasonable doubt, and I suppose they succeeded in that.

I read about the victims, starting with Gwen Primrose. I like her, as a character anyway – she's intriguing. From a posh family, a whip-smart first-class finance graduate who never worked a day in her life. So she went out and proved she was clever but never needed to use her degree. Instead, she married an MP, had two kids and stayed at home.

Simon Primrose next. Upper middle-class. Studied business and finance, and worked in banking before setting out to become a politician. Climbed the ranks of the Tories at a rate of knots. He became a minister at thirty-eight, just six years after his political career began. Oversaw a major infrastructure project, and made a controversial call that ended in a terrible train crash, killing nine people. The media pounced and his political aspirations died. The Southgate disaster ended his political career. Devilishly handsome, roguish, enjoyed whisky and rugby.

The plane touches down and I pack away my notes.

After passport control and customs, I find the Avis counter in the airport. The queue moves slowly but before long I'm in a car and following the navigation toward Auckland City.

I call Esteban, my producer.

'Sloane,' he says. 'I've got Tara on the line too.'

'Hi Tara.'

'So you arrived okay?' she says.

'I'm here now, on my way to the hotel in Auckland. What else do you have for me?'

'Nothing yet. I've been in touch with the prison,' Esteban says. 'And I can get over there to join you in a week or so. Tara's booked for late next week. Aren't you, T?'

'Yep.'

'At this stage,' Esteban continues, 'we haven't managed to get in touch with Bill directly and we're not going to be able to do this without him. The prison are receptive but they're making us jump through the usual hoops.'

'What if I go to the prison directly?'

'Sloane, no,' he says. 'This is one door you won't be able to kick down, gung-ho does not work with corrections people. We need to be softer there. And Bill won't speak, apparently. Even if we fast-track the visitor's application he needs to approve your visit.'

'What about his lawyer?'

'His original lawyer, Laurence Berry, is now retired, but he is happy to speak to you about the trial,' Tara says.

'Good,' I say. 'Schedule it.'

'One problem is he is insisting that you go to him in Wellington, he won't speak remotely, only in person.'

'Doable,' I say. 'And the other lawyer, can he get us access to Bill?'

'James McMurry is his name and he told me the only person Bill Kareama trusts, or rather *trusted*, was this psychologist, Te Kuru Phillips. But he's also not keen to talk.'

'The psychologist. We went back to him, right?'

'Yep, but he hasn't responded again,' Tara says. 'And I called the number for his office and left a message.'

'Okay,' I say. 'Leave it with me.'

TK

I WALK AMELIA to school. Kiss her at the gate, then head toward my office. Don, who sleeps rough in nooks and alleys near my office, greets me as I pass.

'Morning, Doc,' he says.

'Kia ora, Don,' I say.

I drop a coin in his cup. There's fresh graffiti on the wall outside my office. I crack the door and head upstairs. The first client of the day is new – she's booked for 10 am. At five minutes to ten, I hear the bell and go downstairs to unlock the door to let her in. She's short, with blonde hair, dark eyeliner and a warm smile.

'Hi,' she says in an Australian accent.

'Hello, Sarah, isn't it? Welcome, come on up.'

She follows me up the stairs.

'This is a new client form,' I say, handing her the iPad once we are in my office. 'If you want to take a seat and get started on that.'

She's attractive, with large eyes that give her a sort of intensity. Her gaze doesn't leave my face.

'The form won't be necessary,' she says. Her voice is familiar.

Shit. It's her.

'Sorry?'

'I confess I'm not actually here for an appointment.'

I swallow, try to keep a neutral expression. *Sloane Abbott.*

'I'm sorry,' I say. 'If you're not here for an appointment, I can't help you.'

She clicks her tongue. 'I'm here to talk to you about Bill Kareama. I won't keep you long.'

'I know who you are,' I say.

'And I know I have an hour booked into your calendar. I don't want to waste your time. I'm going to pay.'

'That won't be necessary. Please just leave.' I give her the calm, flat voice I otherwise reserve for cold-callers.

'Te Kuru, please, just give me five minutes?'

'Te *Kuru*,' I correct her.

'Te *Kuru*, sorry. Look, I read an interview you gave – you were so passionate. You worked for years to get him out. What happened?'

'I'm going to ask you one more time to leave,' I say. 'Before I call the police.'

She smiles. 'Really? You're going to call the police? I don't know what happened with you but from what I've read, you were Bill's champion, the only person who cared about him and, if you still do, or even if you only care about justice, you have to see this as an opportunity to help get the truth.'

'I have all the truth I need,' I say, my voice even. 'Sorry. I can't help.'

She doesn't speak for a moment and now I see why she's so good at her job. Her green eyes fix on mine. The silence is a flame that warms my cheeks. 'Is that right?'

'That's right. Now, if you wouldn't min—'

'We have tens of millions of listeners. My team and I, we can open doors, we can get him a retrial.'

'I don't think you can, Miss Abbott.'

'Call me Sloane.'

'No.'

She looks exacerbated. 'You tried your best, you tried for years. But you're just one man.'

I shake my head. 'He won't acknowledge his guilt. That's the only way he's getting out early.'

'Would you?'

'What?'

'Acknowledge your guilt if you were innocent?'

I look past her, exhale. I think about my daughter, my ex-wife. I think about promises.

'Okay,' I say. 'Let's sit, at least.'

She takes a seat and I sit across from her, keeping the coffee table between us. 'What exactly is it that you want from me? I won't go on your podcast. I can't help in any material way. I won't get involved in it all again.'

'I'm told he won't speak to anyone, other than you and his lawyer.'

'You already tried James, then?' Figures.

'James was happy to meet but he told my producer the only person Bill trusted was you.'

Trusted. Not *trusts.* The past tense is a fist that lands somewhere below my sternum.

'I can't convince Bill to do anything,' I say. 'He's stubborn – you won't change his mind or influence him.'

'What happened?'

'What do you mean?'

'With you. How does someone go from filing endless motions for new trials, giving media interviews, committing so much time and resources to someone, to one day just giving up?'

'That's all there is to it. I gave up,' I confess. 'It takes a lot out of you.' It's not a lie but then again it's not entirely the truth. 'Look, I can't help and I won't. It's not my place. So good luck with your podcast.'

'Sure,' she says, standing. She reaches into her bag and pulls out a card. She places it on the table. 'Now you have my number. I'm visiting the house today, by the way.'

'I wouldn't bother,' I say, getting up too. 'They won't let you in.'

'Who?'

'The owners.'

'They're giving me a tour this afternoon actually.' She must see the shock on my face because she says, 'Huh, you've never been inside.'

I'd tried when the house was sold to get through, to talk to them. It was boarded up for years, functionally derelict, but they restored it.

'Well, that should give you a good starting point,' I say.

'James also told us that Bill wrote an account of the events.'

'He did. I originally suggested it as part of his therapy, but I think he came to see it as a vehicle for proving his innocence.'

'And you have a copy?'

'I can't share it without his permission, sorry.'

'Of course,' she says. 'Well, I will leave you to it.'

'Who else are you speaking with?'

She turns back, her smile even bigger. 'The trial lawyer, Laurence Berry, a few people around town. I'm hoping to track down some of the people who worked at the property at the time.'

I nod. I shouldn't be surprised. I'm not really, but I am struck by the power of her platform, how many doors that might open which were slammed in my face.

'Elizabeth Primrose, hopefully.'

'Good luck with that,' I say. What about Tate Mercer-Kemp – what if she gets him? And Fleur? I clear my throat. How long will it take her to get onto Maia and what will happen when she does? Will she give up and find something new?

'I can't help directly,' I say. 'But . . . I do still care.'

'So why can't you help?'

'It's a long story but the short answer is Bill's a hopeless case. You'll see that in time.'

She looks confused, then her eyes go from me to the window, the buildings outside, then back to my face. 'All we need, all I want from you is to get me access to Bill. That's it. I don't care about anything else. I just need that one thing. You need to tell him that this is his best shot at proving he didn't get a fair trial. And you're a smart man, Te Kuru.'

Didn't get a fair trial. Not *he's innocent,* or *not guilty.* Sloane is concerned with the legal system more than whether or not he did it. 'Call me TK,' I say.

'Right, well, from what I've read about you, you're a genius. You finished high school two years early, studied at university as a teenager, a doctorate by twenty-one. A wunderkind.'

'What's your point?'

'You're smart enough to know that I'm his best shot. If he's innocent, if there was a genuine case of misjustice, then I'll get to the bottom of it. You may be intelligent but you're not as dogged as me. You don't have my investigative skills, TK. I appreciate you gave years of your life to this cause but I can bring fresh eyes and new energy.'

I believe her. I feel the anxious butterflies.

'If you're half the investigator I think you are, you'll be on a plane home by the end of the week,' I say.

'I guess we'll see. From what I've read, Bill Kareama never stood a chance.'

Spots of rain appear on the window.

'Alright,' I say, eyeing the clock. 'I think you better go.'

'Can I get your mobile number, TK?'

I sigh. At least if she can call me, it will stop her from turning up again.

'Just in case I find something you might be interested in.'

'Sure.' I scribble on a page from my notebook and tear it out. Once she's gone, I call James.

'TK,' he says. 'Long time no speak.'

'I won't keep you long, just had a surprise visitor.'

'Yeah?'

'A famous podcaster looking into Bill's case.'

'Well, she's persistent,' he says. 'Which is a good thing. I'm away until next week but I've organised to talk to her when I get back. You're not, umm, you know, back on the case are you?'

'No,' I say. 'No, I'm not.'

BILL

'LET'S SEE HOW we rub along for a few weeks, and then after a month, we can decide whether to continue on,' Gwen told me.

I planned to last a lot longer than a month. I'd worked out that after twelve months, if I saved every dollar, I'd be pretty set up. I'd have enough for a house deposit, for some travel.

Gwen had liked my menu plans – 'Fine for everyday food,' she'd said – but left the choice of what I'd cook that first night to me. I decided to play to my strengths and went with a classic: roast lamb, crunchy potatoes, roasted kūmara, buttery peas and rich gravy. The sort of meal I'd been cooking most of my life. Elle, being a vegetarian, could only eat the vegetables, so I would include a side salad with grains, pulses and grilled artichoke. Still, I was a little nervous.

The kitchen was the size of a generous one-bedroom apartment, with a huge walk-in pantry, a double oven and gas burners. It had everything I could want – close to a professional kitchen. It had a competently sharpened set of knives but I'd brought my own with me. Any good chef will tell you: we use our own knives always and no one else should touch them. My set was a gift from my old boss in Melbourne. When I eventually moved up to sous chef at Noir, he gave me his old Mac knives and a steel to keep them sharp.

I got into a rhythm pretty quickly, on my own in the kitchen, with no interruptions and just doing my thing. I'd always been able to lose myself in cooking, really sharpen my focus. It was no different here: it was just me and the food.

But I knew a lot was riding on this one meal, and by the time I was garnishing the lamb, I was sweating – from more than the hot oven. This was it – the moment of truth. The family were already seated at the table, the cutlery set. Gwen had a glass of white wine in front of her. The rest had water. I used the caterer's trolley laid with a folded, white tablecloth to freight the dishes out.

'Bon appétit.'

'Smells delicious,' Gwen said.

From the kitchen, through a crack in the door, I watched Gwen. Her eyes were on her husband. He must have started eating, because he soon murmured, 'Mmm, the lamb is tender.' She gave a small smile, took her knife and fork, and started on her own meal. Then, with the decorum of the queen – elbows in, chin up – she ate every last morsel.

Simon came to me in the kitchen later, as I started on the dishes.

'The gravy,' he said. 'It was a little salty. Otherwise, it was all very nice.'

'Thank you.'

The family all went on with their evenings. That was it, the nerves disappeared. Hands in grey dishwater, belief took hold. *I can do this.* Everyone likes to eat good food, and the rich like good food most of all.

After a week or two of nerves, I started to feel more at home at the Primroses. I knew how to work the kitchen, how to cook and plate, and they all seemed to like my food, especially Chet. I quickly realised my responsibilities went beyond just cooking, though. Doing the dishes, tidying and even serving were all part of the role.

Breakfasts were no trouble, mostly they all wanted the same basic stuff, which was easy to whip up to order and serve fresh. I had Elle and Chet's lunches ready and on the bench by the time Gwen's soft-boiled eggs were done. Gwen ate the same small salad for lunch daily (tuna, blanched mixed greens), and Simon got lunch at the office. So I could spend most of my day planning and prepping the family's evening meal, which was to be served at 7 pm sharp, unless advised otherwise.

And the house: well, it seemed to get bigger by the day, I was discovering new rooms and alcoves – the basement alone was as big as any house I'd lived in. Two storeys, five large bedrooms, living room, a formal dining room, two loungerooms, an office, a study, three bathrooms and beautiful grounds with a generous-sized swimming pool, complete with deckchairs, sun umbrellas and a pool house.

My days were mostly my own, and I only crossed paths with Gwen from time to time. I'd drive the family car, the Range Rover, to get groceries, letting it roar when I got far enough away from the house. Sometimes, if I only needed something small like butter or a loaf of bread, I'd ride my skateboard down to the village. It was just a couple of kilometres and there was a crisp new footpath at the end of our road. It was the only exercise I got, and I made sure I always had my asthma inhaler on me, just in case.

Fleur was always around, but mostly prepared her own meals in our cottage, which suited me. Her au pair duties extended to helping with homework, babysitting, general tidying. She was almost like a fifth family member, sometimes even eating lunch with Gwen, who would often have her fork in one hand and a novel in the other. Occasionally, Fleur sat and watched TV with the family in the evenings too.

One night, when the family had gone to bed and I was cooking in the cottage, testing out a recipe I planned to cook for the family, she came into the living area with a bottle of wine. It was clear she'd already had a couple of glasses.

'So, you drink?'

'Yeah,' I said. 'Sometimes.'

'Not since you arrived, I noticed.'

'No, I didn't want to . . . make a bad impression, I guess.'

'With them?' she laughed, took a sip of her wine from the mug she was using. 'I think you are okay. They don't mind a few drinks themselves, in case you hadn't noticed. You should never let them know you think they're drunk, by the way. Just act normal.'

I didn't go as far as saying I had noticed – but of course I had. Every night, a couple of glasses of wine each. I just murmured my agreement.

'Even the girl.'

'Elle?'

'Back in the UK, I caught her once drinking vodka with her friends. They're all putting on a show, though.'

'Everyone here is.'

'What does this mean? *Everyone.*'

'Well, we put on a show, don't we?' I said, trying to soften what I was really saying. 'You seem a different person around me than you do around them.'

She looked stern. 'It's different. I'm working. It's expected. I am a good little au pair. You're a good little chef. No different. This is not *acting*, is it?' She came into the kitchen area. Reached past me, so close I could smell her perfume, took another mug from the shelf, and filled it before putting it on the bench beside me. 'They listen to me,' she said. 'You know, I can make things easier or more difficult.'

I took a sip. What was she implying? Was she threatening me somehow? I wasn't much of a wine drinker and I didn't really like the taste, but I drank it all the same. I sat down with my meal: cordon bleu with a salad of charred Brussels sprouts. I ate and drank, trying to focus on the flavours, thinking how I might improve the meal.

'I moved with them. They made it possible for me to see a new country. I'm loyal – I could never just leave them.'

'You want to leave?'

She smiled, rolled her tongue over her top lip.

'They wouldn't like that. They decide who comes and goes.'

I laughed but she just lifted her glass to her lips and took another drink.

'It gets a little lonely working over the other side of the world,' she said.

I felt heat in my cheeks. She continued speaking.

'They don't like me to date or to meet men because they don't want strangers back at the house. I make do for now. But, you know. It can be lonely.'

'Surely you can do what you want when you're not working?'

'I'm always working. No chance to meet men.'

'You're not working now.'

'No,' she said, her lips curling up. 'But it's just me and you, Bill. And you have a girlfriend, no?'

I realised the implication of my words too late. 'No, sorry, I meant to say you're not *always* working. Not us . . . not like . . .'

She laughed. 'Relax. I know. I was teasing. You're right, now I'm not working, but I'm always on call. Only when they're asleep can I truly relax. We must be available.' *We*, I noted. 'If you let them down, it doesn't end well. I've seen it.'

I don't know if she did it on purpose but her foot touched mine beneath the table as she recrossed her legs. I took another mouthful of the chicken, a sip of wine.

'We make do, though, don't we?' She drained the last of her wine. She stood and took the bottle from the table. 'Cordon bleu.'

'You want some?' I said.

'No. You plan on serving that to the family, yes?'

'How did you know?'

'Every night, you cook yourself a meal then it turns up in the house.'

She was more observant than I gave her credit for.

'This Pinot Noir is not good. It will be much better with a Chablis, maybe Pinot Blanc. Never a red.' Then she turned and went to bed.

After dinner, I cleaned up and took my phone out into the yard. I found myself looking up at Elle's room where the window was open, the breeze twitching the curtains.

I messaged Maia and she called me back immediately.

'Hey,' I whispered.

'Hey babe, how's it all going?' her voice was crackly, dropping in and out.

'Okay, I just miss you like crazy. It's not the same here.'

There was a long pause. I kept my eyes on Elle's window, feeling exposed in the cold.

'I want to come . . . need . . . see you,' she said. 'Just . . . a night.'

'It's too soon. Let me try to have a conversation at my end.'

'You're not a child. You can do what you like.'

I exhaled.

It didn't feel like the time or place to have this conversation. I could call her from the village in the morning where the phone reception was better. After the call, I went back inside and laid on top of my covers, thinking about Maia, imagining her warm body next to mine. In my room, I was chilled to my bones and aching with loneliness.

Later that week, Elle came into the kitchen and watched me cook. We'd not had much interaction alone up until that point. Simon wanted stewed rabbit, a dish he'd had as a child when visiting his great uncle's farm, so I'd organised it. I was cutting potatoes to go in the stew and Elle was sitting on the kitchen bench, her legs crossed beneath her.

'So what do you do with the wine?'

'I just put a little in the broth. It adds flavour.'

'Like a bolognaise?'

'Sort of. I thought it would be fun to get Chet drunk.'

She snorted when she laughed and covered her mouth. 'Not funny. My dad would kill you.'

'The wine reduces and the alcohol boils out. So it's not really alcoholic by the time you eat. We'll have to find another way to get him liquored up,' I joked.

'I didn't expect you to encourage underage drinking,' she said.

I smiled, not turning away from the task at hand. I took the carrots and began to chop.

'When did you start drinking?'

I wasn't sure if I should tell her the truth or not. 'I was probably twelve,' I said.

Her mouth opened. 'Really?

'Yeah, twelve, thirteen. We would pinch beers from my uncle or my friend's parents. Had my stomach pumped when I was fourteen after I got hold of a bottle of Jim Beam.'

'Goodness,' she said. 'It wasn't like that in London, not at my school.'

'Do you miss it? London?' I asked, keeping the conversation going. It was nice to have someone to chat to.

'Like crazy,' she said. 'I wish I could click my fingers and move back.'

'Miss your friends, huh?'

'I'm making friends here at school, but not many. I do miss my old friends, my old life.'

'It must be hard. Do you still keep in touch with them?'

'Not really. It's the middle of the night over there when we are awake. I can't just call. They're all going on with their lives, I imagine. I try to chat on Messenger and I can email, I suppose. I miss my boyfriend too.' She said it with a pause, like she wanted me to notice. 'I guess he's my ex-boyfriend now.'

The silence begged to be filled.

'What's his name?'

'Harvey,' she said. 'Harvey Bond.'

'Sounds posh.'

'He is posh.'

'How long have you been vegetarian?'

'A few months,' she said. 'Dad didn't like it, *doesn't* like it. He's always making jokes about how it's a phase or that I'll end up famished and anaemic. But I think it's important.'

'Why is that?'

'I just thought it was cruel and unnecessary to kill animals. I would never kill a dog or a cat for food but for some reason we just accept the killing of pigs and lambs. My family have all these traditions: they shoot foxes and birds for fun, they eat all kinds of animals. I don't think they'll ever change.'

There was no point airing my own opinions on the matter. I did agree that her parents were traditional in that way.

'No one actually kills the animals themselves, that's why,' she continues. 'If they did, they'd see how cruel it is.'

'Some do.'

'Butchers, you mean?'

'Not just butchers, you goose.'

'And farmers or people in abattoirs, I suppose.'

'I killed them,' I said, nodding at the skinned rabbits on the chopping board.

Her eyebrows dropped. 'You did not?' she said with a sort of lightness in her voice, as if I must be joking.

'I did. They're a pest, introduced by colonisers.'

'Colonisers?'

'I mean early settlers. I went out to a friend's farm, borrowed his rifle. Your dad wanted rabbit and it's hard to buy at stores. I used to hunt pigs too, wild boar.'

Her eyes narrowed a little – not quite disgust but something close.

'How do you hunt pigs? Aren't they domesticated?'

'Wild pigs, with dogs, out in the bush.'

She slipped from the bench and went over to the rabbit. She prodded the flesh, salmon pink with a tight sheen of pale fat.

'Is it easy?' she said.

'What? Hunting?'

'No,' she says, taking the hind leg of a rabbit between her finger and thumb, like a kid in science class. 'Is it easy to kill? Do you not feel bad?'

I turned and eyed her. *Strange girl*, I thought. 'I don't think about much at all. It takes just a few seconds and I'm always grateful for the food, the nourishment.'

'With a gun? Is that how you do it?'

'That's how I got the rabbits. Pigs it's usually a knife.'

She swallowed. 'You stab them?'

'We stick them. Or slit their throat.'

'Is it quick?' She looked like she might be sick.

'Over in a few seconds. They panic, maybe feel some pain but it's only for a moment.'

'A moment,' she said to herself. Then she left the kitchen. That night, she wasn't at the table for dinner.

'Elle's feeling unwell,' Gwen told me.

'I'll put her dinner in the oven. If she's feeling better later, she can have it then.'

After dinner, the landline in the cottage rang. It was Gwen calling, and when I heard her voice, I was certain I was in trouble. All the talk of drinking alcohol as a teenager and killing animals – it wasn't my smartest move. But I was wrong. She called to tell me Elle was feeling better and that she wanted a cheese and tomato toasted sandwich for dinner. I headed to the house to start cooking. Elle met me in the kitchen, sitting on the bench again, this time in her pyjamas. We talked while I prepared her food, then I sat with her while she ate. She wanted to know more about me, and I suppose I wanted to understand her better too.

The family was out for dinner. Gwen had given me the night off for the first time but I still felt a little guilty, like they might be annoyed I wasn't there when they got back.

Teimana came to pick me up in his old Mazda, parked at the gate. I had said there would be a box of beers in it for him if he drove me. Maia was working, just at the movie theatre, but she'd be home when I got there.

'So,' Maia said, when she got in from work, 'what's it like?'

'It's work,' I said. 'But it's fun.'

'What are they like? The family.'

I thought about it. Teimana was in the room with us, frowning down at the joint he was rolling in his hands.

'They're fine. I mean, they're like most rich people. They don't even realise they're different. Just blind to it. The kids seem cool though.'

'Not the parents then?' Teimana asked, still not looking up. 'The husband and wife.'

'Oh, no, they're okay. A bit demanding. He has some important job.'

'Yeah? What does he do?'

'He works for a company in Hamilton, he's the CEO. But he goes to Auckland and to Wellington a bit.'

Teimana looked straight into my eyes. 'Wasn't he a politician? Over there in England?'

I swallowed. I didn't know. I hadn't asked about their history.

'I don't know anything about his work over there,' I said. Maia, who was resting her legs across my lap, reached out and held my hand. 'Where did you hear that?' I asked Teimana.

'Maia told me their names,' he said. He licked the edge of the paper and closed the joint. 'I looked them up. Must have a bit of money, eh.' He smiled. 'So, they better do right by you, boy, or we will hit the house, clean them out. Bet they got a big TV, jewellery, credit cards.'

He put the joint between his lips and lit it.

'What's it like inside?' Maia asked.

'The house? It's nice,' I said, feeling oddly self-conscious.

Teimana held the joint out to me but I waved it away.

'Eh?' he said. 'Gone straight?'

'Nah, but I better not.'

He held it to Maia, who took it and inhaled.

'Just act straight. Nothing to worry about,' Teimana said, looking at me.

'Nah,' I say. 'I can't.'

He shrugged. 'So, what sort of cars they got?'

'I don't know. Nice ones,' I said, clearly evasive.

'Come on, man,' Teimana said with a grin. 'You know.'

'One of those Range Rovers,' I said. 'And an Aston Martin. Both pretty flash.'

Teimana whistled. 'You get to drive them?'

I wanted to boast about driving the Range Rover but I felt a bit protective of the family. I didn't want him to pry.

'Nah,' I said, lying.

'Do they travel a lot?'

'I've only worked there a few weeks,' I said. 'Not sure what their travel plans are like.'

'And if they go away, will you go with them?'

'Yeah, I'm supposed to.'

Teimana cut his eyes to his sister. He got up and went to the fridge. 'Beer?'

'Yeah,' I said. He came back with two crate bottles of Lion Red, cracking the tops off on the edge of his wooden coffee table. I took a mouthful. *How am I getting home?*

Sometime later that night, Maia stood up and led me away to the bedroom. I could feel Teimana's eyes on my back the entire way until the door closed and Maia threw me down on her unmade bed. She had a book on her bedside table.

'What's this one about?' I said, picking it up.

She smiled. 'It's an old book. Ngaio Marsh.'

'Never heard of her,' I said. '*A Murder at Membrey Manor*.'

'You might like it. She was a famous Kiwi author.'

'Yeah?' I said, turning it to read the blurb. I wasn't much of a reader back then but I now had plenty of time in the evenings. Maia took the book from my hand, her body pressing down against mine. Her hands holding my own above my head, she kissed my neck.

I had to bribe Teimana with McDonald's to get him to drop me back early the next morning. It took all my courage to knock on his door and wake him. I knew I'd messed up. I was supposed to be back that night and soon the family would be getting up. Simon would be waiting for his omelette and single espresso, Gwen her soft-boiled eggs and milky tea, Elle her porridge and fruit, and Chet his Cheerios.

Teimana ate his McMuffin in two or three bites with one hand still on the wheel, then he reached for his hash browns as he tore along the road from Rotorua to Cambridge.

'You owe me, boy,' he said. He gulped down his hot chocolate. At the gate as he dropped me off, he shook my hand. When I turned back, I noticed he was still there, in the car watching. I entered the code for the gate and strode as quickly as I could toward the cottage, with Maia's book tucked under my arm as the sun began to rise.

SLOANE

A WOMAN DESCRIBES the gruesome details of the murders with eerie sound effects – whistling wind, a door creaking, the *shick* of a blade. The host insists hers is the *number-one underground* true-crime podcast, despite tens of thousands of ratings on the listening app – a sure fire indicator that the podcast is well and truly above sea level. They have dedicated an episode to the Primrose stabbings but barely scratched the surface. It's the worst of all the podcasts I've listened to on the case. In fact, all the information they cover is publicly available and there's no recorded interview with anyone involved; just a reading that could be a transcript of the Wikipedia page, with a 1970s horror sound design and 'This episode is brought to you by' every eight minutes. *Underground indeed*, I think before turning it off and shifting my focus to the world outside, the road ahead. Not all podcasters are journalists – I accept that – but this is just lazy.

As I drive, I'm surprised by the absence of native bush. Where I would have expected to see the ferns, scrub, and trees of New Zealand postcards, there are only endless green paddocks alternately speckled with birch-coloured sheep and dairy cows.

The smaller towns seem to have Māori names, while the cities and larger towns still wear titles carried by the British across the sea: Hamilton, Wellington, Dunedin, Christchurch and Cambridge – my destination. Not quite a city, more a large town really. Twenty-one thousand people according to Google but it was roughly half that population when the murders occurred.

Billed as *The town of trees and champions*, the first thing I notice is how quaint it is. A wide, tree-lined main street, a church, a small clocktower, cafes, shops of bric-a-brac and kitschy souvenirs, banks, bars. Service stations, Super Cheap Auto, and a Carpet Court. An opportunity shop. The usual fare. The infamous bar where Bill had his last drink as a free man. I see the bakery, where he sat and ate a pie the morning after he washed the blood off, still there on the main strip. Can't have been too bad for business then.

In a blink, the town is behind me and the navigation has me travelling along a rural road. Townhouses neatly line the street, but the further I go, the bigger the blocks get. A horse truck blows by, going the other way. The house isn't far from town at all. I've travelled just a few minutes before I'm pulling in at a gate. So that was the trip Bill Kareama supposedly ran that night. I find myself wondering if he would even recognise this area now. Before, the aerial photos showed farmland in every direction; now, the house is crowded by new developments. The paddocks have been split up, sold off and built on, and the Primrose mansion stands out like a relic. It's as grand and beautiful as the old photos. I park and take a few snaps on my phone before pressing the intercom at the gate.

'Hello?' a woman's voice.

'Hi, my name's Sloane. I was in touch about seeing the house for a pod—'

'Right, Sloane. Yes, I'll buzz you through. Terrence is here waiting.'

The gate groans open. I walk in and head toward the house. It's a little dated, set about thirty metres back from the road at the end of a paved driveway, overhung by trees on one side and opening up to gardens on the other. It's strange to think the house before me is the site of one of the ugliest crimes in this nation's history. It gives me the creeps, no question about it. But if I'd turned away from everything that chilled me, I'd still be scratching together 300 words for *The Age*.

A golden retriever comes bounding in my direction, its tail wagging, as a woman steps through the front door: late fifties, a strong, wide build, a tired blonde bob and stern eyes. This is someone who plays tennis or maybe golf, and she plays to win, you can just tell. She whistles the dog back to her.

'Hello,' she says, as I step up to the door.

'Sloane,' I say, giving her a smile that goes unreciprocated.

'Karen.' She doesn't offer her hand. 'I listened to your podcast.' There's no warmth in it.

'You did? That's nice to hear.'

'Come on,' she says, turning. 'This way.'

The house feels larger than it looked in the crime-scene photos that I've seen. On the lower level, the floors are now boards, no longer carpet, and the curtains that were once strung before the windows have been replaced by tasteful, white-slat blinds. Karen leads me past the base of the staircase and through the living area into an enormous kitchen. *Bill's domain*, I think.

A tall man is sitting at a high marble benchtop. He turns and looks at me over his reading glasses, assessing me for a moment before he stands. 'Terrence Koenig,' he says with a warm smile, extending a hand.

'Sloane Abbott,' I say. His grip is just a little too firm.

'Please, take a seat.'

He shuffles the pages on the bench, stacking them to one side. Terrence and I both sit but Karen remains standing, her hands on the back of a kitchen stool next to her husband.

'So,' I begin, reaching for my notepad and pen and the voice recorder in my bag. 'I'll try not to keep you long. I just had a few questions about the house.'

But when I place the recorder on the bench, Terrence's hand reaches out, covering it. He shakes his head. 'Listen, we don't really want to be part of your podcast,' he says.

'Sorry?'

Karen speaks now. 'We discussed it and we don't want to be part of your podcast. Please don't record our voices.'

I blink away the confusion. *Why let me in the door then?* Maybe TK was right about these people. 'Okay, sorry, I was under the impression from your email—'

'Yes, you've had your assistant harass us for this conversation—'

'Karen,' Terrence says. 'She's a guest.'

'Sorry, there must be some confusion. Harass?' *What a mole,* I think. Tara doesn't *harass.* I turn to Karen, take her in: the glow in her vein-blotched cheeks, the unblinking, scornful expression. She doesn't speak, she doesn't meet my gaze. 'Let's put that aside. If you're not happy for me to record, that's fine. I can just ask you a few questions about the house.'

'Good idea,' Terrence says, running his fingers back through his steel-wool hair. He has kind eyes, made for smiling, with wrinkles fanning from the corners. 'No recording our voices but I'll show you the house and we can chat about it. Why don't we do that?'

'That's totally fine. I really don't mean to intrude.'

'So you're going to try to get him out?' Karen says.

Terrence gives me a knowing look.

I want to ask her how she can stand up straight under the weight of that enormous chip on her shoulder.

'I'm not trying to do anything other than get to the heart of the story. I want to give my listeners an opportunity to make their own minds up about the case and whether or not Bill Kareama had a fair trial.'

A hack of laughter. But it's Terrence who speaks next. 'Right, well, your listeners should trust the robust legal systems and processes of our country. But that's neither here nor there. We've got a bit of time but we don't want our names or voices attached to this podcast. Right, Karen?'

She throws up one hand. 'Do what you want, Terrence.'

'No, come on. What do you want me to do?'

'Can I speak to you outside?' Karen says. He exaggerates an eyeroll.

'Sure. One moment, Sloane. Let me smooth this over.'

They leave the kitchen via a sliding glass door that leads outside, and I see them walk down a patio until they are out of sight. I feel like I can finally breathe out. That was a little awkward. A few minutes later, only Terrence comes back.

'We've had tourists try to visit the house. People think it's weird that we live here,' he says, sitting again. 'Karen's just worried about exposure.'

'Like dark tourists?'

'I guess. They don't realise how much work we've done. It's not the same house – maybe it is on the outside, but in here we've worked hard and spent a lot of money to make it our own. We completely gutted the inside. All of this is new,' he says, gesturing expansively. 'We knocked over the cottage where Bill Kareama lived. As you can see outside, the land was subdivided before we bought it. And we only bought the place because it was too good a deal to pass up, especially with property prices being the way they are. And I always admired the architecture.'

'I get it,' I say. 'Have you lived around here long?'

'We've been in Cambridge for decades, yes. Some people our age want to downsize but we upsized. The thing is, this house was actually cheaper than our old place.'

It's clear that he wants to use this interview to defend their decision to buy the house. But he makes a valid point. It sounds like it sold for roughly half its value.

'We just think your podcast is going to bring a whole lot of attention to something that is done and dusted.'

'Right,' I say. 'Well, I'm here in New Zealand to record this podcast about Bill Kareama and what happened in *this* house.'

'There are so many unsolved crimes. Why are you bothering with one that is solved? What am I missing?'

I need to quickly get him onside here. If Karen has her way, I'll be out the door before I get any useful info at all. I give a smile, pull my voice recorder from where it sits on the table and put it away in my bag.

'Look, I hear what you are saying. The last thing I want to do is make life difficult for you both. The podcast is happening, there will be growing interest in your house. That's just a fact. What you can do is be proactive. You've said the house has changed a lot, right? And you've given me sound reasoning for buying it, given the climate of the property market. If we talk about that, if I include those details in the podcast, then fans, er, listeners won't have any incentive to want to see it.'

He's watching me closely. 'I retired a few years ago. We only have this house to our name. This podcast could bring out all sorts of ghouls and make resale impossible if we were forced to move.'

'Again, it's a totally valid concern,' I say, looking around me. 'But we will do what we can to direct interest away from the house. It's beautiful,' I add.

'It's not just the house,' he says. 'I was around when it happened.'

'Yeah?'

He clears his throat. 'I was headmaster at St Luke's from 2001 until 2017.'

'You knew the family?'

He nods. 'Not well. But yes, I knew them. Half the town knew them. No one wants their lives to be some show, entertainment. We all deserve that basic courtesy.'

I nod again. 'Have you listened to my previous podcasts, Terrence?'

'No, not yet. I don't much listen to podcasts. I mostly just read books. Karen has.'

'And?'

'She said they were good, maybe a touch, umm . . . well, exploitative is not the right word.'

No, it's not the right word at all.

'Well, I like to think I give the victims the centre stage. I am kind and I treat them with the dignity and respect they deserve. Not salacious, no airing of dirty laundry unless it is pertinent to the case. I like to think I show much more than just basic courtesy.'

I notice in my periphery that Karen has re-entered the room. She speaks next. 'If you get him out and he hurts someone else, you're going to have to bloody live with it.'

'*Karen*, please,' Terrence says. 'She's not going to get him out.'

It's clear Terrence is leading the charge here – that he was the one who agreed to see me, probably against his wife's wishes.

'I just want her to know what she's risking,' she says. 'And I don't want anyone turning up here like we live in some mausoleum.'

'Of course,' I say. 'I was just saying to Terrence that this could actually help.'

'I'm sure,' she says. An uncomfortable silence fills the room.

'Well,' Terrence says at last, rising. 'If you're finished berating our guest, Karen, I might make us a cup of tea and we can get this over with.'

'That'd be great,' I say, as I open my notebook. 'Milk with one, please.' Karen gives me a look and leaves.

As he makes the tea, Terrence tells me more about their decision to purchase the house: when he first noticed it, the history of the property before the Primrose family moved in and its significance in the town as the former home of a very wealthy and famous local horse trainer, before he retired to his beachfront mansion in Mount Maunganui. After the murders, Elizabeth Primrose was the executor of the family trust – initially, she didn't want to sell and wouldn't let anyone knock the house down. But eventually, it was sold on to developers, who failed to get any traction with a redevelopment but managed to offload most of the farmland. The house remained vacant as the suburbs crept closer then finally Terrence and Karen put an offer in. 'I thought our offer was ridiculous, way too low, and I honestly didn't think they'd even consider it. But it was like Christmas when the email came back – they'd accepted.'

He places a mug of tea in front of me. 'Wow, that must have been a surprise,' I say.

'We were gobsmacked. But we hadn't realised quite how much it would cost to tidy it up,' he says, with a chuckle. 'The interior was graffitied beyond recognition. Every window smashed, burn marks on the carpets. The pool had road cones, a shopping trolley, drug paraphernalia in it. The roof was leaking. We paid $1.2 million for the house and the small parcel of land that was left after the rest had gone to developers. But we put in hundreds of thousands of dollars and a couple of years of blood, sweat and tears, literally, to completely refit the house and,' Terrence adds proudly, 'it's come out wonderfully, I think.'

'It has,' I agree. Like any good teacher or school principal, he's affable, unfazed and approachable but speaks with authority. 'And you mentioned you knew the family? Did you have many dealings with them?'

'Only in a professional setting,' Terrence said. 'A late enrolment from memory and the girl had some issues at school. There was a situation with the PE teacher and I was *summoned* by Simon Primrose to fix it.'

'Right,' I say, making a note. 'What came of the PE teacher?'

'He left that year. No harm done. I recall something about misconduct but it's all a little hazy. It was a long time ago.'

'And it was her parents who raised this with you, you said?' I have a sip of the hot tea. It's strong.

'Simon was incensed. He was a strong-willed man.' Again, that chuckle. 'I remember him well. I had to smooth things over once or twice and, as I said, he *summoned* me, for lack of a better word.'

'How does one summon you?'

He sighs but there's the hint of a smile in it as if to say, *Oh boy.* 'Sternly. He called the school, told me if I didn't come and speak with him, the next correspondence would come from either a journalist or a lawyer. I knew he was once a politician and, god, he was an intimidating man. So I had to go and explain the steps we had taken to protect his daughter.'

'Sounds intense for an incident you don't even remember?'

'No, it wasn't so serious. But I have three sons, so I get it. He just did what any good father would do. His daughter was going through a hard time at school, there was this business with the teacher and Simon wanted to make sure we were looking after her.'

'Right, and the teacher just up and left?'

'Officially.'

'Unofficially?'

'He fled.'

I nod and sip my tea again. This is great for the podcast. Suddenly, I have a new person of interest. 'Do you know if the police caught up with this teacher?'

He shakes his head. 'No, this is all very much a secret history. No police or investigation. He didn't break any laws—'

'I mean, did the police interview him regarding the murders?'

I see genuine surprise now. His grey eyebrows sail up his forehead. 'The murders, well, I assume not. You don't think . . . No, he was long gone by then and Kareama—'

'It's just for the podcast. I'm sure it's nothing but listeners would be interested to know what came of him. What was his name?'

'Oh, it was almost twenty years ago and he wasn't there long. I could try to remember.'

'If it comes to you, just let me know.'

'Of course,' he says, nodding. 'Anyway, why don't I give you a tour?'

'That'd be great.'

I leave my tea unfinished in the kitchen as Terrence leads me through to the dining room, and then the rest of the ground floor, pointing out which rooms have changed and how. There are a number of living areas, one of which is a fairly formal loungeroom, while the others look more lived in, with a big flatscreen and soft leather couches in the larger one. It is all tastefully furnished, and very tidy.

We arrive at the foot of the staircase and head up. I feel a cool tickle at my throat. A generous hallway runs one way to two guest bedrooms, Terrence explains on the landing, and the other way to the master bedroom and two more large rooms. There are three bathrooms in the house – a full-sized bathroom up here, an ensuite off the master, and another downstairs.

Terrence shows me the two bedrooms at the south end of the house, both of which, he says, were spare rooms when the family lived here. One is filled with boxes and the other is quite bare, with just a single bed and a dresser.

The next bedroom we stop at is on the north corner of the house; the afternoon sun floods in through the large sash window.

A wooden desk sits beneath a galaxy of moving dust particles. There's a framed photograph of a group of adults standing in front of a school gate – Terrence's staff at the school, I figure.

This is where it happened, I remind myself, my eyes searching for spots of blood I know aren't there.

'This one was Elle's room,' he says. *How well did he know her?* 'Now it's my study and gym.' He points at the stationary bicycle set up facing the window. 'I can at least look outside while I ride.'

He hadn't struck me as a fitness junkie but is in reasonable shape, I suppose, for a man of his age. Despite the warmth of the sun, a cool breath runs over my skin. I imagine a young girl, on the floor before me, blood pulsing from a gaping wound in her stomach. He nods at the window. 'Pool used to be down there. We filled it in, costs a bomb to run the pumps and heating. Anyway,' he says, turning, 'let's continue the tour.'

I follow him out.

'The son was in here,' he says at the next room. He doesn't use his name.

'Did you know him?'

'He was at intermediate school. I never met him but I heard he was a good kid. I always think he was the biggest tragedy in the murders. The boy. He was twelve, for goodness sake. Makes Kareama even more of a monster in my eyes.'

This room is now a home library. Shelves of books, a reading chair, a sewing machine set up on a table and views out over the front lawn toward the road.

'Karen reads her books, does her sewing up here. She didn't like it at first. She thinks the room has bad energy. We've been talking about moving this stuff and using the room for storage instead – setting up a sewing room or library downstairs. I don't believe in ghosts, neither does she. Couldn't live here if we did, but we both agree this room feels off. It gets cold in here if the heating's off, not much natural light, maybe it's just that.'

I could laugh at the irony. The entire house feels off, even for me.

The master bedroom next.

'This is our room, it's all different now. The shape is the same but we replaced all the carpets up here – it was torn up and water-logged. We made the walk-in wardrobe bigger, cutting into the bathroom. We pulled the bath out of the ensuite and renovated it all. I understand the bed used to be over here.' He gestures to the far wall. 'Coming out this way. We decided it was better under the window on this wall because you get a bit of morning sun in summer.' He turns to face me. 'Not a bad view of the front garden, eh?'

'It's nice,' I lie.

'We replaced the old curtains, torn and mouldy things they were.'

'Can I ask, did you notice anything off when you started renovating?'

'Off?' He turns back, hands on hips.

'Anything that might have belonged to the family? Or anything that struck you as not quite right?'

'Well . . . I wasn't sure if I should mention this or not,' he says, rolling up each sleeve of his shirt, slowly. 'Karen thought it'd be better not to. But there was something with the heating.' He stares at me a moment, his expression a question mark as if he's deciphering some hidden code. 'Come on, I guess I'll show you.'

He leads me downstairs and to a discreet door off the foyer.

'I told one of the local cops about it but he didn't seem to think it was important; it might be good for your podcast though.'

He opens the door and hits a light switch to reveal a wooden set of stairs. We head down the stairs, which lead to a cavernous basement space.

'It's not that common to see a basement like this in New Zealand. It's a bit of a flood risk actually. As you can see, we don't keep much down here. When we moved in, we found a couple of things that probably belonged to the Primrose family,' he says, pointing toward the corner. 'And this.'

He nods at a gas heating unit on the wall. Beside it is a six-foot-tall gas bottle.

'Definitely not common in New Zealand. We are a cold country but everyone uses fire to heat their homes, or electric heating. Gas central heating isn't seen too much, especially fifteen years ago.'

'I suppose that's out of the ordinary.' I'm unsure what the exact significance of all this is.

He turns to me and the way the naked bulb shadows his eyes makes my heart speed up.

'No, that's not the strange thing. We use it – it's great actually. It's ducted to all the rooms so it heats the entire place like a dream. The house retains the heat really well, so we only need it in winter. After all this time, we had to have someone come out and give it a service, to check it was in working order.'

A funny feeling comes over me. *I need to get out*, I think. It's this place, it's the history of the house. The bodies, the blood. Bill Kareama fleeing into the night.

'So that's what you thought I'd be interested in?' I say, a traitorous quiver in my voice. *Channel this feeling for the podcast*, I remind myself. *Remember the atmosphere, the ick of the place.*

He shakes his head. 'Not the fact they had central heating like this, no – it was what the technician found. The exhaust of the heater was clogged with leaves, twigs, debris.'

'So after all the years, it got blocked?' I ask.

'No. Not after all these years. The technician said it was practically impossible for that to happen naturally. And it was packed tight, jammed in there. Blocking it. So the carbon monoxide had nowhere to go.'

'Except into the house,' I say, as much to myself as him. An exhaust choked with debris . . . I have that feeling I get when I know I've found something big. The anticipation of this discovery almost eclipses the unease of being here.

'If it was blocked, this basement would fill first, before the carbon monoxide ends up pumping through the system,' he says, running his hand over his head. 'I reckon he tried to kill them this way, then when that didn't work he stabbed them.'

I feel almost lightheaded. 'Why didn't it work?'

'The house is probably too big, too many ways for the carbon monoxide to escape. Anyway, like I said, the local coppers didn't think it was worth bothering with because the case was solved.'

'Have you got any photos of what it was like before it was repaired?'

'Karen has a couple on her phone. I'll send them to the email we've got.'

I walk further into the basement, my heart hammering. It's more spacious than it looks – the further you go in, the more it reveals itself. I move through the gloom toward the corner. Wooden pillars stand, evenly spaced, like tall, pale men watching me pass.

In a corner, there's a dusty cardboard box and an old set of golf clubs sitting like straws in a grubby-looking golf bag. When I go closer, I see there are a few old books inside the half-opened box. *Encyclopedia Britannica* printed on the crimson spines. Not a full set, just a few volumes.

'Yours?' I ask Terrence, pointing to the golf clubs.

'No,' he says. 'They were left here. Simon's, I can only presume. I'm surprised they weren't stolen in the years the house was derelict.'

'The box?'

'Oh, they're ours – I've been meaning to chuck them out, actually,' he says.

'Can I take a look at them?' I ask. 'The clubs?' I can see finger marks in the dust on the golf bag – it's clear Terrence or someone else has handled it recently.

'Be my guest.'

I pull a club out and hold it in my hands, studying it for a moment – a putter. My ex was into golf; on one of our early dates he took me to the driving range to show me how far he could hit. Putting was the only part I actually liked. I swing the club. It doesn't feel right. *Lefty*. I make a mental record of that.

'Mind if I take a photo?' I say.

'Sure.'

'And these were left here with the boxes?'

'That's right.'

I snap a couple of shots of the putter, then of the rest of the clubs.

It's with relief that I emerge into the main house, and return to the kitchen. Karen has already cleared my unfinished mug of tea away.

Terrence takes a mobile phone that's charging next to the stove and scrolls for a while before coming around to stand next to me and showing me an image. 'Here,' he says. I see twigs and leaves, just how he said, jammed into the exhaust.

'Interesting. It definitely looks deliberate.'

He murmurs his agreement. 'I'll send this and some other shots to you.'

'Who was the gas technician?'

'Andrew Mears,' he says. 'Karen's second cousin. He's in town here.'

'Have you got a number for him?'

'I'll send it with the photos.'

I feel warmth in my chest, a tingling inside. I realise this is something, this is exactly why I do this.

Passing through the loungeroom, I notice a number of books on flyfishing and New Zealand history in a bookcase. Shelved beside them, another title catches my eye. *The Primrose Stabbings*.

Terrence seems to notice me looking.

'Ah, the book,' he says. 'Written by the arresting police officer. It makes it really clear they got the right guy. I know it won't help your ratings but you'll come to see Bill Kareama was a bad man.'

He reaches out and takes *The Primrose Stabbings* from the shelf and hands it to me. 'Give it a read.'

'Thanks,' I say. 'I'll add it to the reading pile and get it back to you when I'm done.' I'm not a snob, but the book has a self-published feel to it, the paper thick and heavy and very white. I look at the spine. No logo.

He nods.

Back in the car, I send a message to the phone number I have for TK.

I'm guessing you already know that the heating in the Primrose house was tampered with and set up to pump carbon monoxide into the bedrooms, right?

He might not want to help, he might want to block me out, but he can't ignore that.

TK

I RUSH TO answer my phone when it rings.

'This is a call from an inmate at Waikeria Prison. Please hold the line to accept this call.' I'd called the prison and requested contact but I had no idea if he would call me back. I wait for the familiar click.

'TK.' It's a voice I used to hear every week, multiple times a week.

'Bill,' I say. My heart is thumping. I steady my breath. 'Kia ora, e hoa. It's been a while.'

'Yeah,' he says. 'A couple of years. I didn't think I'd ever hear from you again.'

'Things have changed a bit for me, Bill.'

'Sure,' he says. 'I get it. How's the family?'

'Lynn and I, we separated a year or two back.'

'Sorry to hear, TK. I feel guilty about—'

'No, no, it wasn't your fault. We weren't right for each other, that's all. We're different people.'

'Still,' he says. 'You gave up a lot for me.' He could hate me for just abandoning him but he doesn't. 'So why are you getting in touch? You back with the prison?'

'No,' I say. 'No, look, it's something else.'

'Yeah.'

'You won't like it but I told her I'd ask. I heard from a journalist.'

'Oh,' he says, his voice deflating. 'A journalist. No, no, I'm not talking to—'

'Just hear me out, Bill. You can say no.'

'I'm going to walk out of here one day, TK. I just want people to forget. I just want to move on.'

I promised him we would get him out, we would prove he was innocent. The only promise I've broken. I gave up on him but it's not right to gatekeep Sloane Abbott from him. The least I could do is get her foot in the door.

'She's different, Bill. She's a podcaster, concerned above all else with justice. She has already been in the house. She's found something the police missed.'

He groans. 'Where have I heard that before?'

'I know,' I say. 'I know, but in two of her previous seasons, she got cases revisited and one of them led to an arrest. And she believes you didn't get a fair trial.'

'You trust her, TK?'

My throat feels dry. Do I tell him the truth? *Not entirely.* Or do I tell him what I know he needs to hear? 'I wouldn't recommend you speak with her if I didn't think she could help. The prison director can fast-track her visitor form with your consent. You can tell your story.'

'I have told it,' he says. 'Over and over, but they always change it. They always use those old photos, my old statements.'

'What about your written account?'

'What about it?'

I've still got it on my hard drive. I'd transposed his notes into one document. 'Bill, she's a much better investigator than me and she has a huge audience. She can sway public opinion, which puts pressure on politicians and the courts to re-evaluate your case. They can't ignore her. It's not just the potential of uncovering new evidence; she can get people's attention on the evidence that's been underplayed. I thought she could maybe read your account, at least to give her insight?'

'Nah,' he says. 'Nah, it's not going to help. I wish I never bloody wrote the thing.'

'Don't be like that. It's your story, it's your truth.'

'Truth,' he says.

I sense the bitterness coming back again. I have to keep him positive. 'Bill, why don't you just meet her? Talk to her. She's going to do this with or without you, eh. If you meet her and trust her, I'll give her your written account, your story. If not, you can just move on.'

'Move on?' he says.

'Well, not move on. But . . . you know.'

A long pause.

'Bill, you there?'

'I'm thinking.' I let him consider it – I grew accustomed to his silences long ago. I wonder if he gets any visitors these days. It was just me and James, his latest lawyer for years, and James had other clients, other cases.

'What's her name?'

'Sloane Abbott.'

'Sloane Abbott . . .' he repeats. 'Be my first visitor in a while. Tell her she can come.'

A strange sensation washes over me – is this relief? 'That's a good idea, Bill. You'll have to accept the visitor. I'll let her know today to book it in.'

'Well, you can organise a time with her,' he says.

'Yeah, I can do that.'

'It will be good to see you again.'

'Me?' I say. 'No, Bill—'

'TK, I'm not going to see her without you. I won't do that. I need you there. I can't just trust a stranger.'

Before I can stop myself, I'm looking at the calendar. I can't see him until the weekend, at the earliest.

'Okay, I'll speak with her. We can find a time.' I pick up the photo of Amelia on my desk, stare at her face.

'Thanks, TK.'

I've found myself solely responsible for him before, completely obsessed with the case. It's subtle, the way guilt builds on you, like a pressure on your chest that grows every day until it's all you feel. And now I'm back, helping him, even though I know deep down that Bill deserves to be exactly where he is.

BILL

'SO WHEN DOES Aunt Lizzie land, Mummy?' I heard Elle ask. She was lounging by the pool, as Gwen attacked the garden beds. I was heading from the cottage to the kitchen, about to start on lunch.

'In a few weeks,' Gwen replied. 'Actually, Bill, you should know this.'

I stopped.

'My aunt, Elizabeth, is coming to stay in a few weeks,' Gwen said from beneath her gardening hat. 'She'll be in New Zealand for a week or so before she heads off to see her nephew in Brisbane.' The kitchen window was open, letting in the cool autumnal breeze.

'I'll have to make a special meal when she arrives.'

'You will. Family is everything, Bill, everything. I miss them terribly,' she said. 'Are you close to your parents, are they nearby?' She decapitated a dying rose with her secateurs.

'Mum's dead,' I said. I registered the shock. 'It's okay. She died when I was eleven.'

'Oh, I'm sorry, Bill. That must have been dreadful. And your father?'

'I don't know my father,' I said, suddenly self-conscious that Elle was studying me closely. 'I never have.'

'So, you are an orphan. Well, that's just tragic,' Gwen said, tutting.

'It's okay,' I said again.

There was a small silence before Gwen moved onto the next bush. I made brief eye contact with Elle, who was looking at me like you might a stray dog, and then slipped quickly into the cool of the kitchen. I heard Simon on the stairs, then he passed through the kitchen, and went out the sliding doors to the garden. I began preparing lunch.

'It's too much for me,' I heard Gwen say to him.

'Well, we did have a gardener.'

'He wasn't a gardener. He was a lawnmower, Simon. We need someone who knows what they're doing.'

I thought about Mooks. Seeing Gwen spend hours out there among the flowers and trees, I could see that he was never suitable for this.

Elle stood up and came inside, stood by the door. I could feel her eyes on me.

'How's school going?' I said as casually as I could, tearing up some chicken breast that I'd poached the day before for fresh sandwiches.

Elle looked down at my hands and grimaced. 'It's okay. Fine.'

Only a week later, I would discover that wasn't entirely true.

I wasn't sleeping well. I was distracted, Maia and I weren't chatting as much – it was always hard to find time to talk, and when we did, I'd have to stand outside in the cold. I don't want to blame the reception at the house or the long working hours because I could have made more effort, but still, it made things harder. I'd receive cryptic messages from her, which I couldn't always get a read on.

I guess things must be going well at the house.

My bed's cold.

It's like they were part of a different conversation she was having with someone else. When I didn't know how to reply, I just said nothing. Looking back, I guess that wasn't very smart. But I was young and had my hands full with my new job. Feeding a whole family around the clock didn't leave me with much downtime.

Later that week, Shirley, the cleaner, gave the house a deep clean before Simon had friends over, a bunch of Kiwi fat cats – not exactly what I was expecting. He had a decanter full of whisky, and loads of bottles lined up, some aged ten years, others aged eighteen, twenty-one, twenty-five, thirty. But I knew it was the stuff in the decanter that was the most expensive of all. I once overheard Gwen joke that if they ever ran out of money, they could put the kids through university by selling *the good stuff*.

That night, after a bottle of wine and a rich dinner – eye-fillet steak, creamy mashed potato, red wine jus – the men sat around the living room sampling Simon's whisky. They worked their way through a few drams. Then someone said, 'What about that one?'

I could tell they were all a little drunk, but Simon could pretty much drink anyone under the table, perhaps the single exception being his wife. He was barely tipsy.

'Not tonight,' he said. 'That's one for a special occasion.'

'What is it?'

'It's a special Macallan. Decanted in 1999.'

'How old?'

'Age statement isn't everything,' Simon said.

'But it's fucking old, isn't it?' someone added. A few chuckles.

'It was aged in ex-sherry hogshead casks for half a century.'

Someone whistled.

'Jesus, a fifty-year-old Macallan,' another voice added.

'You ever drink it?'

'From time to time. I opened it less than a year ago.'

I felt the air charge with electricity. 'Go on then. Open it up.'

'I said no,' Simon said. 'It's probably a thousand dollars a dram. And you lot are not worth spending four grand on, not tonight.

It was a gift before I left the UK and you've all had your fill.' He paused. 'Even if I decided to pour a dram, you won't taste it like you should. The best whisky, you don't drink after you've blunted your palate with the cheap stuff.'

'The cheap stuff?'

'True. Nothing on my whisky shelf is cheap per se,' he said with a laugh. 'The *cheaper* stuff. You're drinking a twenty-six-year-old Glendronach. Aged in port pipe.'

'Garden is looking nice, Simon,' one of the men said. I wasn't sure if it was sarcasm or an earnest attempt to move the conversation on. But Simon answered in good faith.

'Kind of you to say, Peter. Although I recently had to fire my gardener.'

'Over-pruned the roses?'

'Not this time,' he said. 'No. His name was Mooks.'

'Who calls a kid Mooks?'

It's amazing what you can hear, listening in from the kitchen, the way voices carry.

'Māori fella?' The voice belonged to the big man I'd heard them call Peter.

'Certainly was. Chef is apparently Māori. But hard to know. Brown-skinned, though.'

I squirmed. I should have left out the sliding door, silently retreated to the cottage, but instead I stepped a little closer to hear better.

'Hiring all the natives then? Cooks a good steak, I'll grant him that.'

'Gwen's idea.' He laughed. They all did. 'I don't mind. The chef's dad disappeared when he was a kid. He made good in a nice restaurant in Australia before coming here.'

'All good and well till one of them nicks your telly,' one of the men said and there were more laughs. 'Or worse.'

'Worse?' Simon said.

'You know.' There was an awkward pause.

I felt heat rising to my face. Did Simon even know that my father was Pākehā and not Māori? It didn't matter. I just needed to keep my head down, keep making the money.

'I guess it doesn't hurt having them around, just got to keep an eye out. But yes, had to sack the gardener but I've got someone else lined up. The son of someone I went to Oxford with is in New Zealand. He came to see me at the office, couldn't remember his dad for the life of me to be honest, but the lad just so happens to be a gardener. I thought I'd give him a job myself.' He paused to take a sip.

'Anyway, how's the golf going, Simon?'

'I need a new putter. There seems to be something wrong with the one I have.' Laughter.

'What are you doing?' I almost jumped. It was Elle – she was in her pyjama shorts and top. I looked above her at the clock on the wall. It was 10.35 pm.

'I was just about to ask your father if he and his guests wanted snacks or tea.'

She went to the cupboard, took a glass out and poured some water.

'You don't have to do that. He can get it himself, or he will call you.'

'Maybe you're right. I better get to the cottage then.'

'Bill,' she said. 'Do you bake?'

'Bake? I can.'

'We used to have shortbread, not the store-bought stuff. Fresh shortbread.'

'You want me to make some?'

'I'd love that. If you're up for it.'

She'd been a touch quiet of late, I'd noticed, maybe homesick. 'I can do that. I'll make some tomorrow.'

'If you do it after school, maybe I'll help.'

'Yeah, that's ok—'

'You know, if you don't mind?'

'No, of course not.'

I went back out to the cottage and took a shower. Long and hot.

I felt it again, that empty feeling as if I was losing everything, the landscape of my life around me changing. I needed to see Maia. I went outside and messaged her.

I miss u so much. I wish I could see u.

I wish u had a car, I wish u could come over. It's been a hard week, she replied back immediately.

Why what happened?

Teimana is in trouble.

Trouble? What happened?

He was arrested. He got in a fght, but they're calling it GBH.

Grievous bodily harm.

Is he out?

On bail til his hearing.

I swallowed.

I could come to u. I can use his car and I don't have work tomorrow.

I looked up at the house, the lights on inside. Simon and his friends. By the time she got here, they would all be gone and the family asleep.

If u want to? I'll sneak u in.

From where she sat on the couch reading, Fleur eyed me as I went back inside, got a can of beer from the fridge and snapped it open. Without a word, she closed her book, stood up and went to bed. It was like she was annoyed, but I didn't care. She was an odd girl, that's all I knew.

It would be so good to see Maia. A touch of the real world outside of that stone wall. I missed her constantly. With the gates and locks, the privacy, *their* rules. With the outside world blocked out, you could forget who you were missing. You could forget who you were.

I slipped out around midnight. No lights were on in the main house and the night was quiet but for the country sounds – the distant call of a cow, the low hum of insects. I walked quietly along the edge of the house to the small gate beside the driveway, opening it from the inside and stepping out onto the road. I stood there and waited. I was still feeling confused and anxious about the way Simon spoke about Mooks, about Māori people in general. I hated it but I wanted to prove him and his friends wrong. After about ten minutes, Maia arrived in Teimana's car and climbed out with a small overnight bag.

'Hey,' she said.

'Hey,' I said, walking toward her and opening my arms. I pulled her body close to mine and kissed her long and slow. 'Come on. I'll take you to the cottage.'

'Are you sure this is okay?'

'We just have to be silent going in,' I said. 'I don't know if I'm ready to have that conversation with Gwen and Simon. They're awkward. It's a British thing.'

'Okay,' she said. I punched the code in at the side gate and she followed me silently up along the side of the house, toward the cottage. Inside, I turned and closed the door, locking it behind me.

'What's this? Who is she?'

I clutched my heart and turned to see Fleur standing in her doorframe.

'Ah, Fleur, this is Maia.'

'Girlfriend?' she said, it was flat and neutral.

Maia looked fierce, staring at Fleur, then she met my eyes. 'Umm, kind of, yeah.'

'You just bring her here? You don't tell me.'

'I didn't know I needed permission.'

'And what do you think happens if I tell them?' She jerked her head in the direction of the house. 'What then?'

'I don't know. It's a free country, Fleur. Am I doing something wrong?'

'You shouldn't be here,' she said, speaking to Maia now. 'I'm sorry Bill didn't tell you. But guests are not allowed.'

'Why not?' Maia said. 'He lives here.'

Fleur didn't answer her. She was looking at me again. 'You like this job? You like the money?'

I shrugged. 'I like her too.'

'Well, take her out. Right now.'

'No,' I said. 'No, I'm not doing that.'

She shook her head, slow with meanness. 'Stupid, selfish man. You'll be gone by the morning if they find out. This is about privacy, Bill.'

'It's fine, she'll be gone before anyone wakes.'

'You know why they like their privacy, no?'

I wanted to argue, but I was curious. A beat passed.

'You don't? Okay then. Well, maybe you should figure that out before you go having friends over again. I'm not going to go telling tales to Simon and Gwen, but I won't lie for you either.'

With the conversation clearly over, I pulled Maia into my room.

Later, despite her protests, I took Maia out around 2 am. What Fleur had said was lodged in my mind like a fishhook. I didn't want to hurt Maia, but I knew she would understand when she cooled off. I couldn't risk losing my job. She wanted to stay and was angry that she had borrowed Teimana's car and driven all this way only to be sent back after a couple of hours.

'Who does she think she is? Why did she even say all that?' she said in a hushed voice, on her way to the car.

'I don't know why she said it but I'll figure it out in the morning. She's a bit weird, you know – maybe it's a French thing?'

'It's not a French thing, Bill. It's a rich thing. You're changing. It's this,' she hissed, throwing an arm toward the house. 'This place.'

I grabbed her forearm, pulling her toward the gate. 'Shh,' I said. 'You'll wake them.'

'This house has made you different.' Her voice was lower. 'The house, the family. You are not the same.'

I gripped her by both arms at the gate. 'No, Maia. I'm growing up. I'm putting my work first.'

'Your work first? Before me?'

'That's not what I mean—'

'They take you in, give you a little money and look what you do for them. You don't have a life anymore. You don't smoke, or skate, or drink. You don't see your family.'

'Just calm down. It's not even been a month, I need to prove myself.'

'No, I will not calm down!' She shook me off and turned away, starting toward her car. 'Leave me alone.'

'Maia,' I said, but the fight had gone out of my voice.

When I got back inside, Fleur was up again, sitting at the table.

'You should be sleeping,' I said.

'I've been sleeping. You woke me. You haven't slept.' She sniffed the air. 'I can smell it on you. You've been busy with your little girlfriend.'

'Stop it.' I was agitated, still wired from the fight with Maia.

'So you broke up with her?'

I just shook my head.

She smiled. I felt empty, drained. I realised a break-up was probably coming – history repeating. I'd left her to go to Melbourne; she took me back. I'd left her again for my career, thinking we could make it work. Maia was right. I was choosing them over her.

'I'll quit in the morning.'

Fleur laughed at that, full-throated. I glanced toward the house as if she might wake the family. 'Is it the sex?'

'What? No.' I felt sick. Maia would be driving all the way home to her brother with angry tears blurring the road ahead. 'It's got nothing to do with sex. I *like* her.'

'Well,' she said. 'Sex is one thing. Bringing people here, that's another thing. You will learn. The longer you are with the family, the more you realise they value loyalty above all else. And they punish disloyalty. Maybe you will be here a long time, maybe not. But you won't quit in the morning. We both know that much. It's true – tell me it isn't. Go on, tell me a lie?'

I swallowed. She had me caught, like a child slowly pulling apart the wings of a moth.

'Break that girl's heart. It won't be so bad. I think you will be happy here.'

SLOANE

MY PHONE RINGS through the car speaker – it's TK.

'Hi, TK.'

'So, you got into the house.'

'I have a knack for weaselling my way into places.'

'I know,' he says. 'I've seen it firsthand.' I laugh. 'Look, I've spoken with Bill. He's agreed to see you tomorrow, so long as I come along too.'

'And you're happy to do that?' I ask, feeling the swelling excitement.

'Yeah, I guess. Just this once.'

I drive past a velodrome near St Luke's. I can't decide if the manicured lawns, pristine gardens and terracotta-roofed buildings remind me more of a winery or a mission. Not a school though, or any school I attended.

'That's brilliant. Thank you, TK.'

'Anyway, I have a client in a minute so I better run. But I'd love to hear more about this heating unit when you've got a moment.'

'Absolutely,' I say. It's clear he's interested again in the case. I'll need to keep him onside.

There is something *pleasant* about Cambridge, despite what happened here. It grows on you. A sort of charm. In the twilight as

I drive down the main street, I see pansies sprouting from hanging pots outside stores, young people on scooters in school uniforms. I wonder if they're at the same school the Primrose children went to. *The town of trees and champions.* Well, I can see the trees, that's for sure. I've spotted a couple of eucalyptus in parks, a reminder of Australia, and the main street is lined with oak trees.

I see a white-aproned butcher dragging in an A-frame sign advertising discounted beef sausages. A dress store has a low bar across its shopfront to prevent ram-raid theft – apparently a real problem in this country – but that brute chunk of steel feels out of place here, like knuckledusters on a pearl-wearing pensioner.

The only motel with any vacancies in Cambridge is the Number One Motor Lodge, which has a jaw-dropping two stars and a rating of 2.1 on Tripadvisor. When I arrive, I realise why it's the last place available. I should have opted for an Airbnb out of town but I guess this will have to do. The sponge-coloured motel sits inconspicuous on the main road, right in the heart of the action. I hadn't even clocked it on my earlier lap.

On the bright side, Waikeria Prison, where Bill is housed, is only about forty minutes away and it's easy to get on the road out of town from here. It is the dullest of silver linings. When I press the button on the desk, a few minutes pass before a surprisingly spritely young receptionist comes bounding down the stairs.

'Hello, Miss Abbott?'

'That's me.'

'Your room is ready,' she says before handing over the keys. 'I can help with your bags.'

'It's fine,' I say. I stare up at the rather large security camera in the reception. 'Thanks.'

'Three nights, right?' she says.

'Yep.' I don't ask about extending my stay because if I survive three nights here, I plan on treating myself to the nicest Airbnb within a fifty-kilometre radius. My room is at the end of a long, grim exterior corridor, lit with fluorescent lights. I hear the muted growl of people arguing and the hack of phlegm dislodged as I walk past closed doors.

My room is equally as bleak. There's an old kettle, a nicotine-coloured AC unit, a soft bed and a twenty-inch TV bolted up so high it might as well be on the ceiling. I let out a long and satisfying sigh. I could fall on this bed and sleep. *No, the pub,* I think. There's still work to do.

I drive back through the main street, guided by my maps to where Bill Kareama had his last drink. Tracks Turf Bar, a wise rebrand from The Pope, given how notorious the murders made the place. Out front there's a covered deck area for smokers, with some-thing I've never seen before: an outdoor pool table, blue, spotted with cigarette burns and drink stains. I pass through the doors and see a place surprisingly busy, humming with locals by the look of it. In my mind, I can see Bill here, hunched over a beer at the bar. I glance around – no one seems to notice me enter, not at first. But when I wander up to the bar with my laptop bag, I clock a few glances. The simple fact of my gender makes me stand out – other than the girl behind the bar, I appear to be the only woman in the place. Although I guess anyone could be in the windowless gaming room. There are a few TVs showing horseracing, a clutch of men gathered around the betting machine in the corner, looking up at the screens with that dead-eyed lethargy I associate with gamblers. Groups of men sit about high tables, nursing handles of beer, chatting away.

'What are you after?' the old publican says. He's got grey hair, pulled back in a ponytail, and a grey moustache. Thick, tattooed forearms that might go some way in deterring any potential troublemakers.

'A wine,' I say. 'Chardonnay.'

He takes a wine glass from the rack above the bar and pours me a generous glass.

'Just the wine?'

'Ah, food too, please. A steak.'

'No steak,' he says. 'Just chips and wedges.'

'Wedges,' I say.

He punches the order into the till, holds a card reader out.

Next, he serves a pimply kid in high-vis with a suspicious-looking moustache. No ID check, must be a local – or the publican simply doesn't care. He pulls a handle of beer. Then he wanders back over toward me.

'Passing through?'

'Sorry?'

'You're not from around here.'

'No, you're right, I'm just in town a few days.'

'Right,' he says. 'Work?'

'Something like that.'

'Where you from? That's an Aussie accent.'

'Melbourne,' I say. 'I'm actually a journalist.'

'In town to cover the big race on this weekend?'

'Race?'

'Cycle race. Roads will be blocked for a couple of hours.'

'Is that why every hotel is booked out?'

He laughs. 'Probably. So it's not that? What sort of journalist?'

'Crime.'

'Crime, eh? Nothing much happening here.'

'It does strike me as a remarkably safe town. I'm actually here for a historical crime. I'm recording a podcast on the Primrose murders.'

Something shifts in his features. His eyes are a little harder now, as they go past me toward the road. 'That right? Well, good luck.'

Good luck. Odd thing to say. 'This was the pub, right?' I say, sipping my wine. 'The last place he had a drink.'

'I was here that night. Pissed as a fart he was, Kareama. Still remember it. You don't really forget stuff like that do you?'

I make a mental note. If he was as drunk as people say, then how on earth did he cover the distance? The speed is enough of a question mark but doing it 'pissed as a fart'?

'So it hurt the town?'

'Of course it bloody did,' he says. 'Everyone was hurt.' Without breaking eye contact with me, he's pulled another beer and placed it on the beermat as a man approaches and puts down his empty. The man recedes with the fresh glass. *Efficient*, I think.

'I mean, economically, sorry to be insensitive,' I say. 'It hurt the town economically—'

'It certainly didn't help. Back then, it was all horseracing here, not much tourism. We've rebranded as a high-performance sport centre since then, triathletes, rowing, cycling, you name it. Got some of the world's greatest drinkers in this town too.' He nods at the people behind me. There's a chuckle. *So everyone is listening.*

'Always this busy?'

'Thursdays, Fridays and Saturdays we are.' He pulls another beer. 'So the podcast, who are you talking to?' This man would be great for the podcast himself – he could give us a lot of context.

'I spoke to the new owners of the house.'

'You did? Strange decision buying that joint, if you ask me. Can't blame them, though. Heard they got it for two muskets and a blanket.'

Another unusual expression.

'Sorry,' he says. 'It's a joke. You know much about the history of this country?'

'I'm not particularly well versed in New Zealand history.'

'Aotearoa.'

'Aotearoa history, right,' I say. I know that much, the te reo
Māori name for the country. 'Sounds like the house went cheap,
though. A bargain.'

'Cheap. You'd hope so. Who else you spoken to? Any of the cops?'

'No,' I say. 'We've been reaching out to them but no one has
agreed to an interview. I have a book written by one of the arresting
officers.'

I take it out now, show him.

'Oh yeah, I knew him. He's moved down Palmerston North.
They all seemed to clear out after that.'

He gets busier as the pub gets more crowded. It's not a rough
sort of place where you'd likely see a fistfight, but it does have a
calloused, locals-only feel. An old Māori man balls a betting slip
and tosses it in the bin before returning to the betting machine.

Now I make a few notes in my notebook. *Texture*, I think. It's
Esteban's word. He wants listeners to feel the texture of the story,
what the story world is made of. *This*, I think, *this pub is not only
context but texture.* I scribble a few more notes then open the book
and begin to read. There's an inscription, with an illegible signature.

For Mr Koenig, I'll never forget Pythagoras' theorem because of you.

So Terrence Koenig taught one of the arresting officers. It really is a
small town. And he was a maths teacher before he became principal.
If nothing else, the author's bias is immediately clear. Within four
pages, he's referred to Bill as *pure evil* and *a monster*. He describes
him as a pathological liar, a manipulator, heartless. He details the
arrest; nothing new here other than the slightly purple descriptions
of how cold and detached Bill seemed that morning, how it was
immediately clear they had the killer.

The barman leans over again, his meaty forearms resting in
front of me. 'I'll tell you who you should speak to. See him,' he

says, nodding. 'Just there.' I turn. He's looking at a Māori man, rail thin, sixties, dark eyes. He's rapt by the screen, the horses running. 'That's your man.' The publican pours me another glass of wine. I tap my card.

'Who is he?'

Just then, the woman behind the bar puts my wedges in front of me. There's enough potato on the plate to feed a rugby team, and a fist of sour cream slathered in sweet chilli sauce.

'He worked at the house, knew the family,' he says. 'And he happens to be Bill Karcama's uncle. Salt of the earth, though. Has nothing to do with him now.'

'Is that right? Bill's uncle?'

'Yep. He got him the job but you can't blame him. You never know what anyone's capable of.'

I turn back once more. The man is at the betting machine. He's in work overalls.

I begin on the wedges, hungrier than I realised. Once I've made a dint in the pile of potatoes and finished my second glass of wine, the barman asks if I'd like another.

'Better not. I'm driving.'

'Where you staying?'

'The motel up the road.'

'Number One? That's not far,' he says, then he looks past me. 'I suppose you don't want to walk in the dark. Here.' He reaches under the bar and produces a business card. 'He's the local driver. He'll be around if you want to pick your car up in the morning.'

I put the card in my bag. 'Alright. I'll have another chardonnay.'

I eat a few more wedges as he pours me another. I tip the last of the glass I've almost finished into the new one after he sets it down before me. Then I stand, and with the ice-cold wine in my hand and my bag strung from my shoulder, I wander over toward the Māori man, Bill's uncle. He doesn't seem to notice me until the horse race on the screen is finished.

'Hi,' I say, reaching out my hand. 'I'm Sloane.'

He gazes at me, uncertain, then toward the bar, then back at my hand. 'Sloane?' He reaches out slowly, shakes it. It's like shaking a block of sandpaper. 'Kia ora. I'm Mooks.'

'Mooks, kia ora, it's nice to meet you,' I respond. I feel my heart thudding. 'Listen, I'm a journalist and I'm investigating the Primrose murders for an independent investigative podcast, which I run. It's called *Legacy*, you might have heard of it?'

His eyes sharpen.

'I'm sure it's a sensitive topic, so I'd understand if you had nothing to say on the matter, but I was hoping to buy you a beer and talk to you about the family. I'm told you worked at the house for a time.'

He sniffs. Looks back up at the TV. 'I did,' he says, his eyes fixed on the screen. 'For a couple months. Gardening, that's all.'

'Right, well, let me buy you a beer.'

'Nah, you're right. I don't drink.'

I look around. *This is a pub. Why come?* Actually, I think I know. His gaze hasn't left the screen for more than a few seconds since I approached.

'But I'll take an L&P,' he adds.

'What's that?'

'He'll know,' Mooks responds, nodding at the bar but again keeping his eyes on the screen.

I come back with the drink and we find a leaner. I don't ask to record just yet. I need to establish trust and there's time for that later. Instead, I ask about him: what he does, who he is, what makes him tick.

'Why did you quit working for the family?'

Now he looks down at a betting slip in his hand before looking back up and meeting my gaze. 'They fired me. I'm more of a labourer, you know, to look after the grounds. They had this big formal-type garden back then and I didn't really know what I was doing. Then I got work at the school – that was okay for a while. I finished up in 2011. But a friend was selling his towing business and he said I could pay it off over time so I started doing that.'

'And you are Bill Kareama's uncle?'

A loaded silence. 'That's right.'

I decide to change tack before he closes down on me completely. After years of interviewing, I know the signs.

'This might be a long shot but do you recall a heater in the basement?'

He picks at his nails. 'Who you like in this one?' he says, nodding at the screen. I turn, see a list of names with betting odds.

'Ah, number seven.'

'Billy's Pride.'

He floats back over to the betting machine, waiting for another punter to finish up before feeding a note into it. When he comes back, he puts the betting slip down on the table. It feels like there's more than money riding on this race.

'So the heater . . .'

He raises a hand. I turn to the screen. The race jumps. 'One sec,' he says. 'We've got the one in green with the red horseshoe.' We watch as the horses round the track. 'Go on!' he says at the top of the straight. 'It needs to get off the rail.' Bouncing out into the middle of the track, the horse kicks on. There's three horses neck and neck, the number seven bobs at the line.

'Did it get there?' he says. I look down at the ticket. Twenty dollars. The odds were fifteen to one. Three hundred dollars. The results come up. 'Billy's Pride.' He smiles.

I feel the adrenaline coursing in my veins.

'I remember, the basement,' he says. 'And the heater.' He takes the ticket, places it into the chest pocket of his overalls. 'You've got good luck,' he says.

'You spent time down there in the basement?'

'A bit. Some tools and things were kept down there. Why is that?'

'Oh, just something I heard, there was an issue with the heating.'

He shrugs his shoulders.

'And Bill, do you have much to do with him now? You got him the job, is that right?'

'Yeah, that's right. But I haven't seen him since the trial.'

'Did you have much to do with him before he got the job?'

'Not really. His mum was my half-sister. She died when he was little, then he went to live with our brother and his family. Didn't think he had it in him, to do what he did. I always thought about how I got him that job – hard not to wonder what might have happened if I didn't do that. Maybe he'd have killed someone else, but maybe he wouldn't. They'd still be alive.'

'No one ever knows what's going to happen.'

'Nah,' he says. 'That's true.'

'So you think he's definitely guilty?'

'Of course he is,' he says. 'I didn't want to believe it at first, but then I saw the evidence and everything. Lied his way into his job at a restaurant in Melbourne, did the same with the family. He's a crook and he's as guilty as sin. But that probably won't help your podcast.'

I finish my wine.

'And what was your perception of the Primrose family?'

'They were fine,' he says. 'Kids were good.' He sips his fizzy drink through a straw.

'And the parents?'

'Well, you shouldn't speak ill of the dead.' His expression is indecipherable.

'You didn't like them?'

'I didn't think they treated me fairly or any of the other staff fairly. But that was a long time ago. They didn't deserve what happened.'

That goes without saying, I think.

'Pick another number.'

'Seven,' I say, again.

'Again? Alright.' He places another bet. Comes back. 'Anyway,' he says and drains the glass.

'Would you be happy to chat for the podcast? I can come to you to record.'

'Nah, I don't want to dredge all that stuff up again. Hard enough being related to him.'

'Sure,' I say, disappointed. 'We can do it anonymously if that would help? Distort your voice.'

'Nah,' he says. 'Others will talk to you, though. But not me.'

The race jumps. This time number seven isn't close. I can feel my heart pounding as it hits the straight, makes a run but finishes sixth.

He screws the ticket up, puts his hat back on and eyes the door. 'I better head off.'

'Sure,' I say. 'Can I ask you one last thing?'

He stops, eyes a couple of the other punters. 'Alright,' he says.

'When you first heard about the murders, before Bill was arrested, did you think there was anyone else who could have done it?'

He looks at me, long and hard. 'I got him the job, like I said. I loved him but the first person I thought of . . .' he exhales slowly through his lips. 'The very first thing that came to my mind was *Bill's killed them*. Then I thought of others, tried to convince myself he wasn't capable of that, but really he was the first name in my mind.'

He turns and heads for the door.

I order another wine, already over the limit anyway. I'll need to get that taxi. It's dark and it looks like rain is starting outside. I read another twenty pages of the cop's book. The publican orders the taxi for me, and I go outside to the car to grab a few things and in just a moment it's here.

'Good night?' the driver asks, as I climb in. He's got a bushy beard and small, dark eyes.

'Yeah, it was fine, thanks. Is there anywhere I can get a bottle of wine from?'

'Of course. Super Liquor is open until ten.' He has an accent I can't quite place – not quite Kiwi – slightly harsher, hybridised.

'That'll do.'

The diet and exercise regime I'd planned is already out the window. I've not hit my 10,000 steps a single day since I won the Walkley, but I could take a stroll in the morning, maybe get up early and retrace Bill's steps. Get a feel for the walking route from the ATM to the house.

We pull into a liquor shop, and I jump out and pick up a chardonnay, Hawke's Bay, while the taxi driver leaves the engine and the meter running.

'Thanks for that,' I say as we pull out.

'Where you from?' he asks.

'Australia, Melbourne. You?'

'South Africa,' he says. 'Been here a while, though. I just have to hide out when we beat the All Blacks, you know.' His laugh is genuine, it's hard not to join in.

I get out at the motel with my handbag, and my gear from the car. I've just got the chain on the door when my phone rings.

'Sloane,' Esteban's familiar voice says when I answer. 'I'm just on a call with Tara, are you free to chat? We want to a run a few things by you.'

'Sure. I just got to my room,' I say the phone wedged between my ear and my shoulder. 'Give me a minute and I'll join you.'

'I'll email you the meeting link.'

I use the hotspot on my phone for internet and join the video call. I am greeted by Esteban's face and an empty chair in Tara's study.

'How's the motel?' he says, as Tara's face reappears on the split screen in front of me. She's drinking from one of those enormous reusable water bottles with a big straw.

'I would describe it as Bates chic.' He laughs. 'You laugh now, but I'm expensing a thousand dollars a night for a health retreat after this to make up for it.'

'Well, at least the Bates Motel has wi-fi,' he says. 'We weren't sure.'

'It doesn't,' I say, standing to open my wine. 'I'm tethered to my phone.'

Tara laughs, as Esteban shakes his head.

'Anyway, news. Big news, in fact. I discovered today that the heating vent at the house was blocked and tampered with.' I find a wine glass, more of a goblet actually, in the cupboard. It's thick enough to stop bullets. I slosh some chardonnay inside.

'The murder house?' Esteban says. 'Blocked with what?'

'Foliage mostly, by the look of it. Just leaves and sticks shoved down there but apparently it couldn't have got in there unless someone did it deliberately. It could have caused carbon-monoxide poisoning.'

Esteban's mouth hangs open for a second. 'Really? Well, I think we have the hook for the first episode. And this is new news? No one knows about it?'

'Hard to say. The new owners obviously know and they informed the police. The gas technician who I'll be contacting tomorrow knows but there's nothing in the media. It wasn't discovered until the new owners moved in. I agree it's a strong opening.'

'Great. Do you want to send through the audio?'

'The new owners wouldn't let me record them. They're private people. They don't want the attention and I don't blame them.'

'Sure,' Esteban says. 'And the psychologist? Are we any closer to getting through to Bill Kareama?'

'Tomorrow,' I say.

'What?'

'I should have led with that, shouldn't I? Yes, I'm meeting Bill tomorrow. The psychologist is coming too.'

'What?' Esteban says. 'How? So many questions. You didn't think to pop that in your schedule so we could see.'

'This is crazy, Sloane,' Tara chimes in. 'You're a genius.'

'It took her two days to crack a psych!' Esteban adds. 'Way to bury the lede.'

'I just booked a session at his practice, told him why it's in Bill's best interest to speak with me. I don't know why he gave up on the case but it's clear he still cares about it.'

'Can you record?'

'Not that first session but hopefully I can establish enough trust and rapport to record next time.'

'If there is a next time,' Esteban reminds me.

Tara takes notes, then at the end of the conversation I ask her, 'No baby yet?'

'Not yet,' she says, 'but soon!'

We say our goodbyes and end the call, agreeing to speak again following my visit with Bill the next day.

After the call, I read more of the cop's book and I'm soon dozing off. I go to the bathroom to brush my teeth; the hot and cold taps are reversed and the toilet-paper holder is hanging on by a single screw. I think of the five-star hotel I stayed in after the awards night in Sydney. It's all part of the story, I suppose.

My room is too close to the road – every time a truck passes, the place seems to rattle. I wake during the night and the alarm clock says 2.13 am in neon red. Even at that time of the night, I can hear car tyres crunching by. A spine of light passes through the gap in the blinds, slides around the ceiling of my room. I toss and turn. I can't identify the exact feeling causing my unrest: trepidation, excitement, fear – or a mixture of the three? All the facts run through my mind. Sleep comes again, a block of it. The clock says 7.31 am the next time I open my eyes.

I get up and call Andrew Mears from Cambridge Gas and Plumbing.

'Sloane Abbott here,' I say. 'I'd like to speak to you for *Legacy* podcast.'

Minutes later, I have an interview booked for the next day. I head back toward the pub, grabbing a coffee on the way. I walk all the way through the town in the morning light but the car is not where I left it. I find nothing but gravel in the parking area beside Tracks Turf Bar. It's been stolen. Just my luck.

'Shit,' I say, quietly at first. Then a little louder. '*Shit.*'

TK

SLOANE HAS ALREADY done what I failed to. She's discovered new evidence in the Kareama case and it's taken her less than twenty-four hours. She thinks she's onto something, and while her energy and drive are a little infectious, I know that her pursuit is in vain. But I can't tell her that – she'll have to find out herself.

All psychologists are familiar with biases, including our own. To counter the effects of a bias, one must first be aware of it, and we are just as susceptible as everyone else. I had been seeing Bill for about a year when I realised I had become emotionally invested in his case. It wasn't transference, it was something else. I *believed* him, and not just that, I believed *in* him. When you come to believe that over a decade of someone's life has been robbed by incompetent police and a dysfunctional judicial system, as I did, it's impossible to walk away. So I quit being his psychologist and started working as his advocate. That began two years of unpaid work.

My old supervisor and mentor called me out in the end. She believed I'd become too attached to the case and that it was possible Bill had manipulated me. We fell out over it in the end, and after I quit, I never spoke to her again. Now, years later, I see that she was right. Consciously or not, I was under his spell. I neglected my marriage and family; my focus was singular and all consuming. Bill's smarter, much smarter, than I took him for. He had me doing his bidding in the real world and had sold me on the idea he was innocent. Something I no longer believe.

All of this is rushing through my mind as I bundle Amelia into the car before 7 am and make the nearly three-hour drive to my parents' house. She's tired and quiet, sleep in her eyes. I am painfully aware that this is not the daddy-daughter day that either of us had in mind – six hours in the car and lunch with my parents, not me. Luckily, Amelia loves spending time with her koro and kuia, and that's what I'll say if Lynn asks, which I hope she won't. My day, my rules, that's what we agreed.

My parents' house looks more or less the same as it always has: the roof tiles have faded and the tree at the front is towering over the southern eave now but otherwise I could have entered a time machine to my childhood.

I knock on the door, Amelia holding my hand.

'Koro!' she screams when the door opens. My father takes her in his arms, hugs her then puts her down. 'Go see your kuia,' he says to her. 'Keeping well?' he says to me.

'I'm alright,' I say.

He turns, letting me inside. 'Cuppa?'

'Love one.'

'Te Kuru,' Mum says, using my full name. I let her hug me when I go inside. She's still got a youthfulness about her, despite the grey that's recently colonised new chunks of her otherwise black hair.

I look around the place and see a thousand moments from my childhood: Christmas trees, bikes, a broken arm courtesy of a pine tree – I could climb like a monkey but not always discern which branches could take my weight. There's also the burn mark in the linoleum from when Anaru, my brother, lit and dropped a sparkler inside the house.

We drink our tea in near silence. Idly, I open my phone. Check my emails, messages. I go to Airbnb, look at the bookmarked listing in Montargis in the Centre-Val de Loire region of France. A homestead, agricultural tourism. I stare at the face of the host. *Fleur.* I could pass it on to Sloane. I check my watch, ninety-four minutes. I need to get back on the road. I take my mug to the sink, tip the rest of the tea down the drain.

'Who are you helping move down here?' Mum asks.

'Oh, just an old mate,' I lie. Is that scepticism on her face?

I am just introducing Bill and Sloane, that's it, I tell myself. Then I can go back to my life.

BILL

THE NEXT DAY, Fleur watched me in the house, discreetly, but I caught her at it. When I brought breakfast through to the dining room, she had a small smile ready for me.

'How did you sleep, Bill?' she asked in front of the family. Anyone could see the bags under my eyes.

'Fine, thank you,' I said. 'And you?'

'No complaints.'

Simon's knife clattered onto his plate. His eyes found me. I returned to the kitchen. It was like that for the rest of the day. Fleur amplified her false sweetness and reserved her nicest smiles for me. I think she relished in my squirming, like she wanted me to know who the apex predator was here, who had the power.

That night, back in the cottage, I slumped on the couch and read through messages I'd sent Maia over the course of the day. She hadn't replied. There was anger and sadness, a warm press at the back of my eyes.

Fleur came out, wearing just her nightgown. I could see the hint of a tattoo up high on her outer thigh. The small shape of a crescent moon.

'What's wrong?' she said, sitting down next to me.

'I'm fine,' I said. I put my phone down.

'Is it about last night? Your little girlfriend?'

I didn't respond.

'Oh, poor baby,' she said. 'You need a hug.' She moved closer, put her arms out.

'No,' I said, shaking my head and edging away from her. 'No, thanks. Think I'll be okay.'

'This work, it's like a cruise ship, or oil rig – good money but hard to keep outside relationships. I think you move on quickly, have some fun.'

Have fun with who?

'Can I ask you something, Fleur? About something you said?'

'Yes?'

'About why they moved here?'

'You still don't know?'

'Know what? I know they're posh and rich.'

'They were famous in England. Not real famous, just sort of famous, you know.'

'Famous for what?'

'He was a politician. I was with them. He seems young but he was in the British Parliament. Very high up. People thought maybe he would become prime minister one day. But it did not happen that way, of course. And Gwen's family, well, they are old posh types. Lots of money and a mansion in the country. So when they marry and have his career and her life, hanging out with princesses and things, they became famous. It happens this way in Britain.'

'So why would they move all the way over here? What happened?'

'Something with trains and contracts. There was an accident. Nine people died. There was a lot of anger. I would be angry too, I guess, if my family was hurt, you know? But there are a lot of people who make these decisions. After a few years, Simon gets blamed, he's a scapegoat. He quits, or maybe they make him quit, but people are still angry. Then after some time, some pressure, they move.'

'And the kids?'

'The photos of their father in the papers – it wasn't good for them. Simon is very smart, you know this, I'm sure. He gets a good job here. Nobody knows too much about what happened at Southgate.' She gestured toward the door. 'It's quiet here. They can just go on living now.'

My head was spinning.

'But listen to me. I know, I *know* this man, Simon. He is not a good man,' she said.

'How?'

'Sometimes, women, young women like me. We see things others do not.'

I stared at her face trying to decipher what she could mean. 'You mean . . . he's inappropriate?'

'I didn't say that,' she said. 'And I can look after myself. If a man doesn't listen when I say no, I might just open him up like a zip.' Then she smiled, her lips pouty and full.

At that moment, the phone rang. I stood and went to it. Maybe Elle wanted a sandwich or Simon wanted dessert.

'Hello,' I said.

'Bill,' Gwen's voice, rushed and low. 'Someone is at the gate asking to see you.'

'Me?'

'Teimana, he said his name was. What's this about, Bill?'

My heart was racing. 'I'll go to the gate and see.'

I left the cottage and made my way past the house toward the front gate. It was easy to imagine Teimana climbing over and flying toward me in a rage. He was smaller than me but strong, with a hair-trigger temper. He was also on bail – I wondered what his conditions might be – could he leave Rotorua? Did he have a curfew?

'Teimana,' I said, as I approached. I tried to keep the fear out of my voice. In the moonlight, I could only see his eyes in his hoodie.

'What'd you do, bro? What'd you do to Maia?'

'Me? Uh, nothing.'

'Nothing? Why's she been crying in her room all day?'

I sighed. 'Look, it's not what you think. We just had a fight.'

'Nah, bro, you're not getting rid of me that easy.' He had come all this way to confront me. I knew he was not going to just leave.

'I've called and messaged her,' I said. 'I didn't hurt her.'

'Didn't hurt her?' A joyless laugh. 'Don't you fucking lie to me. You didn't hit her but you hurt her alright, and now you've got me to deal with, and them.' He nods back toward his car. I see the faces in the back.

'What do you want?' I asked, but I already knew.

'I want to break your fucking face, boy. Why don't you step outside this gate?' He moved closer, his fists closing around the bars.

Shit. Blood drummed at my temples. 'Teimana, please. You don't need to do this. I'll make it up to her. I promise. Just go.'

He turned back to the car. 'My boys came all this way. They won't leave empty-handed.' His eyes went to the house.

'What do you mean?'

'We can come in there and kick your teeth in. Or you can come out here and take it like a man.'

I glanced back at the house. 'Please,' I said, my voice assured. I didn't think about my health, my teeth, jaw, ribs. I thought about my job, my future. I thought about the family. What would they think? Would they feel safe if they saw this violence on their door-step? 'They'll call the police. The family. They're watching and if you hurt me, they'll call the police. Maia said you're on bail.'

'What did you say?' His voice was cold, his eyes wide.

'I'm just saying, there must be another way to fix this.'

He nodded to himself, thinking about it. 'Here's how this goes. We don't hurt you. We leave you alone but we're going to come back when the house is empty.' He paused. 'You're going to call Maia's phone, understand? You don't need to be here. We just need to know how to get in. Then I might forget about what you did to my sister.'

My breath, my pulse, everything was going quickly. There was no way I was going to do that to the Primroses. I eyed the car, then met Teimana's gaze.

'Okay,' I said. 'Okay, but don't come back until I call. I'll have to try to smooth this over, because they're going to want to know who you are and why you came here. But I'll do it. Give me a cut of what you get, though. Is that fair?' I said, trying to add some plausibility to the idea I was willing to help him. I just needed him to go.

'If the meat's juicy enough, boy, we might throw you a bone.'

'They don't go away much but next time they do, I'll let you know.'

'And if you don't, we will be back, and maybe I won't be so kind next time to you or those rich bastards at the house. Got it, eh?'

'Yeah,' I said. 'Got it.'

SLOANE

THE POLICE ARE on their way to investigate the stolen car but I'm supposed to be meeting Bill Kareama in a couple of hours. I make an inventory of all the things that I left in the boot. My running shoes, a notebook, some recording equipment . . . what else? My organs sink. Insurance will cover any losses but what a shitty way to start the investigation. It's a small town. Who would have thought that in sleepy Cambridge a car thief would turn up? I look to the road – dozens of cyclists shrink-wrapped in colourful lycra fly past.

The bar is closed but when I knock on the window, I see a head pop around the corner from the kitchen. It's one of the bar staff and, when I report my car was stolen, he is not very surprised.

'Happens more and more these days. Might be kids joy riding, using it for ram raids.'

'I'm sorry, is there anything you can help with? CCTV?'

'Nah, we only have cameras inside. Have you called the cops?'

'I have actually,' I say.

The police who turn up are young, too young to have been on Bill's case seventeen years ago – not every cloud has a silver lining. They take a statement, details about the car and the time I left it behind last night, the time I noticed it missing this morning.

If everyone is right, they'll catch the joy riding teenagers before long. I'm more concerned about the excess.

I take the card for the taxi from my purse and call the driver from last night. He answers and then arrives shortly after to take me to Hamilton airport, where I'm hoping I can organise another rental car.

'You okay?' the driver says.

I move my palms from my eyes and look up. 'Yeah,' I say. 'I think so. Bad day.'

'It's only ten am,' he says deadpan. 'Plenty of time left for the day to get even worse.' He clocks my expression in the rear-view mirror, then turns to look at me. 'Sorry, I don't mean to make you feel worse.' The light changes, he presses the car on. 'Was just trying to have a laugh.'

I get a better look at him in the daylight. Late thirties, maybe early forties, but already with scruffy, greying hair. *Might have been handsome once*, I think, but now he has a prize-fighter's nose – one who lost a few fights. And the bushy beard isn't doing him any favours, either.

'That's fine,' I say. 'Have you lived here long?'

'A little while,' he says. 'Well, in New Zealand. Only been in this part of the country a year or so. Been living down south.'

'What brought you here?'

'Had an accident at work, hurt my back so now I drive my taxi. Used to shear a couple of hundred sheep a day.'

'Why Cambridge, though?'

'Good question. I like the place, came here for a bit when I first arrived. Seemed as good a place as any to live.'

I was hoping for more insight from a local, someone who could make this all feel worthwhile.

'So what takes you to the airport?' he says. 'Heading off?'

'Actually, it's the closest Avis I could find. My rental car was stolen last night.'

'You're joking? Bad day, alright.'

'I'm hoping to get a new car today.'

'And if you can't?'

'Well, I guess I'll be stuck.'

I'm still holding his card. It looks like it was made in Microsoft Paint but there's something endearing about that.

'Ah well, I can do my day rate for you, drive you wherever you need to go.'

'Oh,' I say. 'What is it?'

'I can tell when a lady needs a break,' he says, putting the car into drive. 'Two thousand a day.'

'What? That seems—'

'Sorry, bad joke. Two hundred a day, plus thirty cents a kilometre for petrol. Fair enough?'

I do the maths in my head – with the exchange rate, that strikes me as extremely reasonable. It isn't much more than a rental, and I could work while he drives.

'Yeah, that's fine. Can you wait around?'

'Yeah, no worries. I'll be available all day.'

'Really?' I say. 'That sounds perfect. What will you do while you wait?'

He reaches over, opens the glove box and pulls out a novel and holds it up. *Michael Robotham.* 'I got more in the boot. You get used to waiting. If you need me on call twenty-four hours, it's four hundred a day. But nine to five, two hundred, no worries.'

'Great,' I say. 'Well, if you can drive me for the next couple of days, that would be a lifesaver.'

He touches his phone, mounted to the windscreen, as he drives, accessing his calendar. 'That won't be an issue. Next couple of days are all clear.'

'Thanks. So right now, I need to get to Waikeria prison.'

'No worries. Are you visiting someone there?'

'Umm, yeah, a guy named Bill Kareama. He murdered—'

'*The* Bill Kareama?'

'That's right.'

'Wow,' he says. 'You know him?'

'I have a podcast.'

'Oh, what's it called?'

'*Legacy*,' I say.

'And now you're doing one about Bill Kareama?'

'Possibly,' I say. 'That's the plan.'

I see him nodding, his eyes on the road ahead as spots of rain appear on the glass.

'That was a big story in New Zealand, real big. I'd listen to that. Messed-up bloke. Wonder what he will say.'

'You think he did it.'

'Oh yeah,' he says. 'I don't know all the details but it's hard to argue, really. Burnt all his clothes, was at the house.'

'And the inhaler?' I say.

'The what?'

I explain the situation, the distance he covered between the scream and when he was seen on the ATM CCTV, and his supposed asthma.

'Probably faked the asthma. I don't know. Maybe the scream was unrelated? A possum or something?'

'Would be pretty coincidental.'

He makes an agreeing sound in his throat. 'Maybe he rode a bike?'

'Possibly, but none was found or recovered. No skateboard or anything.'

'Yeah, I don't know. Just . . . sometimes you can just look at someone and know they're guilty.'

'What exactly does that mean? You look at someone and *know* they're guilty? Just by their looks?'

'Oh, um, I mean, just how he looked in the photos from court and his mugshot. Not, you know, because he's a Māori fella. I don't think that matters,' he adds. 'Sorry—'

'Let me give you a piece of advice from someone who makes a living out of true crime: no one looks innocent in a mugshot.'

'I'm sure you're right. The media probably used the worst photos. But still—'

'Yeah, I get it,' I say. I think of his mugshot, the pink, sleepless eyes, shaved head. 'But we, as society, shouldn't decide who is guilty based on appearance. We review the evidence, the facts and make an informed judgement, leaving no room for reasonable doubt before deciding someone is guilty.'

He gives a thoughtful *Hmm*.

'And I can't get past the most important fact of all: a drunk, asthmatic man cannot cover three kilometres in twelve minutes. Less, given that's not all the way inside the bedroom. That, to me, is the definition of reasonable doubt.'

'Yeah, that is quick. Could he have got a ride with someone?'

'Possibly,' I say. It's a theory I'd considered myself but there was no evidence of anyone else inside at the time of the murders, no one came forward, no cars on CCTV. 'Normally people talk, word gets out and the police will catch wind of it. Accomplices are generally discovered pretty quickly.'

The only thing that might back this was a report of a white Holden Commodore seen driving near the scene after the murders. Police were asking for information on the car in early reports but nothing seemed to come of it. I take my notebook out and write *White Holden Commodore*, then underline it twice. I've been meaning to look into it more.

Dean turns the wipers up, swishing the rain off the windscreen. It grows heavier, hitting the window hard in gusts, like handfuls of gravel.

We arrive at the prison with minutes to spare and buzz the intercom. A boom gate rises and we drive through to the checkpoint to hand over our IDs. They quickly check the car.

'Alright,' the officer says. 'Head on through.'

It's about a kilometre's drive from the checkpoint to the razor-wired walls of Waikeria Prison. We head toward the main gates.

I spot TK there already in the car park, under an umbrella, staring out at the open fields that surround the prison. 'Over there,' I say, pointing. Dean pulls up and I get out.

'Hi,' TK says, looking at his watch. 'I don't have long. Let's go.'

'Sure,' I say. Then he leads me toward the building.

TK

'AUĒ, LOOK WHAT the cat dragged in,' says one of the guards. Someone I'd see here every week when I was on the case.

'Kia ora, e hoa,' I say. 'Been a while.'

'You back for Kareama?' he says, absentmindedly taking the tray with my phone, wallet and car keys and sliding it through the scanner.

'Yep.'

Sloane places her handbag, her phone and a voice recorder on the tray. We pass through the metal detectors.

As she's frisked, Sloane says, 'So my rental car was stolen last night.'

'You're joking,' I say.

'Welcome to New Zealand, hey,' she laughs. 'I've managed to convince the local taxi driver to take me around, thank God.'

'That guy out there?' I ask, referring to the big, bearded fellow who'd been behind the wheel of the car I had seen drop her off.

'Yeah.' She collects her belongings. 'He's been a godsend, actually. I mean, who actually has their rental car stolen? I can't believe my bad luck.'

Now it's my turn to get patted down. 'Well, I'm sorry that happened. Where was it parked?'

'Outside the pub. At least it gives me a chance to work while he drives.' Sloane strikes me as very high-functioning, a Type A workaholic. 'He seems good company too, the driver. Gave me his life story already. South African, worked on a farm in the south – relatively new to the area.'

Finally we are cleared by security and they take us to the visitor's area. Tables bolted to the floor, just like the chairs. Two doors, each manned by a guard. It's all so familiar. I visited Bill in this room hundreds of times; before that, when I was his psychologist, we met in a private space in another building. There are a couple of other people here. A woman visiting a man at the other end. An old man and woman speaking with someone who I assume is their son.

I sit down – the chair is cold, even through my jeans – and Sloane follows, placing her recorder on the table.

'Put it away for now,' I say.

A moment later, the door opens and Bill steps into the room. He's just as I remember him: strong, wide shoulders and thick forearms. Not the skinny boy from the mugshot and photos of the time, but the man who I came to know. Who I came to consider a friend even. He smiles when he sees me. A glint of white among a coarse black beard.

No physical contact is allowed, so I simply nod as he takes his seat.

'TK,' he says. 'Shit, I didn't think I'd ever see your face again.'

You might not have if it wasn't for her, I think.

'Bill, this is Sloane Abbott.'

'Nice to meet you,' she says.

He just stares at her. 'So you want to help?'

Do I correct him? She's not here to *help* so much as to investigate.

'Did, ah, TK explain why I'm interested in your case?' she asks Bill, not wasting time with small talk.

'Yeah,' he says. 'Yeah, he told me about your podcast.'

'That's right. So I guess I am here to help, in a way.'

'In a way?'

'Well, I'm here to get to the bottom of what happened. I'm here to find out the truth.'

I feel the coolness radiating off Bill. He looks at me, squinting as if to say, *What the fuck?*

'Did you do it?' Sloane asks.

Bill stands, ready to leave. She's blown it. 'You're wasting your time with her, TK.' He steps away from the table.

'If you didn't do it, then I'll get you out of here.'

He stops. The guard is already moving toward the door to let him through but he swings around, facing us again. 'You can guarantee that?'

I raise my hand. They both look at me.

'Bill, just sit down, please. Let's have a chat and see what her plan is.'

'Do you guarantee it?' he repeats. 'You find out the truth, you promise you'll get me out.'

Sloane turns to me, maybe she senses a trap.

'He promised me something once,' he says, nodding in my direction.

My heart is thumping in my chest. A long silence. I can't find the words. I can't think of anything to say.

'Look, you don't have to agree to the podcast, not yet,' Sloane says. 'But it's going ahead, Bill, whether you are involved or not. So why don't you help me? Who do I need to speak to? Who was overlooked? Who did they never track down? What really happened that night? You wanted your knives back, right?'

'She's been in the house,' I say. His face doesn't change but I know it means something. No one has been in the house. 'She managed to get inside, check it out.'

'Has TK told you what I want? What I want most of all?' Bill says.
Sloane shakes her head. 'Tell me, Bill.'

'You need to talk to everyone who was there,' he says.

'At the house? When?'

'In the weeks leading up to it.'

'The au pair?'

'Fleur,' he says. 'Of course.'

'Who else?'

'TK will tell you,' he says.

'Who?' Sloane says. 'Elizabeth?'

He turns to me. 'You promised, bro. You found her. You were ready to go – what happened?'

'Just her?' Sloane asks. 'I can find her. I can speak with her.'

Good luck, I think.

'Tate,' Bill says. 'Tate Mercer-Kemp, he was there. He was the gardener.'

'Elizabeth is the most important, though?' Sloane says. 'That's what you want, right?'

He nods. 'Maybe you're smarter than I thought. I want him to talk to her. You found her, TK – talk to her, then I'll do the podcast.'

'You know I can't,' I say. 'I won't. You can't ask that of me.'

He shakes his head. 'I've always told you, TK, and you wouldn't listen. She put me here. I can't tell you who did it and I can't tell you why, but she lied. She's probably the only one who knows the truth, the only one who can really get me out.'

'Sloane can see her,' I offer.

'Nah,' he says. 'It has to be you. You told me you found her. Go see her, talk to her, then I'll do whatever you want. Sloane can have everything I wrote and as many interviews as she likes.'

'Can Elizabeth explain away what Maia told me, Bill?' I say, letting my frustration get the better of me. He looks hurt.

'I could explain it but you never gave me the chance, did you?'

'What?' Sloane says. Then to me, 'What's he talking about?'

I know it'll be unfair on Bill to tell her.

Just as quick as it began, it's over. Bill's walking away. He turns back once. 'Good to see you, bro. I know you'll do the right thing.'

BILL

'SO HER BROTHER just turns up?' Gwen said.

I nodded my head. 'I don't know why he would come here.'

'And how did he know where we live, Bill?' The note of accusation hit me in my throat like a dart.

'I don't have a car,' I said through a sigh. 'So when I went to see my girlfriend, he gave me a lift.'

Fleur's eyes pinned me to the spot. She could've told them that I let Maia into the cottage, on the property. Even if I didn't lose my job, there was no way I'd be able to do that again. Teimana had sealed that door closed. But maybe one day, after all of this was over, in a year or so, I could take the money I made and we could find each other again. I had to tell myself that, to soothe the ache of loss.

'And you are sure he won't come back, Bill?'

I swallowed. 'Yeah, he won't be back. I made it clear that his behaviour was unacceptable. I told him I ended the relationship with Maia because it was distracting me from my work.'

At that, Simon smiled, but Gwen's eyebrows were still drawn and her mouth was slightly sour.

'It's fine, Gwen,' Simon said, standing from where he was leaning against the desk. He moved around behind it, rested his hands on her shoulders. 'It's different this time.'

It's different this time. What did that mean? Had this happened before?

'Nothing to worry about, eh Bill? Just a lover's tiff, a protective older brother, and our man here has sorted it all out.'

I nodded. 'That's right.' I exhaled with relief.

The next afternoon, Elle and I baked shortbread.

'What was it like growing up here?' she asked.

'Boring, I guess. Nothing like England.'

'Would you ever move to the UK? You lived in Australia.'

Despite the task and the conversation, my mind was elsewhere. What if Teimana did come back? It didn't feel like an if – more a when. What would I do? What would happen if I never sent a message to him giving the greenlight to rob the place? Would he forget? Move on? I could report the breach of bail but that might just make matters worse. Teimana was not the sort of bear you should poke.

'I don't know. Maybe. I like the idea of London. The good thing about being a chef is you can work anywhere,' I said. 'What do you want to do, you know, after school?'

'You will laugh.' Elle had her father's slightly pinched eyes but her mother's small, upturned nose and heart-shaped lips.

'No, I won't, unless you say chef, then I probably would laugh.'

'I want to be a vet. Mummy and Daddy don't approve, though.'

'What do they want from you?'

'Probably to marry well and have kids.'

We cut the shortbread and put it in the oven. I set the timer and started cleaning up. While I washed the dishes, she dried them and put them away. I was surprised, although perhaps

I shouldn't have been, to see her put the bowl, the spoon, the measuring cups all away in the right places.

'What now?'

'We wait,' I said, wiping down the sink. 'Do you know what vets do? I mean, day to day?'

'You sound like Daddy.'

'Really? Just another old man being condescending.'

'Is my father really condescending, Bill?' For a split second I wasn't sure if she was joking. Then that big smile cracked open. 'Relax,' she said. 'You're not old. You're basically the same age as me.'

'Not quite.'

She laughed and left the kitchen. I watched her as she sat in a deckchair, gazed back in at me. I looked away, made myself busy prepping the evening meal.

Thirty-five minutes later, dinner was prepped and the timer went off. Elle jumped up and came in, looking at me expectantly.

'Go on,' I said, tilting my head to the oven.

Elle awkwardly pulled the tray out of the oven and set it on the bench. We both looked over it, bent close together. She went to grab a piece and I reached out to stop her.

'You'll burn your fingers.' Our hands touched for just a second.

She looked at me, then back to the shortbread. 'It's perfect. Well done.'

'You did most of the work.'

'You're different,' she said. 'I mean, different to other people. I knew older guys but you're not like them.'

'I'm a bit rough around the edges.'

'It's not that,' she said. 'You're nice, you don't treat me like I'm some stupid girl.' She ran her tongue over her top lip, turned back to the shortbread. Then she reached out and broke a piece away. It steamed in her fingers and she blew on it before popping it in her mouth. Her eyes widened. 'My goodness, that's delicious.'

I tried a piece. 'I prefer it cold and crunchy.'

'Me too but I couldn't wait. So buttery.' She smiled, her nose wrinkling between her eyes like her mother's did.

She's just a friendly kid, don't see it any other way, I told myself. But I couldn't help it. We were flirting, subtly, but it was there. I knew I needed to stop.

'We need to let these cool,' I said, untying my apron.

I went to the cottage. Fleur was there, sitting as she did around the back near the pool house wearing her bikini in the sun, her pale skin stark against the dark fabric. I didn't think it was quite hot enough, but in her big glasses and with a book in hand, she looked quite comfortable.

'What?' she said when she saw me looking over.

'Nothing.'

'You can stop staring.'

I began to wonder: what use is an au pair for a seventeen-year-old girl, Elle, and even a twelve-year-old boy, Chet? I knew she drove them around, tidied up after them, did some general house chores, but she must have known that her time with the family was limited. Another few years at the most.

I continued walking before stopping at the door and turning back. Elle was still in my head. I was frustrated, I suppose. Fleur made me feel like the joke was on me, like I was a naïve little boy. 'You always flirt, always say things to get under my skin. Why? Is it fun for you?'

She lowered her glasses. 'It's not fun for me, no.'

I let my breath out. 'You sent my girlfriend home, you made me feel so guilty. You're the reason we broke up.'

'I'm the reason you still have a job.'

I would have laughed if I wasn't so annoyed at her.

'Young love never lasts anyway,' she added.

'How would you know?' I said.

'Sorry?'

'You've worked for the family for ten years, right? Since you were a teenager.'

'I've had my share of young love,' she said.

'Really?'

'I was seeing a man when we moved actually.'

I sighed and started unbuttoning my chef's whites.

'Gwen and Simon are out today,' she said. 'I'm just warming myself in the sun. It's innocent. You are the one who stared at me.'

I shook my head. 'I wasn't staring at you, Fleur. You know that. Stop with your games, please.'

I went inside and ran a shower so hot it scalded my skin. I stood under it, looking up at the ceiling. I reminded myself how good the pay was, reminded myself that the short-term sacrifice was worth it. But what about Maia? She'd not messaged me again. We were so close before I started here and it went sour so quickly. And Fleur? I couldn't read her – and I suppose she sensed that. She liked to mess with my head; I could feel myself being manipulated. That's when the door to the bathroom opened.

Fleur stood. She reached up her spine and untied her bikini. I turned away, I didn't know what to do. She came to the door of the shower and opened it.

'What are you doing?' I said, covering up. But I found my eyes moving from her face to her body. She pulled her bikini bottoms down and stepped out of them.

'Little lamb, you really can't read women. Or are you just afraid to make the first move?' Then she reached for me, leading with her hand. A curl of breath on my throat. 'Need the woman to take control,' she spoke into my neck, then softly kissed the skin at the base of my throat, pressing me back against the wall. I raised my hand to her chest, to hold her off, but she took it in her own.

I found myself kissing her then grabbing at her with both hands. My mind, just for a moment, wandered back to the house, to Elle, before I lost myself in the moment. Fleur reached for my hand, brought it up to her throat. I squeezed gently, turning her and pressing her back against the wall of the shower. She bit my lip hard. Everything seemed to sharpen into absolute clarity. Her breathing grew heavy, almost to a groan. The wine, the comments, the lounging around in her bikini. She was right, I can't read women – I had missed all of the cues that led to this. I released the grip on her throat and placed both hands on her thighs, lifting her, feeling the water scorch my back. We both released our breath at the same time.

'Our secret,' she whispered, breathless, right into my ear. I didn't feel guilt for Maia. I didn't think deeply about the manipulation, how easy it was for Fleur to get what she wanted. Not in that moment. That would all come later.

SLOANE

OUTSIDE THE PRISON, I talk to TK as he leans against his car. He runs his palms back over his head and I see the veins in his forearms. He and Bill had been having their own conversation, all subtext. I had no idea what was happening most of the time, but it's clear the ball is in TK's court now.

'That was tense,' I say, which is an understatement. I can see Dean, my driver, sitting in his car across the car park.

'It's all bullshit,' TK says, clearly pissed. 'He's been saying that for years. She's the key.'

'Elizabeth Primrose? You found her?'

He shrugs, regains his composure. 'Look, I think this is the end of the road for me. I can't help.' He looks past me, his hands on his hips. 'He's asking too much.'

'I don't get it.'

'I shouldn't have come. I knew it would be hopeless. I just don't want to let him manipulate you or me.'

Manipulate? 'What do you mean by that?'

Now his eyes meet mine. 'Think about what he's asking of me, then ask yourself why?'

'Because he thinks she knows the truth?'

He shakes his head. 'He wants to drag it all back up, bully everyone. It's so traumatic, so dark for those involved. Maybe he just wants to punish them for putting him inside.' He folds his arms and the shirt hugs his biceps. 'Does it even matter to you if he did it?'

'Of course.'

'You said all that matters is he didn't get a fair trial, like that's the most important thing. Your main principle is justice, right? Not moral correctness.'

'What are you saying, TK?' He is so hard to get a read on, I'm not used to it.

'If you knew he did it but you also knew that he did not have a fair trial, would it matter?'

Of course it would matter – the most important thing for a democratic society is a robust and fair legal apparatus.

'It's better that ten guilty people walk free than one innocent person go to prison,' I say. I hear how trite the words sound as I say them.

'That's not what I'm saying. If you knew beyond a shadow of a doubt that Bill murdered that family *but* he also didn't have adequate legal defence or a fair trial. What then, you'd still want him to walk free?'

'Please, TK. I don't know what this is about. How can you be sure he did it?'

'Speak to his ex, Maia. Speak to his trial lawyer, Laurie Berry. Then come back to me.'

'Maia? Have you got a contact for her? I can't find her.'

'I don't have her contact details,' he says. 'She found me.'

'And you're one hundred per cent certain that whatever she said is true? People lie. Unless you've seen video footage of him committing the crime, you can't be sure, TK.'

I watch his face, the complex shifting emotions. 'I spoke to almost everyone,' he says quietly.

'The au pair?'

He shakes his head.

'Elizabeth?'

Again, he shakes his head. As smart as he is, I can see now he's as biased as anyone . . . what did Bill do to him? Or what did he discover?

'Well, that's not everyone then.' I shake my head. 'How can you make a judgement on Bill's guilt without speaking to the two most important people in the entire investigation?'

'I wouldn't necessarily say they're the two most important.'

'Really? From where I'm standing, they are. Look, just consider it, okay? I don't think he's asking too much.'

'I did find her,' he says. 'But I couldn't. I just couldn't.'

I need his help, I need to know what he knows. 'Well, I'll go talk to her then.'

He looks uncertain. 'It has to be me and he knows I won't do it. This is his way of seeing me again, to get to me.'

Or maybe Bill really believes it's his only chance of getting out, and maybe TK is the only one he trusts enough to do it. I have to try to get through to him. 'I read you're a genius, TK. Accelerated into university, destined for greatness.'

'Don't believe everything you read.'

'No, but how does someone like Bill Kareama manipulate someone like you? How do you *misread* someone like him when that's what you studied to do – read people, understand them?'

'Slowly,' he says. 'And precisely, that's how he manipulated me. He's not dumb, he's very clever in fact. He told me exactly what I needed to hear. My job was to help prevent him from reoffending, but he twisted everything and had me convinced he was incapable of offending in the first place.' He takes his keys from his pocket. 'At the start, there were two things that made me think he was innocent: one, he's too considered and in control to impulsively stab the family – he would've had to have planned it. I could see no evidence that he did that. And two, the inhaler, the running, it never made sense.'

'What changed?'

'I was wrong on both counts. This blocked heater proves premeditation.'

This new piece of evidence has only further convinced him of Bill's guilt. TK unlocks his car, lowers himself into the seat.

'What can I do, TK, to convince you to help?'

He's so distant, so removed, but coming here and helping me is a hint that he is still interested if not invested.

'It doesn't matter if he manipulated you or lied to you. All that matters is whether or not he should be in prison. You are one man – you might think you have all the evidence, but that's why we have *twelve* jurors, not just *one* judge. We don't want one person deciding the fate of another based on their own interpretation, influenced by their own biases.'

He looks out past me, a thousand-yard stare, for what feels like minutes.

'TK?'

He doesn't respond. He just nods then closes his door and starts the car. His window slides down.

'TK?' I say again. 'Please. I can organise your travel, pay for it. I can do whatever you need—'

'You're right.'

'What?' I say, confused.

'I shouldn't be the one to decide. That's not how justice works.'

'Wait . . . you're going to do it?'

'I'll call Bill tonight and tell him. If that's his terms and if it means I can hand the reins over to you, I'll do this one last thing for him. You can try to get the retrial, then let a jury decide all over again. Whatever happens, I don't think Bill is coming out.'

'TK, thank you. I promise you, this is the last thing I will ask you to do for me, really.' I am not so sure, but we can cross that bridge if and when.

'Okay,' he says and sighs. 'I've got a long drive ahead of me. I'll text you later tonight, when I've booked a flight.'

'Bye,' I say and wave as he pulls away. I am trying to contain the excitement, stop the smile I feel tugging at the corners of my mouth. I've got him. I've got TK.

As Dean drives back to Cambridge, I think about the women in this case. My gut instinct tells me that they might hold the key. There's Elizabeth, perhaps the most elusive of all, who Bill is fixated on. There's Fleur – according to forums online, she runs an Airbnb in France. And then there's Maia, Bill's ex – I don't know much about her, other than the fact Tara can't find her.

TK's spoken to Maia, but she's not on the record anywhere else. It's highly unusual. Why did she never testify? Yes, the original case was infamous for its lack of witnesses; barely anyone was called on to take the stand. I suppose it's possible that the prosecution thought the evidence was so compelling they didn't need a great deal of witness testimony. But surely Bill's lawyer wasn't so incompetent as to fail in getting in touch with his ex? At the very least, she could have provided a character statement to prove he was never violent and never spoke ill of the family. Or maybe that's just it – maybe Maia was never called to testify by the defence because the prosecution could squeeze information out of her that would implicate Bill further. Maybe she disappeared to protect him.

Back in the motel room, I grab my laptop, sit on the bed and launch the daily meeting with Esteban and Tara. Tara is sitting in a child's bedroom by the look of it and Esteban is in his home office.

'I know we have to talk work, Sloane, but first things first: I am an aunty again!' Tara bursts into a smile.

'Oh my god, congrats!' I say. 'So how's the bub?'

'Bub is great – on the small side, but a full head of hair! Baby boy, named Joe.' She holds her mobile phone up to the webcam and shows me a photo of a tiny thing with a shock of thick black hair.

'Aww, he is teeny,' I say. 'And how's your sister doing?'

'Great,' Tara says. 'She'll probably be out tomorrow or the next day. Then I can head back to mine.' She gestures to the room behind her. 'Or over to join you, depending on . . .'

'Yes, true. So sweet, Tara. Anyway, let's get started,' Est cuts in. 'How did the meeting go, Sloane?'

'Well, I wouldn't say it was a success.'

'What happened?'

'He's not exactly what I was expecting – quite shrewd, standoffish and didn't want a bar of me. TK, on the other hand . . .'

'He was friendlier with him?' Esteban says.

'Kind of. He wants TK to find and speak with Elizabeth Primrose.'

I think my internet must have dropped out because neither of them move or speak, until finally Esteban runs his hand over his forehead.

'Well, of course, that was part of the plan for us too. We've been trying to track her down.'

'Good. TK also said I need to speak to Maia, Bill's ex. Another thing we need to work on. Plus he mentioned the lawyer, this Laurie guy. What time is my flight on Tuesday?'

'Early,' Tara says. 'Out at 9 am and back in the afternoon. They're in your email.'

'And he's happy to go on the record, the lawyer?'

'Yep. That's what he said,' Tara says.

'That reminds me,' Esteban says. 'Can you send your recordings through?'

'Oh, I've not made any yet.'

'Okay,' he says. 'Well, time to get cracking. We need a clear angle of attack here. I'm thinking if we can structure the season so we have different suspects for each episode, with Bill the final suspect in the final episode and leave that question unanswered. This is all contingent on what we find but that's how it's shaping up.'

I'm endlessly grateful for Esteban's clarity of vision. It's a good idea, given how many people are involved in this, but a better ending of course would be if Bill got his retrial, if we actually made a difference.

'So, who are the suspects?' Tara asks. 'Can we run through them now? I'll get a list going.'

'Sloane?'

I run through what I know in my head.

'From the cop's self-published book, self-aggrandising as it was, I did at least get a picture of who was at the house, and who had alibis.' I pull out my notebook. 'According to him, the former gardener was out of the country and instantly eliminated as a suspect. Fleur, the French au pair, was not at the house either, and her alibi was confirmed by a man she was seeing in town. Bill was arrested about six hours after the crime and charged with the murders less than twenty-four hours later. That's a total of twenty-eight hours. How much investigation can happen in a little over a day? Can you really check all these alibis, eliminate all other suspects?'

'I agree, it doesn't exactly sound thorough,' Esteban chips in. 'Definitely worth us looking into everyone again, our way.' He grins.

'I'll send you Bill's account to read when I get it – we might learn more from that about who else was around. That will probably give us a more comprehensive list, but at the moment we have the obvious ones. Fleur, ah, Bill, Mooks. This teacher who was apparently inappropriate.'

'Anyone else?' Tara says.

'Simon,' Esteban adds.

'Simon, yes. The murder–suicide theory.'

'We might need to conjure a couple more or zoom in a bit on certain suspects. The first episode, we summarise the murders and the result of the trial. Open it with the emergency-services call.'

'What's the hook?' Tara says. 'At the end of episode one?'

'The gas heater,' I say. 'That's it for me. It opens up the idea the stabbings weren't the first attempt. It eliminates the idea that this was an unplanned crime of passion, not premeditated. The killer is calculating, clever.'

'I agree,' Esteban says. 'And it's a scoop. We explain it was only discovered after the house was sold two years ago and the police did no further investigation.'

'Then,' Tara says, 'we give the listeners context on each *suspect*, lead them toward uncertainty that it was Bill.'

'Before we give them their respective alibis,' I say.

'That's right.'

Esteban's eyes are moving across his screen and I can tell he's reading.

'What is it, Esteban?' I say.

'I'm on a subreddit here. There's a couple of mentions of another potential suspect – Teimana Coates, Maia's brother. He was on bail, but his sister confirmed he was home all evening.'

'Bail for what?' I say, immediately. I can feel the heat of a lead flare in my stomach.

'Maia is his alibi?' Tara said at the same time. 'That's . . . not exactly watertight.'

'It's not,' I agree. 'Teimana. Hmm, the name is familiar.' Had I read about him online?

'Bail for assault, by the look of it. Oh god, wait, hang on. It says here he went to prison for manslaughter, two years after Bill.'

'What?' I say. *How are we only finding out about this now?*

'He and another gang member beat a man so badly he died the next day in hospital. It was a drug debt apparently. Spent seven years behind bars.'

'And he wasn't even looked at as a suspect in the Primrose murders?' I say. 'That is unbelievable. How incompetent were these lawyers?'

'If the police cleared him, and he had an alibi, there's not much the lawyers can do,' Esteban says.

'Well, let me track him down,' Tara says. 'He's out now. He might want to talk. I'll keep your calendar loaded, Sloane. We've got the neighbours next week – she called emergency services, heard the screams. She'll be able to eliminate the theory a possum or cow woke her.'

'Right,' I say, still thinking about Teimana.

'Any idea when you'll have a car again? Things will get busy.'

'Maybe we can organise it if you guys come over next week, as planned. My driver is reliable and cheap enough to see us through this week.'

'Sure,' Esteban says. 'But this goes without saying: please make sure you're not leaking anything to him or anyone else. We've got a helluva scoop with this carbon-monoxide poisoning theory.'

'I know, of course,' I say, trying to think over what Dean might already know or have overheard. 'Anyway, same time tomorrow?'

'I'll send you both a calendar invite,' Tara says.

TK

'ALRIGHT, MUNCHKIN?' I say, when I get to the door at Mum and Dad's. Amelia doesn't rush into my arms anymore like she used to but I squat down and wait for her to pull her blue gumboots on. 'You have fun?'

'She had a ball,' Mum says, coming in to stand beside Dad. 'You get everything done that you needed to?'

'All sorted.'

'The other day when you were here,' Mum says, 'you were reading about Bill Kareama in the paper.'

'Was I?' I say but I can feel the warmth of her gaze – I never could get away with lying to Mum. Amelia stands with her gumboots on and slings her backpack over one shoulder.

'He's in there again today, the newspaper.'

'Oh, right.'

'Apparently, a podcaster from Australia is here and on the case.'

I stand up. I feel both of my parents studying my face. 'Well, I wouldn't know much about that.'

So the news is out. I suppose it will help Sloane turn up leads, open new doors.

'Big news,' Dad says.

'When do you head down to Milford Sound?' Mum asks.

'Tomorrow,' I say. I'd booked it in a while back. Four days of trails through the most beautiful part of the country.

'Good idea to get out and in nature. Do you good.'

I just nod. *Do I tell them about the change of plans?* They worry about me. No one wants to see their children depressed but I'm better now, balanced even. I kiss my mum goodbye.

'C'mon darling,' I say, and lead Amelia to the car. 'Better get you back home to Mum.'

I buckle her in, and start the drive to Lynn's, my mind not on the road. Of course Sloane's arrival would be news, *everything* is news in this country, and the arrival of a star Australian journalist to investigate one of our most infamous crimes would definitely rate a mention. I wonder if her producer sent out a media release to drum up attention. It's getting harder and harder to block out, the thrumming excitement underneath it all. What Sloane said got to me – her commitment to justice is principled, unwavering. It shouldn't matter if I have come to believe Bill is guilty. She's right. That's not how the justice system should work.

'Why are you frowning?' Amelia says.

'I'm thinking,' I say, as I hold the wheel.

'What about?'

'Just work, honey. Nothing really.'

A few hours and about fifty rounds of I Spy later, I drop Amelia at her mother's then return home to pack my bag. There's a flight in the morning at 9 am. It's not cheap but it's Sloane's money, not mine. I book it and text her the details. It doesn't feel at all real, and every part of my psychologist's brain is screaming at me that this is a bad idea, risky behaviour for me, psychologically speaking. But the same training knows this is precisely why I've decided to do it. Unfinished business can be a powerful motivator – for better or for worse. Bill knows how to get under my skin: he reminded me of the promise I made. The promise I broke.

I head out to the garage, stare at my weight rack. I step into the rack and bend to lift the loaded bar off the floor. Over and over, until my back is numb and my body is trembling. Again and again, for an hour, more, until I can barely stand. While the bar rises and falls, my mind is clear and blank. There is no room for cognition, not when your brain is full of pain and adrenaline. Afterward, I shower, holding myself against the wall, and breathe. Maybe this will finally be the closure I've been seeking all these years.

Bill calls again in the morning. I tell him I have booked a flight. I tell him it's the last thing I'll do for the case. He doesn't thank me, he just grunts. Just as I am going to hang up, he speaks.

'Send the podcaster what I wrote, my account of what happened. And tell her I'll see her next week.' The line goes dead.

I fire Bill's document through to Sloane's email just before I put my laptop in my carry-on. I lock up and head outside to wait for my taxi. I reach the airport and soon enough I'm boarding a plane bound for London. Twenty-one hours in this tube. I'll be back on Friday for my clients next week. Everything will return to normal. No one will notice I was gone at all.

PART TWO

Detective Marsden: Take your time. We just want to understand what happened.

Bill Kareama: I just found them. I . . . I just wanted my knives.

Detective Marsden: We know, Bill. You went there to collect your knives. They never should have kept them. They were yours and it was unfair. You had every right to be angry.

Bill Kareama: I wasn't angry.

Detective Marsden: Frustrated. You went there a little drunk, a little frustrated. You didn't know what you were doing.

Bill Kareama: I knew what I was doing. I was getting my knives.

Detective Marsden: But you went upstairs — your boot prints are all through the blood, Bill. An eyewitness has you leaving the property right before the police arrived. You closed the window and left a bloody handprint on the window.

Bill Kareama: I . . . something was wrong. I knew something was wrong. The door was open. I didn't touch them or do anything. I went inside because the door was open.

Detective Marsden: Why were you wearing gloves?

Bill Kareama: Because I wasn't supposed to be there. That's why. But I didn't stab them.

Detective Marsden: Do you know what I think, Bill? I think you were wearing gloves because you'd gone to that house to hurt that family. I think you wanted to maybe scare them, take your knives and leave. But you lost control. You were frustrated, angry that they fired you, angry that they had kicked you out. You were drunk and you lost control, just for a minute. That's all it was.

Bill Kareama: No, no, no. I didn't want to hurt anyone. I didn't.

Detective Marsden: So it was an accident. The first one. You were scared. You lashed out.

Bill Kareama: That's not how it happened.

BILL

'ALRIGHT, MATE?' THOSE were the first words Tate Mercer-Kemp said to me. It was his standard greeting.

After his first shift as the new gardener, he came and sat in the sun outside the cottage and insisted we have a beer.

'Ole Simo won't mind too much. You work hard, right?' he said. 'You deserve it.'

So I sat with him, one ear aimed inside for the phone in case the family needed me.

'Trust me, my father gave me the word on him. He was a real booze hound at uni. He knows men need a cold lager after a hard day's work.'

'Oh, he's the same young man your father knew,' I said, laughing. 'Still enjoys a drink.'

He smiled at that. He wore a blue hat low over his eyes. It had a pair of crossed oars and a crown on it, *OU* emblazoned on one side and *BC* on the other.

'Oxford University,' he said, pointing to one side, then moving his finger to the other side. 'Boat Club.'

'You row?' I asked. Talk about posh, I thought. Another one.

'Once upon a time,' he said, sucking a mouthful of beer from the can. 'So, what's the deal with this French bird?'

'Fleur?' He was direct, indiscreet. 'Oh, no, nothing. She's nice.'

'Not your type then?' he said, showing that grin I would grow accustomed to. 'You don't like gorgeous young women or what?' He gently prodded my ribs with his finger.

'It's not that.'

'Wouldn't surprise me if she tried it on with you. Strapping young lad you are, aren't you?'

'I don't know about that.'

I wanted to change the subject. There was every chance someone might overhear and think I was comfortable with the direction of the conversation. Fleur and I weren't an item; it was just sex. But it was happening most nights, in her bed, or mine, on the couch, the kitchen table. Last time, we were both fully dressed. She pulled down her leggings and pulled me into her against the kitchen bench in our cottage. Afterward, she plucked a dark strand of hair off the chest of my chef's whites before retreating to the bathroom to fix herself up.

'So what brings you to New Zealand?' I said.

'A change of scene, see the world.'

'Cambridge seems an odd choice, though. Pretty quiet here.'

'I started in Auckland, and I am working my way down. But this feels like the real New Zealand. Auckland is just a city, like any other. You know what I mean?'

'I do.'

'I was travelling with some mates. They all kept on going, working their way south. I'll probably get bored here, eventually. Might move on somewhere with a bit more happening.'

'Where were you in England?'

'London,' he said. 'The one thing I miss is the women back there, stuck up as some of them are – they all get loose after a couple of vodkas or champagnes. The posh ones too. Looking forward to when little miss Primrose is of age.'

I cut my eyes to him. 'Elle?'

'Oh, she's a sweetheart, isn't she?' he said, before clocking my look. 'I'm just having fun with you, mate. She's off limits, even for a debauched prick like me.'

'Can I ask you something?' I said. 'Do you know much about what happened with the family back in England?'

He finished his beer. 'I know a bit about them, yeah.'

'I heard he was a politician.'

'High up in the Tories. All thieving bastards in that game but he seemed alright. My dad spoke highly of him. But I heard a bit about it back home. All the tabloids love a scandal.'

'There was a train crash?' I said.

I couldn't read his expression. 'You know about that?'

'Yeah, I heard.'

'I think it's best you don't let them know you know. They probably moved here to escape all that Southgate drama. But yeah, he was public enemy numero uno for about a week, then the media moved on to speculating on some royal affair.'

'What did he actually do?'

'Well, he wasn't driving the train, was he? That's the way I see it. He made some decision about safety standards, that's it. Someone had to decide. If you're angry at him, you gotta be angry at all politicians for everything that goes wrong.'

'I guess,' I said.

'Anyway, you got any more of these?' he said, holding up his beer. 'Could do with another one before I head home.'

'Might be a couple more in the fridge,' I said.

'Why don't we hit up the bars? Go sample some of the local produce, you know?'

'On the clock. Maybe another time.'

'Ah, you stiff. Well, I'll hold you to that. So what do you and Frenchie get up to for fun if you're always on the clock?'

I shrugged. 'I'm just trying to make some money,' I say. 'I'll have my fun later.'

'Well, put in a good word for me then, will you?'

I smiled. 'Sure. Where are you staying?'

'Just in the village. The local grocer has a flat out the back of her place. Easy enough to come and go.'

'Nice,' I said. 'Probably better than this cottage.'

'The view's not as good,' he said, referring to Fleur, and again I had to laugh.

'Anyway,' he said. 'I better get back to the basement. There are tools in there that haven't been used since before the family moved here, I think. Most of it is shite, but some of it is in pretty good nick. I don't think the last guy knew what he was doing with the gardens, to be honest.'

'Yeah right, I'll let you get back to it.' I squashed my beer can and headed back to the cool familiarity of the kitchen.

One afternoon a few weeks after Tate arrived, I was out on the small concrete patch, behind the pool house near the edge of the pine forest with my board when Chet came out.

'Bill,' he said. 'Can you teach me to skate?'

He'd seen me out there, practising kickflips, shove-its. He knew I'd skate to the shops sometimes.

'I guess I could show you a thing or two.'

'Kids at school skate, or some of them do.' I'd noticed he was wearing his jeans a little lower, not baggy or fashionable, but he was making an effort to fit in.

'Well, maybe we can practise out front. I'll need to tighten the trucks on my board a bit.' The driveway was wide and paved, with a slight decline to coast along toward the gate. I wasn't sure how his parents would feel about him skateboarding but he was determined to learn.

So from then on – always at the same time, afternoons before Simon got home from work – I taught Chet how to skate. I started by teaching him how to balance, then to kick-push. He was a slow learner but he got there in the end. Soon he wanted to know how to ollie and kickflip.

'So what's new at school?' I said, watching him time and again *almost* ollie.

'Nothing, just the same old stuff.'

In his school uniform, with the limbs that seemed too big for his body, he reminded me of a foal finding its feet. He'd taken his leather shoes off and put on his sneakers.

'What's the same old stuff? You making friends?'

'Not really,' he said. 'Just a couple.'

'Well, you'll be at high school next year, right? Then everyone will have to make new friends.'

'Yeah, I guess. That will be easier. It's just stupid, the teachers are stupid, the other boys are mostly annoying. And Elle hates that school anyway.'

'I get it. But she came to that school after everyone else had already been there for years, at least you'll be starting with everyone else.'

'They're just all mostly obsessed with this centenary thing at my school. It doesn't feel like my school in London.'

'What's the centenary?'

The tail of the board clapped against the stone again. He gave a grunt of frustration.

'You'll get there,' I said. 'Just remember, slide your front foot as the board comes up, and bend your knees.'

'The centenary' – another failed attempt – 'means the school started one hundred years ago. They're having a celebration at the end of the year. We are doing stupid events and old students are coming back. I've got to write a letter to my future self and put something of personal significance in my shoebox for the time capsule by the end of the term.'

'That doesn't sound so bad.'

'No, but it's just stupid. I don't care about the school. I just want my London friends.'

A crack and the board lifted. Just a little. Maybe half an inch. A big toothy grin.

'Did I ollie?'

I showed him with my thumb and forefinger. 'This high.'

He cheered and jumped off the board. He ran around, making a plane with his arms. 'Get in! I can ollie.'

I sensed a presence and turned back to see Gwen at the door, her fingers pressed to her cheek. She smiled.

'Come on in, Beckham,' she called from the house.

'I'm Giggs!'

'Alright, Giggs, homework time. And Bill, it might be time to get started on dinner. I've got a meeting at Elle's school tonight, so we might eat a little early.'

SLOANE

EVERYONE KNOWS HOW it ends: my chef's knife snapped in Simon's chest. Each member of the family stabbed.

That's some opening line. I've not been this excited about reading something since *Normal People*. After that cop's self-published piece of crap, this is a page-turner. Instead of the antichrist, the impression I get of Bill is that he is a quiet, slightly neurotic chef who just wants to go about his business.

I'm flying through it, having to force myself to slow down so I don't miss anything. As I read, I make notes. There are some big unanswered questions: did Fleur view her romance with Bill the same way he did, as a casual fling? And Teimana, what came of his threats? He is the biggest red flag of all so far, especially given he was later sent to prison for manslaughter.

I tidy up my notes so far and send them in an email to Tara and Esteban. *Here's your suspect list.* I'm sure they're doing the exact same thing right now, scrutinising the text for any clues. I'm halfway through but my time is up – I've got an interview soon.

I find Dean waiting in the car park with a strong latte in the cup holder.

'Got you a coffee,' he says, as I take a seat in the back.

A bloom of warmth. 'Thank you. That's so thoughtful.' I am sure it helped that Tara transferred funds to cover his day rate for three more days this morning.

'Noticed your order yesterday. Thought it would save you a stop at the coffee shop.'

He hands the coffee back to me and I take a mouthful. My first coffee is generally the highlight of my day and this one is surprisingly good. It's like someone has taken a leaf blower, pressed it to my ear and blasted the fog from my brain.

It was another bad sleep last night. I had nightmares about a stalker kicking down the motel door. Telling me to repent, take back my lies. With all the hate mail and threats from defenders of my last case, well, it's easy enough to block it all out in the daylight hours, less so in the motel, with its dish-sponge mattress and creaky doors.

Just as I'd finally fallen into a deep sleep, a text from TK had woken me. He was at the airport, he said, waiting to board a flight to Heathrow. I'd replied immediately, wishing him a good flight and asking him to text me when he landed. I still can't quite believe he'd agreed to go there.

'Where's the first stop?' Dean asks.

'Eleven Coventry Street. I'm meeting a gas technician.'

'Righto,' he says, in his strange hybrid accent. Then we're off.

I think about something else from Bill's account. The basement, the heater. Tate Mercer-Kemp had access to it. *Maybe Tate should be back on our suspect list*, I think.

Dean drops me off at the address, and I see a ruddy-faced man in his late fifties, with patchy stubble and an off-white work polo that strains to cover his impressive beer belly, loading some gear into a van.

'Hello,' he says, as I approach. 'Sloane, is it?'

'That's me,' I say offering my hand.

'Andrew Mears,' he says and thrusts his hand out to shake mine with a warm grip. 'Come on, I got an office out back.'

I set my voice recorder on the desk and sit across from him. The rubbish bin is almost spilling over; one of the slats of his aluminium blinds is bent in the middle like a greeting card. 'I don't know how much I will use, but if I could record that would be great. It might just be for my notes, but I'll need you to sign a release form.'

'No worries,' he says. 'I told my daughter I was going to be on your podcast and she couldn't believe it.'

'She a listener?'

'Oh yeah,' he says. 'Almost thirty years old and an absolute true-crime junkie. Loves the Golden State Killer.' *Loves a man who strangled and raped dozens of women?* 'She's working, otherwise she'd be here. Big fan.'

'That's nice to hear. Thirty you said?' I do the maths. She's a little older than Chet would have been now. 'What school did she go to?'

'St Luke's.'

'She didn't know either of the Primrose kids, did she?'

'Nah, but she could tell you about the school. What it was like. She remembers it all.'

'I might grab her phone number if that's okay?'

'Sure. Of course. She'd love to talk to you.'

'Alright, let's get started. First, I'll get you to explain what you found in the gas-heating system at the former Primrose house.'

'Oh, right,' he says, somehow surprised we're actually going to talk about what he agreed to. 'So, I've been doing this for twenty years, right. Seen everything under the sun, or so I thought. Until I was called out to that house.'

'Did you know that's where you were heading when you got the call?'

'Yep, everyone in town knows the address and I'm related to Karen, she called me. Most of my work is in Hamilton but it's nice when you get work closer to home.'

'Sure,' I say.

He digs at the corner of his eye with his stumpy forefinger. 'I'd actually installed the original unit for the Primrose family.'

I pause, glance up. 'You did?'

'Yep. Way back when. Was one of my first big gas jobs, actually. I was a plumber originally, then I got into gas refrigeration and heating. It was more lucrative and a growing trade.'

'Okay, I might come back to that, if that's okay. But first, what did you find when you went to repair it for Terrence and Karen?'

'Leaves, sticks, all sorts of crap jammed into the exhaust.'

'And there's *no way* it could have got there naturally?'

'Ah, shit, no – no way. Firstly, the exterior cover is designed to prevent anything getting inside or blocking it. They stick out and have lots of points of exit, so you can't just block it there, and you can't just shove leaves through the filter. Secondly, it was all jammed in the one spot. It wouldn't build up like that. Someone's clumped it together and stuffed it there.'

'And you think it had definitely been there for a while?' I ask.

'Dry as paper,' he says. 'But it might have been wet when it was stuffed in – it was kind of solidified, if you know what I mean. Been there for a long, long time.'

I'm convinced that this was the first attempt at murdering the family.

'So in your opinion, how did it get there?'

'Someone removed the cover, pulled the filter out and pushed the junk in there. They would have balled it all up like that and maybe pushed it in deep with a broom handle or something.'

'So it was definitely deliberate, in your opinion?'

'It was absolutely deliberate, I'd put my house on it.'

'And it couldn't have been, say, a kid mucking around?'

'I'd say that Kareama did it and that he knew exactly what he was doing,' he says.

'Do you remember anything unusual from when you installed the system?'

'Not really. Beautiful house, that's all. Not much like that around here. Big job too, running the vents to all the rooms – but it's all wood so there's space between the levels to get it through. Was the biggest house I'd seen. I wouldn't live there now.'

'No,' I agree.

'Happy with my three-bedder on five acres out of town. That'll do me just fine, thank you.'

'Did you speak to the police?'

'After the murders?'

'No, after you discovered the heating?'

'Yeah,' he says. 'Terrence must have told them. Cookie, the local copper, came and knocked on my door. Told him what I found.'

'Cookie?'

'Adam Cooke – he's the head of the Cambridge police force.'

'Right, and nothing came of it?'

'Not that I know of. Cleared the blockage, good as gold.'

It's a closed case. What incentive would the police have to investigate it anyway? Reopening old cases is the last thing police need or want – they've enough on their plate.

'What tools would be required to block the exhaust?'

'Well, a couple of spanners. From memory, it's just bolts holding the cover on, so a wrench or the right-sized socket. It's really not so sophisticated.'

No special skills or tools. Maybe a single Google search. It could have been done with things lying around the house or in a toolbox in the basement.

I continue to ask Andrew questions: about Cambridge, about the Primroses, what he knew of Bill. After forty minutes, I think I have mined everything Andrew knows about the town, and realise he needs to get back to work.

Dean starts the car as I approach. The last thing I want to do is spend the rest of the day in that motel.

'Listen, do you want to get a bite?' I say as I pull the door closed behind me.

'A bite?'

'A pub meal, maybe?'

'Umm,' he says. 'I'm fine. You can go in. I'll wait.'

'No,' I say. 'My shout. Come on, it's the least I can do.'

'Alright. George Union?'

'What's that?'

'Near your motel, the old church with the pink doors.'

'That's a pub?'

'Yep. And a brewery.'

'I'll need to do a bit of work.'

'Fine by me. I'll bring my book.'

George Union is both very cute and very huge. Like a baby elephant. There's hanging ivy, rustic tables in the large courtyard under louvered shutters. The church part of the pub is even better. At two in the afternoon on a Friday, it's busy and I suppose it will only get busier as the after-work crowd rolls in. I order fish and chips, Dean gets a steak and we find a corner table. He's got that Kiwi bashfulness, despite being South African, but when he warms up he's good for a bit of banter.

Dean has a non-alcoholic beer with his steak and I drink a glass of wine, tapping away at my keyboard, filling out the shared spreadsheet that we always use at the start of a case. *Record everything* is my rule – you never know when a small detail will become significant, and three sets of eyes are infinitely more useful than one. It's a good system, it hasn't let us down.

'How's the book?' I say, closing my laptop. He's finished the Michael Robotham and is now tearing through a vintage Val McDermid.

'It's alright,' he says. 'Pretty good actually.' He lays it face down on the table.

'You read a lot?'

'I guess so. Got more free time now.'

'Have you read any books by *En-gai-oh* Marsh?'

He laughs. '*Ngaio* Marsh? I've read a few. Criminally underrated.'

'Have you read *A Murder at Membrey Manor*?' It's the book Bill had mentioned in his story.

'It's a classic,' he says. 'Not her most famous but one of her best I'd say. A clever ending.'

'What happens?'

'I don't want to ruin it.'

'Go on. I probably won't read it.'

'Each member of a family is found stabbed. Only the father survives. At first, the detective believes it was committed by the butler but it turns out it was the father.'

Sounds awfully familiar.

'The father gave himself a non-lethal stab wound to cover his tracks.'

Coincidence or inspiration?

'Hmm.'

'So did you get anything for your podcast today?' he says.

'A bit.' I probably shouldn't spill the beans. He knows I visited a gas technician too – that's close enough for me. Esteban warned me about this. The last thing I want is my scoop getting out before I have a chance to record the podcast.

'So your podcast, you think it might not have been Bill Kareama then?'

'I don't want to speculate too much. Suffice to say, it's becoming clear there are certain things the police may have overlooked.'

'When does he get released otherwise?'

'Another few years,' I say. 'He'd be eligible for parole now if he acknowledged his guilt. But if he doesn't confess and his conviction is one day overturned, then he'd also be up for a decent whack of compensation.'

'How much?'

'I'd say millions.'

Dean looks thoughtful, creases forming between his eyes. Then he opens his book again and continues reading. I can't help but smile at that. The pub is getting busier, the tables filling around us. Nearby, a young group of men are watching something on a phone, sucking down their cold glasses of beer.

I notice a group of women in one corner, looking over toward us. They're draining cocktails as fast as the bar can make them. Looks like the nascent stages of a hen's party, with one of the women wearing a bridal veil and a sexy pink slip dress.

I go to order another round, wine for me but soft drink for Dean. There's a queue at the bar. I turn back and see one of the younger women from the hen's party over near Dean, chatting. Or . . . flirting? She's leaning on our table, her face close to Dean's. When I get our drinks and start back, she seems to clock me and smiles as she clears off.

'She trying to pick you up?' I tease, watching her walk away.

'I think you've got a fan club actually.'

I turn back to see a few of the women looking our way. Thirties, mostly white: right in the true-crime demographic. I think about the article announcing my arrival in town to investigate the Primrose murders. Esteban had sent out a media release thinking it'd help draw people out of the woodwork. No doubt it ruffled some feathers too. With my notebook out, I check my interview hit list. I spend some time drafting up my interview questions for the lawyer tomorrow.

'I might walk back to the motel,' I say, swallowing the last of my drink. Bill's version of events is at the front of my mind.

'No problem,' he says. 'Well, let me know if you need a lift anywhere in the morning.'

'I've got to get to Hamilton airport. Nine am flight.'

'I'll pick you up at seven-thirty.'

At the motel, I lie on the bed. I have an hour before our daily video catch-up. An hour of unbroken time to get back into Bill Kareama's mind.

BILL

FLEUR DECIDED WE should stop sleeping together. It was pretty weird how quickly it started, how bright and hot that flame burned before it went out. About a week after she'd called it off, we were both drinking coffee in the cottage in the morning.

'You ever want children?' I asked. Even though I didn't want to be with her, I was curious about Fleur. Following the Primroses halfway around the world didn't feel like much of a life.

'No,' she said. 'Probably never. I'm getting old.'

'You're not too old.'

'I guess not. You?'

'Oh yeah,' I said. 'I want a big family. Three or four children.'

'Your poor future wife. What about her? Maybe she wants a career.'

'Well, hopefully she'll want the same thing as me.'

'You didn't get any feelings, did you?' she asked.

I couldn't help but laugh at that. 'No, I don't think so.'

'Well, me neither, so that's good. You're okay as a friend but no more.'

'I see you as a friend, don't worry.'

'Good boy,' she said. 'I don't need to ask but you haven't said anything about this situation, no?'

'To the family?'

'To anyone?'

I thought about Tate. What had I said? Nothing. 'No.'

We were interrupted by a thud on the door of the cottage. It swung open.

'Bill,' Gwen said. 'What are you doing?'

I lifted my cup as if it was self-evident. 'Coffee,' I said. I eyed the clock on the microwave. Too early for breakfast still. 'Did you want me to come to the house?'

'Elle is taking a couple of days off school.' She clenched her jaw and looked uncharacteristically fierce. 'She's a bit unwell, I'm going to go to the shop and was thinking you could make some minestrone soup?'

'Sure.'

'Well, I'll pick up some stock and ingredients. Fleur, if you could keep an eye on her.'

'What sort of illness?' Fleur asked.

'Who knows? Maybe homesick, maybe a bit under the weather. She's really not herself.'

Elle emerged later in the day, as I was serving up the soup.

'Do you want it in your room?' I said. 'I could put it on a tray?'

She looked up at me. There were tiny spiderwebs of red veins in the white of her wet eyes. She looked down at the soup. 'I'm not hungry.'

'Okay,' I said. 'Well, it's here if you want it.'

For three days, she stayed home from school, barely eating. Fleur kept her company, and on the third day Simon and Gwen went to the school in the afternoon to meet with the principal.

After they returned, I could hear them speaking in hushed tones in Simon's office. Chet was practising the piano and Gwen raised her voice a few times, but I couldn't hear her words.

Fleur came into the kitchen. 'Someone at school,' she said quietly. 'He was leaving notes for Elle.' The piano music stopped.

'That's what she's upset about?'

Fleur looked taken aback. 'Of course. It's disgusting.'

'Oh, I know. I mean . . . what sort of notes?'

'I don't know what they said. Maybe threatening? Maybe harassment?'

A throat was cleared, and we both turned. Chet was there, my skateboard in his hand. 'Can I use this, Bill?'

'Of course,' I said.

About ten minutes later, Elle came down and crossed the room without a word. She reached for a glass, filled it with water, then left. I could see the birdlike bones of her ribs and spine through her light pyjama top. Fleur followed her out.

I kept on with my day. I'd been experimenting with some bread recipes, thinking it might be nice to bake some home-made loaves for lunches. I hadn't mastered it yet. It was quiet in the house, and as I kneaded, I looked out to the garden, where Tate was moving mulch under the trees with a rake. He looked up toward Elle's window, then his eyes fell on me. I could feel it, an undercurrent. Over the past week or so, he had cooled. No more beers outside the cottage.

When he came in to use the bathroom, he slowed at the door to the kitchen.

'Go on then, cook,' he said. 'Make me a sandwich, extra mayo.' I laughed but Tate barely smiled before continuing on. I threw the dough in the bin, it was not right, and pulled out the loaf from the supermarket.

Later that week, Gwen's aunt Elizabeth, or Lizzie, turned up with a nimbus of grey hair and pearls strung from her neck. She was very elegant, but seemed nice from what I could see. Elle seemed to like her anyway, which was a good sign.

Things were still tense around the house – according to Fleur, Simon had been pressuring the school to take more action about what had happened to Elle, and the principal had even come to the house to discuss the issue.

I was also tense, not so much because of what was happening with the family, though I did feel sorry for Elle, but more because I was constantly on edge about Teimana. I hadn't heard anything from him yet, but I knew it was a ticking timebomb. He would expect me to deliver on my promise sooner or later. I'd tried texting and calling Maia a few more times, thinking that maybe if I was back on good terms with her, Teimana would let it go. But I had given up when I got no response. A couple of times, I felt so stressed that I knocked on Fleur's door at night, only to be rebuffed. It didn't feel good being rejected, especially after what had happened with Maia. I didn't blame Fleur for the break-up but she was a catalyst.

The first night Lizzie was there, Chet also had a friend over. It was twilight, but in the pine trees it was dark enough to play spotlight – hide-and-seek with a torch. Chet and his friend Marco coaxed me out to join them. Half an hour wouldn't hurt. I'd spent the day preparing a Beef Wellington, with pastry from scratch – Gwen's request – and the oven was warming up. I had forty-five minutes before I'd need to put it in. That week, I planned to make extra special meals – slow-cooked lamb shanks, steak and ale pie, rich British fare.

Walking down through the garden with the torch, I aimed the beam of light toward the pines, scanning through the trees. Before long, I discovered Chet at the fence line, then together we found Marco. Chet took the torch back toward the pool house and started counting. My turn to hide. I opted for a dark enclave between the blackberry bush and the wooden fence that separated the garden from the pine forest.

'Ready or not!' I heard Chet call.

After a while, I heard other voices coming from the pine trees lining the boundary of the property.

'I've been meaning to visit for some time, but it's been so difficult to get away,' Lizzie said.

I heard Gwen's voice responding, but couldn't quite make out what she was saying. I heard Lizzie's laugh tinkle.

'And your help,' she said then, getting close to where I was crouching down, out of sight. 'Where did you find them?'

'A couple of locals,' Gwen said. A gate whined open then closed. The torch passed over the blackberry bush so I moved a little deeper. A prick at the back of my arm – I recoiled from the barbs. 'Hard to find good people but we like them. And Fleur came with us.'

Chatter from behind me. Chet had found his friend and now they were both searching for me.

'Yes, I remember Fleur,' she said. 'The au pair. Are the kids getting a little old for an au pair?'

'I don't think so. Simon thinks we will move her on in a few more years, but Chet is still young, and it's been good for Elle to have someone here who is familiar. Our new gardener, Tate, is from back home. His father was an old uni chum of Simon's.'

'That chef, he seems a bit rough around the edges.'

My chest filled with hollow air, a balloon inflating.

'Mummy,' Chet said, emerging from the pines. 'Have you seen Bill?'

'Bill, no. I'd imagine he's in the kitchen.'

'He's playing spotlight with us.'

Lizzie made a noise in the back of her throat.

'Oh, well, no. I haven't.'

Chet and Marco continued on searching.

'I thought you'd be a bit more careful about who you let in the house, Gwen. Especially given this business with the notes. Are you absolutely sure that it is someone at the school?'

I could see Lizzie's back, the two of them silhouettes before the lights of the great house. Gwen's head was turned toward the cottage.

'We've looked at the handwriting,' she said. 'We thought it might have been him, Bill. But it's not. It has to be someone at her school.'

'Just be careful, won't you? I'd err on the side of caution. How hard are good chefs to find?' The two continued up toward the house.

'Harder than you'd expect,' said Gwen tightly. It was the last thing I heard before I lost the rest of the conversation.

I exhaled, feeling dazed. Why the hell did this lady have a problem with me? We'd never even had a conversation. I thought about the hours I'd put into perfecting the pastry that day, and felt anger rise from my gut.

A moment later, a blinding light hit me. 'Found you!'

I climbed out of the bush. Gwen and Lizzie were thankfully back inside the house by then. I knew that Lizzie was important to the family and I didn't want to give her any reason to dislike me. There was no telling the influence she had over the family. Elle, after all, was named after her, but Gwen was right. Good private chefs were not easy to find.

'Sorry boys, I better get dinner on now,' I said abruptly, starting back toward the house.

BILL

'IT IS NOTHING,' Fleur told me in the morning, when I told her what I'd overheard Lizzie saying to Gwen. 'They're suspicious of everyone because there was a psycho who came to the house in London.'

'Who was he?'

'Who?'

'The psycho who came to the house?'

'Who said it was a man? Only men can be dangerous? Is that right?'

'It was a woman?'

'An older lady. She was maybe forty. Her husband was killed in the train crash. She came to their home in Kensington with a knife but didn't get past the gate and the police were called. They moved after that – they could barely go about their life. Just walking outside to get the newspaper someone might say something. Can you imagine being so despised? Perhaps this is why they stay so often inside the property here. Force of habit. Simon is not so afraid, I think. He travels a lot, speaks at business forums, makes himself very public, but Elle and Gwen, maybe Chet, they are all still fearful. Of course. Why wouldn't they be?'

I couldn't hide my shock. 'Aren't you scared as well?'

'I have nothing to fear,' she said. 'I did nothing wrong. I'm nothing but a helper. What could I possibly do to stop what happened with the train?'

I cooked hearty lamb shanks for Lizzie that night. Steak and ale pie the night after. I did everything with a smile. I can't say if I won her over or not, but after her time in the house I still had a job.

Simon was away for a conference in Queenstown for two nights the following week and Lizzie had gone up to Auckland for the night, so Gwen decided to host drinks with some of her friends – mostly wives of Simon's colleagues over from Hamilton. Gwen had gone out that afternoon while I prepared appetisers: beer-battered fried brie with a cranberry dressing, citrus-cured ceviche, oysters, spiced hummus, breadsticks and venison carpaccio, my old boss's recipe. Gwen wanted sophisticated snacks to match the bottles of Veuve Clicquot.

That evening, Fleur came in as I was putting the finishing touches on the appetisers.

'Fancy,' she said, as I slid my blade through the fish, and laid the thin slices in a bowl. 'Gwen's spent a lot to impress these people.'

'Yeah, I suppose,' I said, focused on the task at hand.

'All the champagne,' she said, eyeing the case of bottles.

'Mmm,' I said. I didn't have time to chat. But Fleur was clearly worked up.

'They just have no idea, you know,' she said, as I sliced through another fillet. 'I was poor growing up, so I know. My mother owned a wool store, then she had me and my two brothers and she closed up shop to look after us. My father was a truck driver.'

'Working class,' I said, without making eye contact. 'No oysters and caviar in your home?'

She turned to lean back against the bench beside me. 'No. My father spent long hours going up and down the country. He slept when we were awake and he would take painkillers like candy. He retired early. I say retired but he just couldn't get work so he got a pension.'

'How did you end up with this job? With such a posh family?' I asked, my interest growing. She had never really opened up to me about her family life before.

'I applied through an agency. I had experience and had been through all the training,' she said. 'And they'd had a couple of different nannies in the past. I guess I just clicked better. But these people were so different to me. Maybe this is why I always felt a little out of place in London, with all the other families in the Primrose circles and their Norland nannies. I was younger.'

'Why did they go through so many nannies?'

'Simon,' she said. She smiled to herself. 'He's difficult to work with. I think Gwen also wanted a genuine French au pair to introduce the children to another culture. I spoke French to Elle and Chet when they were little.'

'Makes sense,' I said, mostly because I couldn't think of what else to say.

'Does it?' she asked, an inscrutable look on her face.

'Err,' I stammered.

But Fleur cut me off with a loud laugh. 'Oh poor naïve Bill,' she said. 'You're almost as sheltered as they are.' She gestured with her head to the loungeroom where Gwen's guests were making a small racket.

Annoyed, I loaded the platters onto the trolley and left the kitchen. I didn't have the time or patience for Fleur's games tonight.

It occurred to me, as I delivered the canapés then topped up glasses and moved about in the background, that Fleur likely knew almost all of the family's secrets. She was helping that night with the drinks, but soon I began to realise she was also getting drunk, stealing away to the kitchen to throw back glasses of champagne. It was out of character for her to let herself get like this.

Earlier, Fleur had turned the pool pump off and set candles on trays to float on the surface. Now that the light was dying, she lit the candles on their trays and pushed them out. She returned to the loungeroom, and nodded to Gwen, who led her guests to the poolside for dusk.

I checked the food then went out to the garden where they were all gathered.

'Tom said Simon was talking about getting away for a holiday,' one of the women who was very attractive said. 'Somewhere tropical.'

'Seychelles, maybe,' Gwen said. 'If he can find time. It'd be good for the kids; they've struggled to settle in. Although I've thought it would be nice to get back to London to see my family and our old friends.'

'Seychelles?' another woman said.

'It's a sunny little paradise,' Gwen said.

'I know it,' a different woman added. 'Big flight. Fiji is far enough for me, if we want somewhere tropical.'

'Well, that's an idea,' Gwen said.

I wondered if Gwen's friends knew about the controversy in London. They must have known he was once a politician, but what else?

'So,' Fleur said, moving around to top up glasses, 'Simon is your husband's boss, no?'

'Well, yes, that's right,' the attractive woman said, a puzzled expression on her face.

'Ah, I see,' Fleur said. 'And none of you work, have jobs?' I hoped I was the only one who could tell her words were dripping with booze.

A few small laughs. 'We all have our kids and families.'

'So that makes me the only working woman here, I suppose.'

I approached the table to collect empty plates, something compelling me to intervene.

'No family for me!' she said as if delighted.

A couple of the women laughed politely.

The air was full of tension. Fleur's contempt was rising too close to the surface. Gwen reached over and touched her hand. A stiff gesture, but her back was to me so I couldn't make out her expression.

'Would anyone care for more food?' I asked awkwardly. My presence was a stone dropping through the surface, breaking the tension. The group all turned to me, their eyes lighting up.

'You could twist my arm to eat a little more of that, ah . . . what did you call it?'

'Carpaccio?'

'Oh yum, me too,' the attractive woman added, eyeing me up and down.

Moments later, the conversation was buoyant, superficial again.

Fleur smiled archly, an undisguised flirtation in it. 'He's very good with his hands,' she said to the group of women, pointing to me.

Thankfully, they all seemed to miss the comment, everyone but Gwen, that is, who turned her head sharply to Fleur, then leaned closer and said something into her ear. Fleur straightened up, her mouth set in a tight line. She headed toward the cottage.

Gwen turned back to me.

'Thanks, Bill. And if there are any more oysters, could you bring them out?'

'Of course.'

'The kids have eaten?'

'Vegetarian lasagne,' I said. None of those women had the money for a full-time private chef, that was obvious. They were impressed.

Back in the kitchen, as I shucked the last few oysters and prepared a little more of the carpaccio, I could still hear them.

'Where does one find a chef who can make carpaccio like that? We had it in Italy years ago. It's phenomenal.'

'You'll have to ask him how he does it.'

'Easy on the eyes,' someone else said, as if I couldn't hear.

'Didn't know you were that way inclined,' another of the women said.

'What does that mean?' Gwen asked.

'Well, you've met Harry? White as snow,' she said.

Gwen seemed to ignore it. 'He apprenticed under a top chef in Melbourne. We're very lucky to have him.'

'Well, Tom is at least two promotions away from a private chef for us.'

The polite murmur of restrained laughter. I felt like Gwen was outside of the joke, like it was on her.

Before long, the drinks had wrapped up. I assumed Fleur was sleeping out in the cottage. When the women cleared off, I brought the glasses and dishes in from the table and Gwen helped me clean up, insisting she did her part. She blustered about, tidying up, going from room to room, constantly changing direction like those moments before a storm when the wind is not sure which way it's blowing.

'Not my sort of women, really,' she said, mostly to herself. 'Can't say I didn't try but they're really not my kind of people.'

'Mmm,' I responded, my hands in dishwater.

'The cleaner can finish the dishes when she comes tomorrow. Why don't you come sit with me?'

But Shirley came in the afternoon. I would still need the kitchen tidy for breakfast.

'Oh,' I said. 'Umm, sure. Now?'

'Yes, come on. You can change out of your dirty chef's clothes, if you like.'

173

I knew that was more of a command than a question, so I went out to the cottage and put on a clean shirt and jeans. My tidiest clothes. I didn't see Fleur – the door to her room was open but she wasn't in there.

Back inside, Gwen was sitting in the loungeroom with a glass of wine, a record on.

'Wine?' she said.

'Yeah, okay,' I said.

'I suppose Fleur can come back now. She stunk of alcohol. What was she thinking?'

'I'm not sure,' I said.

She shook her head. 'So, you two,' she said. 'How long has that been happening?'

I didn't know how to respond to that. I just shrugged. 'I don't know—'

'It's pretty obvious.'

'Yeah, we . . . I suppose we were seeing each other, like that, but not anymore. It ended weeks ago.'

Gwen took a sip. 'Well, I suggest you don't let Simon find out.'

I didn't know what to say to that. 'Okay. Like I said, it's over now.'

'You're both consenting adults. You can do as you please.'

I took a quick sip of the wine.

'You don't like it, the wine?'

'No, it's fine.'

'What do you drink? Beer?'

'Beer. Whisky.'

'Whisky?' she asked, an eyebrow rising a fraction.

What I meant was Jim Beam, mixed with Coke. But when I saw her place her glass down on the table and stand up, I knew she thought I was talking about scotch. She crossed the room.

'Peated? Unpeated?'

'Umm, either,' I said. I had no idea what the difference was.

'He has everything. I don't know much about any of it but I know this one,' she said, reaching up to the shelf with the decanter, 'is a good one.'

'Oh, no. I can't—'

'Shh, just enjoy it.'

She took it down and brought it over, taking a glass from the sideboard.

'Please, I don't need a—'

'Shh. You're on the clock, Bill. And I'm telling you to have a drink.'

The pour was generous. She didn't offer ice, or Coke, or water. She just put it down beside my wine glass. I knew it meant this wasn't to be mixed or diluted or chilled.

I left the wine and lifted the glass of whisky. She watched me. I brought it to my nose, caught a strong, heady whiff.

I took a sip. I couldn't keep the grimace entirely off my face.

'Wow,' she said, she laughed. 'Not the response I was expecting.'

'It's strong.'

'It's whisky.'

'I like it. I just wasn't ready.' It was true. Maybe knowing it was expensive made it nicer but it tasted nothing like anything I had tried before. It was like Christmas cake in a liquid form, with a hearty kick of heat deep in my chest.

'You should enjoy it. It's not cheap, I know that much.'

I thought about what Teimana might steal if he came to this house. A decanter full of whisky would probably be the last thing on the list. How could anyone know the value of any of it? That's when she noticed something else.

She stood up, went back to the whiskies but peered instead at the shelf of antiques, ceramic swans, a teapot that looked like it could be Indian.

'Is something wrong?' I said.

She turned back to me, her mouth open. 'Something is missing.'

'What is it?'

'A comb,' she said. She narrowed her eyes, scanned about the room as if searching for it.

'What sort of comb?'

'It was a family heirloom. My great-grandfather, he was one of the first to visit New Zealand actually. He gave it to his wife, my great-grandmother. It's extremely sentimental – and valuable.'

'I'm sure it will turn up.'

She was trembling. 'It's been passed down for over a hundred years. It's just . . . well, it's one of those silly old superstitions but it's our history.'

Something caught in my throat.

She went on. 'It's passed down from mother to daughter on our wedding days. It's supposed to protect us. The comb.'

I took another sip of the whisky. And another one. With each sip, it grew better and better. I wanted to enjoy it – maybe that's the trick. Wanting to taste it, seeking out flavours in the spirit. And soon I did enjoy it and, before long, it was finished.

Gwen had sat silently since discovering the missing comb. She held her glass of wine but didn't finish it before she stood and went to the stairs. Touching my shoulder as she passed.

'I'm going to bed.'

Then she was gone. I heard a door open and close upstairs and the house was still. Knowing I'd never have an opportunity to do this again, I went and poured another small glass of the whisky.

Someone stepped into the loungeroom and I almost jumped. It was Elle. She had her journal in her hand.

'How long have you been there?'

'Not too long,' she said, her eyes in sallow loops. 'I wasn't eavesdropping.'

'I know,' I said, wondering if she'd been there long enough to hear what was said about me and Fleur. If so, half the Primrose family now knew we'd hooked up. *Damn.*

She left the loungeroom, and started back up the steps, her journal held tight to her chest. I returned to the kitchen, downed the last of the whisky in my glass and finished the dishes.

Back in the cottage, Fleur's door was closed. I poured a glass of water and found a Panadol to take through to her but when I opened her door I found her room empty. Where was she? I went outside, back to the pool, where the candles had long since burned out. I checked the deckchairs beside the pool, scanned the garden in the moonlight. A mist was creeping across the paddocks toward the house. It was already cold and there would be a crisp layer of frost on the grass in the morning.

I went back to the house, searched downstairs in every room. Still, I couldn't find her.

I watched TV in the cottage until the shows stopped and an old movie came on. I was just waiting until I fell asleep. I woke when the door opened, startled to see Fleur. The clock on the microwave told me it was after 3 am. Hours had passed.

'Where have you been?' I said.

'I went for a walk.'

'A walk where?'

She was angry with Gwen, that much was clear, but no one had seen her since nine o'clock.

'I just wanted to leave this place for a while,' she said. 'Sometimes I go for walks at night, nothing for you to worry your pretty little head about.'

'You embarrassed her,' I said. 'And she knows we hooked up now. She warned me not to let Simon know.'

Fleur laughed at that, going to the sink for a glass of water. She faced me and took a sip. 'They won't fire me.'

'Why not?'

'Because they can't.'

I looked into her eyes. 'Why?'

'I know where the bodies are buried.'

'Half the house knows about us – Gwen and Elle.'

'Poor Elle, her little heart will be breaking.'

'It's not a joke,' I said, my voice angry. Elle was going through something and Fleur seemed to take joy in her misery.

'I'm not joking. The girl has a crush but we both know you're not good at reading these things.'

I sighed.

'Well, good night,' she said. 'You better get to sleep soon if you don't want to miss breakfast.' And then she disappeared into her room, closing the door firmly behind her.

The morning came around, bringing three hangovers with it: one for Fleur, who tried to chase it away with three black coffees before 9 am; one for Gwen, who wandered down looking dishevelled in her dressing gown and picked at toast with jam and milky tea; and one for me, despite only having had two glasses of whisky and a bit of wine. The three of us were also united in blocking out the drama of the night before: Fleur's gaffes in front of the women, Gwen and my chat in the loungeroom. We all just pretended like nothing had happened.

Chet, the only one in the dark, came over and punched me on the arm as I served breakfast. It was our joke.

'What are you doing, mate?' he would say, as he struck my arm.

'Morning, sport,' I said, gently punching him back.

Elle was supposed to be studying for her mid-year high-school exams and disappeared to her room the moment she finished breakfast, but who knows what she was getting up to in there. I had no reason to go see her but I wanted to explain the situation, or at least chat to her. I don't know what I wanted exactly – maybe just to relieve my own sense of pressing guilt. So after cleaning up, when Fleur was out in the cottage and Gwen was on the phone in the loungeroom, I climbed the stairs and tapped on Elle's door.

'Mummy?' she said. There was something a little disconcerting about the fact the kids still called their parents Mummy and Daddy. It was old-timey, like something out of a fairytale – something I'd never dreamed of calling my mum.

'Umm, it's me, actually.'

'Bill.' I heard the squeak, like a chair turning, then footsteps. She opened the door. 'Yes?'

'I thought I would just explain what you might have heard last night.'

'Oh,' she said. 'You and Fleur, right. That's fine. No explanation needed.'

'It's just, I don't want you to get the wrong idea.'

'No,' she said, squirming. 'Honestly—'

'We're not in a relationship or anything.'

'I'm not a child,' she said. 'I don't, like . . . I don't really care. Don't worry.'

She almost sounded mean.

'Sure,' I said. 'Okay.'

'Bill?'

I turned and saw Gwen coming up the stairs.

'What's happening here?'

'He was just asking what I wanted for lunch, Mummy. A salad would be nice, thanks, Bill.'

'Bill,' Gwen said. 'Please don't disturb her. She has her exams starting in just a couple of weeks. Go on, downstairs.'

Lizzie returned that afternoon. Again, I overheard something I shouldn't have. They were sitting in the loungeroom and Gwen told her about the missing heirloom.

'Well, I think it's probably the chef,' Lizzie said. 'It seems obvious to me but Simon will want to talk to them all, I'm sure.'

I balled my fists and walked away before I heard anything more.

BILL

I OPENED THE front door to the Primrose mansion, collapsed my rain-slicked umbrella and found them all there in the foyer, shoulder to shoulder, like a police line-up: Tate, Shirley, Fleur. Everyone who came and went from the house.

'Bill, come here,' Simon said from where he stood beside Gwen. I'd been out collecting groceries. 'Put those in the kitchen first.'

'Sure,' I said, pulling my shoes off. I did exactly as I was told, returning to where the three others stood.

'Now, we're going to do this ourselves before we involve the police. If you confess, well, we will decide on the appropriate action – but so long as our property is returned, you won't be charged.'

I watched him, his cheeks crumbed with stubble, his eyes hard and flint-coloured.

'What's this about?' Fleur asked. The only one who possessed the courage to open her mouth.

'This,' Simon said, with a grim emphasis on the word, 'is about a family heirloom that has gone missing. And someone here took it.'

I pulled my hands out of my pockets, held them together behind my back. *They can't know that*, I thought. *Others have been and gone, including the women from Gwen's drinks.* Did I look guilty? Why was Simon staring at me?

'So,' he said, his eyes now roaming. 'Anyone want to come forward?'

'Well, it wasn't me and I've got work to do,' Tate said.

But Simon stepped closer, towering over the smaller man. Tate had a scar beside his mouth and when he smiled it cut through his left dimple. But at that moment, when I turned to him, I saw it was an angry pink colour. I realised he was afraid of Simon. It didn't matter that his father knew him – Simon still intimidated Tate.

'It's for me to work out who took it, Tate. Not you. I'm sorry but this is how it must be done.'

'When did it go missing?' Fleur again.

'Well, in the last week. We both recall seeing it last Friday, in the loungeroom.' He walks to the loungeroom door and opens it. 'And it looks like someone also helped themselves to my whisky.' There's even more colour in his cheeks now.

I raised my hand and his eyes locked on me.

'You!' he said, coming forward.

'Simon,' Gwen said by way of intervention. 'Bill had a small glass of your whisky.'

'What?'

'I offered it to him. He did such a great job of the dinner and canapés, I wanted to give him a treat.'

'You did? A treat?' He straightened, his body stiff and tight. 'What did you think, Bill? Up to scratch?' There was no warmth in his voice.

I didn't know what to say. 'Umm—'

'Well?'

'Umm, yes,' I said. 'It was, ah, very nice.'

He laughed but it didn't break the tension. It seemed to heat the room a few degrees instead. 'Discerning palate. Wouldn't have picked it.' Then to Gwen. 'I didn't realise we were giving out the good stuff to the help, Gwen. Maybe next time, pick one of the other ones.' He tried to laugh again but it was clear this had thrown him.

'If he's stealing your whisky,' Tate piped up then, 'maybe he took the comb?'

Simon was entirely motionless apart from the thumb of his right hand, which was rubbing the knuckle of his left.

'Tate, are your ears working?' he said, without looking away from Gwen. 'My wife just said she gave it to him. He didn't steal it.' Now his eyes shifted to Tate's face. 'Did you see him take the comb?'

I turned just enough to see Tate's face. I could have hit him for trying to throw me under the bus like that. I felt more pressure in that moment than I'd ever felt in a commercial kitchen. Everyone seemed to be burning up, including Gwen, but it was clear Simon wasn't going to stop. This was the environment he thrived in.

Tate shook his head.

'No. Okay. Shirley?'

The diminutive cleaner just shook her head.

'Fleur, Bill, either of you see anything?'

We both shook our heads.

No one was going to raise their hand and Simon didn't have any evidence either way. He just wanted to strongarm a confession out of one of us.

'Well, what if we search your things then?' he said. 'I wonder what we would turn up?'

Fleur was shaking her head. 'No, Simon. That would be invading our privacy.' A surge of relief rinsed up in my chest. *He can't search our rooms.*

Annoyance flitted across his face. 'Well, we all live together, don't we? What privacy are you talking about?'

'Only Bill and me. The rest do not live here,' she said, her voice small. 'And that's our space.'

Simon studied me. 'Someone might have had extra motivation to take it, I can't say. But I'm going to try something different since this isn't working. You might have thought it didn't mean so much to us, or that you had some claim, some right to take our possessions. I'm going to give the culprit one week to return it. Put it back on the shelf in there. No games or tricks. If it is here at,' he checked his wristwatch, 'midday next Thursday, let's just say lunchtime, then we won't take it any further. We won't even try to figure out who took it. Put it back and all is well. If not, then it might be time for all of you to start looking for work elsewhere.'

Simon suspected me. It was something he said. *Someone might have had extra motivation.* And the whisky. He didn't like that.

'So you're going to clean house?' Tate said. 'Sack us all?'

'That's right,' Simon said. 'And I'll report it to the police. Unless it's returned, then everything will be fine.'

When we were all dismissed, I saw Lizzie sitting at the dining table. She watched Fleur and me as we passed.

The sick feeling in my stomach got worse when, that night, I found a folded letter on my bed. I opened it and realised who it was from. Elle. My heart lodged somewhere in my throat.

I'm not going to pretend to recall the exact details of the letter but it went something like this:

You know I'm shy. I can't just say this to your face because I feel a little nervous around you still ... even after all this time. I know I'm younger but I'm eighteen soon and my father is just overprotective. I know there are reasons that nothing can ever happen between us but I want you to know that I like you. I like you more than I've liked anyone else. I tried to meet other guys my age, through friends at school, but I've always had a crush on you, Bill. It hurt to know you were

with Fleur, I can't say why. I guess because she is
so different to me, much older than me, and I thought
maybe part of me wanted you for myself. I know
nothing will come of it but I just wanted you to know.

I reread the note a number of times, thinking about how hard it must have been for her to write, about how awkward it might make things now. She was lonely. If I was honest, so was I: Maia had completely blocked me out – she hadn't even so much as messaged me since Teimana had turned up at the house.

But Elle was not the answer to my loneliness, that was too complicated and was the definition of playing with fire. Fleur hadn't been the answer either. In some ways, being with her had just made me feel more lonely. I'd never really been the kind of guy to have a no-strings-attached sort of thing. I stuffed the letter into a drawer in my wardrobe, and tried not to think about it. I thought maybe I could pretend I never read it.

Aunt Lizzie left two days later. I was happy to see the back of her, but Gwen looked like she might cry as she hugged her at the door. Elle and Chet squeezed her hard too, and Elle looked downcast.

'Be good for your parents and I'll be back again before long,' Lizzie said, pinching Elle's cheeks.

Afterward, as Elle passed through the kitchen out to the garden, she couldn't look me in the eye. I acted as normally as I could. I prepped lunch, then gave Chet a skateboard lesson, sucking a few puffs from my inhaler to keep my asthma at bay. In the afternoon, we played a game of chess at the kitchen bench – Chet had decided to teach me, as payback for the skating. I was hopeless but it was alright; Chet was a nice kid, and hanging out with him sometimes felt like what it must be like to have a little brother.

During the week that Simon gave us to return the comb, I did see something. I told the police later but I only wish I'd told the family. I saw Tate in places he shouldn't have been.

First, one early evening, I saw him emerge from the cottage as I was cooking. He slipped up the side of the house and left before I could talk to him.

The second place was the basement. He was down there alone and came up with a toolbox in hand as I was bringing the groceries in from the car. 'Billy boy,' he said as he passed me. I nodded and he continued on.

He was also turning up around the house at all hours, when he wasn't working. One night, late, I found him inside. He had left for the day hours earlier, gone home, yet there he was in the kitchen, staring out into the yard, his face like a skull, his eyes made dark by the shadow from the downlights. 'Getting cold now,' he said then smiled.

SLOANE

HOLY RED HERRINGS, this is huge.

This dodgy Tate character. Fleur and Bill, ending the way they did. Fleur acting out. The daughter's crush on Bill: I wonder if it ever went further. The prosecution had painted Bill as a predator, but this account makes it clear he is deeply uncomfortable with the attention. Even the cleaner, what was her story? The stolen heirloom – well, it could have been any of them, really. The persons of interest just keep multiplying. There's more than enough here for a series. I feel a tingling sensation in my gut – the one I get when I know I am onto a good story. An *excellent* story.

I still think that if we can find out who tampered with the heating, we will likely find the killer. It could have been Bill, of course, and if it was, it would make sense to place the detail about Tate in the basement in his personal account, to point the finger at him. But how could Bill have known that the tampered heating would ever be discovered? He wrote his account years after the murders, as part of his therapy with TK, and no one even knew about the heating tampering then – no one knew about it until I came along. Surely Bill wasn't counting on it being revealed seventeen years later? What seems more likely is that Bill himself hasn't connected the dots, that he didn't know about the heating. Otherwise, it could have been raised by his lawyers in his trial, as a possible defence.

The business with Simon and the train disaster is also more notable than I'd realised. It wasn't even mentioned in Bill's trial, and media coverage of the murders didn't reveal much about Simon's political career at all, aside from the fact that he'd once been a minister in the UK. But a simple Google search of *Southgate train disaster* yields hundreds of results, from news articles and government reports to blogposts and endless images of the carnage. Two photos come up over and over: one of the train carriages, derailed and corkscrewed; the other of one of the victims – a boy with blood covering the bottom half of his face, howling as a woman holds him.

I feel sure that we can get an episode out of the Southgate train crash. An episode on Tate. An episode on Fleur. An episode on the theft of the heirloom. Maybe even an episode on the class and racial politics that were playing out under the roof of the Primrose mansion. Bill might not have been clear at the time as to why he was a target of suspicion. But I sure as hell have a theory. It was more important than ever that TK track Elizabeth down and get her insights into the house, and what was happening at the time.

I refill my wine and check my emails. Then I notice there's something on the mud-coloured carpet, a white square slipped under my door. My heart slams. I reach for it and turn it over. It's a polaroid image of a burnt-out white Holden Commodore in a paddock. Is this the car that was seen on the night of the murders? Underneath the photo I see a line of words: *Meet beside Lake Te Koo Utu 12 am for the truth. Come alone.* It's almost midnight now and I know better than to meet a stranger alone at night. I message Dean; this is important and I can't miss my opportunity. I hold my breath, see three dots appear on the screen. Is this asking too much of him? He said twenty-four hours a day but did he mean it?

I can come. Give me fifteen.

I do a quick google. Lake Te Koo Utu is close, in the park practically across the street. I'd seen it during the day. On the map, the lake is in the middle. It'd be pitch black in there, surrounded by trees.

As I wait for Dean outside in the car park, questions pinball in my brain. How did I miss the note sliding under my door? I was sucked in by Bill's story, but still. And how did the note sender find me? Did they follow me? Maybe. The bar we were at earlier was full of patrons – anyone might have noticed me. The hen's party certainly did.

Dean arrives at 11.55 pm. 'It's a creepy place at night,' he says as he climbs out of the car. 'You did the right thing to call me.'

It's a walk – we don't even need to drive. We cross the road, through the heavy fog, walk to the end of the block and reach the park. A glowing cross appears to hover in the night sky, but as we get close I see the pole holding it up.

'It's dark down there,' I say, eyeing the path through the bush toward the lake.

Dean looks about, using the torch on his phone and aiming it at the ground ahead. It lights up an orb of fog around us. 'We can go back.'

'No,' I say. 'No, this is important. The car . . .'

How much do I say? A photo of a burnt-out car. We take the stairs slowly. The path wraps back and forth, in a descent that leads us eventually to the lakeside. It's dead quiet: the light of the town, the traffic sounds, every sign of civilisation blocked out by darkness and fog.

'Hello?' I call.

'It said beside the lake, right?'

'Yep.'

'They could mean up ahead. Let's go a bit further.'

I can barely compel my feet to carry me forward. What if this is a set-up? What if someone brought me here to hurt me? Adrenaline makes my arms and legs feel somehow both weak and strong; I could collapse or lift a car.

Dean doesn't speak; maybe he's afraid too. The trees cast a black shadow, but soon picnic tables emerge from the fog and I think I see people gathered around them – shapes in the dark. But there is no sound or movement, there is no one there.

I want to run, turn and fly back up the hill, out of this darkness. But we press on tentatively. We walk together all the way to the far end of the park.

'Maybe it was a prank,' I say.

'Maybe,' he says.

We pause for a moment, waiting.

'Is there another way back?' I ask, a wobble in my voice. 'Along the street? I'm not really up for the return trip.'

'This way.'

Dean leads me up another climb, this time more open and light. We reach the road and start walking back. He leaves me at the motel.

'Sorry,' I say.

'Oh, no, don't apologise. I'm glad I came. I'll see you in the morning.'

'Thanks.'

I head back to my room, open the door and find another note, this time scrawled on a torn piece of newspaper.

I said come alone. Tomorrow. Same time. Last chance.

TK

THE GROWL OF the engines gets louder, the plane lightly trembles. I take a Valium in my palm and tip it down my throat. I grip the arm rests.

The older woman next to me gives a sympathetic look. 'Bad flyer?' she says.

'If we get even a hint of turbulence, you might find me cowering under the seat like a dog.'

'Well, I'll make sure we get there safely,' she says, with such conviction I almost believe her. 'Don't worry.'

I sleep off and on throughout the flight, and in between I listen to podcasts and watch a couple of movies. Eventually, we begin descending through the clouds to Heathrow airport. I brace for touchdown.

The airport is chaos. I'm just grateful I only brought carry-on. Immigration is apparently unconvinced that a near forty-year-old would travel alone across the planet for a few days with just a small bag of clothes, so I get a little extra attention in an interview room but I'm not too concerned – my train to Edinburgh doesn't leave for a few hours.

I take the Elizabeth line to Paddington station and find a Pret A Manger nearby to caffeinate. It's four in the morning New Zealand time and my eyes are drooping out of my head, but it's not the first time that caffeine has helped me to march through the fog of sleeplessness.

As I sit and refuel, I hear the familiar sound of a variety of British accents and dialects around me. I've missed London – the people, that is, not so much the food or coffee. The hours pass too slowly as I sit in front of my laptop, reading back through the coverage of the Southgate train disaster, looking at those images. Sloane's latest text had suggested I have another look into it. She must have some kind of theory, I guess, or maybe she just wants it as background for the podcast. I scroll through a few different articles. I can sense the anger that the families must have felt. The failures of politicians *always* disproportionately affect the lower classes, the marginalised and disenfranchised. And they always get away with it.

I look at the time and head to the platform, more waiting. Eventually, a train pulls in, slows, stops. I find a seat in a mostly empty carriage and soon we are away.

Outside, towns pass, broken up by the rolling green countryside. The gentle, rhythmic sway soon rocks me to sleep and, when I open my eyes again, I see the sea, a golf course wrapping the coast. We're not far away. I drift off again and the next time I wake we're pulling into Edinburgh station.

From the platform, up the elevator, I emerge into the heart of the city. It's a storybook world: grimy sandstone buildings from an age of kings and queens; a brutalist tower stands like an obsidian dagger pointed at the sky; a castle overlooks the city from its hill. How different this trip would be if it wasn't accompanied by the anxious butterflies my task brings with it.

The Airbnb I booked online is in the old town, not far from Harvey Bond's architecture office, not far from what I suspect is his home. *Harvey Bond*, that's a name you won't find on any court transcripts, nor on any of those morbid true-crime forums online. But that's the name that led me to this place, halfway across the planet.

It's mid-afternoon but I'm overwhelmed by a sudden fatigue. I close the blinds, pull my shoes off and lie on the covers. The dark mouth of sleep swallows me whole.

BILL

IT WAS THURSDAY. Simon had not gone into the office and his ultimatum was set to expire in a few hours, at which point he said he would fire us all and involve the police. As lunchtime approached, there was no sign of Tate.

I returned to the cottage, found the bag I'd arrived with, stuffed all of my clothes inside it.

The cottage phone rang. Fleur answered it.

'Yes,' I heard her say. 'Okay, we will come over.'

We lined up once more before Simon, only three of us this time.

'It seems,' Simon said, 'Tate has disappeared and, with him, I assume the comb is gone too. I have contacted the police and I'm sure they will catch up with him, but until they do, I'm asking you all to let me know if you see him anywhere near the house or around town.'

We all nodded.

He cleared his throat. His eyes settled on me for a beat.

'Alright, back to work.'

Fleur marched from the room without looking back. I could see an incandescent glow on the back of her otherwise pale neck.

Simon's eyes stayed with her for a moment before turning back to Shirley and me.

'Chop chop.'

'I'll get into my whites,' I said, following Fleur to the cottage. Unlike me, she had not packed her things. She must have known Simon wouldn't fire us all, that it was all a bluff. But whatever rapport we had built up had evaporated the moment that comb went missing; our banter was gone and Fleur was a different woman. Quiet, more serious. There'd been a few nights that she had not returned to the cottage until late, creeping in during the small hours.

'What did you do with it?' she asked me, facing me with wet eyes.

'The comb?' I said. 'Why would I steal that?'

She huffed, shook her head. 'I'm not an idiot. It obviously wasn't Tate.' She drew a breath. 'They wouldn't fire you. Gwen would have understood but you were too cowardly to put your hand up.'

'What's going on, Fleur? You've changed. The last few weeks, you've been different.'

'What do you mean? Maybe you just didn't know me before. Now you know.'

'They wouldn't be happy with you sneaking around,' I said, giving her words back to her from months earlier, when I had Maia visit.

'I don't care what they think.'

'You don't like any of them?' I asked. 'You really don't?'

'And you do? Maybe you hide it from yourself but it's bubbling away – every time they lord over you, make demands of you, mispronounce your surname and disrespect your culture. If you don't feel the rage now, you will eventually. But we all do strange things for money.'

'It's a job. No one likes their boss.'

She shook her head. 'You had so much potential, Bill. I thought you were different.'

I don't know why, but that stung. I felt anger swelling but the phone rang before I could respond. I reached to answer it.

Without missing a beat, Fleur said, 'Chop chop,' the words slow, soaked in sarcasm. I scowled at her and picked up the receiver.

It was Gwen, wanting us back at the house. I went to my room to quickly pull on my chef's whites.

Back at the house, Simon was calm, sitting on a bench beside Chet at the piano. He played at one end while Chet played at the other. Gwen sat with a smile, watching the boys in the loungeroom through the open French doors, and Elle sat with her new iPod and headphones on, reading through her notes for an upcoming exam. Everything seemed perfectly normal. I began to clear some glasses and cups and saucers from the morning, stacking them on the trolley to return to the kitchen.

When Fleur came back to the house, she had her lips painted red and eyes bright, as if she could not be happier to be there. She went to the laundry and came out with a basketful of washing, proceeding to fold, her eyes fixed firmly on the back of Simon's head as he sat at the piano. By then, I was sitting with Gwen, showing her the menu plan for the week, and compiling my shopping list with a pencil and pad.

'Bill,' Gwen said. 'I've been meaning to tell you. We've got important guests coming to visit from the UK.' *Important* guests. 'I want to make sure we put on a great feast.'

'Sure,' I said. 'When?'

'In a few weeks' time, end of the month. I'll let you know closer to the date, but it might be worth thinking about what you'll cook. Doing a few test runs if you need to.'

'Of course.' *And what were you going to do if Simon had fired me?*

But inwardly, I relaxed. Despite Fleur's coldness, this moment felt like a turning point, the house returning to normal after the chaotic period in which Tate was there. The sun was shining in through the windows – we were in the middle of a warm spell, the last before winter hit, and a flighty lilt issued from the piano where the boys played.

Back in the kitchen, I could hear Simon begin to sing, his voice surprising me, and when Chet joined in, it was a moment of real beauty. At the conclusion of the song, I heard clapping.

'Bravo,' Gwen said.

'Keep practising,' Simon said to Chet. 'You dropped the E a few times in the arpeggios, but you're getting better.'

'For this dinner,' Gwen said, entering the kitchen later that day. 'I've been thinking I'd like a bit of local flair, show off the New Zealand cuisine.'

'I could use natives, a nice seafood main,' I told her, searching my mind. 'Kingfish ceviche with grilled kūmara okonomiyaki. A kiwifruit terrine for dessert.'

'What did you make last week? The fluffy dessert, like a large meringue?'

'Pavlova.'

'Yes, pavlova. That's a New Zealand dessert?'

'It is.'

'Sounds Russian, or Baltic,' Simon said, coming in from the loungeroom. 'Pavlova,' he repeated, affecting a Russian accent. 'I'd have thought an authentic New Zealand dish would have a name like ruarangawhakeapoopataha.'

Gwen snorted. I tried to smile but my cheeks felt tight. Fleur's words came back to me. *Every time they disrespect your culture.*

'No,' I said, forcing a hint of laughter into my voice. 'Who knows where the name came from?'

'Well, Russian or New Zealand, I think a pavlova would be great for dessert. And maybe a couple of starters too.'

I thought about Elle. 'Maybe a vegetarian starter?'

'Elle can do without,' she says. 'You made scallops wrapped in prosciutto once?'

'I can do those again. For sure. Anything else?'

'No, we can discuss it closer to the day. One of Simon's old colleagues from London will be here with his wife,' she said. 'We'll also be joined by the British High Commissioner to New Zealand. She helped us out a lot when we arrived. She will be up from Wellington,' Gwen added. 'And we might add a few more, to make up the party. I am still deciding.'

I didn't even know what a high commissioner was but it sounded important.

'Easy enough. I'll get the ingredients fresh the morning they arrive.'

That night, I messaged Mooks, a keen fisherman. If he could get either kingfish or snapper on the morning, it'd be extra fresh. He messaged back straight away.

No worries, nephew. Should be fine just remind me a couple of days before. I'll take the boat out in the morning then you can come see me in the afternoon.

My mouth watered, just thinking about the meal I'd prepare. I lay in bed, running through menu options in my head – sauces, sides, even plating. I'd make it a meal to remember.

BILL

'KIA ORA, NEPHEW,' Mooks's voice came down the phone line. Sometimes even the best fishermen come back empty-handed, and I had a back-up plan just in case. But any doubt disappeared when he said, 'We've had a good morning. Enough snapper to feed the whānau, and I picked up a haku from a mate in Maketū on the way back this morning.'

'Fresh kingfish?' I said.

'Speared this morning.'

I exhaled, relieved. 'What time should I meet you?'

'What is it? Eight now? I've got work at the school at ten, so any time before then,' he said. 'Or this afternoon.'

'I'll come now.' I took two fifty-dollar notes in petty cash, wrote *$100 – fresh fish* down on the ledger I kept for Gwen. It was above market value, sure, but Mooks had earnt it.

After clearing breakfast away, I jumped in the Range Rover and drove to meet Mooks outside the school grounds. He was dressed in his overalls, looked as tired as an old bulldog.

He shook my hand then went to the boot of his car. 'Big feed, eh?'

'They've got guests,' I said. 'Important guests.' Including the family, I was cooking for eight.

His black eyebrows flew up. '*Important*, eh? Hope they're looking after you and I hope you're getting paid.'

'Yeah, I'm doing alright, Uncle.'

'Don't forget your kaupapa, eh, boy.'

I met his eyes, his serious gaze. 'I hear you, Uncle. It's just mahi.'

He lifted a chilly-bin out of his boot and handed it to me. I gave him the cash. He tried to give one of the $50 notes back.

'Nah, it's their money.'

'Your money, boy. They don't need to know. One hundred is too much.'

'Take it, Uncle,' I said, pushing it away. He folded it and put it in the chest pocket of his overalls.

'A few kina in there too.'

'Fresh?'

'Fresh as.'

'Beauty,' I said, already imagining the ways I could incorporate them into the meal. 'In their shell?'

'Yeah,' he said. 'Three of them.'

I whistled. 'Well, if they don't eat them, I will.'

'I got them for you, nephew,' he said. 'Better get to work.' He closed the boot of his old Toyota.

'Before you go,' I said, reaching into the pocket of my coat, 'there's something I want you to help me with.'

I pulled out an old t-shirt and put it in the boot. Wrapped inside was the carved-bone comb. I unfolded it, and Mooks leaned in for a look.

'What's this? Heru?'

'I don't know where it belongs but it's not with them,' I said.

He just nodded and wrapped it back up. 'I'll take care of it.' Then he set off toward the school gates.

On the way home, I picked up the rest of the ingredients, most from the small organic grocer they liked in Hamilton. I'd been gone for the morning, and when I got back, I cooked a quick macaroni and cheese for the family lunch. Simon was out all day and Gwen dragged Elle out of the house in the afternoon.

Shirley came through and spent a few hours cleaning – she polished the silver, dusted everything and set the table up with a starched white cloth and candles. Everything was perfect, *nothing* was out of place. A new gardener had arrived early that morning, not a full-timer like Tate but a landscaper hired as a once-off to bring everything up to scratch. I could see him out in the gardens, working away.

Shirley, I later discovered, had even cleaned the cottage. Our beds were freshly made, the windows cleaned inside and out. She must have worked all morning and most of the afternoon.

Gwen and Elle came back with their hair done, arms full of shopping bags. Gwen inspected the house and the grounds, before coming in to check on my progress in the kitchen. Satisfied, she eventually retreated upstairs.

After a while, Simon came to the kitchen to assess the situation and check that everything was ready. He was wearing a sharp dinner suit, slacks cinched around his narrow waist, his brown hair neat and cheeks cleanshaven. He gave me a long, hard look.

'We need to talk about something,' he said. 'But it can wait until after tonight. Just make sure everything is perfect.'

'Of course,' I said, with a knot of unease in my chest.

I did my prep, head down in the kitchen. Gwen soon appeared wearing gold earrings, a thin pearl necklace and a glamorous black shift, and she and Fleur set the table – well, Fleur was setting it, Gwen was following her around, making small adjustments. They had four bottles of Bollinger lined up like soldiers in the fridge, with a bottle of vermouth and martini glasses in the freezer. A bartender and waitress turned up, hired for the night. They were both in black with white suspenders and starched white aprons. Simon barked instructions in the dining room when Fleur came through to the kitchen.

'The first guests are here,' she said quietly. 'They're in a Rolls-Royce. She is stunning, the woman. Much younger.'

She poured the welcome drinks, two glasses of champagne. The waitress came through and collected them. Soon I could hear the murmur of conversation and music playing from the record player. A light jazz number. The second couple arrived.

The chat was boisterous; old acquaintances coming together – I could hear Simon laughing heartily. I was focused on the task at hand but couldn't help listening, snatching lines of conversation here and there.

'The colonies haven't changed you too much, old boy?' one deep voice said.

'It's a bit like the countryside back home, reminds me of our weekends in Dorset.'

The rest of the guests arrived. After letting them in, Fleur mostly stayed in the kitchen with me: on a night like this, it was kept formal. I knew despite her eyerolling that Fleur enjoyed playing spectator with me. There was a lightness to her that I hadn't seen for weeks.

Glasses clinked and I sent the canapés out. Oysters, ceviche, prawns and the star of the show: fresh kina, like tiny, mango-coloured tongues, served with oyster forks on caviar, in their original spiked black shells. The colours contrasted beautifully and the plating was striking.

'That fish is divine,' one of the women said.

A general murmur of agreement.

'Less so that horrible orange creation,' another voice said. Laughter. Heat rushed to my face.

'Try it,' Gwen said. 'I enjoyed it.'

'Don't spit it out!' A man's voice. They howled.

'It's a popular local dish, kina,' Gwen said, reciting the information I'd conveyed earlier when running through the menu. 'It's a delicacy.'

'Kina?' another voice. 'No, it's sea urchin. Japanese, I think. I'm surprised anyone considers it edible. I've certainly never understood it. It's ghastly. Like a bad oyster.'

'Yes, the Japanese eat it but they eat anything from the sea.'

'If you scoop it out, you can get to the caviar at least.'

Sweat ran down from my brow as I finished garnishing the sides. I tried to block the voices out but I couldn't. I thought about Mooks and how much he loved kina. My mouth had been watering as I prepared them and now they'd be coming back to the kitchen half-eaten and spat out. *People have their own tastes*, I reminded myself. *Not everyone loves everything I cook.*

'Simon,' Gwen said. 'What do you think? It's nice, right?'

'I love you, Gwen. But let's not pretend this tastes nice. If *this* is New Zealand cuisine, I think we should book flights home.'

This was met with the biggest round of laughs of all. I slammed my knife through a carrot, over and over until it bit into the edge of my thumb knuckle. A pearl of blood, bright red.

'Gwen, why don't you show us the gardens? Before we lose the light.'

'This way.' I recognised Gwen's voice, polite as ever. 'Nothing like what we had at the Dorset house but we do the best with what we've got.'

'I'm sure it's just lovely.'

'Well, if you met the first gardener, you would understand. Should have guessed from his name,' Simon's voice boomed through.

'What was this chap called?'

'Mooks,' Simon said, his voice charged with derision. They all laughed again.

'Sounds like something from *Sesame Street.*'

'Could have been a muppet, let me tell you. Had to fire him in the end, over-pruned the roses. He was another one of Gwen's charity projects.' More laughter.

The fish they'd loved so much had come from Mooks; he'd never hurt a fly and was a hard worker, generous. In that moment, I hated Simon. I felt sweat forming in the collar of my shirt.

'It's important to give everyone an opportunity, Simon.'

'Indeed,' Simon said. 'I'm just asking for competency as well. Black, white, yellow. I just want someone who can do the job.'

BILL

THEY SET OUT through the gardens with champagne in hand – the women in their dresses, their shouldered furs, neat rows of pearls strung about their pale throats. The men in dinner suits – cartoonish, penguin-like black coats and slacks. The guests looked exactly how I'd imagined from the kitchen, confirming what I suspected about these people and their lives.

The two men were both older than Simon, one grey-haired and the other with a lick of wispy black hair combed tight across his otherwise bald scalp. One of the women was younger and beautiful, as Fleur had said, but she was bone thin with sharp cheeks and a sort of sleepy, dull gaze; the other looked around Gwen's age – mid-forties, without Gwen's hard edges. They walked down through the gardens, circling back along the side of the pool. Gwen pointed things out as she went and the group would stop, heads tilted in admiration.

'So posh, no?' Fleur said, carrying the tray of oyster shells back from the dining room. 'Thought we escaped all this when we left London.' She poured herself a small glass of champagne and threw it back. 'Going to be a long night for us. It may be over by 9 pm but that will feel like an eternity.'

When they came back inside, I sent out another round of appetisers before starting on the snapper fillets for the mains. There were four snapper in total, which was more than enough for a fillet each. I'd cleaned and scaled the fillets that afternoon. The mussel chowder was steaming on the stovetop and the home-made garlic bread was in the oven.

A few minutes later, I heard whooping and voices raised as Elle and Chet obviously joined the party for dinner. Their arrival signalled it was time to start serving the sit-down meal.

Despite having everything under control, anxiety squeezed my organs, made my throat feel like it was full of cotton wool. *What if the fish was dry? What if the chowder was over-seasoned? And what did Simon want to talk to me about later?*

On cue, the waitress, a young woman with dark hair, appeared in the doorway, and the chef in me took over. I plated, seasoned, garnished, wiped. I broke the bread, giving it an artisanal look. The soup was ready to serve. The trolley disappeared out the door, and I leaned back and sighed with relief. Fleur flashed me a smile.

Sometime between the soup and the main, Simon came to the kitchen.

'Bill,' he said. 'Great job in here, chap. It's all going well.'

'Thank you,' I said.

'Could we ask you to come on out here a moment? Our guests would like to meet you.'

Three bottles of champagne sat empty on the bench. I could see the glow of the booze in his cheeks, the dewiness of his eyes.

'Now?' I said. 'I'm just about to put the fish on.'

'Now, yes. The main course can wait a moment, can't it? We won't keep you long. They want to see who is producing all this marvellous food.'

'Sure,' I said. 'I'll be right out.' I only needed to dress the salads, fry the fish and season the potatoes.

'When you're ready.'

I took a deep breath. As I walked in, I saw the waitress standing near the wall, with her hands behind her back. Every face in the room turned to me as I entered – each of them smiling, all but Elle, who just looked tired.

'Bill!' Chet said enthusiastically. I gave him a quick wink.

'You're telling me that the chef who has been making all this wonderful food is sixteen years old?'

Laughter. My smile was held in place by thumbtacks. It was almost as if I was a street performer playing for tips. It felt like I wasn't getting enough oxygen, like I was standing beneath a heat lamp. I just wanted the privacy of the kitchen.

'He's a prodigy, like I said,' Gwen said, with pride. I looked to her, saw her eyes heavy-lidded, her head tilted as if in admiration.

I wanted to say something, but even if I had the words, it didn't seem that I was expected to speak. I focused on the small things, the details of the room. The candles were burning on the table. Music floated just below the level of conversation.

'Very fresh seafood,' the younger of the men addressed me. 'Interesting citrus on the ceviche.'

In the preceding week, I'd tested out different combinations, settling on squeezed lime juice, crushed kiwifruit and coconut cream with a hint of sumac and wild manuka honey.

'But what was that orange gunk at the start?' the other man said with a smirk. They all guffawed.

'Oh, Richard.'

'That was kina,' I said. 'It's not for everyone.' I stole a glance at Elle. She was looking down at her empty plate. Chet was staring at me.

'No,' the older man named Richard said. 'Although I think my hounds would have liked it.' He laughed at his own joke.

'Stop it,' one of the women said, though her tone suggested she could listen to him spout on all day.

'I liked it,' Chet piped up.

'You wouldn't even try it, Chet,' Gwen said, laughing gently. 'Now Bill,' she looked back at me, 'why don't you tell our guests a bit about your life in New Zealand?'

It struck me then that she and Simon had never asked about this before. They didn't know anything about me, really, other than the basic biographical details I'd given them when I applied for the job.

'My life,' I said, turning to Simon. 'Yeah, umm—'

'Well,' Gwen added, with a look like she was helping me out, 'your life has been so different to ours. So maybe you could help us understand your culture and background.'

If the floor had opened up and sucked me down inside, I would have welcomed it.

'Go on,' Richard said. His shoulders were back and his waist-coated belly touched the edge of the table.

'Well, I grew up in New Zealand. I'm a Kiwi.'

'He's an awesome skater,' Chet said, but no one seemed to hear him. I flashed a half-smile his way – it was the best I could muster.

'And you were raised by your uncle, right?' Gwen said.

I swallowed. 'From the age of eleven. After my mum died.'

'And your father?' the beautiful thin woman asked.

I shrugged. 'Well, I didn't really know him actually.'

Someone clicked their tongue.

'Now, Bill is a Māori,' Gwen said. She bleats it like a sheep – *Mah-ree.*

'Is he?' Richard said. Not *Are you?* As if this singular fact of my existence required outside verification.

'Yes,' I said, finding my voice at last. 'Yeah. I am Māori.'

'And your father? He ran off.'

I nodded. I knew what they were thinking. 'My dad was white,' I blurted out. Eyebrows rose.

Elle looked up sharply. Her eyes probed mine with an intensity I hadn't seen in her before. She gave a very small shake of her head, before looking away again.

'He could almost be Portuguese or Spanish.' The older woman spoke this time. I was a bug pinned under a microscope, wings impotently flapping. 'European features, if you don't mind me saying. The nose and eyes. Green eyes.'

'It's not a bad thing, Deirdre,' said the other woman.

'Do you have the tattoos?'

Tā moko. I searched the room, there was no getting out. No 'break the glass' escape to end the awkwardness. I sensed the waiter and bartender could also feel it. That's when Fleur reached for the champagne bottle and set about topping up glasses.

'Can you do the haka?' Dierdre asked sweetly.

Gwen looked on, puzzled. 'The haka?' she said.

'You know, the dance.'

Gwen had set this in motion, but now I could see that the momentum was taking them somewhere even she didn't want to go.

I went to shake my head.

'Yeah, go on,' Richard said. 'Give us a rendition.'

'He's just a normal guy,' Elle said suddenly, quite loudly. 'Daddy, this is awkward.'

The music seemed to dip, they all turned to her. Simon wore a stern face. Chet was scratching at a spot on the tablecloth with the tip of his index finger.

Elle herself had tasted a couple of glasses of champagne. 'Bill shouldn't have to perform,' she said.

Simon cleared his throat. 'He's a big boy, darling. He can speak for himself.'

I met her eyes. She looked as mortified as I felt.

'No,' I said. 'It's fine. But I don't think my chef's whites give me the freedom to perform a haka, though, unfortunately.'

The tension fell away. A few chuckles.

But Elle put her glass down so hard I thought the stem might snap.

Gwen turned to her. 'Very well, Bill,' she said, as though calming a wild animal.

But Simon continued speaking, 'No, no. They can all do the haka over here. Even the whites. Just like the All Blacks. You can do the vocals, can't you, Bill?'

Fleur wasn't supposed to top up glasses. That was what the waitress was for. I caught her eye as she moved around the table. Something passed between us, an understanding, a moment of kinship.

I cleared my throat, searching the room again, the silence going on like a coin falling down a well.

That was when Fleur spilled the champagne. Tipping over a glass.

The wine poured down into the older woman's lap. She stood suddenly, sending her chair tipping back, clattering against the floor. The waitress came forward, conjuring a large cotton napkin.

'You klutz, look at me.'

'It's okay, dear – it happens,' her husband said, but he didn't rise to help her. He was staring at Fleur, just like the rest of us.

'It's only bubbles, it'll come right out,' Gwen said. 'Fleur, make yourself useful and get more napkins please.'

'I'm so sorry, my hand slipped. It was clumsy.'

Elle stood, clearly upset. She walked out without a word. No one seemed to notice, except Gwen who went after her.

Simon made eye contact with me, an unreadable expression. He nodded back toward the kitchen and that's where I went, my ears burning as they mopped up Fleur's mess. I made a start on the next course, their comments racing through my mind while I tried to focus on the food instead. I reached for the pan but I'd left the burner on. I scorched my palm, a blister rising across my lifeline.

At the sink, running cold water on the burn, I caught snatches of Gwen and Simon trying to salvage the evening.

'We will have to save the haka for your next visit,' Simon said, to laughter, the atmosphere light and cool, like someone had cracked a window and let the heat and pressure escape.

'It's a war dance, isn't it? Supposed to intimidate the opposing forces, I suppose.'

'How effective was this jig against our muskets?'

I was angry and my hand was pulsing from the burn. The anger spiked, deflated. I wrapped my hand and put a latex glove on before going back to the stove. When I took the handle, this time holding a tea towel, I noticed I was shaking, my entire body trembling with a strange new energy. Something I felt like I couldn't control. Something I knew could spill over at any moment, a tide of rage sweeping through the house.

'Do you people even hear yourself?' Elle's voice cut through the chatter. Gwen must have coaxed her back into the dining room, but she wasn't having it.

'Oh, darling, don't start.'

'Sit back down,' Simon's voice.

'No!' Steps flying up to the second storey. A slammed door.

There was a moment or two of pregnant silence.

'Hormones,' Simon said, the joke dying in the air like a shot bird.

I cleaned my large chef's knife, laid it down and stared at it. Admiring for a moment the clean, sharp edge.

TK

I WAKE AT 3 am and I know I won't be sleeping again. It's the afternoon in New Zealand and there's no point forcing my body clock onto GMT for the few days I'm in the UK.

I go back to Google, punch in his name. I open the article I'd read all those years ago.

> TOWNHOUSE IN EDINBURGH BAGS PRESTIGIOUS DESIGN AWARD
> The annual British Home Interior Design Awards backed by *The Sunday Times* has chosen the overhaul of a full townhouse in New Town as the winner of the grand prize. Owner and architect Harvey Bond said he was delighted to be on the shortlist but never dreamed of winning. He spent the last year working on the project with his wife Lucy.

I continue reading the article, looking at the photos of the renovated home, zooming in to a small, framed photo of a smiling couple on a mantelpiece – a detail no one else probably noticed.

> The pair had long admired the property before they bought it. It sits in an unusually wide cobbled street – famous for being one of only two roads in New Town where a horse and carriage could complete a U-turn.

I stop reading and toss and turn until light presses the curtains from outside. I am up, showered and dressed by 7 am – a coat and jeans, there's no hint of clouds but it's still a crisp morning. I head straight to the New Town neighbourhood by foot, taking in the city around me. Using Google Maps, I had quickly worked out which street it was, but finding the actual house from satellite images proved more challenging.

Arriving, I look down the wide cobbled street. There is nowhere discreet to stand, no bus stop or cafe or restaurant; nothing but the bland residential facades of three dozen old brick townhouses, crowded together like teeth. I could doorknock each one, if it came to that, but how far could I get before raising suspicion?

I walk along the footpath slowly, eyeing each house as I go, with the vague hope I might spot something familiar. What about their mail? Maybe I could come back at night and check the letterboxes, try to find a letter with the surname 'Bond' on the envelope.

I get to the end and turn around to double back, my hands in my pockets. I'm almost back where I started when I hear a dog barking. Glancing over my shoulder, impossibly, he is there. Harvey Bond. He's in exercise gear, leading a dog down the front steps of one of the townhouses.

I make a note of the house he left. I stop to tie my shoelace and watch him pass, then I go back. I knock on the door.

A long time passes. She's not here. What if this is all wrong? What if I am wrong?

The door swings inward.

'Yes?'

It's an older woman, with an accent I can't quite place.

'Hi,' I say. 'I might have the wrong house.'

'Who are you looking for?'

'Is this Harvey Bond's house?'

'You're looking for Harvey? He's just left.'

'No,' I say. 'I'm not here to see Harvey.'

BILL

KEEP YOUR HEAD *down. Breathe.*

They continued talking, the subject changed for now to hunting, I think. I heard someone descending the stairs. I took my inhaler out, sucked it in.

Gwen's voice reached me in the kitchen. 'Well, Miss Primrose will not be joining us again this evening, unfortunately. Chet, you may be excused too, you can go and watch some telly, if you like.'

I heard Chet's chair scrape back, and the adults bid him goodnight.

Things quietened down after that. I plated up the main, and the waitress served it. The portion I'd sampled for myself had been perfect, the fresh fish melting in my mouth. I was relieved to only hear a satisfied silence and scraping of cutlery as the meal was enjoyed. One course to go and then this night would be over.

Soon enough, the men were outside with their cigars, moving on to whisky. The women remained inside, drinking martinis. I watched the men out near the garden as I prepared dessert, layering the pavlova with whipped cream and fresh fruit. I studied the way they leaned in when they spoke, looked over their shoulders to make sure no one was listening, then they'd all bend back like the petals of a flower opening, gripping shoulders and yellow teeth aimed skyward. I wondered if it was the good whisky they were drinking. I'd forgotten how it tasted already.

The women were chatting about people I'd never heard of, friends from back home, or politicians and socialites. When the men came back in, I was plating the desserts. Again I listened to the chat, close to the door.

'So,' Richard said, 'did you have any more trouble over here?'

'Trouble?' Simon said.

'Well.' He cleared his throat. 'The Southgate situation.'

Southgate, I thought. That was the train crash.

'Oh,' Simon said. 'That nonsense is well and truly behind us now.'

Gwen cleared her throat.

'You don't think it is, Gwen?'

'Well, I think Simon gets half as much stick about it here.'

'I don't get any stick at all, *darling.*' There was a note of warning in his voice.

'No,' she said. 'I guess you don't. You're right.'

'Contrary to the evidence, Gwen thinks we are somehow at risk. Like that lunatic with the knife might turn up again and skewer us like pigs.' He laughed.

My hand was still softly trembling as I drew a wedge of the pavlova and laid it over passionfruit coulis on a large, flat plate.

'There was one minor threat,' Simon said offhandedly, 'but it was not related to Southgate at all.'

'Oh, gosh, what threat?'

'It's not what you think. People lash out sometimes when they're let go.'

'Lash out. What do you mean?'

'Nothing really. Just the usual stuff, you know: *One day you will get what's coming. I'll get you while you sleep.*'

'Simon.' Gwen's voice was tight. 'When did this happen?'

'Oh, after the gardener was let go.'

Mooks. My uncle *threatened* them?

'And you didn't think to tell me?' Gwen said.

'Oh, lighten up. It's not a real threat.'

'You two always attract the mad ones, don't you,' a man added, trying to ease the tension.

'*One* mad one. *Two* if you include the woman in London. But he really was hopeless, the old gardener, *and* he broke our shears so I deducted his last pay. He wasn't happy but fair is fair. I told the police. I assume they warned him off.'

I thought about the fish again. Mooks had caught and supplied them. For a moment, I wondered if he might have done something. It didn't sound like him; he was so placid. But then again, I know all people have something inside, a hint of animal they hide away.

'The police know, that's the important thing. He turns up here, you call them and they take him away.' A woman's voice.

'We've had a bad run of it with help. Or the gardeners at least. Rogue breed, aren't they? The first one threatens me after we let him go. The second one disappears with a family heirloom.'

'Goodness,' a woman exclaimed.

'This second one, Tate Mercer-Kemp, well, I never would have given him the job, but his father was apparently an old boy at Oxford with me. Thought I'd look him up to tell him what his son got up to, but to be frank I can't even remember the chap.' They all laughed at this. 'I'll be rolling up the sleeves myself next.'

'Simon Primrose in the garden,' a man's voice bellowed. 'I'll believe it when I see it.'

'I'm not joking. Lucky we've got Fleur and Bill, although who knows what they're getting up to. Probably plotting something.'

When Fleur came back into the kitchen, she looked worse for wear – the night had tired her out too, I supposed. She looked so tiny in that moment.

'Thanks,' I said. I reached out, took her hand in mine and squeezed.

'What for?'

'The spill, for distracting them. You didn't have to.'

'A slip of the hand,' she said. 'Don't flatter yourself.'

She snatched her hand back. I followed her gaze to my chef's knife behind me, lying on its side near the sink.

'Be careful. It looks very sharp,' Fleur said, with a joyless grin – all canines and wide eyes. She began to move her head slowly side to side. 'You don't want anybody to get hurt, no?'

'No, of course not.'

'They were humiliating you. You see that, right? They did that to make you feel small, worthless. It was a game.'

'They're just oblivious,' I said. 'Harmless, really.'

She laughed. 'If you say so.' She picked up the knife and held it before her eyes. 'As sharp as a guillotine.' She put it back on the bench. 'Chop chop.' Then she left the kitchen.

I continued listening in to the conversation in the dining room.

'What say we have another whisky, Simon?'

'Your pick.'

'What's that in the decanter?'

'Macallan,' Simon answered.

'Which Macallan?'

'Sherry cask, fifty-year-old, a parting gift from my old friends in London,' Simon's voice was slightly tight. 'But we normally save that for the help.' Simon laughed. 'Gwen gave Bill, in the kitchen, a dram. Ten thousand quid at auction and she's dishing it out like Johnnie Walker Red to the bloody cook.'

The room erupts.

'You're a card, Gwen!'

'Go on then,' one of the men said. 'Pour us a nightcap, good lad.'

'Your offspring in bed, I take it?' one of the women asked.

'Chet's sleeping,' Gwen said. 'He's not been one hundred per cent of late.' Chet had thrown up in the night once earlier this week, then again last night. 'Elle's in her room. She's out of sorts too. I think that's why her behaviour this evening was so . . . so out of character. She's been having a hard time at school.'

'Teenagers.'

'No, not teenagers, *Simon.*'

'No?' a woman's voice.

'No,' Gwen said.

Simon spoke next. 'Her physical education teacher was leaving her the most explicit, crude notes. We called the school and had him fired.'

'You're joking? What is going on in this country? Who is in charge?'

'Sounds obscene. Is it worth suing the school? They're supposed to care for your children.'

'The principal was very apologetic. He came to the house, grovel-ling. They acted on it very quickly,' Simon said. 'But honestly, I think if things don't get better, we may have to return home or send her back to boarding school. Chet's the only one really settled, he's loving it here now. But Elle would do anything to go home.'

'Did they arrest him, the teacher?'

'No,' Simon said. 'We pushed for it but apparently they didn't have enough proof. They just moved him on, offered their apologies.'

'Elle hasn't quite been the same,' Gwen said. 'That's probably what was behind her little outburst earlier. She's become very sensitive.'

'She's always been such a sweet girl,' said one of the women. 'How did you find out about the notes? Did she tell you?'

'The cleaner,' said Simon. 'Stumbled upon them in her room.'

'That old chestnut,' said one of the men. 'Got the cleaner doing your snooping.'

I thought about Elle's letter, the fact the cleaner had been through the cottage. I thought about Simon's chat earlier. *We have something to talk about.*

'You'd be surprised what the cleaner turns up, actually.'

BILL

I DIDN'T REALISE Elle had entered the kitchen until she spoke.

'Sorry they put you through that,' she said, slurring a little and almost loud enough that she might be heard in the next room. I turned to face her, keeping my hands in the soapy water.

She stepped in beside me and took up a tea towel to help. The lens of privilege hadn't obscured the real world for her as much as for the others.

'It's fine,' I said. 'I'll finish these.'

'No. You do too much for everyone already. I bet they won't even thank you.'

'It's my job.' *And the pay is definitely enough.*

She put her hand on my forearm. 'Why have you got one glove on?'

'Just a cut,' I said, not mentioning the burn. I was off my game.

'Is it okay?'

'It's fine. It's my job.'

She took her hand away. 'You're not even four years older than me, Bill. You don't need to take everything so seriously. If you bottle it all up, you'll snap.' She didn't laugh but her liquid smile told me she was joking. 'Have a mental breakdown like me.'

'You're not having a mental breakdown. You're just a teenager.'

She touched my cheek now. Her hand was so soft I thought my skin might graze it. I reached up, took her hand away. She looked like she was about to cry. Something seemed to break away from her, detach completely.

'If only you knew. Something happened, Bill. I've not told anyone. Something bad. I just—'

The door opened and Simon was there. He caught sight of us close like that.

'I thought you were asleep,' he said, eyes a little bloodshot and a current of anger running through his voice. 'Bedtime, now.'

'*Daddy.*'

'Don't *Daddy* me. It's midnight. You were supposed to be in bed hours ago.'

For the first time, I was seeing Simon properly drunk. He swayed and his gestures were bigger, louder.

Elle gave me a look that didn't do me any favours – her father's eyes fell on me, sharp as the point of the boning knife I was cleaning in the sink. She walked past as though she'd lost sensation in her legs, dragging them out of the kitchen.

Simon stepped closer. 'Bill, I like you. You're good at your job.' His sharp Adam's apple rose and fell as swallowed. It was clear he was trying to act more sober than he was. Perhaps this was the little chat he was talking about earlier. He pointed at the door and said, 'That's my daughter. Do you understand me?'

I nodded.

'I don't want you to . . .' he grimaced, made a gesture like a man bouncing hot coals in his hands, 'be hanging around the house, chatting with her. You just be friendly, do your job and mind your own business. You got it?'

'Yeah. Sorry, did I do someth—'

He raised his hand. Let his breath out slowly. 'Let's not beat around the bush,' he said, his voice hard as glass. 'You don't lay a finger on her, you understand? I don't think I could make it any clearer than that. You touch her, act untoward, take advantage, and you'll regret ever stepping foot in this house.'

'I would never—'

'No, you wouldn't,' he said. 'You would never. You're smarter than that. *A lot* smarter than that. You're from a different world to her, you're not the same. The chap who was leaving her notes, he'll never work as a teacher again, he'll never set foot in this town again. If I could get my hands on him myself, I don't know what I would do, but it wouldn't be pretty. Same goes for you, Bill.'

After he left, I just felt numb. For the first time, I started to wonder if the money was worth it. I finished the dishes and tied off the rubbish bags. I wiped down the benches. Outside, the sky was clear and bursting with stars. I took the rubbish around the side to where the plastic bins were. I thought everyone had gone but then I saw a car parked in the driveway. Someone was sitting in the driver's seat, looking up at the house. *Was it Teimana?*

As I got closer, the engine started. I can't be sure, maybe I'd imagined it, because the last I'd heard he had left the country. Still, I thought for a second, before the car sped away, that Tate was the man behind the wheel. I watched the red tail-lights fade in the distance, before the car rounded the bend.

BILL

THE FOLLOWING WEEK, after days of hiding out upstairs – 'sulking', Fleur called it – Elle actually left her room and went to her post-exams party. Gwen and Simon practically fell over themselves, they were so happy to see a glimpse of the old Elle. I have to admit, I was happy to see her like that too.

She came home safe and sound at around midnight. I'd been sitting outside the cottage, looking up at the stars in my Swanndri coat and trackpants. After four beers, I was tired but couldn't sleep; I hadn't slept well since that dinner party a few nights earlier. A light came on inside the house and I saw Elle through the kitchen window. She went to the sink and poured a glass of water, swaying slightly as she filled it and then drained it all in one go. Then she got another glass. That's when I saw Gwen standing behind her in her dressing gown, her arms crossed. Gwen had complained about headaches that week, so she'd gone to bed early, but she was up again. Fleur, who had picked Elle up, came back out to the cottage.

'Up late,' she remarked.

'Can't sleep,' I said.

She went inside the cottage.

The light went out in the kitchen and came on upstairs in Elle's room.

I sat for a while longer, finishing my beer and scanning the stars in the dark sky, watching the pale ghosts of my breath rise.

I sent Maia a message. It was probably the hundredth unanswered message I'd sent her.

That's when the door to the house opened. I leapt. Someone was coming out. I narrowed my eyes, trying to make the figure out in the dark.

They weren't moving quickly, more stumbling. Elle. I didn't speak. I just watched her. What was she doing? Going for a swim? It was freezing. She walked straight past the pool, toward the cottage. She didn't notice me until I spoke.

'Elle?'

She jumped, hand pressed to her sternum. 'Oh, it's you,' she stage whispered. 'My God, you gave me the fright of my life.'

'Shh, you'll wake everyone. What are you doing out here?'

'I just wanted to . . .' she looked around, as if uncertain. 'Oh God, I don't know. Just chat.'

'It's too cold out here. You should go to bed.'

She was swaying. The alcohol was the only thing keeping her warm. 'No, no. Umm. I just . . .' She pressed her hand to her head as if in pain. 'You've never told me if you see me . . . like that.' She took her hand away.

It was easy to think that Elle had it all. I wondered when I met her what it would be like to be her: two loving and wealthy parents, a sharp mind and the sort of looks that would always open doors. Her troubles seemed so slight, her future so unblemished and wide open like the dark vault of stars above us. But, as with everyone, she had her insecurities. Life wasn't so easy for anyone.

'I know you like me,' she said. 'I can tell you feel something. And I go to university next year. I won't be living here.'

'Yes, I like you. But not in *that* way,' I said, choosing my words carefully. I glanced up at the dark house.

'But I think you do,' she said. 'I've seen you look at me.'

'Look, Elle, it's not like that. Obviously I think you're, you know, attractive. But we're from different worlds. It just doesn't work.' *Different worlds* – Simon's words tasted like dirt in my mouth.

She took my hands. I gently pulled them away. 'Come sit with me at least. We can just talk.' Turning, she walked toward the pool area and opened the gate.

Against my better judgement, I followed her to the deckchairs, sat down on the one facing her. All the sharp, white-hot feelings I had about Simon, Gwen and their guests were softening now. I felt calm.

'Mum and Dad's room is on the other side, and they're sleeping. They won't know we're out here.'

'Listen, we can be friends but that's it. You're like a sister.'

Even in the dark, I could see the sadness in her eyes. 'No, we're not siblings. We're just two people. Stop thinking about my parents, your work. Think about yourself and think about me.'

'I really can't. This isn't how the world works. I got your note and I was just afraid, that's all. I don't know what to say.' I was angry at the family still and I did want her, but not for the right reasons.

'Please,' she said. 'It's Daddy. He's doing this. He's always doing this.'

'You're drunk.'

'It doesn't matter.'

'I'm too old for you.'

'He was twenty-four and Mummy was nineteen when they got together. That's a bigger gap than between us.'

'This is different.'

'It's not.' She stood up from her deckchair.

'No,' I said. She straddled my lap and tried to kiss me.

I placed my hands on her shoulders, pushed her back.

'What are you so afraid of, Bill? I'm almost eighteen. I will be soon.'

Her lips met mine, our teeth gently clashing.

I kissed her back.

She pressed her face against mine, harder now. Her hands firm on my cheeks. We stopped kissing for a moment, our faces close, the moment stretching between us. There was only stillness.

'I want you,' she said, her lips so close to mine.

'No,' I said. 'Stop, Elle.'

I tried to pull away but she pushed me back into the chair, pressed her body into mine. I let her. Maybe she did want me, but I knew she'd been having a hard time, so maybe she just wanted someone, anyone, to hold her. I put my arms around her.

A door opened. I froze.

'Get your hands off her, you animal!' The voice boomed across the yard. A torch was on me, bright like a hunting spotlight.

'What? What's happening?' I said, blinded by the glare in the dark. 'Wait. It's not what you think.'

Elle stood up, straightened her clothing. 'No, Daddy,' she said. But he was already striding toward us.

I looked in his hand and saw the large, steel fire poker. Before I could react, he was upon us, waving the weapon in front of him, thrusting it. I held up my hands but he kept coming.

'Stop!' I said, scrambling to my feet. I turned and leapt the pool fence, falling hard over the other side. Then I was on my feet again, my heart pounding, my head swimming. The lights came on inside. I turned toward them, squinting against the glare. Fleur's light came on in the cottage.

'What were you doing to my daughter?' Simon seethed, his rage stretching his voice thin.

'It's not what you think!'

'I've been watching from her room!' he said, pointing with the poker. He climbed the fence himself now.

'Daddy, stop!' Elle screamed, her voice breaking at the point of hysteria. 'Leave him alone.'

My eyes adjusted. I could see Gwen in the brightly lit kitchen, the phone pinned to her ear.

Simon was mad, too far gone. I'd seen it in bar fights and on the rugby field, when someone completely loses control. I knew he would kill me if he got close. My throat felt tight, my asthma slowing me, but I sprinted past the cottage until I was forced to my knees, sucking in mouthfuls of cold, stinging air. I took my inhaler, pressed it to my mouth and squeezed, the cool air instantly relieving the tightness in my throat.

Fleur was there suddenly. 'Go,' she said. 'Run.'

'Fleur!' Simon's voice boomed. 'Where is he?'

I started again, racing toward the gate. Sirens.

The police. Gwen must have called them. They would stop him. I ran down the driveway, the wail of the police car growing louder. I took another hit of my inhaler then saw the lights. The gates began to open in front of me. I raised my hands.

In what felt like seconds, the police had pinned me to the ground, put handcuffs on me and dragged me to a standing position. They loaded me into the car and closed the door, left me in there with my shock. I looked for my inhaler, but I must have dropped it somewhere in the process.

In front of the house, Gwen was watching in her nightgown, Fleur close by. A second car turned up. More cops got out, spoke to the family.

It would all be straightened out, I told myself. But I already knew there'd be no going back. The way Simon gripped the poker, it was clear to me he was capable of anything. He'd warned me, stay away. I was drinking, stressed, and made a mistake. I also realised that it wasn't just me he was capable of hurting.

Then they took me away.

BILL

I WAS RELEASED from the police station the next morning, although I was advised that I might still be charged. I wasn't to leave town, not until they said I could.

Had Elle set the police straight? I assumed so. Simon couldn't have stopped her from talking to the officers and telling them what really happened. I needed a day or two to clear my head and for the police to clear me completely. Then I'd go back to Rotorua.

The police had collected my phone and wallet, but all my clothes and other belongings were at the cottage. I called into the grocer, the one who'd leased a flat behind her shop to Tate when he was here. I'd been a pretty good customer of hers, so she knew me and was happy for me to take the flat straight away. I told her some story about the cottage being pest-sprayed. One-fifty a week if I paid upfront, she said.

I doubled back and withdrew a wad of cash from the ATM, returned to the grocer, paid for some basic food items, paid a week's rent and collected the key.

Once I let myself in and opened a window to air the place out a little, I messaged Fleur, and asked her to drop around with the rest of my things. Then I lay on the lumpy sofa, feeling like I might cry.

When Fleur turned up a few hours later, she just held out my bag. 'Here.'

'What's going on?'

'I don't know.' Her voice was flat.

'Well, what are they saying I did?'

'Simon said you grabbed Elle, forced yourself on her. You were drinking.'

'The police, they said there's no charges. I didn't do anything.'

She shrugged. 'Elle won't leave her room. I don't know what happened but the house is not a happy place to be.' She exhaled. 'I better go.'

'Elle will tell you. It's him, he lost it. She came onto me. You know she had a crush.'

But she just turned away to leave.

I wondered if Simon could coerce Elle into a false statement to the police. My mood swung from rage to disappointment, from melancholy to a simmering resentment. How could Fleur turn her back on me? How could Elle not set the record straight? Would people in this town think I had forced myself on a teenage girl?

When I checked my bags, everything was there. Everything except my knives.

I went to the liquor shop and bought a bottle of Jim Beam and a bottle of Coke and went back to the flat. I needed to slow down my brain, numb the anger. I drank for half the afternoon, and then, as the evening came around, stumbled to a bar.

I sent Fleur another message. *Meet me for a drink, I have a plan.*

I ordered a beer and sat alone; the bartender served me in silence. To my surprise, Fleur messaged back.

Okay. Want me to bring Elle too? Maybe the rest of the family will come. Good idea.

She always was sarcastic.

I'm so angry. I don't know what I'm going to do. I have to come to the house.

No, you don't, stay away. You'll be arrested. Just move on.

Let's see.

I could have just continued getting drunk alone but I was in a tailspin. The bar filled up; I got chatting to a couple of girls my age, backpackers passing through. I kept bending the conversation back to the family and what had happened, and the women soon got bored of it and me. My story and my anger. This all would come up later in the trial, when the prosecution painted me as obsessed, unstable, *volcanic*. I slowed down my drinking and went to another bar: The Pope.

I walked in under the Lion Red signs. I ordered a beer and found an empty seat at a booth in the corner. I couldn't be alone but I couldn't stay there all night – I felt restless, my mind still processing everything that had happened. I needed to talk to someone who would understand. I called Maia. This time, to my surprise, she answered. I stumbled out of the bar and talked to her on the walk back to the flat.

According to my mobile-phone record, we spoke for four-and-a-half minutes, but it felt like much longer. I know I told her I loved her, that I was sorry for everything. I told her I'd been chased from the house.

After the call, I sat and drank the rest of the Jim Beam in the flat. Despite how much I drank, I still remember everything that happened from there so clearly. Every second of it is etched into my brain.

BILL

THERE IS AN ATM with a security camera between the flat and the corner of the main street. The camera captured me stumbling past it, a little after midnight. Winter was beginning, when the earth clenches its fist and grass hardens in the frost. I wore my black wool gloves, not to hide my prints but because I was cold. I wore a black hoodie and jeans. I turned and passed the pub. I walked all the way along that quiet country road to the Primrose house. The only sound I could hear was the thud of my feet on the road, and the fog limited my visibility to no more than fifty metres ahead. It took me about twenty minutes to get to the house.

Creeping in through the gate and up along the edge of the property, I was careful not to make a sound. I knew the back door was often left unlocked, and if it was locked the spare key would be under a nearby pot plant. It turned out I didn't need a key – the door was wide open. I should have known then that something was wrong, but in my drunken, stoned state, it barely even registered.

Inside, I instantly felt it. Everything was too still, too quiet. I could hear the heater humming and yet the place felt cold. The home phone trilled like an alarm, startling me. Who was calling at this time? It kept ringing and ringing.

I stepped closer to the back door, ready to flee. A dog was barking somewhere on one of the neighbouring properties. Why wasn't anyone answering it? The phone in the hallway near Elle's bedroom or the one in Gwen and Simon's room should have woken them all.

Another ringing – not the landline this time, but a mobile in one of the bedrooms, a tiny polyphonic sound. Still no one stirred. That was the moment I knew something was really wrong, that something evil lurked in the shadows of the house. It compelled me on, deeper, up the stairs, silently, one foot after the other.

The nightmare began when I opened Elle's door. Blankets strewn across the floor. Blood . . . a patch of black, slick as oil, and Elle, lying in it. I turned on the light. Blood oozed from a wound. Crimson-sprayed floral wallpaper. She was completely still. There was too much blood. I knew what it meant. I shook her and pulled her too me. I howled. 'Elle! No, no, no.' An involuntary drumbeat of denial. 'No, this isn't happening.'

I ran for help.

What I found only worsened the nightmare. Gwen, on her side, one hand hanging out from under the covers, her head tilted back and throat open. More blood, too much blood it seemed for two human bodies. Staked in Simon's chest was my chef's knife. I reached for it, tried to pull it free. But it was too slippery to grip.

I fought to control my breathing. I didn't have my inhaler and I could feel the panic growing. I don't know why but I left. My footprints leaving a bloody trail down the stairs to the back door. I was drunk, I wasn't supposed to be there, I was sleepless and confused – I knew how it would look. I panicked.

I ran.

The police arrived before the ambulance and fire engine. The first cop car passed by me where I crouched in a ditch at the road's edge, with its sirens blaring and lights strobing. Then an ambulance flew by and eventually more police cars. I stayed low, watched them pass. None of them stopped for me. I backtracked to the main street, avoiding main roads. I was wired but cognisant enough to stay down, avoid being seen – or so I thought. I later discovered one of the neighbours had seen me bolting from the property.

Of course I was going to have to give an interview, and I knew how things looked, but I really believed that they would catch the *real* killer, that they would realise it wasn't me. It was a stupid belief. I looked guilty and the police would be baying for my blood.

When I got back to the flat, I stripped and took a shower. I scrubbed under my fingernails until they were raw, until Elle's blood was scorched from my skin. I dried myself off roughly, and got dressed in clean clothes. I went out the back and found an old steel bin. I burnt the clothes I'd been wearing.

I lay on top of the blankets, fully dressed, my eyes wide. I'd never felt so lonely, so depressed, such despair, not since my mother died. I called Maia again but this time she didn't answer. I didn't know how to process it all. I just lay there. I couldn't cry. I couldn't move or do anything. I was just still.

Logic departed long before I got up and went out to the pie shop. Time had changed, it wasn't a sequence: before, after. Truck, trailer. Time was jumbled, folding over on itself like an omelette. I was there at the house, then I wasn't. I was walking out of my flat, then I was standing up to answer the knock at door.

I was holding Elle's body, then I was being handled by the police, turned around, my wrists bound in handcuffs. Then I was scrubbing my nails, then I was eating the mince and cheese pie, staring out at the morning fog.

I was running through the streets, trying to get home, terror pulsing in my veins, thinking about Maia, and how simple my life could have been. I was walking back in the morning light, then I was in an interview room at the police station. Completely dazed and clueless.

When asked why I did it, I answered, 'I hated him,' but the rest of the sentence didn't come. I was taken by grief. I wanted to say, 'I hated him but I wouldn't do that, not to anyone, but especially not Elle.'

When they said Chet was dead too, I felt sick. I hadn't seen him. They found traces of me all through the rooms, all but Chet's – I hadn't been in there but still they were convinced I killed him too.

They formed a narrative. Shoe prints. Hair. A witness from a neighbouring house. Someone had heard the scream and had been calling to check on them, to make sure they were okay. The scream, the police told me, was when I pushed the knife into Elle's stomach.

'If you're telling the truth, why did you run?' the detective asked.

'I don't know.'

'Why didn't you stay and help? Why didn't you perform CPR or try to stem the bleeding? Why didn't you try to save her?'

'I knew she was gone.'

'You thought she was gone,' he said, his palm striking the steel table between us. 'You thought she was gone but she wasn't. When she wakes up, she's going to tell the world exactly what you did.'

And that was how I found out that Elle had survived.

PART THREE

Elizabeth Primrose: It was definitely Bill?

Detective Marsden: Bill Kareama is the alleged murderer, yes.
    We have arrested him and charged him but we need you to
    try to remember what you saw that night.

Elizabeth Primrose: I—He was in my room. He . . . he . . .
    I don't know. I just remember him being there.

Detective Marsden: Take your time, Elizabeth. I know it's
    hard. Just tell us what Bill was holding when you saw him
    in your room.

Elizabeth Primrose: I don't know, I don't remember.

Detective Marsden: You don't know if he had anything in his hand?

Elizabeth Primrose: If he did this to me, and . . . if he hurt
    my family. Oh God. I can't.

Detective Marsden: We can come back. We can take a break.

Elizabeth Primrose: Maybe he had a knife. I don't know. I just don't know.

Detective Marsden: It might be easier, Elizabeth, if we write it all down and you can read it and tell us if it is what you remember. Would you like that?

Elizabeth Primrose: I think I need a break.

Detective Marsden: Okay, let's have a break. We've almost got enough. I just need you to try really hard to remember what Bill was holding when he came into your room, okay? Can you think about it while we take a break? Then we will type it up and get your signature, and that's all we need. What he did to you, and to your family, was unimaginably cruel, but he's going to pay for it, I promise.

TK

'I'M HERE TO see Lucy,' I say.

'Lucy. Is she expecting you?'

'No,' I say. 'I don't think so.'

'Who is it?' a voice calls from inside the house.

My heart is pounding. I've planned this far, but now I'm here, and I can barely believe it. I see her coming toward the front door. *It's her.*

'Someone is here to see you,' the older woman says, turning back.

'Yes?' she says. 'What is it?'

'Hello,' I say. My heart is going even faster now. Lucy Bond, that's her new name. 'My name is Te Kuru Phillips, TK for short.'

Her confusion is growing. It's my accent. A stranger with a New Zealand accent. I see her eyes go past me, then return to my face.

'Yes? What do you want?'

I clear my throat. I eye the woman who answered the door, who is still standing there, behind her.

'Listen, Lucy, I want to talk to you about . . . Bill.'

Her expression changes. Something approaching horror. She swallows, it then turns back to the woman, face composed again.

'Rosemary, could you check the twins please?'

'Yes, love,' she says and retreats into the house.

She turns back to me. 'How did you find me?' It's a low hiss, the seams of the words fraying. 'You need to go before I call the police.'

'Listen, Elle, ah Elizabeth.'

'Don't call me that,' she spits.

I've found her. She's changed a lot – she has some hard-living lines around her mouth and around her eyes – but it is undeniable. I'm staring at the face of the girl who survived.

'I'm his psychologist, okay? Bill's psychologist and I don't want anything from you. This isn't for anyone else.' The words fly out of my mouth. 'I've come halfway around the world for this and I just want to talk.'

A line forms down the centre of her forehead. 'About what?' She huffs out a breath. 'To bring up the past? You people just don't give up, do you? It's not enough I lose my family. It's not enough he stabbed me. Now I have to hide away from people like *you*.'

I meet her gaze, try to keep my expression neutral. 'I understand. I don't want to retraumatise you. In fact, I've known you were in Edinburgh for a couple of years and I didn't want to come. I wouldn't have come.'

'Why have you then? Why not leave it alone?' She is looking around the street, to see if anyone is watching on. 'Why?'

'For years, I was certain Bill was innocent. I know the case inside and out. I spent countless hours with him. Whatever happened, no one can deny that Bill did not get a fair trial. There were elements of the case that were never properly explained or investigated—'

She closes her eyes tight as if in pain and it stops me in my tracks.

I force myself on. 'I know it doesn't compare to what you went through but I lost years of my life – I lost my marriage and myself – to this case. For me, for my own sanity,' I say. 'I just want to talk for five minutes, that's all.'

She rubs her chest, soothing her heart. 'You're trying to get him out?'

'I was,' I say. 'But it all depends on what you tell me. I just need to know some things. That's all.'

'My husband will call the police if he finds out you're here. *I* should call the police. How do I know you're not a journalist? How did you find me to begin with?' She's flustered, angry.

'You could Google me for a start to see I really was his psychologist in prison.'

'You want him released after everything he did?'

'He could walk out of that prison tomorrow if he confessed to the crimes and acknowledged his guilt.'

She's defiant, her jaw rises. 'Why doesn't he then?'

I shrug. I don't know the answer but the logical one is: *He didn't do it.* If I was cynical, I would say because if he can get off his charges, the payout he would get would be huge. Similar cases have yielded millions. 'That's the question. All I know is he didn't get a fair defence or a fair trial.'

'No . . .' she says, her breath shaky. 'No, he was there . . . the evidence . . . the police. I saw him standing over me. I remember.'

Her reaction is typical, clinically. If you believe something for seventeen years, it's not going to undo itself in a matter of minutes. I don't know what I was expecting. Some clarity on the statement she gave police, perhaps. Her lawyer and a psychologist argued that she should not be made to testify, even in a pretrial hearing. Given the nature of the crime and the risk of retraumatising the witness, the judge granted the request. It became a legal precedent when it comes to minors.

'I'm not trying to get him out, not anymore. I just want the truth.'

Something catches in her eyes. 'I don't want to talk about the case. I didn't then and I don't now. I gave my statement and it almost broke me.'

'You've got kids now?'

She doesn't respond.

'I understand that this is the last thing you want back in your life right now. Really, I do. I've built my whole career around understanding trauma.'

She could have slammed the door in my face by now. She could have called the cops. But she's still here, listening. So I keep talking.

'But something tells me that you don't really have the closure you need. That there's a part of you that still has questions too. I know it's scary, but could you try trusting me, just for ten minutes?'

A silence hangs in the air.

'You get ten minutes. There's a garden up the road. I'll get my coat.'

When she emerges again, wearing her coat and holding her head high, I think of her mother, how much she looks like the old photos of Gwen.

'Are you going to tell me how you found out where I was?' she says as she leads me along the street.

'I tried to contact your friends from back then and known family. Since you disappeared so soon after the trial, it was the only thing I had to go on. Bill mentioned a name: Harvey Bond. Said he was someone you'd dated before you left London. So I set up a Google alert with his name. I set up a bunch of alerts, to be honest. I was a bit, ah, obsessive about it. And then, a couple of years ago, Harvey Bond won a design award and there were a few articles published about it.'

'Oh,' she says, so quietly I almost don't hear it.

'I saw a photo in the background of one the shots of the interior. I thought it looked like you. I looked up marriage notices and saw he married Lucy Smith, which to me sounded a lot like a made-up name.'

She just nods. 'It was only a matter of time, I suppose. I'm just glad you didn't find it on one of those vile websites where armchair detectives re-litigate solved crimes from their homes.'

'You read about the case still?'

'No,' she says. 'Well, sometimes. I'll have too many glasses of wine and google my old name just to see what's out there.' She shakes her head. 'I'll have to ask Harvey to try to get the articles taken down. I love Edinburgh but we could always move again.'

'Well, my lips are sealed,' I say. 'But I'm deeply sorry that you have to live this way.'

'We have a good life. I never forget. I think about Mummy, Chet and Daddy every day, but sometimes, for brief moments, the pain is absent. I don't think about what he did to us.' She exhales. 'Obviously, Harvey knows, our close friends know. I can keep my scars hidden, assuming I never wear a two-piece bathing suit. But we are very private people with a small, close circle.' She leads me along the street to a fenced-in park. She uses a key to open it, before leading me to a bench where we sit a few feet apart.

She folds one knee over the other, and sits tall with a remarkably straight back. She's very like the photos I've seen of her as a girl, except more drawn; her face has lost that youthful roundness, her nose seems slightly sharper. She has her ankles locked together and rubs her bottom lip with her fingernails as she talks.

'I don't know exactly what you want to know, but I'm not going to talk about my family or . . .' she pauses, and the cords stand out in her neck as if it causes her pain to even think about it, 'the specific details of their deaths.'

'No, of course. I don't want to cause you to relive it.'

'I've spent almost two decades working through it with therapists, my husband. I'm still not quite at that place yet.'

'That's fair enough,' I say. 'The main thing I want to know is the nature of your relationship with Bill before, well, before what happened. I want to know what you remember.'

'Well, people seem to think he groomed me. But I was just shy of eighteen when we met. And he was young. I would say he was much more naïve than I was; he wasn't as turbulent and emotional, but he was naïve in other ways.'

'So there was nothing inappropriate?' I think about Bill's version of events, how he resisted her, how Simon warned him away from her. He told it in a way that made me think Elle was the one who pursued him.

'Nothing untoward. It's all hazy and I suppose my memories are skewed by the context that he then killed my whole family and tried to kill me too. But I liked him, and I liked the attention. I liked the fact he treated me and spoke to me like an adult and not a little kid. I missed Harvey so much, and all my friends back in London. I guess I developed a crush.'

'How confident are you in your memories?'

'Not very,' she says. 'I know what trauma does. I know what time does.'

'Trauma is an intensely distorting lens to view your life through. Especially when you believe this man did . . . what he was accused of. It can't be easy.'

'All of his behaviour was strange. That's how I see it now. I don't think he planned it. But then . . .' She throws up her hands. 'I just want him to be guilty. I don't want this . . . this doubt. He did it. I know he did it. He's a monster.'

I think again about something Bill raised a lot with me. 'You kept a journal, didn't you?'

'I did.'

'But you lost it.'

'Sometime in those last few weeks. It disappeared.'

'Any idea who might have taken it? Or could you have misplaced it?'

'Bill stole it,' she says. 'He wasn't supposed to go into my room but he was always in places he wasn't supposed to be. He'd come to the house at night sometimes. I think I'd written how much I missed Harvey and maybe it made him jealous. Who knows?'

She stares off into the distance, through the trees that edge the park.

'If Bill didn't take my journal, then maybe Daddy did. Daddy found a letter I wrote Bill and he was mad about it. But my journal, I wrote my secrets in there, things I observed.' She clears her throat, holds her head up to keep the tears in her eyes from falling. 'You can't just do this.' She shrugs one shoulder. 'You people really have no idea what it's like. If he was released, I'll still think it was him. I can't just stop believing that. What would it mean for me if I'm wrong? The real killer has just been walking around?'

'I am sorry, Elle, really I am. I know this hurts. But your statement, it was pivotal in the trial. So I have to ask: do you remember seeing him with the knife, standing over you?'

She shakes her head. 'I don't know. I can still see him with it when I close my eyes, but it feels like a dream. The police told me what happened. I just didn't want to imagine it, or think about it. I signed the statement.'

'You gave the statement.'

She subtly shakes her head. 'I signed it. They asked me questions and I just signed it. I can see him holding the knife.' She's frowning now, concentration straining her features. 'He was there. I remember him there. I saw him in my room. They said he stabbed me, and, well, he had to have had the knife. It was *his* knife.'

'I am so sorry. I know how important closure and resolution is.'

Finally, she looks at me. She gives her head the tiniest shake. 'The man who did this to me, and my parents, the man who stabbed my brother in his heart, he was convicted and put in prison. Don't take that from me.' I expect to see tears starting – they're there in her eyes but they don't fall.

She turns her eyes from me. The gate opens and someone else comes through with a toddler. She gives them a small nod as they pass. When she speaks again, the tears shudder in her voice.

'You know, when I had the twins, the first thing I thought, the first thing I felt, was this acute sense of loss. Every time I feel a big emotion, I think of my family. I think how much joy it would have brought my mother to meet her grandchildren. I think of everything my children miss out on, without their uncle and their grandparents. Do you know what that's like? Do you know how much *guilt* I have felt? My entire life I think about the fact that I'm alive, I'm living, I'm going on and they're dead.' She sniffs hard, raises her chin.

A sudden sinking feeling of loss washes over me. You see someone who has lost something they love and it makes you take stock, clutch at the things that you care about, things you might have otherwise forgotten. I want to have a coffee with my parents, tell them I love them. I want Amelia in my arms, her head nestled on my shoulder.

'If you could click your fingers and make me believe he's innocent, that would make it harder to keep doing this.' She moves her palm through the air. 'To go on living. If you could make me believe it wasn't Bill, that just means someone else's innocence was destroyed. That would mean the person responsible got away with it.' She clears her throat. 'I can't remember anything of that night, really. I woke a week later with a hideous wound below my ribs and to the news that my family was dead. The police told me Bill had been charged with murdering my family and attempting to murder me. I remembered him standing over me, and so that's what I told them. If he didn't do it, he still found me there. I was alive but he left me to die.' There's such anger, such pain in that final sentence that I feel a shiver run through me.

'That's more or less the version of events I know,' I say. 'He was in the house, he was there.'

She turns her wrist, looks at the tiny watch strapped to it. 'That's ten minutes. I better get back.'

'Can I ask you one final question?' I say.

She turns to me, her eyes still shining. 'Last one.'

'Is there anyone else, other than Bill, you thought of when they told you?'

'Told me what?' she says, then it dawns on her. 'About my family . . .' She smears her eyes with the back of her right hand. 'He's going to be worried, Harvey. When I go home with puffy eyes.'

'I'm sorry.'

'What will come of it? Nothing. There's no point me thinking about it.'

'I'm sorry, Elle.'

'Don't,' she says. 'Not Elle. Elizabeth Primrose died that night. She's never coming back. Don't say that name.'

I feel like I'm slowly tumbling into a crevice. This is exactly what I feared would happen; I'm just causing more hurt. I wish I could hug her, tell her I care about her, but who am I to her? Just someone picking at an old wound.

'Fleur.' She says it so quietly I lean a little closer as if I misheard. 'If you'd asked me when I woke up, I would have said Fleur. I don't know why. I know now that she was with a man, so it wasn't her. But she had a meanness about her and she was a liar. She was blackmailing my father.'

She shivers.

'Blackmailing?'

'I don't recall all the details. It tore me up a bit, I wrote about it in my journal too.'

'What about Tate?' I say.

She shrugs. 'He was a little uncouth. I didn't trust him. But he was out of the country.'

I've had a sense about Tate and Fleur, and in Bill's notes, he thought he saw Tate when he was supposed to be out of the country at the time of the murders. But then again, it wouldn't be the first time Bill misled me.

'That was your last question,' she says. 'I just want to go home.' She stands and starts toward the road. I follow her only so far as the gate. She turns back. 'I hope it was worth your while.'

I think about the journal. 'Me too.'

SLOANE

THE FLIGHT TO Wellington is up and down in a little over an hour, carrying me to the southern end of the North Island. I catch an Uber from the airport to the suburb of Lyall Bay.

Laurence, or Laurie, Berry has got the sort of house you would expect for a retired lawyer of his experience. It overlooks the surf on the crescent-moon beach, a two-storey modern luxury home – black steel window frames and a pale timber facade. A charcoal Mercedes convertible is tucked in the driveway, where I find a diminutive but barrel-chested man stroking a chamois over its bonnet.

'Sloane?' he says as I approach. He takes his sunglasses off.

This is a man who has, without a doubt, seen his fair share of long lunches. He smiles, showing me a set of teeth fresh off the shelf, luminous against his slightly unnatural tan.

'Sloane Abbott,' I reply, nodding. 'Thanks for seeing me.'

'Oh, no problem, it's a real pleasure,' he says. A labradoodle comes over, yapping. Laurie smears his palm down his thigh before offering it to me. He practically crushes the bones in my hand. 'Come on up.'

He takes me inside and up a set of stairs.

'I'll show you the view outside,' he says opening a bi-fold door. 'Ladies first,' he says. 'Maybe I'm not supposed to say that – who knows these days?'

'I don't mind.'

'And nor should you. I can barely keep up with all the rules now. It's a good thing I'm retired.'

I don't say I agree that it's a good thing he is retired.

'Called it quits a few years after the Kareama case,' he says, as he follows me out onto the deck. It's breathtaking. I suppose he quietly disappeared to this gorgeous house in what appears to be prime Wellington real estate. Now he leans against the banister.

'See the ferry coming in?' He points out to the rippled strait and I nod. 'That's how you get to the South Island. If it's a clear day, you can spot a few surfers out there, braving the cold. Not like your Aussie beaches. Wetsuits year round down here. Especially if we cop a southerly. We have a saying in this part of the country: *You can't beat Welly on a good day.* Problem is, we don't get too many of them.'

'You a surfer?' I ask. *Got the tan for it,* I think shadily.

'Couldn't think of anything worse, bobbing out there like an iceberg. No, I sail a bit, otherwise I prefer to stay on terra firma. Come on, let's get a cuppa inside.'

'Coffee, if you have any?'

'We've got plenty. Bought an espresso maker when I stopped going to the office.'

'Black, please.'

'No worries.' The house is open plan. Laurie keeps talking as he goes to the kitchen to make coffee. 'So you're doing a podcast on the case?'

'That's right.'

'Well, I'm a fan of yours. Listened to the one you did on the missing teacher. It got to where I would be hanging out for the next episode. Great stuff.' He's got something about him, Laurie. As much as I didn't want to like him, he sort of grows on you. He's familiar, chatty, but I remind myself why I'm here – he was responsible for defending Bill and he failed on that front.

'Thanks. I'm glad you enjoyed it.'

'No, thank you for flying down.'

I reach for my recorder. 'So, can you tell me a bit about the challenges of the case?'

'The challenges?'

'When you took it on, what was it like?'

He sniffs, I see him shake his head. 'What went wrong, you mean?' he says to himself. 'You've met Bill Kareama?'

'I have.'

His long, grey eyebrows fly up his forehead and stay there. 'And you understand client–lawyer privilege?'

'I do. I'm not asking you to breach it.'

'What went wrong?' he intones, drawing a breath. 'I don't want this part recorded. We can do that after.'

'Sure,' I say.

'Okay. Well, for starters, he's not an instantly likeable guy. Not bad-looking but softly spoken, a bit shy; he would break eye contact, fidget constantly. He came across as standoffish. Those were some challenges. I'd say we got unlucky with the jury. Nine women, almost all Pākehā – that didn't help.'

'Sure.'

'The cards were stacked against us.'

'What was he like back then to deal with?'

'He was fine, other than changing his story every ten minutes. I know we cop stick now from people who weren't there but we couldn't make head or tails of half the things he said. No real evidence to back up most of his claims. Timelines didn't match.'

He brings the coffees and a plate covered in a variety of biscuits over to where I have taken a seat at the dining table.

'Sweet tooth,' he says. 'Help yourself. Anyway, Bill tells us the girl was in love with him, but there's no real proof other than some drunken kiss, which ended in his arrest. He talks about a letter she sent that never turned up.'

I murmur encouragingly, though it's already clear this guy likes to talk. I blow on my coffee.

'Look, we can get into all the details, but the main reason our defence fell over and the appeal was refused was because the evidence overwhelmingly pointed to guilty. The girl identified him in the house, with the knife. They found boot prints between the rooms. He *acted* very guilty and some of his statements in those early police interviews flirted with confession. It was an open-and-shut case, and frankly, I don't think it will make for interesting listening. We tried, but Bill Kareama did it. He stabbed the Primrose family.' He pauses to bite into a biscuit.

I jump in before he starts up again. 'But there are things that don't make sense. Many people believe he's a good candidate for a retrial.'

'What people? Whoever they are, I can't see them getting too far with it, not after all this time. If I had a do-over, I think I would focus purely on the physical evidence the police relied on so much. It didn't work, not the way they said.'

'In what way?'

'Well, the timeline with the asthma for one. And his footprints between the rooms didn't quite fit their narrative. The order of the stabbings as they alleged were Chester, then Simon, then Gwen, and finally Elizabeth. They said Bill didn't leave any DNA traces in Chester's room because he was careful and calm, because Chester was the first one, but they also claimed it was not planned, so how calm could he have been?'

'So it *is* possible he was wrongly convicted?'

'No,' he counters. 'I know he got a raw deal in the investigation and he didn't make it easy for himself. But that's not all I know.'

I pause on this. I'm wondering why he didn't want this part recorded – it's good stuff. 'What is it that you're not telling me, Laurie?'

'I've got all my private notes, everything from the trial. You can't take it away but you can have a look. Copies of crime scene photos, witness testimony, our original interviews with witnesses. But nothing that's not publicly available goes in the podcast. I mean that. I still know the top lawyers in this country and I know what you journalists are like. This is privileged. Fair enough?'

'Sure,' I say. *So why are you showing me at all?*

'The thing is I think you need to see it all to have a full picture of Bill Kareama. Then we can chat.'

'Understood,' I say.

I hear footsteps and turn to see a blonde woman with grey roots and smiling eyes. 'Hello!' she says, her voice bright. 'Sloane is it? We're such big fans!' She comes over and introduces herself. 'I'm Laurie's wife, Helen.'

'Nice to meet you,' I say.

'It's important work, what you do, and now you're looking at the Kareama case?'

'I am. I'm doing a podcast and possibly helping to get him a retrial.'

She frowns. 'Oh, right, that's a bit different.'

'Well,' I say. 'We're looking at the failures of his first legal defence and the context of that trial.'

Her smile slips. 'The failures?'

Now I put warmth in my voice. 'Not that Laurie could have done more. I just mean the lack of witnesses, the myopic investigation.'

'Well, sometimes there's nothing you can do.'

'Come on,' Laurie says. 'I've got it all out for you, ready to go.'

He leads me down the hall to a book-lined study. A computer sits on a desk in the corner, and Laurie has set up a trestle table in the middle of the room, with notes, papers and photographs laid out in neat rows. I go closer and see stacks of handwritten notes, copies of numbered crime-scene photographs, tiny cassette tapes with letters and codes on the sides.

'You may be wondering why I kept all this stuff and why it's in such good condition. I was always very methodical, like most lawyers. I have drawers and archives from all of my cases going back to the early eighties, and Bill's was certainly my most high-profile case.'

'Well, I'm grateful you still have it all.'

Running my eyes over the photos is a jarring experience – some are of a shoe or a coin beside an evidence marker, but some show the bodies strewn across the beds. One is just an empty bed, blood everywhere. I've seen some of the crime-scene photos but not these. I squeeze my molars and don't look away. Chet looks so young, so peaceful. No sign of a struggle. Gwen looks less peaceful – I can't look at her throat. There's much more blood in Elizabeth's room and she's not there. By this stage, she was in an ambulance, I assume. Simon got it the worst.

While reading Bill's story, I'd gotten lost in it – I'd almost forgotten that this happened to real people with dreams, ambitions, fears, anxieties. People like me. That's what it is about; it has to be about the victims first. Bill, yes. But these people too. How can I look away, how can anyone get used to seeing images like this?

'You can take photos of the photos but not of my notes.' He clears his throat. 'I take it you're familiar with the so-called "buried bodies" case?'

'No, I'm woefully ignorant about New Zealand crime,' I say, finally turning away from the images. He's leaning against the door, his hands in the pockets of his shorts.

'Oh, it's not New Zealand,' he says with a chuckle. 'No, the buried bodies case is a touchstone for legal ethics and expanded the definition of client–attorney privilege. Lawyers for a man who was on trial and likely to be convicted of murder were advised by the defendant that he had killed two other women.' He clears his throat into his fist. 'The defendant gave them the locations of the additional bodies which had at that point not been discovered. The lawyers went out and found those bodies. The lawyers were pillars of their community, and they knew the victims' families. And yet they chose not to tell the police, or the families who were still searching for the missing girls. It came out at the trial, via a slip of the tongue, that they had seen the dead girls' decomposing bodies. They knew about the locations but did not report it.'

'Jesus,' I say. 'That should be the end of their careers, discussion over. It's morally impermissible.'

'Morally, perhaps. But ethically,' he says, 'that's another story. Clients must be able to trust their lawyers. They are all entitled to fair, unbiased representation.'

'I agree but—'

'But we all have a gut reaction to it. It *feels* wrong, doesn't it?'

'What happened to the lawyers?'

'After some debate, legal scholars unanimously agreed that the lawyers had acted ethically. In telling the police or the families where the bodies were, they would have breached client–attorney privilege. They're sticklers, lawyers.'

'Don't you mean *we're sticklers*?'

'Oh, I'm not a lawyer anymore.' He smiles. 'Do you agree with it in principle at least?'

I think about it. 'A positive moral outcome is more important than a positive ethical outcome. They *never* should have gone to check if the bodies were there. If client privilege is so important, how was it going to enhance the chances of a better outcome for their client in the case? But I agree with the ethical side of it. Guilty or not, ethics are there for a reason.'

'Clever,' he says. 'Finding the bodies wouldn't change the outcome of the trial, and if they'd told the families, anonymously even, it wouldn't have changed the outcome of the trial. He was guilty as sin. Already going down for murder. When the bodies were eventually discovered, it would always be tied back to him anyway. But we don't call on lawyers to make these complex judgements – that's what a code of ethics is supposed to be for. A reference, to assist in decision-making.'

'So do you agree with the findings of the case or not?'

'In my view, it's okay to breach client–attorney privilege in very particular circumstances. But what do I know? I'm no longer a lawyer, and you . . . well, you're just here to see my notes. I'll leave you to it. Let me know when you're ready to record.'

'Thanks,' I say as he leaves the room.

I look at the spread of papers on the table before me. It would take weeks to read through it all.

I begin to sort through the notes, skimming them for anything that might jump out as relevant. After about half an hour, I've not made much progress. Laurie is a thorough notetaker, I'll give him that. He has even kept records of phone calls he made to the prosecution, a list of subpoenas, and a page about items of discovery from the family's banking records. I find an invoice from Shirley Brown, the cleaner. I read the emails between Bill and Gwen before he took the job. *This is how it all started,* I remind myself.

I turn back to the photos, studying Elizabeth's room. It is tidy except for the bedding and a small pile of clothes in the corner of the room – it doesn't look like a typical teenage girl's room, but I guess she wasn't exactly typical. I force myself to look at the other crime scenes, the other bedrooms. In each of the other photos, the bodies are clearly lifeless – if not for the blood and poses, the beds and rooms look normal, undisturbed. Why did they not fight back? Why did no one wake? Why did only one person scream?

I notice a small stack of old cassette-style videotapes and a camcorder that must be twenty years old sitting on the table. A cable snakes from the camcorder to the computer monitor, which is on. I pick up the tape on top of the pile – but the case is empty. I turn it over in my hands, squinting at the writing on the label.

'I want you to promise me that it won't leave this room.'

I almost jump. 'What is it?' I say, turning to face him, holding the case aloft.

He's standing in the frame of the door. 'You'll see. I can always destroy it, maybe I will. If you claim it exists, I'll hurl it in the fire.'

I study his features for a moment. He is particularly grave and I know one way or another I need to hear what is on that tape. 'I promise. Whatever it is.'

'Go on.' He nods at the camcorder. 'Hit play. It will give you some context.'

I do.

On the screen, Bill sits on a plastic chair, his head in his hands. I forget sometimes just how young he was, he's just a scared kid here. My heart is hammering as I watch him. He looks around in what I guess is a police interview room, except something is off. It's not a cop asking the questions but a much younger Laurie. Shirt open near the neck, sleeves up, slacks cinched tight around a much narrower waist.

So if you didn't do it, why did you touch the knife? Can you explain that?

I tried to pull it out.

You tried? Are you saying you couldn't do it?

Bill exhales, he can't look up. God, I can see what Laurie means. He looks guilty – it's hard to trust someone who just stares down at his hands.

No. It was slippery.

Why did you close the window in Elizabeth's room?

Despite the low quality of the recording, I can see his eyes rise, focusing down the camera lens.

Because I didn't want anyone to hear her screams.
What? Bill?
I knew they'd stop me, if someone heard.
Bill, let's end it there. We can take a break.
She just kept screaming and screaming.
Hey, turn that off.

Younger Laurie looks up, strides toward the lens and the recording cuts in a flash of static.

I turn and look into Laurie's eyes.

'It got worse,' he says. 'I feel bad we lost the case, but as the years have gone on, I've reflected on it. He more or less confessed, numerous times. The sort of things the police would dream of. That is to say, *credible* evidence to prove his guilt. Not under duress. So if your intention is to paint Bill Kareama as the victim in all this, then perhaps you should think again.'

Laurie is watching my face as I process this information. I realise I have just been schooled in legal ethics – but as damning as the footage is, it doesn't undermine another foundation of democracy: that everyone is entitled to a fair trial. And Bill did not get that, irrespective of how guilty I might personally think he is. Laurie didn't believe he was innocent and I can see why. But it is also true that, as his legal counsel, Laurie was biased.

The book, *A Murder at Membrey*. Maybe that really was his inspiration – he planned on framing Simon. I start to hypothesise, consider alternative theories. Bill tampered with the heating, then when it didn't work, he went there with his knife?

'The buried bodies case,' I say slowly. That's what this is about. He *knew* Bill was guilty. 'You knew but . . . client–attorney privilege.'

'We were making these recordings to play for small focus groups of mock jurors. Then we would take opinions on whether or not he was believable, general sentiment, that sort of thing, and see which answers worked and which didn't.'

The Bill in the tape does not match the Bill I have created in my head. I realise the guy in my head is based on Bill's written account. I've hardly questioned the veracity of it, but through it, Bill has painted an innocent picture of himself. In it, he manages to point the finger at everyone else – Fleur, Tate, Teimana, even Mooks.

'I still get hate mail. People implying that we conspired to put him in prison. I get called racist by strangers, which is frankly offensive. Do they ever look at how many Māori men I've kept *out* of jail? Are they ever grateful for how much I've done for Māori in this country?' I baulk. 'It all starts anew, the hate mail and hit pieces, whenever the case is back in the media, and I'm sure your podcast won't help.' He chuckles ruefully. 'But that's life and I'm a big boy. I can deal with trolls.'

'Maybe he was just stressed, when he said that,' I offer. 'Or maybe he didn't want anyone to hear the screams because he knew he would be in trouble. He would be *stopped* by police.'

'Maybe, but it didn't happen just once. At times, he would say he didn't mean to hurt anyone,' he says. 'And in my forty years in the legal profession, I was never so certain of my own client's guilt. I know I shouldn't think or say that, and I still gave it my best, but it was a lost cause. Now then, if you want, we can turn your recorder on and I'll answer your questions. On the record but not about that.' He nods in the direction of the screen.

'Sure,' I say. 'It's quiet enough in here.' But my mind is jagged on the video. I steady myself, gather my thoughts. 'Let's start with Elizabeth. She gave a statement but didn't testify, right?'

'She identified him at the scene. She saw the knife in his hand, which was later identified as the murder weapon.'

'So she saw the knife but she didn't see Bill stab her?'

He shrugs. 'It happens. People are so traumatised. They might remember only certain details.'

'And Fleur, the au pair. Did you speak with her?'

'She had a solid alibi. She was at a motel in town with a man, her lover. The police, as prejudiced as you might think they were, did check all alibis. Everyone was where they claimed and with who they claimed to be with.'

'Who was her lover?'

'Michael someone. She was investigated – our job was not to present other suspects, suspects who had confirmed alibis. Our job was to try to find reasonable doubt where really none existed.'

I silently wondered about the legitimacy of that claim – presenting other suspects as possible perps is a pretty common defence strategy.

'What about Teimana? And Tate? Were they ruled out by water-tight alibis too?'

'Teimana? Remind me . . .'

'Maia's brother.'

'The ex's brother? Yes, rock-solid alibi. An officer checked in with him in the morning as per his bail conditions, sister was up late with him too and there was no evidence he'd left the house. And Tate . . . ?'

'Tate Mercer-Kemp.'

He looks confused.

'Do you know who I'm talking about? He was a gardener at the property.'

'Bill's uncle? He did raise a couple of red flags.'

'No, the next one. He was out of the country at the time of the murders.'

'Oh,' he says. He looks vaguely annoyed. 'I don't recall—'

'You didn't speak to him?'

'If he was out of the country, as you say, that would be why. I didn't speak to the pest-inspection guy, or the aunt who visited once, or all the cleaners, or the gardeners, waiters and tradespeople who came and we—'

'What about the teacher?'

'What teacher?'

'The teacher who was sending Elizabeth notes.'

He stares into my eyes, his cheeks incandescent. 'I'm not on the stand here, Miss Abbott. What exactly do you expect a defence counsel to do?'

'A little more than the bare minimum,' I say sharply, unable to choke back my outrage.

And now his cheeks are almost purple. 'The bare minimum.' He surprises me when he opens his mouth and laughs. 'The teacher was not a suspect. Your alternative theories might wash well with uninformed listeners but they don't pass the sniff test. There's no evidence of anyone else being inside the house on the night of the murders. The au pair is accounted for, the ex's brother is accounted for, the gardener was out of the country. This teacher, from memory, had left town weeks before. I'm not a detective. I work with the evidence. I work with the law.'

'And Mooks, the other gardener, Bill's uncle, who was also fired?'

'Police checked him out. He wasn't in town on the night in question and we couldn't produce any evidence to the contrary.'

Not according to Bill's account, I think. Mooks also said he wouldn't speak ill of the dead. Could he have been involved?

'We all know they zeroed in on Bill,' says Laurie. 'They had their guy and, despite a rather shoddy investigation, they got a conviction. But you'll hear this a lot: Bill doesn't always tell the truth.'

'Does anyone?'

'No, but he was particularly egregious when it came to his fabrications and fantasies. He tells us the girl was in love with him but there's no proof. He talks about a letter she sent that never turned up. I thought she'd help us, given Bill claimed they were close; he said she would support his character, but her statement was actually the prosecution's silver bullet. And we had real trouble finding anyone else who could give positive testimony about Bill.'

'What about Elizabeth's screams? They should have helped the defence as well, given that they gave a timeline for Bill to travel from the ATM to the house. It's an impossible distance for him to cover.'

'The jury didn't think it was impossible.'

'And on the screams. Only Elizabeth screamed, no one else did. She fought back but there's no evidence anyone else did. Did you have a theory about that?'

'No,' he says. 'No . . . that's always been a question mark. We could have maybe pushed that point a little more.'

Damn right you could have, I think.

An Uber whisks me away to the airport, despite Laurie's offers to drive – four hours is enough time to spend in that man's company. No wonder he wanted to see me and not just talk on the phone. It's like Laurie needed someone to understand, to prove he wasn't completely incompetent. He was clearly distracted by the small fact his client admitted he was there when Elizabeth was screaming, and that instead of calling for help, he just closed the window.

Security is almost non-existent in the domestic terminal of Wellington airport. I take a seat, begin rereading my notes, flicking through the photos I took of the crime scene images. I listen to my recording with Laurie.

I hear Laurie's words again: *In my forty years in the legal profession, I was never so certain of my own client's guilt.* Nothing is black and white, but the grey area in this case gets smaller by the day.

'Paging Sloane Abbott. Could you please make yourself known to flight staff at Gate 11.'

I push my laptop into my bag and run. *Shit.* The flight attendant gives me a stern look as she scans my ticket. I bolt down the bridge to the plane.

'Sorry,' I say to the woman in the seat next to me, as if I have only inconvenienced her. The overhead lockers are full so I jam my bag under the seat.

As the flight attendants carry out the safety demo, I run through our list of suspects, our episode plan. There's one piece of the puzzle I've not inspected closely enough yet: the PE teacher with the creepy notes.

I reach for my phone, to switch it to flight mode, and see a message from TK. It's the last thing I see before we take off.

Elizabeth's journal disappeared before the murders. She confirmed she may have had a crush on Bill but she can't really remember much from those days – a trauma response. She doesn't know if she saw Bill with the knife or imagined it. False statement?

TK

A PUB LUNCH sees me through – haggis, chips, peas. As the saying goes: *When in Rome, eat like a greedy pig.* I pass out at around 7 pm, barely making it under the covers before my heavy lids fall. It's 2 am when I wake again, jetlag winning the battle against my circadian rhythm. And I know I'm probably not getting back to sleep because my mind is already gnawing the fat of Bill's case, just like the old days. I'm breaking down all the new information from Elizabeth. If I was convinced Bill was guilty, she's introduced a fraction of doubt for me. Maybe Bill knew what he was doing sending me here, maybe it wasn't just to interrupt her life. Maybe it wasn't narcissism but a genuine belief that she could help him.

Years ago, when we started to petition the Governor-General and campaign for a new trial, I got in contact with Tate Mercer-Kemp, but he told me in no uncertain terms to go away. I called his work, emailed him a number of times but, after that first contact, he didn't respond. What social media he had was private. There was no way to find his address or personal number. The one thing I have is his employer from his LinkedIn profile. I reach for my laptop, white light blasting any remnants of sleep.

This all feels so familiar. For years, all I did was research the case: I lost my job, then what money I had went toward paying forensic experts or flying around the country talking to people about the case. Bill became *the other person* in my marriage, and soon my wife and I drifted apart. Friends stopped inviting me out for dinner or to gatherings because I'd inevitably end up arguing with *someone* about Bill's case. It took almost everything from me, and now I feel myself sucked back in. But I remind myself that this is it, this is the last roll of the dice for Bill Kareama.

After a few hours, I pull myself up, shower and pack. My train back to London departs at 6 am. I'd allowed a few days in the UK to find Elle and Tate. But now I think about Fleur. She is easier to contact than the others, running an Airbnb out of her farm near Montargis, south of Paris. Onboard the train, I track down the Airbnb listing online. It's sparsely booked for the next few weeks, and tomorrow night is free. I send a booking request. Next, I check flights and book one for midday tomorrow. I start to mentally prepare for Tate. I call the advertising agency where he works.

'Hi,' I say to the woman who answers. 'I was hoping to speak with Tate Mercer-Kemp?'

'Sure, give me one moment . . . Actually, it looks like he's a bit tied up at the moment. Can I ask what it's in relation to?'

I don't want to lie – it will make the conversation much more awkward when we do finally speak. 'Sure. I'm investigating a historical crime. I just wanted to chat with him if he had a moment, that's all.'

There's a long pause. 'Right,' she says. 'I'll be right back.'

I wait on the line for a few minutes. I finally hear a formal English accent down the line. 'Yes, hello?'

'Hi Tate, my name is Te Kuru Phillips. I'm from New Zealand.'

He groans. 'I know what this is about.'

'Good, I don't need to fill you in then. I guess I just wanted to chat with you about the brief period you worked at the Primrose home in Cambridge. I'm in London this afternoon, I won't keep you long.'

'Are you a cop?'

I pause. 'No. Not a cop.'

'A lawyer?'

'No,' I say. 'But—'

'Well, in that case you can fuck right off back to where you came from.'

The line cuts out.

I hold the phone in my hand, staring at it, my finger hovering over the call button. The message was pretty clear. The old man sitting across from me watches me with open suspicion as the train jerks along. I raise my eyebrows at him and he turns to look out the window. The morning English countryside rolls by outside the window. Stone walls, brambles.

It's easier to hang up a phone than it is to slam a door in someone's face or kick them out of your office – that's just how people are wired. I look up the street address of the company Tate works for. I'll do it the hard way. I'm not looking forward to it, but I'm short on time, and shorter on options.

In London, I take the Tube to Shoreditch and check into a hotel before dropping my duffel bag in the room and heading straight back out.

The advertising agency Tate works for is in an office tower in the financial district. I find a cafe across the road and sit with a coffee, watching the revolving glass door to his building.

I've studied his face on LinkedIn: designer stubble, blue eyes, slightly pursed lips, Clive Owen good looks. But the photo could be years old by now.

I order lunch and keep working on my laptop. I need to get him somewhere he can't sic security on me, somewhere that doesn't require swipe-card access. What time would he finish – could he work late? Could he have a car in an underground car park and I'd never even see him leave? This begins to feel like a folly, but I'm here now.

I bide my time. The waiter is patient with me. I order more coffee and sip on it slowly. People are coming and going, and in among them I see two men leave the building together – one looks a lot like the LinkedIn photo. It has to be him – an arrow of a man, lean and tall, blue eyes, capped with dark, slick hair. He's with one other man, slightly older, greying hair at the temples, carrying a brown leather satchel.

I pay as quickly as I can and get out the door in time to see the pair turn at the next street corner.

SLOANE

MY PHONE STARTS to vibrate in my hand as I stride from the gate, through the airport toward the pick-up area. Tara is calling.

'Hi,' I say.

'How did it go with Laurie Berry?'

'Good and bad,' I say.

'Go on?'

'The interview went well. I'll send through the recordings along with some photos.'

'So what was the bad?'

'He showed me something we can't use, a recording of a mock cross-examination. I promised we wouldn't make it public. But, basically, it shows Bill confessing to closing the window so no one would hear Elizabeth screaming, and so no one would stop him.'

'But . . . he always said she was unresponsive when he arrived. He always said that he thought she was dead.'

'I know. Honestly, I'm beginning to think we might be spinning our wheels here. I've gone on with the assumption he's potentially innocent. But now I don't know. You should have seen this recording.'

268

Dean is waiting for me outside of arrivals. I wave to him, he opens his door and comes to grab my bag.

'Sometimes,' Tara begins, 'people say all sorts of things under duress.'

'I know. But he wasn't under duress. It was a mock-up.'

'It could have been like a false confession, or it could be a real confession that meant something else. Maybe he did close the window because she was screaming, but that doesn't mean he stabbed her. Maybe he just didn't want anyone to hear because he knew the police would stop *him* and blame *him*.'

'Maybe,' I say. 'I just don't know. It was a little demoralising.'

'I wouldn't accept it at face value, Sloane. And I think we might be asking the wrong question, maybe we shouldn't be asking why he closed the window . . .'

'What do you mean?' I say, lowering myself into the front seat of Dean's car.

'Maybe we should be asking why the window was open in the first place?'

'It was hot?' I say.

'I have a theory,' she says. 'Her room was north facing, right? So it got the sun, Bill wrote about it in his account. But it was getting colder, coming into winter. Sloane, what if Elle was the only one who fought back because she is the only one who could? What if she was the only one who screamed because she was the only one who was conscious when she was attacked?'

'The heating.'

'Bingo.'

I almost feel dizzy, I know exactly what she's saying. Could she be right? 'Listen, I'm with the driver so I better go but I have a plan.'

'Okay,' she says. 'Talk later.'

'Can I get some charge?' I ask Dean once I have hung up.

'Help yourself,' he says, holding out the cable for my phone. 'Good trip?'

'Yeah,' I say.

As he drives me back toward the motel, I scroll through the photos again. My eyes are fixed on the crime scene in Elizabeth's room.

Pieces start to fall into place . . . What if they were all supposed to be dead before the killer turned up? *Tara,* I think, *you genius.* In the crime-scene photos of Elizabeth's room, I see the clothes piled in a heap in the corner.

Dean hums along to the radio, 'Slice of Heaven'.

'Change of plan,' I say. 'Don't take me to the motel.'

'Where are we going?'

Terrence Koenig is already at the door when we pull up.

'Hi,' he says, frowning as I walk up the steps to him. 'Sounded urgent on the phone. What's going on?'

'Can I come in?'

He hesitates. 'What's this about?' He eyes the car behind me. Dean already has his head down, nose in a book.

'I have a theory. I need to go upstairs.'

'What theory?'

'It might be nothing, I just need to see Elizabeth's room.'

'Alright,' he says. I watch his knotted calves as he climbs the stairs ahead of me. 'Can you at least tell me what you're looking for?'

'Chet didn't move or fight back. Gwen and Simon showed barely any sign of a struggle. But Elizabeth fought and survived. I'm just checking a theory as to why.'

'Her wounds weren't as significant. She could fight back because the injury was non-fatal.'

'But the killer stabbed Simon a number of times and Elizabeth only once. What if they fled because she fought back? What if the others were weak and sleepy?'

I stride up the stairs and turn right on the landing.

'Weak and sleepy? Simon Primrose?'

I walk in and pull open the curtains in what was once Elizabeth's room. The sun streams in.

'Were the windows double-glazed?' I say. 'When you bought the house?'

'The ones that were still intact were.'

'Can we move this?' I ask, touching the top of the desk.

'Why?'

'I need to check something.'

'I'd like you to start making sense at some stage.'

'It will make sense,' I say, my heart pumping as I grab the desk. Together, we drag it away from the wall.

Bingo.

A heating vent in the corner, right where the clothes in the crime-scene photos were piled.

'She blocked it,' I say out loud to myself. 'With clothes.' Terrence is staring at me, a confused look on his face. 'She was too hot in this room,' I say loudly, feeling a buzz run through me. She blocked the damn vent and opened the damn window, releasing the carbon-monoxide out.

'It does get warm,' he says.

It was seven degrees the night of the murders. Bill mentioned Gwen was getting headaches in the days leading up to the murder; Chet had been vomiting. Both symptoms of carbon-monoxide poisoning.

I find myself thinking in podcast terms again, imagining this all falling into the architecture of the season, of each episode. I've become invested in the case, deeply invested, but my journalistic instincts are telling me above all else to follow this. I've found something big and loud, something enthralling, something investigators missed. This discovery destroys the theory that the family must have known and trusted the killer – they were sedated.

'I've got to run. I have a meeting with my producer in ten minutes, but one last thing: when you were principal, you said there was a complaint from the family? A teacher was leaving Elizabeth lewd notes?'

He scratches his jaw. 'Like I said, we moved him on. That was months before the murders.'

'Months or weeks?'

He draws a breath. 'No, it seemed like a while. I can't remember but we forced him out.'

'And you were sure these notes were from the teacher, as alleged?'

He looks up, runs his tongue back and forth over his bottom lip. 'The teacher denied it at the time, but of course he would. To be honest, we had to act quickly; there was a lot of pressure from the parents. Simon could be a persuasive and intimidating man. In fact, he wanted more information on the teacher but we couldn't do that.'

'But you looked into it thoroughly?'

'Yes. It was a brief but thorough investigation. We realised it could have only been one man. He was young, it happened after his classes.'

'Did he admit to it?'

'No.'

'How certain are you that it was him leaving the notes?'

He clears his throat. 'I was one hundred per cent at the time. But I suppose it's *possible* that Bill Kareama was putting the notes in her schoolbag at home, maybe in her PE uniform. Unlikely but possible. I also later learned that his uncle was working at the school as a groundskeeper. He might have been doing Bill's bidding, who knows?'

I didn't buy that at all. It wasn't Bill writing the notes. It was the teacher. The young predatory teacher with everything to lose, who was never even questioned about the murders.

TK

I RUN AT first, closing the gap, weaving through the human traffic.

Tate is only half a block ahead but still I struggle to keep up, my laptop satchel swinging against my hip, bumping into pedestrians like an unwieldy fifth limb.

I tail them for five minutes until up ahead Tate opens a door, holding it for his colleague, before disappearing inside. *Another office*, I think. Lengthening my stride, I quickly catch up and find it's not an office but a restaurant. I can see Tate and his colleague inside, speaking with the maître d'.

'. . . the booking is for five,' I catch her saying as I enter.

'The others won't be far off,' Tate says, his voice as rich and plummy as home-made jam.

'Sure,' she responds. 'Right this way.'

I wait for her to return, noting that the restaurant is only half full. There are fake candles on each table offering meagre light, the booths and tables are matte black.

'Hi,' I say. 'Table for one.'

'Just you?'

'That's right.'

She scans me with her eyes. Jeans and an old t-shirt may not fit the dress code. Self-consciously, I run my fingers back through my hair, paste on a smile. She looks past me then back to her iPad. She touches the screen.

'This way.'

As she leads me, I catch Tate and his colleague out of the corner of my eye. I see a free two-seater near the table where they are taking their seats.

'Could I have that one?' I say, pointing.

She stops. The table I've asked for holds plates crusted with dried food and glasses with melting ice. There's a flash of annoyance in her eyes, before her expression is neutral once more. 'I'll have someone right over to clear it.'

I take the seat facing Tate's table. I can't quite catch any of the conversation but their body language is heightened, they're exuding nervous energy. When the maître d' leads two men and a woman to join them, Tate and his colleague spring to their feet. Handshakes all around.

A waiter comes over and gives me a menu. I have a quick look and then order a lemonade and an entrée of calamari. Under almost no other circumstances would I pay thirty pounds for an entrée and a soft drink but needs must.

Tate's colleague, who I sense might be his boss, appears to be doing most of the talking. His hands fly about seemingly of their own accord and he has a ready smile. It's clear this is a sales pitch. Tate won't want it interrupted. That's my advantage.

I need to get Tate alone. I wait for now, chewing the calamari that's just arrived, watching from the corner of my eye. After two drinks and entrées, Tate stands and excuses himself from the table. Chance presents itself. After a few seconds, I rise, follow him to the men's room.

I take a spot at an adjacent urinal. I feel a strange sense of calm, despite this being one of the more insane things I have ever done – no stress, just clarity.

'Nice spot, this,' I say.

I sense his head turn in my direction but he doesn't speak.

'Kiwi?' he says after a moment.

'That's right.' I do my fly up, go to the sink. Turn the tap. 'Listen,' I say, washing my hands, watching his back in the mirror. 'We can talk in here or out there but it seems like an important meeting for me to interrupt.'

'What?' He turns his head, his hackles well and truly raised.

I continue washing my hands under the warm water. *Play it cool, TK.* I take a warm towel from the stack, squeeze it between my hands.

'The meeting you're having. Closing a deal? Whatever the case, this won't take long and it's probably best if we don't involve your colleague and clients.'

Two strides and he's practically on me. I turn. It's not often someone can meet me eye to eye, but Tate's tall, and hovering like a wasp readying its stinger.

'You called my office,' he says. 'Who the fuck are you?'

I can smell the wine on his breath, his nose just an inch from my own. 'TK Phillips,' I say, without taking a step back.

'Big fucker, aren't you? Think you can intimidate me?'

'Not at all. I've come to talk to you about Bill Kareama.'

'And who the fuck is that then?' He's doing a good job of acting confused.

'Come on, Tate. Let's not play games. Bill Kareama, the alleged murderer in the Primrose stabbings.'

He closes his eyes, as if exhausted, then opens them. 'You're one of *them*,' he says. 'One of the headcases who think I'm somehow involved in some murders on the other side of the planet.' His rage grows as he talks. He grips the front of my shirt. I don't flinch. 'And now you're fucking up my work. You think you can just turn up and threaten me?' A vein pulses in his forehead.

There are small tricks, verbal cues you can use to bring someone back from the cusp of rage. I need to develop a connection, make him feel like I'm on his side, and establish my authority on the matter.

'I know exactly how you feel. I shouldn't be here. I shouldn't have to be here – it's frustrating for me too. I just want to do my job.'

Something shifts in his eyes. 'What do you mean you shouldn't have to be here?'

'Well, Bill, the man charged with the murders, has time and again identified you as a person of interest. It's fuelling all the crazies and the conspiracy theorists. I just wish there was some way to get word out that you had nothing to do with the murders.'

'Me? Are you deranged? Of course I had nothing to do with them.'

'You know that. And I believe that,' I say. 'I do. But others don't. Help me get to the bottom of it.'

He releases me before reaching into his pocket and starting toward the door. 'I'm calling the police. This is harassment.'

'Tate, I can help you. I'm not a crazy. I'm a psychologist. I've been involved with this case for years.'

He turns back, phone in hand. 'If you knew anything, you'd know that I did *not* work at the house. Back then I told the police. I never worked there – some people can't get that through their skulls.'

'What do you mean?'

'Something wrong with your ears? I didn't visit them, I didn't speak to them. I never met them. My father was in the same year as Simon at Oxford but they didn't know each other. They were two of thousands in the same year.'

I think about Bill's version. Could he have made this all up? Tate goes to leave again. I reach for his forearm. 'Wait, listen, I'm not leaving without an answer.'

He snatches his arm back, squares up to me again and for a moment I brace for a blow.

'You can call the police. You can do whatever you want. It won't be a good look with your boss, though, will it? Or you can squash this once and for all by just talking to me.'

'No. Fuck off.'

My face feels hot, I'm losing him. 'Tate, this will keep happening. People will always assume you were involved. A big-name podcaster is recording an entire season about the case.' I reach for my own phone. I punch her name into Google, pull up the story. 'She's going to bring huge attention, your name will come up a lot whether you like it or not.' I watch his face changing as he looks at the screen, the news article. 'Do yourself a favour – tell me the truth now. You're going to be famous for all the wrong reasons otherwise.'

He shakes his head, seething. 'A podcast?'

The door opens, someone else walks in. Not from his group. They go past us to the urinals. 'You want to talk?' He reaches into his pocket and pulls out a small, steel card case. He takes a card, hands it to me.

'Call me in an hour. I'll talk to you, then you can fuck off and never contact me again.'

SLOANE

'WHAT A DAY,' I say at the start of our Zoom call. 'There's *a lot* of interesting stuff I discovered today, but a few things we might need to run past our own lawyers.'

'This sounds juicy,' Esteban says. 'Is the defence lawyer happy to do a follow-up if need be?'

'Maybe. Although it did get a touch heated.'

'Have you been playing nice, Sloane?' Laughter bubbles in his voice.

'Not really, no. But Tara figured something out – the mystery of the gas heating and why only Elizabeth survived.'

'Did you now, Tara?' Esteban says.

'If we can track down the coroner from the time, that could help confirm things,' I say. 'But I'm guessing they didn't check for carbon monoxide in the blood.'

'Tara, what is this theory?'

She explains about the heater, the windows and the potential poisoning.

'And I checked the room – the clothes were covering the vent,' I add. 'Elizabeth had blocked the heating vent. Her room was always too warm.'

'This means pre-meditation,' Esteban says. 'Not a frenzied stabbing?'

'It does,' I agree. 'Say Bill went back later thinking they'd all be dead but found Elizabeth alive in her room. I think the others really did die from carbon-monoxide poisoning or were at least subdued by it. It would explain the lack of struggle, the blood patterns. The police must have turned the heating off that night and it was never put back on. The blockage wasn't discovered until years later when the Koenigs moved in.'

'This still doesn't answer how Bill got there so fast: the issue of the inhaler and his run,' Esteban says. 'But more importantly . . . do we really want a podcast where we just further confirm that our man is guilty?'

Something with blunt teeth is gnawing away at my conscious. The forum, the people discussing how horrible I am, how racist I am. This outcome certainly doesn't help. I can see it now: *The only person of colour in any of her podcasts and she chooses a mass murderer.*

'This doesn't prove Bill did it,' Tara insists. 'It simply suggests that whoever *did* do it gave it more planning than just turning up and grabbing a knife.'

'That's true,' Esteban says. *But what about Bill's interview tape?* 'Anyway, what else is on the agenda?'

'We're pretty clear for the next day or two,' Tara says.

'I haven't updated my schedule. I'm meeting someone tonight.'

'Who?'

'I don't know,' I say.

'What does that mean?'

'It means they're anonymous. And something tells me I won't be able to record. They left me a note.'

'No,' Esteban says. 'Wait until I arrive next week. You need to keep safe.'

'I am,' I say, holding up a whistle I bought yesterday. 'Plus Dean, my driver, has agreed to watch from a distance.'

'How much money do we owe this driver?' Esteban says with a laugh.

'A bit.' So far, Dean has been the best money we've spent this season. If he hadn't agreed to keep watch tonight, I wouldn't be going at all.

Tara speaks. 'Where are you meeting this person?'

'In the park,' I say. Even as I say it, I realise how insane it sounds.

'Sloane, are you sure that's a good idea?' The easy tone is gone from Esteban's voice now.

'I know what I'm doing.'

'Tara, can you talk some sense into this woman?'

'Be safe,' Tara says. 'And share your location.'

'Don't encourage her.'

'Seriously, stay safe,' Tara adds.

'I will.'

After we've finished the call, and I'm sitting in the room, I'm not so sure I'm doing the right thing. I reread the anonymous note, trying to see a face or a name in the swirls of the handwriting. *Who could it be?* I study the polaroid, the burnt-out car. There's no guarantee that it's even *the* car – it's a flimsy connection at best.

I kill some time ordering and walking to pick up what turns out to be a pretty ordinary pad see ew from the local Thai place and bringing it back to the motel for dinner. But as midnight approaches, my nerves crackle. I put on a coat and head for the door.

Dean messages me. *I'm in my car near the park.*

Thank you, I respond.

The air is crisp and the fog limits visibility. It's the sort of night the murders happened on. The illuminated cross floats in its own halo among the mist. I'm conscious of my own heartbeat as I approach the dark well of the park.

'Sloane,' a woman's voice issues from the shadows. I turn and see someone standing near the top of the path. She has her hood up, so I can't see her face clearly.

'Hi,' I say. I feel my pulse in my throat. 'Sorry, you gave me a fright.'

'Come on,' she says, her voice almost stern. I can't see her eyes.

'Where?' I say. 'Where are we going?'

'Let's walk.' She leads me into the dark, and I feel fear like a rash covering my skin, closing my throat. She's ahead, at least. If she were behind me, I might be compelled to run.

'Where are you taking me?'

'Through the park.'

'Who are you?' I say. 'I don't want to go any further until I know who you are.' She stops but doesn't turn back.

'Maia. My name's Maia,' she says. 'You know who I am.'

'Wait, you told my assistant you weren't prepared to speak to m—'

'I told her I didn't want anything to do with the podcast.' She faces me and takes her hood down, but in the dark I can still barely see her face. 'You're not recording?'

'No,' I say.

'Can you show me? Your phone, I mean.'

I reach into my pocket, take my phone out and hold it up. The light catches her face – I see dark eyes, a woman around my age. She's pretty, that's obvious. Her hand comes out and, despite my better judgement, I give her the phone. *Bad idea, Sloane.* No, I trust her. I have to trust her.

'Alright,' she says. 'Nothing else in your pockets, no recorder?'

'No.'

'Mind if I check?'

'Sure, fine.'

She steps closer and pats me down, feels the motel room keys in my pocket but nothing else.

'Okay,' she says, handing my phone back. 'Come on, let's walk and talk.'

She walks on. I keep my phone out, flicking on the torch to see the steps.

'Sorry to do it like this,' she says. 'It had to be at night, when my kids were asleep. Drove all the way here last night but I saw that man and I left.'

'Why the anonymity, Maia?'

'Because if it's just you then it's your word against mine.'

Your word against mine.

'I can deny it ever happened. I don't want anything to do with Bill Kareama or any podcast. I just wanted to move on and it took a long time to get over.'

'Right,' I say, reaching for a handrail to take the bottom steps. 'So why meet me at all?'

'Because you contacted me and inevitably you will contact my brother. I guess you want to solve the mystery, fill in the blanks.'

'That's right.'

'Well, I hope this helps you understand things more clearly. The thing is, I know Bill is guilty.'

'He told you?' I ask.

'No. But this is what I do know: Bill Kareama didn't run to the house. He got a ride that night.'

'What?'

'The white Holden Commodore, it was a stolen car. Someone drove him there.'

Fuck. My head is swimming. 'By *someone*, do you mean Teimana?'

'By someone, I mean no one. My brother did not touch that family – he had nothing to do with the murders.'

'But he drove Bill there? That's what you're saying, isn't it?'

'I just want you to know, any doubt you have about his innocence, get rid of it. Bill has asthma but it doesn't matter because he
didn't run. He called a friend for a ride.'

Teimana. Bill's last phone call before the murders was to Maia.
She told the police that they just spoke about the family and Bill was
angry. But . . . maybe he called Maia's phone to speak with Teimana.

'Bill told this friend that he would help him rob the house.
He said that he would go up and make sure they were asleep, then he
would let his friend inside. The friend picked him up, took him
to the house and waited at the road. Then he heard the screams.
He panicked, he had so much to lose.'

'He was on bail,' I say.

She ignores this. 'The screams sent a chill down his spine. He
sped away and he's glad he did, because then he saw cops coming.'

'Teimana drove Bill,' I say.

She stops walking abruptly, turns to me in the dark. 'He never
set foot in the house but he couldn't talk to the police about it.
The next thing we heard, Bill had been arrested for the murders.'

We're beside the lake. I turn my torch off but I can see her nodding.

'One man went to prison,' she goes on, 'but you can bet every
dollar you have that *both* of them would have gone down if the
cops knew he was anywhere near that house. Bill was smart. The
friend was a prospect for a gang and if Bill said anything, his time
inside would be a lot harder than it has been.'

'Right,' I say. It's making sense now. The last piece of the
puzzle. Bill did it, he really did it. Any doubt that lingered about
his Olympic pace is gone. Of course he got a ride. 'So the friend
never went in the house?'

'No,' she says.

'And the car?'

'He got back that night and told me what had happened, then
when the news came out about the murders, and the police were

looking for a white Holden Commodore . . . Well, he torched it. I won't say where but you'll never find it. The plates are gone. And even if you found the car, and the plates, it wouldn't prove anything.'

'And you believe your brother's account? You have no doubt?'

'I do. I know it might be hard to believe, but he doesn't lie to me. We had a rough childhood and he took it harder than me. You know about his troubles with the law, gangs, drugs. You don't understand how hard it was for us as kids – we had nothing.' She heaves out a sigh. 'I'm not making excuses for the crimes he did commit. But he was always honest with me. And I saw him that night, he was shaken, but he had no blood on him or anything like that.'

'Where's Teimana now?' I ask.

'My brother has a family now. He's a great father and he loves his children. He's involved with the church. He's a new man. The last thing we need is for the police to find another reason to bring him in. But I thought it was important for you to know, because there are some who still have their doubts that Bill was the one who did it.'

We're coming back up toward the road now. *Could she simply be bitter about Bill dropping her?*

'And you think Bill was capable of doing that, of murdering the family?'

'I do,' she says. 'I didn't want to believe it at first but he'd changed. That family, that house, turned him into something he was not. He treated me like shit, discarded me, left me broken for years. He was selfish and I didn't see violence from him, but I saw how smart he was, how calculating he could be. He could look you in the eye and tell you the sky was green and you might actually believe it until you looked up.'

'Maia, can I talk about an anonymous source for my podcast? I won't even allude to you or your brother. Journalists have a right to protect their sources, so the law can't compel me to mention your name. Just this single fact about the car.'

She looks at me, and even in the dim, I can see the shock in her eyes. 'You'll still do the podcast?' she asks. 'Even knowing this? Why would you?'

'Well, I don't know,' I say quickly. 'I need to process this, think this new information through.' But I am already imagining how this could tie in to the episode plan we already have. We've discovered so much the police missed, the trial missed. I want to find a way to share it. But can we do that if the conclusion is still that Bill did it?

'Did you tell this to his psychologist?' I ask her.

'I told him what I've told you,' she says. 'Broke his heart but he wouldn't leave me alone until I spoke to him. He just wanted to know the truth. Then when he had it, he was just silent for a while.'

This is it. This is what made TK give up. This is what he couldn't tell me. Bill's case, his only defence, was predicated on a lie. He didn't run from town, he didn't walk. He was driven by Teimana. The timeline works perfectly.

Bill Kareama murdered that family in cold blood.

I send TK a message when I get back to the motel, after Dean has left. *Spoke to Maia. I get it now. The car . . . Bill did it.*

I'm surprised when a message comes back. It's almost 1 am.

I thought that too.

Thought. Past tense. Has he changed his mind again?

You're a hard man to read, TK. Outside of Maia, Teimana and Bill, does anyone else know the truth about the Holden Commodore?

I see the three dots appear. He's typing.

I'm a bit tied up at the moment but I can call you in the morning, your time. Only Teimana and Bill know the truth. Maia has her brother's story but she wasn't there so it's a second-hand account.

Another message comes through.

You've got as far as I ever did on this case, Sloane. You're at the point I became disillusioned, but after speaking with Elizabeth, I'm not so sure. I wanted confirmation but she only gave me more doubt. We need her journal.

I shoot a message back: *It's long gone. I could ask to search the house again but someone would have found it during the renovations, surely?*

Who knows?

I'm so wired. I can't sleep so I open my laptop and start rereading Bill's account. There has to be something here, a message hidden in the text.

This case has challenged me in a new way. I thought the only thing that mattered was that everyone had a fair trial, an honest defence. The buried bodies case comes back to mind. Ethics over morality. What wins out?

TK

IT'S A NICE bar, with a low ceiling, burgundy wallpaper and dark-wood wainscoting. Men in suits fill the space, squeezing their pints. I'm not exactly dressed for the occasion, but I don't care. Tight booth seating that could have been pulled straight off an old train. Wading through the bodies, I see Tate already sitting in a dim corner. He has a beer in front of him and glances up from his phone as I approach.

'Busy place,' I say.

'Yeah,' he grunts. 'Not getting a beer?'

'I don't drink.'

He rolls his eyes.

'Cool place, though,' I add.

I watch the barman pump a handle forward and back like drawing water from a well, a pint glass slowly filling.

I slide in opposite Tate as he takes a mouthful of beer. He makes a circular gesture with his finger, as if to say, *Let's get this over with.* I place my phone on the table and open the voice recorder app. He eyes it for a moment.

'Do you mind?'

He sucks his cheeks in, thinking. 'I'd rather not be recorded, thanks.'

I take my phone back, put it in my pocket. 'Don't know what the sound quality will be like in here anyway,' I say. We're having to practically shout as it is. 'Anyway, I'll try not to keep you too long. You said you never met the Primrose family, or specifically Simon Primrose?'

'What's that?'

'Did you ever meet Simon Primrose?' I ask, leaning closer.

'Not once, never in my life.'

'And yet Bill Kareama identified you as working for him?'

'The ramblings of a convicted murderer, I assume,' he says. 'You're a psychologist, right? So what do you think: do murderers ever lie?' He puts on a gormless expression, the sarcasm as thick as butter.

'So you remember the details of the case, then? You know he was convicted?'

He sips his pint. 'Of course I do. I had to explain to my parents, my ex, my friends why I was somehow implicated in it. Thankfully, I'd left New Zealand when it happened, so I didn't need to explain much, but it was the rumours that I *worked* for the family. That's what pissed me off. I even talked to a lawyer. I was thinking about defamation but we gave up on it.'

'So Bill just came up with your name out of thin air?'

'I guess.'

Elizabeth mentioned it too. 'One of the victims also gave me your name,' I say.

Now he frowns. 'I'll tell you what I told the police: either someone with the same name was there or someone was pretending to be me. I never set foot in that house. I was snowboarding in Queenstown, a thousand miles away. When the stabbings happened, I was starting my internship in London. Got about two hundred witnesses.'

A roar of laughter behind me. The pub is raucous. 'But you *were* in New Zealand at one stage?'

'Briefly. On a holiday. I was backpacking, drinking and partying. Then I came home.'

'The Tate Mercer-Kemp who was working at the house, he was from London, the same age as you, and his father was at school with Simon Primrose,' I try. 'It's unlikely there'd be two people of the same name with those details in common.'

'My father never knew Simon Primrose. I've checked this out myself – they were both at Oxford, but that's it.'

'Do you know of anyone who might have impersonated you to get the job?'

'It's beginning to sound like this is all a lark.'

'Bill Kareama may be wrongly imprisoned. Someone may have been impersonating you . . .' Something else occurs to me. 'They might have stolen your identity and then relied on your travel records as their alibi. This isn't a lark – it's deadly serious.'

He looks past me toward the bar. 'I was travelling with a uni mate and a couple of lads he knew. Me and my uni mate were only in New Zealand for two weeks; one of the others, he stayed on.' Tate focuses, as he tries to remember. 'From memory, the other guy went to Australia.'

'Do you remember your itinerary?'

'We never had an itinerary. We were twenty-year-olds going overseas to try to get laid in hostel bars.' He scratches his jaw. 'We got there then made a plan.'

'Are you still friends with the others?'

He shakes his head. 'Not really. I hear from Chris now and then. He's living in Wimbledon, we were good mates over the years, but you start a family and drift apart after a while. But the others I've not seen in years. I didn't know them as well. I saw Tom at a music festival maybe twelve years ago, just bumped into him. Hadn't changed much. I don't think I caught up with Michael at all after that trip. We weren't very good mates, to be fair.'

'But you were contacted by the police, or lawyers about the murders at the time? And you told them all of this?'

'Yes, both,' he says. 'It was all a bit mad. I told them I never knew the Primroses, verified the date I flew out of New Zealand and then I just stopped answering. They went away not long after that.'

'If someone was impersonating you,' I think aloud, 'it's likely that it was a person who knew you. Someone you spent a little time with at least.'

He finishes the last of his beer. 'Do you have any photos of this other Tate?'

'Nothing. I've looked at all the images available from those months in the house and he isn't in any of them. I never questioned it before.'

Taking his pint glass, he stands and goes to the bar. I can barely believe what I've uncovered here. Whoever the gardener at the house was when Bill was there, it's becoming clear that it was not the real Tate Mercer-Kemp, but an impostor. Just like that, we have another very viable suspect.

'So you didn't go to the town of Cambridge at all?' I ask Tate when he gets back.

'We didn't stop there, no. Not from memory. We just did a bus tour, "Kiwi Experience" it was called. I linked up with a few other Brits on the tour and we went on to Queenstown. I just wanted to get out of Auckland.'

'Nothing wrong with Auckland,' I say. 'That's where I live.'

'I hope it's better now than it was back then. We stayed at a dodgy backpackers in the CBD. I was robbed.'

'Robbed?'

'Yeah, it was a total pain in the arse. I hadn't bothered with travel insurance. I had to get my folks to wire me some money. Lucky they didn't get my passport – I'd put it in a locker at the hostel.'

'When did it happen?'

'The first Friday night. We were wasted, me and the boys. We went out with some others from the hostel, mostly Aussies, I think, hit a few bars then we all split up and I blacked out. I woke inside my room at the hostel but with empty pockets, some other stuff nicked from my rucksack and a killer hangover.'

'Drank too much?'

'Must have.'

'Tate, is it possible you were targeted? That someone spiked your drink to steal your ID?'

He laughs. 'Come on, this is mental.'

If he was drunk, it wouldn't have taken much, a crushed-up sleeping pill maybe? Or Valium? Something that would intensify the effects of the alcohol.

'You have to admit that it's a possibility,' I say, looking him in the eye. 'It would at least explain how your name got mixed up in this whole thing.'

He takes his phone from his pocket. 'It was the early days of Facebook. I made one or two posts back then.' Pint in one hand, phone in the other, he scrolls and scrolls.

While I wait, I reach into my bag and pull out my old note-book. It was my Bible when I was working on Bill's case. My notes are a tidy, leaning scrawl. I find the page I used to profile Tate Mercer-Kemp.

Shorter than Simon and Bill: around six foot.

The man in front of me is well over six feet tall.

Harelip or scar near mouth. Rough way of speaking but could act posh.

Wrong on all fronts.

Dark hair, dark eyebrows, blue eyes.

Roguish grin.

Roughly the same age as Bill, eighteen to twenty-two.

Tate places the phone down on the table, slides it to me. 'Here,' he says. 'These are the only photos I have of the trip.'

I pick up the phone and start to flick through the images – a blurry series of photos from a night out, awkward arm-out selfies in bars and at parties. The old haircuts and fashion make me feel nostalgic. Some landmarks and landscapes without anyone in them. Holiday pics have changed since those nascent days of social media.

In the photos he is in, Tate, the real Tate, had a sort of fringe with hair sticking up at the back – he's thinner and much younger. Evidently he was a fan of fluoro singlets and the type of dark glasses that cover half your face. In one photo, he's posing in front of a couple making out on a dance floor with a big grin. In another, he's bent over in front of a Māori sculpture, a coy look and his fingertips covering his mouth. I feel a flash of annoyance. I stop on photos with large groups of people, enlarging them and scanning each face.

'No photos of the night you got robbed?'

'They got my camera. I bought a new one in Auckland.'

'Any photos of your mates?'

'Here,' he says, taking the phone back. He turns it around and I see them, the four with their arms around each other.

Behind them is a long table covered with what looks like Jäger bombs. A pale blond man with blue eyes. A black man with short-clipped black hair and a huge grin. Tate, in a singlet again. Then there's the last of the foursome. Thick stubble, but there's a slight pull of skin across his cheek. A scar, hidden under a three-day beard. He has straight dark hair and a hard look about him, despite the cheesy grin. I take the phone, zoom in.

'Who is that?' I point.

He leans over the table, looking down. 'That's Michael,' he says.

'I think that's our man,' I say.

'But he was out of the country too.'

'Where?'

'Well, I think he went somewhere in Australia.' He takes his pint, holds it, thinking for a moment. 'Sydney, maybe.' He drains the last mouthful of beer.

'How do you know?'

'He left. He was only there for a week or so. After I got robbed, he wanted to go somewhere else.'

'You said before that you woke up with empty pockets and other missing items. What items?'

'My camera. My watch. My book, weirdly. Even my old Oxford rowing club cap.'

The background noise fades to a low hum. An Oxford rowing club cap. My senses heighten as adrenaline surges through my body, like I'm in danger. The scar, the dark hair, the age, the theft, the cap. It has got to be him.

'You alright, mate?'

I find myself nodding rapidly. 'This guy, Michael. What was he like?' I say.

'Yeah, nice bloke, loved a pint.'

'And you met at university?'

'Nah, through a uni mate,' he says. 'We'd hit the bars together, that's it.'

'Do you know where he is now?'

'Not really.' The pub's getting louder. 'He stayed in Australia after our trip, as far as I'm aware.'

'You didn't have any contact with him after?'

'Just on Facebook, now and then. But I don't think he's on there anymore.'

This man assumed an identity, bluffed his way into the house. *But why?*

'Where did he live when you knew him?'

'Bristol, but he's from London.' He squints. 'West somewhere, maybe Acton. Michael O'Rourke.'

Electricity sparks in my brain, a storm of connections. *Michael O'Rourke.* Why do I know that name?

Tate is staring at me. 'Listen,' he says, 'if we're done here, I better get moving.'

'I need to find this man. I believe he was the one impersonating you at the house.'

'Michael?' he says. 'You must be having a laugh.'

'No,' I say. 'Did he always have stubble?'

'Yeah,' he says. 'And he's got that scar but . . .' I can see the wheels turning in his mind. 'Nah, it can't be. Can it?'

'I'll find out,' I say. 'Can you text this photo to me now?'

'Sure, I guess.' He picks up his phone and after a minute hands it to me. I enter my number and press send. My own phone vibrates in my pocket.

'Do you have a contact for him at all, email, phone?'

'No,' he says.

'What about family or an old address?'

'Nah, I didn't know him that well, didn't know his family or go to his place or anything like that.' He looks up, his expression almost pained, as if he's lifting a weight. 'I remember one of the lads telling me his dad died,' he pauses.

There's a din in the bar, men cheering about something.

'Anyway.' Tate stands, taking his phone from the table and his coat from the seat next to him. 'Good luck finding this guy, I guess, if that's what happened,' he says as a farewell.

'Thanks,' I say. 'I'll be in touch with whatever I find.'

Then he's swallowed by the crowd. There's a group standing nearby, watching me, waiting for me to stand up.

'You leaving, mate?'

I stand. 'All yours.'

SLOANE

MY PHONE. IT'S vibrating on the pillow beside my head.

'Sloane speaking,' I say through a sleepy exhale.

'Miss Abbott. Detective Adam Cooke from the Cambridge police.'

'Oh, hi.'

'So, not the news you probably want to hear, but I need to let you know that your rental car was discovered this morning near the Desert Road, an hour and a half south of where it was stolen. We did not recover any personal items and the car is a write-off, unfortunately.'

'Oh,' I say, my stomach sinking. There goes the excess. I see the time on the alarm clock. 'You're right, not the news I want to start the day with.'

'We have your list of the items that were in the vehicle and if we manage to recover anything we will let you know.'

'Right, thanks.'

By now, I'm used to the frank and direct language of the police but this is brutal.

'We can print you out a report to pass on to your insurer and the rental company.'

'I'll walk down now,' I say. 'I can pick it up. I'm not far.'

'Sure.'

I push through the doors of the Cambridge police station with a take-away coffee and a layer of hastily applied make-up. The cop behind the counter watches me approach with slightly suspicious eyes.

'Yes?' she says.

'I'm here to see Detective Cooke.'

'Detective Cooke,' she repeats. 'He knows you're coming?'

'He does.'

She disappears through a door. A moment later, a side door opens and a beanpole of a man with a neat moustache comes out.

'Here,' he says, holding out the statement. 'Joy riders, probably.'

'Any idea who they are?'

'No, but we normally catch up with them in the end. We pulled a couple of prints.'

'Right. How long have you been on the force here?'

He smiles, there's warmth in it. 'I'm not going to give you anything for your podcast, Miss Abbott.'

He knows exactly who I am. 'Have you all agreed to block me down here at the station?' I say, trying to keep the hint of scorn out of my voice. 'Not a good look if you ask me. Especially given some of the things I've uncovered.' I sip my coffee. The only reason I walked down was to possibly open this locked door.

'I wasn't around back then but we tend to direct such inquiries to the media team.'

'Why did the Cambridge police force not investigate the teacher who harassed Elizabeth Primrose?'

'Thanks for coming down,' he says. 'If there's nothing else related to your case, I'll leave you to it.'

'Did you investigate the gas heating at the Primrose house?'

He turns away, starts back toward the door. 'Thank you, Miss Abbott,' he says with his back to me.

I sigh and leave. It's still early, just past 7 am. I wander back toward the motel. I have an email from Tara. She's reread Bill's account and has some notes, 'new angles of attack' she calls them. One thing immediately stands out to me.

Time capsule. It's a long shot, she's written, *but the timeline checks out. The letter and the journal disappeared around the time the capsule went down.*

Could it be? The centenary was seventeen years ago. How long does a time capsule go in the ground for? A decade? Twenty years? Fifty? I take my phone and call Esteban.

'Sloane, it's 6 am here,' he says. 'I assume this is big news.'

'I got a message from TK,' I say.

'Oh yes, he met with Elizabeth? It was really her?'

'He has. He mentioned the journal again, which Bill wrote about. She confirmed it existed. In it, she wrote all about what was happening in the house and at school, then it disappeared a week or so before the deaths. It's important.'

'This *is* big news,' he says. 'Did TK talk more about Elizabeth? Will she do an interview?'

'No. Listen, Esteban. Tara has an idea about the journal and the time capsule. She noticed that the journal disappeared around the same time as the centenary. It could be down there, the letter she wrote Bill could be down there . . . anything could be in that time capsule. The police didn't check, I'm sure of it.'

There's a long silence. He sighs. 'It's a good idea. But I don't know where to start with that. I'll make some calls to the school; maybe we can offer a donation. There might be privacy issues. Should we aim to try to open it up after Tara and I arrive?'

'My driver is on his way. I'm heading to the school now.'

'You don't think we need more tact?'

'It's easier to say no on a phone call than to my smiling face. Let me try to open the door first.'

I hear a long exhale. 'Just don't burn any bridges.'

'I won't. Oh, and they found the rental. It's a write-off. I'll call Avis soon and organise a new one.'

Esteban exaggerates his sigh down the phone. 'Okay. Talk later.'

⸻

'It's a beautiful property,' I say to Dean as we arrive at the school. I leave him waiting in the car as usual, find the front office and encounter a middle-aged receptionist, who tries her best to keep the gate closed to the principal.

'You say you want to speak to Mrs Pelham for your podcast?' she says, as if this is the most befuddling of riddles.

'Yes,' I say. 'We're investigating an historical crime. Trust me when I say it's in the school's best interests.'

'Right,' she says slowly. 'The principal is very busy today.'

'I'm sure. Can you call her and let her know that Sloane Abbott from *Legacy* podcast is here?' I wonder if Terrence Koenig could get me through the door.

'*Legacy* podcast,' she repeats. She taps something into her computer. *Is she googling me?* She looks at my face, then back at the screen. *She is definitely googling me!*

She picks up the phone and punches in three numbers. When she speaks, she dips her head and turns away. I step back, give her the privacy she obviously wants.

She hangs up. 'Right,' she addresses me. 'There's an assembly today at nine, so ten o'clock is the earliest Mrs Pelham can see you.'

'Perfect,' I say. 'Thank you.'

While I wait, I go outside and begin calling excavator services in the area. The only one that can do it today sets his price suspiciously high, but I'm desperate to get it done. I tell him I will call later to confirm, then I sit and wait.

When the time comes to see the principal, the receptionist leads me down an immaculate walkway to her office, where I find a large, polished desk and a low, stiff-backed chair for visitors. A few minutes pass before the door opens again and a portly woman, with wiry black hair and shrewd eyes, enters the room.

'Sloane Abbott,' she says. 'Annabel Pelham.' We shake hands. Hers is tiny, her grip strong.

'It's a pleasure to meet you.'

'So,' she says, going behind her desk. 'What's this about?'

'The centenary time capsule,' I say, cutting to the chase. 'I'm investigating the Primrose murders and we've had a number of breakthroughs. I have reason to believe a key piece of evidence may be in the young Primrose boy Chester's time capsule.'

'The time capsule?' she repeats. 'I wasn't here when it went in the ground. But it's not due to come up for another thirty years or so.'

'I know,' I say. 'But if I can find an excavator who can do it, I can guarantee we will return everything to exactly how it was.'

She leans back in her chair, taps a beat on the table with her middle and index finger. 'It's not so simple,' she says. 'You don't just come in here and decide we're digging it up.'

'I spoke to my producer and we are happy to make a small donation to the school.'

'It's not about money.'

A change of tack. 'No, it's about justice. And publicity. Your school has an opportunity to be on the right side or the wrong side of history, and given the reach of the podcast—'

'To be frank, Miss Abbott, I don't see why you think your podcast is so valuable to this town, or this school. Nothing good will come from any of this.'

'My latest podcast had *tens* of millions of listeners around the world,' I say. I hate how it sounds.

She blinks rapidly. 'And what should that mean to the school, exactly?'

'Well, I'll likely describe how we go here today to my listeners and I'd love to be able to say that you cooperated with this very small request.'

She's watching me closely now, with an unreadable expression.

'Or I will report that the school, and you specifically, refused to cooperate until we had a police order.' I'm doing precisely what Esteban didn't want but I know I'm close. Her eyes go above my head to where a clock is fixed to the wall. 'And I will get a police order. They're very interested in my findings so far.' Not *exactly* the truth.

The corners of her mouth shift up, but there's no joy in her eyes. 'That's not how things work around here. You don't waltz in and make threats.'

'We can bury it again, immediately after. One way or another, we need Chester Primrose's box.' It can't be a legal issue – no contract would have been signed with the students at the time. I know she can do it.

She sighs.

'The boxes are supposed to stay in the ground for fifty years.'

Make her the hero of the story. I continue speaking, sweetening my voice as much as I can. 'I'll need a witness too; someone I can interview for the podcast. Someone who pulled the strings to make it happen, someone who can talk about the school and its prestigious history.'

She wets her lips, wears a stern look of concentration. 'How long will it take?'

I resist smiling. 'A few hours, I'd guess. We can do it after school tonight, when everyone has gone home. And we can even put fresh concrete down immediately.' I'm writing cheques I'm not sure I can bank but I'll say anything to get that time capsule open. Hell, I'll lay the concrete myself.

'I still don't really understand what significance you think the Primrose boy's time capsule box could possibly have. If it were a legal matter, I might see things differently, but this just sounds like you want content for your podcast.'

Based on the frequency with which she's checking the clock, I know I don't have much time. I summarise. 'There were one or two pieces of evidence that disappeared from the house at around the time the capsule went into the ground. Police didn't necessarily need them for a successful prosecution, but the missing items could give us important context and insight into the victims. Some still believe Bill Kareama is innocent; this might prove his guilt once and for all. But on the flipside—'

'It could prove his innocence?'

'Potentially,' I say. I'm close. I can see a decision being made in her mind. I press her a little more. 'But listen, if you don't have the power to make that call, we could petition the board of trustees—'

'That wouldn't be necessary.'

'No?'

She ponders this for a moment. Her dark eyes are fixed on mine now. 'There's one condition.'

'Name it.'

'I would like you to address our assembly, something inspiring. We can schedule in a day.'

I straighten my spine. 'Sure,' I say. 'I'll do it.'

'And when you've done what you need to do, everything will go back in the ground as it was.'

'Assuming there's no evidence to share with the police, sure.' I really will need a witness when it comes out for anything we find to ever be permissible in court anyway. And if I can convince her to record for me, it would make great extra content for the podcast.

'Come back tonight after six,' she says. 'It'll be dark but we've got floodlights.'

I can barely keep the excitement in. 'Thank you, Mrs Pelham. I'll be here at six sharp. And this probably goes without saying, but I'll need you and anyone else involved to sign NDAs.'

She gives a stern nod. 'That shouldn't be a problem.'

Dean takes me back to the motel and I make a few more calls. A local handyman is happy to lay concrete tonight – this is getting costly, but I just hope the juice is worth the squeeze. While I wait for the rest of the day to pass, I work.

When I return that night, Principal Pelham, the school's groundskeeper, Ian, and I meet Bradley, the excavator I've hired, out the front.

Pelham takes charge and delivers a military-like briefing to the two men at the school gate. I let her – it is her school after all, and I do not want any last-minute changes of heart.

The time capsule is located at the southern end of the expansive school property – in a purpose-built bunker-style underground storage unit. Ian the groundskeeper produces a map, which the excavator studies closely.

'Seems straightforward enough,' says Bradley. 'I'll tow the digger through the grounds, and we'll get started.'

Bradley heads to his ute, which is parked in the school zone out front, then follows the groundskeeper who leads the way on a ride-on mower. Pelham and I trail them in a golf cart, which she drives. *Sometimes this job is weird*, I think, imagining how I will describe this scene to listeners.

'Well, here we are,' Pelham says to me, as she pulls up and gets out of the cart. 'I hope this is worth it.'

With the NDAs signed, work begins. The excavator bucket pulls the soil up until a concrete slab is revealed. The groundskeeper and the excavator bend and lift away the lid, beneath which is a cavity. It appears to be about two metres deep and a few metres wide. Groundskeeper Ian lowers a ladder into the pit. I start recording on my phone.

'Cold in here,' Ian says, as he climbs down. He scans the space with a torch. It looks like a low-budget bomb shelter inside. Through the haze, rows of boxes on steel shelving appear.

I bet all those years ago, no one expected that this would be how it was unearthed – a podcaster forcing her way in to investigate a mass murder from the same year it was buried. I'm imagining a fifty-year reunion, the shadow of Chet's brutal death hanging over all of them.

'Here we are,' Ian says. He starts to rub dust away with his thumb to look at the names. I am holding my breath. Minutes feel like hours.

'Chester Primrose!' Ian says eventually, holding a small box up. Something catches in my throat. *This is it.*

As the groundskeeper begins to climb the ladder, Bradley reaches down and takes the box from Ian's outstretched hand. Bradley hands it to the principal.

'Fence this area off for now. We will need to close it back up once we're done with this,' Pelham says as a dusty Ian emerges.

'Alright,' he says, pulling himself up and onto the grass.

'You've got me until ten,' Bradley says to me. I nod. Esteban won't be over the moon with the cost of all this but it might just be worth it.

Pelham checks her watch. 'Come on,' she says. She takes me in her golf cart to the main office, the precious cargo on the seat between us. It's getting dark – they'll want to get on with closing the hole up.

'Well, the moment of truth.' The wind from the drive ruffles Pelham's short black hair. I feel excitement, as morbid as that is – I can't help it. If the letter or the journal is in here, it will at least prove one way or another if Bill was telling the truth about Elizabeth's feelings toward him. And maybe we will learn more about who was sending her the notes.

'I'd like to take photos of whatever we find, and if nothing is relevant, we can put it straight back down.'

She takes me through to her office and baulks when I pull out two pairs of latex gloves.

'Is that necessary?' she asks.

I nod.

'If you insist,' she says. 'And when will you record our interview?'

'I'll have my assistant find a time that works in the coming days.'

She puts the gloves on, removes the cover of the box. My stomach is a helium balloon, floating up under my sternum. The box is full: a yoyo, a sealed pack of Pokémon cards, a few pieces of paper, a tiny Tech Deck skateboard, a full-sized skateboard wheel, photographs of Chet with his family and another boy around his age. Then I see it. A tan moleskin journal with two words on the cover: *Elle Primrose*.

'Well?' she says. But I can't speak. I try to swallow. My throat is dry. Tara was right again. She will be the first person I message. My eyes close and it must take longer than I think to open them because Pelham speaks again. 'The notebook. Is this what you were looking for?'

I reach out a gloved hand, taking the journal like an artefact that might disintegrate between my fingers. I place it on the surface of Pelham's desk.

'I don't think this will be going back down in a hurry,' I say.

'This was the sister's? Why is it in his box?'

'If this had been discovered before the trial, detectives and lawyers would have pored over every word.' I take my phone, start recording and open the first page, then the next, then the next. The name *Bill* jumps off the page at me, on almost every page. He wasn't lying – the girl had a crush, more than a crush at a glance. I keep going until the words stop and the pages run blank, crisp from the subterranean years. Its author's youth, her family, cleft away just a week or two after the words stop.

'Is that all you need?'

'I might take photos of everything else.'

She moves a few of the items around, lays the pieces of paper out flat. I see a letter. *Could it be the missing letter Elizabeth wrote to Bill?*

'What's on that sheet of paper?'

Pelham picks it up carefully, holds it before her eyes.

'The students were encouraged to write to their future selves. This looks like Chester's letter.'

I take a photo of it but I don't read it.

'I suggest we close the bunker up and leave all of this out. The police will need to see it.'

'The police? You think this might reopen the Primrose case?'

'It could,' I say. Any doubts I had about this year's podcast series are gone in an instant. This will be a blockbuster.

I message Tara: *You were right. You bloody beautiful, big-brained angel. I'm looking at the journal right now. You might have cracked this thing wide open!!*

TK

HE LOST HIS *dad.* I think about it the entire Tube ride back to the hotel. The Tube. It clicks. I know where I've seen him and I know where I've heard that name before: the black hair; those cold, blue eyes. *His dad died.* I google *Southgate train disaster,* scan through the images that come up. The little boy on the train. The blood from his shattered jaw. It's the most famous image from the disaster. Those eyes. It's him. It has to be him. *Gina O'Rourke comforts her son after her husband died in the train wreck.* A woman with red hair holds a twelve-year-old boy's bleeding face hard to her chest. Jesus Christ. I break out in a cold sweat. I can hear my heart in my ears.

Next I search *Gina O'Rourke.* An article from 2001.

Widow of Southgate victim arrested outside Primrose house.

This was the woman Fleur told Bill about. Michael's mother turned up with a knife at the Primrose house in London. I click through to another article, scroll fast. Steve O'Rourke is the man who died. He was a goalkeeper for Sutton United Football Club, a league-two soccer team. He played in the early nineties. There's a photo. The caption: *Steve leaves behind his loving wife, Gina, and son, Michael.*

Michael O'Rourke. My blood is humming in my veins as I march from the Tube station to my hotel. Means, motive and opportunity, he had them all, and, in Tate, the perfect alibi: no one was going to search for a man who supposedly wasn't even in the country at the time. That's how Michael O'Rourke got away with it. *Bill . . . he really could be innocent.* The worst place at the absolute worst time. Luck, fate, call it what you like, but it's starting to look like it's been deeply unkind to Bill.

I order some room service and plug my phone in to charge. I have a name now: Michael O'Rourke. And I know his family lived near Sutton in the south of London. I run a few searches and find a *G O'Rourke* listed online in the White Pages – there's an address and a phone number. As easy as that. *Who still has a landline these days?*

I call the number. A woman answers.

'Gina O'Rourke?' I say.

'No,' the voice says. 'Is this a telemarketing call?'

'No, I'm calling Gina on behalf of a journalist.'

'A journalist? Hang on, I'll just get her for you.'

A tingle of static runs over the skin of my face. 'Thank you.'

'Saying he's a journalist,' I hear, in the background.

A moment later, a new voice comes down the line, 'Yes?'

'Hello,' I say. 'My name's TK. I wanted to speak to you and your son.'

'My son?'

'Yes,' I say. 'I'm helping with a podcast.'

'Oh,' she says. 'What's this podcast about?'

'Simon Primrose.'

A long pause. 'What about Simon Primrose?'

'Well, it's about his death, and the death of his family.'

'What's that got to do with my son?'

Think, TK. I can't exactly tell her the truth.

'The producer wants to know what Simon was really like. I thought it would be good to speak to families who were affected by the Southgate disaster.'

'Affected?'

I clear my throat, wait for her to speak.

'Look, I don't really want to talk to any journos about this and my son won't either.'

'Well, I'd be happy to ask your son myself, if you could provide me with his phone number,' I say. I hold my breath.

'I don't have his number,' she says in a gravelly voice. 'He doesn't live in the UK anymore.'

Shit.

'Well, not to worry.' I press on. 'We'd still like to talk to you, if you don't mind? I won't take much of your time – I could come to speak to you in person, if that's better?'

'I said no.'

She's going to hang up.

'It's paid,' I blurt. 'We will pay you for an interview. Fifteen minutes, that's all.'

'How much?'

'One hundred pounds.'

'One hundred quid for fifteen minutes?'

'That's right.'

'What's the name of this podcast?'

'It's called *Legacy*,' I say. I hope Sloane doesn't mind me borrowing her credibility to get in the door.

'*Legacy*. Alright, bring the money and we can talk. Tomorrow?'

'Sure,' I say, thinking about my midday flight to Paris. 'Can we do morning, say eight?'

'Make it nine,' she says. It's going to be tight, but I'll make it work.

In the morning, I'm up early again. I pack my carry-on, check out of the hotel and take out one hundred pounds from an ATM on the walk to Liverpool Street Station. The Elizabeth line has me in Acton by half past eight.

Gina had told me she lived above a Nepalese restaurant with her husband and step-daughter. The restaurant is easy enough to find, and like most of the stores along the high street, it's closed at this hour. I see stairs at the rear of the building. I climb to the front door, raise my hand and knock.

'Just a minute.' A woman's voice. The door swings inward. I see her behind the security screen. It's the same woman in the images from the train disaster, but more than two decades on she's changed in all the ways you'd expect. She's in a nurse's uniform.

'Hello, ma'am,' I say. 'I am TK Phillips.'

'You here for the podcast?'

'Right, yes. That's me,' I say, ducking down slightly so our eyes are level.

'You're early. I said nine.' She pushes the screen door open to get a better view of me. She looks at my luggage and raises an eyebrow.

'I'm heading to the airport after this,' I explain, hoping it doesn't rattle her.

'Alright then, you better come in,' she says wearily. 'Leave that there for now.' She leads me into a small well-kept flat. A young woman sits on the couch staring at her phone. She doesn't rise or even look at me until Gina says, 'This is Chloe.' Then she gives a tiny wave and I see there's a baby in her arms. This place can't be more than two bedrooms.

Gina sits us down at a round dining table in the kitchen. 'Tea?' she says.

'No, thanks.'

'Alright,' she sits across from me, takes a vape from the table and draws on it before putting it down again. 'Where's your stuff?'

'Stuff?'

'I assume you have microphones.'

'Oh,' I say. 'I'm recording on my phone today.' I place it on the table. I can taste artificial grape flavour when I breathe in.

'And the money?'

'Here.' I take the bills from my wallet and hand them to her. She counts five twenty-pound notes, folds them and stuffs them in her pocket.

'Alright,' she says, touching her phone so the screen comes to life. 8.46 am.

'So,' I say. 'Tell me about the day of the disaster.'

I feel sick with guilt, making this woman revisit what was probably the hardest day of her life, but I can't just dive into questions about Michael. She may be protecting him or she may clam up if she realises why I'm really here. I'd distorted the truth, but it wasn't a complete fabrication: I am here on behalf of a podcast, but also on behalf of Bill too.

Gina runs me through the day she found out her husband had died. The details of the train crash are not new to me, but hearing them from her brings home the extent of the tragedy in a very real way. It's no wonder Simon was a pariah after this – nine people were killed, families forever changed.

When she mentions her son, I use it as an opportunity to tackle the question head-on.

'And Michael? You said he doesn't live in the UK anymore?'

She shakes her head. 'No,' she says. 'He left England a long time ago. I don't blame him really.'

'Oh,' I say. 'Where did he end up?'

'I have no idea. He went overseas, New Zealand, Australia, travelled all over.'

'You don't know where he lives now? You don't have a contact number for him? It might be useful for me to get his story.'

She shifts in her seat, folds her arms. She's shutting down. 'I can't help you,' she says. 'And I don't have a contact for him.'

I'm not sure if I believe her. 'How was he after the accident?' I say, trying to re-establish the connection.

'How do you think? He was badly hurt – his dad had just died.'

'Do you think he left the UK to escape it all, the memories of what happened?'

'What's this all got to do with your podcast?'

'Well, the decision Simon Primrose made concerning the safety . . .' her eyes seem to glaze over, 'and how it affected all the families involved. I think hearing from the children affected and how it's shaped their lives – that is important.'

She's silent, eyes closed for a moment. She takes the vape and draws deeply on it, still holding it in her fist when she crosses her arms again.

'Where are you from?' she says through the smoke.

'Me?' I say. Is this a test? 'New Zealand.'

'Are you going to tell me what this is really about?'

I eye the door. 'The crash and the Primrose family.'

'Why do you keep asking about Michael?'

He could be here, somewhere in the flat. Or . . . he could still be there in New Zealand. We're both looking at my phone, the little flicker of sound registering on the voice recorder app.

'You don't know where he is now or what he's doing? Did he stay in Australia?'

'He went over to New Zealand and he hasn't lived back here since. Last I heard from him he was working on a farm,' she says.

Something clogs in my throat. Sloane's words come back to me: *Gave me his life story already. South African, worked on a farm in the south.* The taxi driver, the one with the beard who was driving her around . . .

Impossible, I think. It just doesn't make sense – and yet I have this nagging feeling. He could be putting on a South African accent to disguise his British one – I think of a horror story out of Australia, every psychologist remembers it: a client was putting on an Irish accent to fool his psychologist and was stalking her. Michael O'Rourke might have never left and he might be keeping an eye on Sloane to make sure she doesn't discover his secret. I take the phone, jam it into my pocket. *No*, I think. *This is insane, TK*. It can't be.

'Sorry, I've got a flight to catch. We might have to wrap things up.'

I need to call Sloane right now. What's the time in New Zealand? It must be late.

SLOANE

'BACK TO THE motel?' Dean asks when I slip into the front seat.

'Yes, please.'

'So, what did you find?'

'Something big,' I say, my heart still racing.

I upload the video recording of the journal and send it to Tara and Esteban, then screenshot each individual page to read in the car. Her handwriting is neat.

'At the school? What could you be searching for there? With the excavator?' *Shit*. I can already see word getting out. I've got the NDAs for the others.

'Dean, I probably don't need to ask you this but you've not mentioned anything to anyone about me or what I've found?'

'Me? No. I mentioned to a couple of driver mates I've got a good gig driving you around but nothing else.'

'Right,' I say. 'I might need you to sign something, if that's okay. A non-disclosure agreement. Sorry if it seems over the top, but we've got to be really careful.'

He smiles. 'No worries, I know what an NDA is,' he says. 'You didn't find a body, did you?' he jokes.

'Not quite so exciting. Just a journal,' I say. My phone is almost flat, I plug it into Dean's charger. My skin tingling and hands lightly trembling. 'Actually, not *just* a journal: Elizabeth Primrose's journal.' I still can't believe it.

'A journal,' he repeats.

'Mmm,' I say, not really listening. I open the first screen shot and I start to read.

What life is there for us here? In this strange new country, this town where everything runs at half speed, where people smile when you pass. Obviously it will take a little while to get used to it but I'm struggling to adjust more than anyone else. It's different and they treat me like an oddity, as if my accent is a large scar on my face. In London it was common to hear so many different accents, even different languages, that I suppose I took it for granted that the rest of the world was a bit like that, but it's really not. My classmates are all alike, with the exception of the exchange students.

Isn't it bizarre that so many people here are of British heritage and yet they act like I'm from another planet? Daddy calls it a bicultural country. Māori and white, he says, but at school it's almost exclusively white, or Pākehā, as they say. There's one Māori girl in my class, we get on really well.

Daddy's the one who settled in the fastest. He's back to playing golf, he has friends, he travels. Other than a chef, he's basically set us up within the space of a couple of months. Mummy's busy with the house, but she'll make friends. Even Chet is doing better than I am. He's made one or two friends at his school. He's much more adaptable, happy-go-lucky Chet. As much as he annoys me, I'm glad he's settled in.

I'm sure he misses his friends, God knows I miss mine. Daddy said it would be easy to keep in contact using the internet but it's much more difficult than I thought. They're on messenger when I'm asleep and they're asleep when I get home from school. I miss Harvey most of all. I know we promised to keep in touch, I know we promised to see each other again in the future. I love him, and he said he loved me too. We speak on the phone when we can but it's hard because we both know it will be months, maybe years, before we see each other. He must feel it too.

Anyway. Time for sleep. Hopefully things get better soon.

I feel a little sick, reading while in a moving car, but I can't stop. Or maybe it's a matter of consent – I have this queasy feeling that I should not be in this girl's head. But it's important for the case. It's important for Bill. I flick to the next entry.

Mummy hired a chef today. She was raving to Daddy about how young he was for someone with such experience. He can start immediately and he can live in the cottage. Perfect for Mummy and Daddy, who demand loyalty and dedication. They'd had trouble finding someone, there'd been a couple of interviews and Mummy must have been getting tired of cooking all of our meals. I wonder how long he will last. The gardener already got fired. I hope he can cook good vegetarian.

He's going to live in the cottage with Fleur, poor him! I still can't believe she travelled halfway across the *planet just to keep working with us. Daddy said it was because it's a good job and she likes us, but I know the truth. We don't need an au pair, not full time. I'm basically an adult and Chet's a teenager. It makes me sick to think about it. What if he's doing it again?*

Next entry.

I've not heard from Harvey for a few days now - we promised to talk every day. In an odd way, I've found as time has gone on, I've missed him less. Not more. Less. The heart is a strange organ. I've read that somewhere. I think it's true. Maybe I will get a tattoo of that.

So much is happening at home: the gardens are a mess, Mummy is doing them herself, doing the best she can after Daddy fired the old gardener. Daddy also came to school to have a meeting with Mr Koenig and Mrs Darcy. I don't know what it was about, but I assume it was me. Mummy and Daddy are worried I haven't settled into the new school well.

In other news: Bill the new chef is great. The food is nice, and he always makes an extra effort to prepare veggie options for me. Daddy thinks I'm getting anaemic without meat because I've been sleepy and a bit down, but I think I'm just homesick.

Bill is young actually, just a few years older than me. And he's got nice, kind eyes. Chet is obsessed with him, probably because he rides a skateboard. I think he is sweet, not up himself like most guys. 'Common', Aunt Lizzie would say, but I think he's the exact opposite. Uncommon. Kindness is uncommon. I wonder if he has a girlfriend. Sometimes I see him with his phone outside, sending messages. I wonder who she is and what she looks like. I bet she is really beautiful.

School isn't much better but at least I'm making a couple of friends and some of the teachers are really nice too.

I flick to the next image and find more.

It's been an eventful week. Chet has taken up skateboarding, and I've found him snooping through my things. He shouldn't be in my room, he's a little pest and Mummy and Daddy won't tell him off for it. They just criticise me and let him do what he wants.

One of the girls at school asked if I wanted to come drink at her house. I didn't know what to say, or how to say it, or what happened between my brain and my mouth that caused me to spurt out some ridiculous story about a non-existent family commitment. Why am I so bad at making new friends now?

I've been talking to Bill a bit more, watching him cook. I told him I want to learn, but mostly I just want someone to talk to and he's a good listener. He asks questions, smiles at the right moments, he likes stories, my stories. He's kind of good-looking. But obviously not someone I could ever see myself with. What on earth would my parents think? Daddy would disown me. Or worse.

So she was attracted to him. Another entry. I read on.

News. So much news. My goodness, there's not enough pages in this book to capture all of the gossip but I'll keep it brief. Daddy hired a new gardener. Tate is his name and he has been hanging around like a bad smell. Coming to the house even when he's not working. I even found him in my room!! When I asked him why, he simply told me he wanted to see how the garden looked from above, he wanted to make sure all the flowers looked pretty for me. He said it so politely that I almost missed the smirk underneath it all. I don't really trust him, but Daddy says he went to school with Tate's father and that Tate is an Oxford man.

There's something else that's happened that has completely freaked me out. A note in my school bag. It said: I'm watching you. You are beautiful. It must be some kind of sick joke from one of my classmates.

So this is where the notes begin: after Tate arrived. I flick to the next image and find the next entry.

At school, I found another note in my bag. I think it was from one of the boys but I can't be sure. I don't want to put the words down here in my journal but it was gross. Someone telling me what they wanted to do to me. I threw it away because I am sure they just want a reaction from me.

At least MK has been nice to me lately, even though I didn't really like him at first, he is not so bad. I feel like I can talk to him, and it's good to have a friend here, an adult I can talk to when I need to. There is also Bill, but there's things I don't want to tell him because he might think I am just a silly kid and I don't really want him to see me like that because you never know what could happen in the future.

MK . . . who is MK? Tate Mercer-Kemp?

Another note in my bag today! It's scaring me. This was less disgusting but somehow worse. I didn't notice it all day but I found it when I got home. Someone in my PE class must have put it there or . . . maybe our teacher. No, our teacher is nice, he's always been so kind and friendly. I don't know what to do, if it's a bully then it would only please them to see me go to the teachers or the principal. I wonder if I should tell someone? Get some advice . . . what would MK say? What if it's really from a boy? This is what it said:

I know how you look at me. I know what you want and you're going to get it soon. I promise.

Do I ignore it, hope it goes away? I can't imagine who would think I'm looking at them that way. I'm not interested in any of the boys. I don't know what to do. I don't want to go to school anymore. I just want it to stop.

I feel tightness in my throat. Was it really the teacher or someone else?

Tate has disappeared!!!!! He stole something, a family heirloom. Mummy's comb. I knew it in my bones that he was bad, even if he acted nice sometimes!! Daddy was very angry. He seems like a different person in this country . . . maybe it's this house? The way he lined all the staff up and berated them. I just wanted to go down and hold Bill's hand. I hate it when Daddy treats people like that.

I'm liking Bill more and more. Maybe it's a distraction, but I don't know, it might be more than that. He ACTUALLY hunts animals but for some reason it doesn't upset me. He kills them himself, with his own hands. He understands what it's like, where food comes from, not just the supermarket but the natural world. He treats me like an adult and talks to me about ideas bigger than school and family. Maybe he feels what I feel? He calls me goose sometimes. Is that flirting or am I just some silly girl he works for?

I don't know anymore what I feel for Harvey. I feel disloyal sometimes when I am talking to Bill, because I know I like him too. Harvey sent me a message the other night and it just said: When will you be home again? And I couldn't give him an answer because I just didn't know. He told me once he loved me, and that he would always love me. He told me one day we would marry and have loads of kids. I don't know if I believe it anymore.

Another entry on the next page.

I've been studying for the mid-year exams, but there's a lot to catch up on in the curriculum and I've been distracted. There was another note at school, I told one of the girls in my class, Tania. She said I had to tell a teacher. She said it's definitely Mr du Plessis, the PE teacher, but I don't think it is. I still think it has to be someone playing a prank.

Fleur is acting weirder than normal! She is disappearing at nights. I'm up late a lot and I see her *sometimes leaving the cottage and walking down toward the road. Maybe she's met a man. Or maybe she's planning on leaving. Maybe she's finally had enough.*

The next entry.

I heard Mummy and Bill talking after her garden party. BILL SLEPT WITH FLEUR!!! It sounds like it's over now but WHY HER!!!!

Fleur, who blackmailed my father. Fleur, who came to our house knowing why the previous nannies hadn't worked out. Knowing what Daddy had done with them. I still remember it when I was only seven or eight. Mummy was away, I was supposed to be in bed. Leaning against the door and listening as Fleur told him what she knew about him: she told him that she knew previous nannies from our home, and they had all reported him, that he was touching them and stuff. She said she would tell the press, the papers. Daddy's career would be ruined. I felt sick listening, I didn't believe it then but now ... it must be true, because why else wouldn't he have just fired her there and then?? She sounded so fierce, she sounded like she was capable of anything. And now Bill and her ...

I think this means he is single now. And maybe that he is lonely, like me. I feel like to be honest, I should tell him that I have feelings for him. I will write him a letter. I will tell him how I feel. It's the easiest, least awkward way to do it.

The letter is real. My head is swimming. I could cry. The tragedy of it all – this innocent girl with her naïve concerns is about to have her life destroyed. And Simon had been inappropriate with other staff, Fleur was holding it over him. It does feel icky, entering her world like this, but I need the truth. I look up, take a few big breaths.

'Mind if I open the window?' I say.

'Go ahead,' Dean responds. 'Feeling sick?'

'A little. I can't stop reading.'

Before #MeToo, guys like Simon Primrose probably thought themselves untouchable. And he likely tried something on with Fleur. No doubt that's what caused the confrontation Elizabeth overheard. I read the next page.

> Coiling, twisting anxiety. It's constant. I feel sick every time I see a shred of paper in my bag. Who is putting them there? Bill hasn't said or done anything since I left him a letter in his room, it's like he just screwed it up and tossed it in the bin. Or maybe Daddy has intervened in some way. I wish he had no control over anyone or anything. I wish he would just let me live and make my own decisions.

The following entry is longer.

> It's not every day the principal calls on you himself. He told me he knew I was having trouble settling in. Perhaps Mummy and Daddy noticed how down I've been, how much I miss home. Maybe they prompted it. He called me to tell me he would do everything he could to make it easy for me to find my feet and study. He seems like he really cares. If I had any courage or any sense, I would have told him then and there about the notes but I couldn't. I just smiled and told him everything was okay and I'm perfectly happy. I lied.

There was something else too. I saw Tate!! I'm sure of it. He was at the gate this afternoon, looking up at the house. In the middle of the night, I heard footsteps in the house too. Could that have been him? When I told Daddy, he said it couldn't be him. He said he checked with the police and that Tate had left the country. So am I seeing a ghost? Is that what's happening? Daddy said it must have been Bill or Fleur I heard in the house.

Bill also reported potentially seeing him in a car after he'd supposedly left the country. What if the immigration records were wrong, or . . . what if Tate was not who he claimed to be? My phone rings, startling me. It's TK. He's awake.

'Hello, TK?' I check my watch, it's almost 10 pm, which means the morning in London.

'Sloane,' he says, breathless. 'Listen, I think you need to be careful.'

I feel heat at the back of my neck. 'Careful? What do you mean?'

We're still driving, surely we're close to the motel. *Wait, how long have we been driving?*

'Someone was impersonating Tate Mercer-Kemp, it's possible he used the real Tate's departure as an alibi. That person, Michael O'Rourke, well, he might still be in New Zealand. Apparently he was working on a farm.'

I feel dizzy. The motion sickness seems to be intensifying. I look up at the road ahead, lit by headlights. The white lines slide beneath, flashing. The country outside is dark.

'What do you mean?' I say.

'Look, it might be nothing, but I just remember something you said about your driver.'

'My driver?'

The phone flies from my hand.

I yelp and look across. Dean has grabbed the cable and tugged. He snatches my handset from where it falls between us.

'What are you doing?' I demand. He ends the call.

'The journal,' he says. 'I'm going to read it.'

My head swims. 'What the fuck?'

Your driver . . . working on a farm. Dean?

He has a strange energy in his eyes. 'Let's not play games, Sloane,' he says, pulling into an unfamiliar road. *Actually . . . where the fuck are we?* 'Surely you've figured it out.'

Figured what out? Am I looking at the man who claimed to be Tate Mercer-Kemp?

I reach out. Dean holds me off with his forearm. I see blood where my nails catch his skin.

He presses me away, against the door, not with a great deal of force but enough to show me how easily he could subdue me.

'Give me my phone, Dean!'

I feel like my heart is going to give up. This moment feels unreal. Is this really him? Has he been driving me around, watching and waiting to see what I found out? Has he been fucking *enjoying* this? The car slows. He angles it onto the shoulder of the road and pulls up.

'You're him,' I say. TK wanted to warn me. Tate, or his impersonator, is still in the country. 'You were there, back then. You knew the family.'

His expression doesn't change. He just stares me in the eye, my phone squeezed in his fist.

TK

MY FLIGHT, IF I make it in time, leaves in two hours. The call with Sloane ended abruptly but reception could be patchy in Cambridge. *What if she was with him?* No, it's late in New Zealand. It's likely she would be back at her accommodation. I try her again anyway. It goes straight to voicemail. She'll call me when she wakes again, I'm sure.

A black cab stops for me on High Street, Acton.

'Heathrow,' I say.

He starts the meter and off we go.

Tate Mercer-Kemp is actually Michael O'Rourke, whose father was killed in the Southgate train disaster that many believe Simon Primrose was responsible for.

What does this mean for Bill?

I think about the gas heater, the fact Tate was never investigated because he was supposedly out of the country. Now we know that someone with an axe to grind was in the country, was in the house.

I check in for my flight, get through security. I board the plane, chew my usual pre-flight Valium and brace for the inevitable panic as the engines start.

After I land at Charles de Gaulle, I pick up a rental car fairly seamlessly. I am racking up the expenses for Sloane, but it'll all be worth it to her, I hope. Fleur's Airbnb in Montargis is about ninety minutes from the airport. I plug my phone in and open Google maps. But the car's phone charger is busted. I am almost out of juice, so I briefly consider turning the car around, but I want to get on the road, and there's a GPS anyway. I manage to switch it to English, and punch in the address. Bingo.

I head out of the airport, my blood pressure rising as I negotiate my way through Paris. Once I am out of the city, I relax a touch and just concentrate on staying on the right side of the road. Beautiful scenes flash by the window, but I am not in a mood to appreciate the views.

If Fleur cannot confirm that the Facebook picture I have of Michael O'Rourke is the man she knew as Tate Mercer-Kemp, then it's game over. I've come here for nothing. At least she might also be able to give me a little more insight into the relationship between Bill and Elizabeth.

I press my foot down, and in eighty minutes exactly, I'm pulling into a country lane. I follow the unsealed road for a couple of kilometres, before I am notified that I've reached my destination. I park the car, get out with my bag and stretch my legs, surveying the picturesque property.

The house is classic French bucolic style, with a white painted exterior, old stone features and creeping vines. The Airbnb accommodation is self-contained in a converted stable about fifty metres from the main house. The check-in instructions said to knock on the farmhouse door, and that Fleur, the hostess, would be there to introduce herself and show guests around.

I walk up to the house, as a diminutive woman appears at the front door. She is thin, her dark hair streaked with elegant grey strands that some women would pay a hair stylist good money for.

'Te Kuru?' she says. 'Welcome, bienvenue!'

'Hi,' I say. I put my bag down, offer my hand. She takes it. 'Call me TK.'

'TK,' she says. 'Welcome to my home.'

'It's beautiful,' I respond, looking about.

'Thank you. We try to keep it looking nice but it's easy in this part of the country.'

'I bet.'

'What brings you all the way to France?'

'I've never been.' A non-answer but right now is not the time to tell her why I'm really here.

'Well, you have good weather while you are here. Anyway, let me give you a tour.'

She leads me into the house. 'This is my home, but where you will stay is the stables, or écurie. It once was used as a real stable, when we bought the property. But no horses anymore, and we converted it. We do have a few of our own cows, sheep, a small orchard, a very large vegetable garden.'

'It's a lovely property,' I say. 'Can I quickly charge my phone?'

'Sure,' she says. 'We have an adapter if you need it.'

She takes my charger and plugs it in in the kitchen.

I follow her through the main part of the lodging, the dining area, with a flatscreen TV mounted to one wall. She holds some keys out to me. My hands are shaking a little as I take them, and she seems to notice.

'Too much coffee,' I say, by way of explanation. 'Helps with the jetlag.'

'It must be late back home, no?'

'Very late, or very early. So, your family lives here?' I say.

'Just my husband. He is working but won't be long.'

I can't say precisely what I was expecting of Fleur. She was, by all accounts, distraught about the killings, catatonic. But now she seems balanced, happy, a normal middle-aged woman.

'Your English is very good,' I say as she leads me to the rear of the house.

'Thank you. I lived in London for a while and I actually spent some time in New Zealand, this was years ago.'

'How did you find it?'

She sighs. 'It was the worst year of my life in New Zealand, actually. It was stressful, my job.'

Do I tell her now? *I know, Fleur. I know what happened. That's why I'm here.*

Her look is weary in the fading light. She reaches and turns the light on. She shows me a sad smile. 'Maybe that's a story for the morning. Let me show you the bedroom.' And like that, the moment is gone.

SLOANE

'YOU WERE THERE,' I say again. 'At the house.'

He ignores me. 'What's your passcode?'

'Why?'

'Please, don't make this any more difficult than it needs to be.'

I suppose I don't have a choice. '1989.'

'Original,' he says. I don't tell him it's not actually my birth year. It's a Taylor Swift album. Hardly seems relevant given the circumstances.

'The journal, it's in your photos?'

'Yes.'

He's perfectly calm, which should help keep me calm, but it has the opposite effect. It's like this is an everyday situation.

'What do you plan on doing with this, the journal? Will it be made public?'

'I don't know,' I say. 'It doesn't have to be.'

We're not near my motel. We're not near anywhere I recognise. There are no houses out here, just endless, dark fields. It's much more barren than Cambridge.

'We can't prove anything,' I say, my voice desperate. 'You realise that. We don't have any proof of who you are or what you did.'

I eye the door handle. I could run.

'No one drives along here,' he says.

I reach for my seatbelt. Press the clip gently. His eyes cut to me.

'Don't do that,' he says. 'Stay right there.'

'I'm just taking my belt off, okay. I'm getting more comfortable.'

'What did I do?' he asks, staring at the phone, reading.

'What?'

He turns to me. 'You said you don't have any proof of what I did.'

'I don't know what you did, that's the point. I mean, if you did anything—'

'What do you think I did?' he says, his eyes on the screen. He's reading the journal entries.

What does he want to hear? I feel both electrified and numb, as if I wouldn't be able to move even if I wanted to. 'I think you were angry, you lost your father. I think you changed your name—'

'I was angry?' he says.

'Maybe not angry. Aggrieved, frustrated. I don't know. Maybe you didn't hurt the family at all. Or you didn't mean to.'

'You believe I killed them, the family?'

'I think you couldn't bear what Simon Primrose took away from you, how much his actions cost you.'

His eyebrows narrow. 'It wasn't just Simon's fault,' he says. 'He just did what anyone would do in his position.'

I continue speaking. 'Maybe you wanted revenge.'

He gives a small, cynical laugh.

'You played your part to gain access to the house. You discovered a way you could get him back – you could punish him and take from him what he took from you. You didn't care about his family or who else got hurt; they would all just go to sleep.' I'm seeing it all with such clarity now. 'You studied the heating. You blocked the exhaust.'

He looks up at me, an impossibly calm expression on his face. He is a sociopath, a cold-blooded killer.

'Tate, the real Tate, left the country, as he'd planned to do and as you knew he would. You'd rigged the heating to poison them, but it hadn't worked yet despite the cold, so one night you snuck into the home, you turned the thermostat up. You hid. You waited. You got Bill's knife – you knew he'd be the one everybody thought did it. You probably went into the master bedroom first; they were out of it but not dead. And you stabbed them. First, Simon and Gwen, then Chester. You didn't realise Elizabeth, Elle, was conscious. Her window was open, she wasn't poisoned.' I can see him there, creeping through the house. 'When you went to her, she fought, she screamed and you panicked. You stabbed her last. Then you fled.'

He has stopped reading the phone now. He just stares at me.

'But I can't prove any of this,' I say. 'No one else knows, not my team, not the police. No one. You don't need to do this, you don't need to hurt me. I can't prove you did anything at al—'

'No,' he says. 'Of course you can't.'

I move an inch closer to the door. I could reach the handle and run. I need to keep him distracted.

'We won't do the podcast. We just won't do it. You're right. I don't even know who you are. I don't know your real name. Bill practically confessed to his lawyer, and I found out that the white Holden Commodore gave him a lift to the house. So, we say it was Bill. It was him all along. We release a press statement with those new facts, and no one will ever question it again. I'll go back to Melbourne, you will never see me or hear from me ever again.'

'Sloane, you do know my name,' he says.

'You know, I think Simon had it coming. That train crash, all the people who died. All those families, their lives ruined. His nannies, too – you know he was assaulting his nannies, he was cheating on his wife and he bullied his son. He was selfish, he moved his whole family across the world because of his ego. And . . . and . . . the way he treated Bill, the way he treated everyone. He was a bad man. I know that. I can leave this alone, I can.'

But I know that he can't let me go. Another inch closer. I slowly reach for the door handle, my eyes fixed on the centre console, anywhere but his eyes. I can feel my pulse at my temple, heat all over my body. I have only one shot at this.

I snatch the door handle, push and run.

TK

'UNFORTUNATELY, YOU MUST go outside to reach the room but it's a nice place to sleep,' Fleur says.

'Sure,' I say, following her.

She leads me out past a firepit between the buildings.

'This was once full of hay but now we have insulated it, and divided it up to make a couple of rooms.' The cicadas' ceaseless trill rings over the land.

'The stonework is beautiful.'

She turns back. 'You think so? We replaced the roof last year. It was hard to find slate that would match the original tiles.'

I glance up, eyes wide in the fading light. I notice newer bricks halfway up the wall; they're a good match to the old ones but the grout gives them away.

'Patch-up job?' I say.

'Oh, that, yes.' It looks fresh.

'This is your room,' she says, opening a bolt then turning the handle. The door swings outward. She gestures for me to enter. I look back, take in the landscape under the darkening sky.

'Go on,' she says. I turn, step forward. It's dark. 'The light switch is just inside, reach out to your left.' I go further into the dark room. Then I see a bucket. *A bucket?*

New roof? Is it leaking? But that's not the only thing that doesn't make sense. There are no windows, no evidence of new insulation. Something else pings my senses. *The bolt – it was on the outside.*

I turn back. 'Fleur,' I say. She's standing there, watching me, silhouetted by the twilight sky above the distant trees.

The door closes. I run forward, reach for the handle. The room becomes dark. A rusty bolt slides into place.

'I'm sorry, TK,' she says, her voice blunted by the steel door between us. 'You'll have to stay in here for now.'

'What's going on?' I say. I try to keep the panic from my voice but it's there nonetheless, thrumming just below the surface. A thought lodges like a shard of glass in my brain: *She knows who you are.*

'What is happening, open up!'

A long pause. Is she there?

'Fleur? Answer me, what are you doing?' I bang hard on the door with my fist.

'You are friends with Bill Kareama,' she says. 'Aren't you?'

I swallow hard. My phone is in the house.

'Please, just open the door. I can explain.'

'I looked your name up, we do it with all guests. I read about you, your friendship with him. We've had other people come stay over the years, people interested in the case. But never someone who actually knows Bill, someone who lied about their intentions. We're going to have to figure out what to do with you when my husband gets home.'

'Fleur, you don't need to do this. I just want to talk.'

Footsteps. She's leaving. I feel my way to the light switch. I let my vision adjust and look about. She has me trapped, like a bug pinned to a board, quivering.

'Fleur?' I call. Then louder. 'Fleur!'

I can think my way out of this. The bucket – can I use it to break through the door? What about the roof – could I scale the wall, tear through the tiles? It's madness, I realise. Strength, brainpower; nothing is getting me out of this room. I stop and listen for any sign of what's to come, but I hear nothing but my own ragged breath.

SLOANE

MY HEART LURCHES as I launch out of the car and sprint back the way we came. The ache of fatigue weighs heavy on me after just a few seconds and my jeans might as well be shackles. Dean's out of the car before I get far. I don't look back, just go, each breath heaving out of scorched lungs.

'Hey!' he calls. 'Stop!'

But it's too late. I can't stop. Instead, I run along the straight road, blood pounding in my ears. I taste copper in my throat. It's empty out here, no light all the way to the horizon. How far will I make it before I collapse? His footsteps clap the road, closer and closer. I turn toward the fence, the desert terrain beyond it. I jump, hit it, my feet catch and I tip over the other side. The ground flies up, knocks my breath from me. Glancing back, I see him shoot toward me. I get up, go again. His feet hit the grass. He's so close. I sprint ahead into the unknown.

'Help!' I yell.

His voice is behind me but terror has blocked out all stimuli except for the burn in my chest, the ache in my calves.

'Help!' Fear contorts my voice. 'Please! Leave me alone!'

'Stop, Sloane!' But I don't listen. Then he hits me. A hard tackle from behind that wraps me up, turns me. Somehow, I hit the ground softly, we roll. I scream but he covers my mouth. I brace for a blow, or a knife. I squirm and kick.

'Stay still for God's sake,' he says.

I can't stop, the panic has seized me. I manage to raise my knee but it just slides impotently up his thigh. His grip loosens and I try to twist out but he soon has a handful of my hair.

'Are you insane?' he shouts. 'Look around!' But I won't. His weight presses into me. I'm wild, savage, incensed. I'm 100 per cent instinct, biting the air, kicking out, limbs thrashing.

'Stop! If you run off out there, no one will see you again. We are in the middle of nowhere.'

He's pointing. I follow his finger with my eyes.

'There will be a bloody frost tonight.' He sounds angry but his eyes have softened. 'Not to mention the fog. You'll get lost.'

He takes his hand from my mouth. My breathing is loud, like an animal snared. I feel the cold on my spine. It tastes like blood in my throat.

'Please, just let me go. I won't go to the police.'

'No,' he said. 'You won't.'

'Please?' I beg. I can feel tears now.

'Stop, Sloane. Just listen. You've got it all wrong.'

I don't believe him. 'Just let me go. Let me go! Please, Tate.'

'Tate?'

'Michael, whatever your real name is.'

He stands, pulling me up, hauling me over his shoulder like a sack of potatoes. Despite how much I kick, scream, scratch, try to bite him, I can't escape his grip. He takes me back toward the fence. He doesn't put me down as he climbs over. I feel like a child, weak now with the fatigue setting into my bones.

'Let me go!' The adrenaline is fading. I think about the images from the murders. He did that. He killed those people.

'Don't run,' he says. 'It's freezing and you'll get lost out there. Trust me.' He lowers me, grips my upper arms.

'Just leave me here. I can get home. Please, just leave me. Your secret is safe.'

'Listen to me,' he says, bending down so his eyes are meeting mine. 'I didn't stab them. I didn't kill them. I don't know what happened that night.'

'The heater?'

He draws a breath, glances past me. I sense for the first time since I met him that the mask is slipping. He's about to tell me the truth.

'I brought you here to talk. I want to tell you everything but first I want Elle's journal. I need to finish reading it all. That's all I want, Sloane.'

TK

IT'S BEEN A couple of hours. I stopped banging on the door a while ago; this building is not close enough to any of the neighbours to be heard. The cicadas' song is like an alarm out there too. There's no room in my head for Michael O'Rourke, or Sloane, or what's she's found out; it's filled instead with a constant hum of panic. Time passes, the cicadas die down and I hear the sound of a car engine. A few minutes later, voices growing louder. Arguing. My high-school French is impotent against the rapid-fire speech.

Then there's one word I recognise. *It can't be*, I think.

The word is 'Michael'.

Michael? Why would they be talking about Michael? My heart pitches against my sternum. I feel sweat on my brow, heat all over. I'm in trouble.

Michael O'Rourke . . . Fleur was seeing a man. He was her alibi; there is CCTV footage of her arriving and not leaving until much later. The police didn't know what Tate looked like so they wouldn't even question the man who confirmed Fleur's whereabouts. It's so simple. The perfect alibi. The perfect crime. Could her husband be the same man? Could her alibi from that night, and the man she's arguing with outside, be Michael O'Rourke? No . . . I squeeze my eyes closed, thinking through it all. *No, it can't be.*

But if it is true, what would they do to keep their secret?

More arguing in impenetrable French breaks my stream of thought. His accent isn't like hers. Panic races through my veins like a narcotic.

The bolt slides open, the door swings. I see the shape of a man in the dark. He steps into the light. Even through the stubble, I see the way the skin pulls where a scar runs from the corner of his mouth over his cheek.

I've found him.

Fleur met him at the house. They shared a hatred. They were in a relationship. They framed Bill.

'Why are you here?' he barks in crisp English.

I keep his gaze, but it doesn't clear the fist-sized stone in my throat. 'Please—'

'Why are you here?!' This man has an aura of easy violence.

'Please, just let me go.' My voice wavers.

He shakes his head. 'Tell me why you came to our house.'

'I just wanted to talk.'

'Talk? You flew halfway around the world *just to talk.* You don't have a phone?'

'I don't have your number,' I say. 'I didn't think Fleur would respond over the phone.'

'You are Bill Kareama's friend,' he says. 'Did he send you?'

'Psychologist,' I say. 'Not friend.' I see a vein at his temple. 'And friend too, yes. He is, or he was, my friend, but I'm trying to speak with everyone who was involved in the case.'

'Why lie your way into our home?' his voice booms. 'Why didn't you tell Fleur when you arrived?'

'Okay,' I say, realising honesty might be the best option. Or something close to honesty. 'I wanted to tell her, I was going to.'

'And me?'

'I don't even know who you are.'

The look in his eyes suggests he knows I'm lying.

'Look, I can just leave.'

He takes another step closer. I'm cornered like a rat. Something has changed in his eyes, a wildness has come over him. Fleur speaks, more French darting from her mouth. I sense she is urging him to stop, but it's possible she's encouraging him.

'Fleur,' I say, speaking over his shoulder. 'There is a record of me coming here. The GPS on my phone, the GPS in the car. The Airbnb booking.'

'Why is that important?' he snaps.

'It's important because I can be traced here. It means I'm leaving your property right now, and you can't stop me.' I step forward, but he doesn't move. He's shorter, but with wide strong shoulders and that wild look in his eyes.

'Is that right?' he says.

Then he speaks French again, turning his head to direct his words over his shoulder. His words become louder, harsher. She gives a terse nod then retreats, closing the door behind her, locking it. It's just him and me. He's sent her back to the house, but why?

'They'll arrest you, Michael. They will know. And they will extradite you for the murders of Simon, Gwen and Chester Primrose, along with the attempted murder of Elizabeth Primrose.'

He grins, the scar on his face curling a little. 'You don't know what you're talking about.'

'You got the job. You blocked the exhaust of the heating unit. But it wasn't enough.'

The door opens behind him. Fleur is in the door frame. He turns back. I see it now, what's in her hands. A hunting rifle. She holds it, aimed in our direction.

'No,' I say. 'You can't do this.'

'You're a big man, we don't want you hurting us.'

'You framed Bill, didn't you? You stabbed them to punish them for what happened to your father.'

He says something in French, and Fleur comes closer, she holds the rifle out to him. *They're going to kill me.* This is happening. I try to slow my breathing, watch as she holds it upright, and he reaches back.

I don't think. I take my chance. I step forward, hit him hard in the face, a big-fisted punch, my whole body behind it. I hear a crack. We both lurch to the floor. Fleur screams. I find my bearings, reach for the gun. We grapple on the ground. I feel steel and clench my hand around it. Fingers press into my eyes. I howl but don't release the barrel. I throw out an elbow, feel it hit something hard.

The gun loosens. I pull it. It comes free, sliding from Michael's grip. I roll over, scramble to my feet and aim it. Michael stands slowly, raising his hands.

'Big fucker, aren't you?' he says. Blood runs from his nose, he turns his head to spit onto the dusty floor. Fleur is back in the door frame.

'Put it down!' she screams.

'It's okay,' Michael says. 'He's not going to use it.'

'Where's my phone?' I say. 'Give it to me!'

'Do you understand how much it takes for a man to be violent?' Michael says gruffly, coming a step closer. 'Violence only comes easy for psychopaths; others live with it forever. They relive it, over and over.'

'I'm not messing around, where is my phone? I'm calling the police, you can't just lock someone up, pull a gun on them.'

He ignores me, steps forward once. 'When I slaughter animals, I know it changes me a little each time. I'm grateful for their meat, I know it is necessary, but it is trauma. To hurt a human is

343

trauma – you know this, as a psychologist. You know what a person goes through when they see violence firsthand, when they experience it. But each time, it gets a little easier. Each time, something calcifies inside until violence is all they know. But it is hard at first.'

It chills me how calm he is with a hunting rifle pointed at his chest. I check the safety. It's off.

'Don't fucking move,' I say. 'Fleur, if you don't go get my phone right now, I will shoot your husband in the head.'

'Put it down!' she yells.

'You know that if you pull that trigger, you will never be the same. You will see my face every night when you go to sleep, every morning when you wake. You will lose your identity. You will be a killer. I'm giving you a chance to escape.'

'You're giving *me* a chance? Get down on your knees, right now.'

I just need to get out of this room, to my car. I need the police. He steps forward. 'Take your chance. Go on. Put the gun down. Walk out that door.'

I shake my head. 'Don't come any closer.'

Another step. He could reach out and grab the end of the gun. I back up. I don't want to do it. My hands are shaking. I could shoot his leg. I could slow him down. *Centre mass.* Isn't that what they say? I aim lower, right at his navel.

He steps forward again. 'You're afraid, you're more afraid than I am.'

'Fleur,' I say. 'Stop him. It doesn't need to be this way.'

Fleur issues another line of panicked French. Michael shakes his head, grins. '*Non,*' he says to her.

This time, when I move away, my back hits the wall.

'I don't have a choice,' I say, more to Fleur than Michael. 'If you move forward again, I will pull the trigger. Don't do it. Just get on your knees and we will all get out of here alive.'

He shakes his head, the swaggering look of an insolent boy. My hands are moist. I can hear my breathing but I steady the gun with both hands. He steps forward, reaches for the barrel. I brace, tense everything. I squeeze the trigger.

SLOANE

'I WAS ON track for a career in rugby when I hurt my back in the last year of school,' Dean says. 'It was all I knew. But suddenly I was in rehab and I realised I needed a plan B, so I studied teaching. I tried to get back into playing but the injury would come and go, and eventually I decided to travel instead. New Zealand was my first choice. I was twenty-two and St Luke's was the first position I applied for.'

He clears his throat, leans against the car. 'They offered me the job immediately. Physical education at an elite private school, in an affluent country – it seemed easy enough but I should have known better. There was so much more to my job than teaching the kids during the day. They wanted a rugby coach, probably more than they wanted a physical education teacher. So I did both, helping out with the First XV as the forwards coach and also running Year 12 PE.'

It's cold. I hold my elbows, shivering.

'Why don't we sit in the car?'

I shake my head, still rattled by everything.

'Anyway, I moved for the job and took the opportunity to live in this great country. They put me up, in a small shack on the farmland that St Luke's owned beside the school, which meant I didn't have to pay rent or expenses. We hate the All Blacks in South Africa but we love Kiwis. We have a rich shared history and a rivalry. I enjoyed my time here, at first. It's safer for one, and I could save more money. I didn't have much of a social life but it was the ideal job.'

'You were her teacher, Elizabeth's?'

He nods. 'It's a strange dynamic, being just a few years older than the students and teaching them. I was in good shape, looked after myself. I didn't touch a drop of alcohol and worked out at the school gym most nights. Not so much a gym junkie these days,' he says, patting his belly. He stands further from me now, in the cold, moonlit air. It must be almost midnight. 'I'd hear occasional comments from some of the girls. Just between themselves.' He takes a moment here. 'Then there was the graffiti. A student had written something in the girl's change room.'

'What did it say?'

'It was juvenile.'

'What?'

'Well, *Mr du Plessis is hot.*' He laughs. 'Honestly, I thought it was just a stupid thing to do but the school made a big thing about it. Mentioned objectification of teachers at an assembly. Next thing I know, there's a witch-hunt for who wrote it. When the student was caught and questioned about it, she said that I was flirty with one of the students. She said there was a rumour I'd hooked up with the student too. That there was a relationship between us. After that, everything went out of control.'

'You're telling me that was a lie?'

His eyes are fixed on me. My adrenaline is fading, replaced by a trembling fatigue and a chill to my bones. I feel I could collapse but I'm not out of the woods yet. I don't know what he wants.

'You think I'd confess like this if there was any chance it's true? It derailed my life. To have that accusation levelled at me.'

'Who did they say you'd hooked up with?'

'Elizabeth Primrose,' he says. 'I get it, we were friendly. Both expats. She was new, some of the other girls didn't like her – she was pretty, you see, and had that accent. It turned out the rumour started because she'd told someone she was into an older guy but she couldn't say who.'

Bill. 'So you left, just like that?'

'It turns out she had been getting these notes – who knows where they were coming from, but they put two and two together and blamed me. Lots of pressure from the parents.'

'They fired you?'

'If they did, I might have had some legal recourse. No, the principal gave me a redundancy,' he says. 'They forced me out. Word spread. I'd been fired because I was sexually harassing a student. Parents speculated, probably hearing rumours from their kids.'

'How long had you been at the school?'

'A few months,' he says. 'I started in the first term and was let go in June. I had to sign an NDA and I got the remainder of my year's pay as redundancy, but I had to move out of the house. Obviously, if anything came out it would tarnish the reputation of the school, and it was clear a scandal was brewing.'

'Why did you stay in Cambridge? Why not leave?'

'I did leave, for a while. But I never taught again. I was a labourer, mostly, until my back couldn't take that either. That's when I started driving cabs.'

'And came back here?' I ask.

'Yeah, I came back a year or so ago. I liked this town, despite what happened to me. I started over. I have Alison, that's my wife . . . we have a good life, we're happy.'

'So why keep this from me? Why drive me around without telling me your connection to the case?'

'I'm a taxi driver and you were a fare. It's good money, good work. And I knew if you found out, I'd end up on your podcast. Alison's been on my case, she wanted me to tell you. I said I would but I had to pick my moment, and to be honest I had to make sure I could trust you not to just sensationalise what I went through. It took me a long time to get past it, almost no one in town remembers me from then and I want to keep it that way. I never thought about all this clearing my name until you mentioned Elle's journal, just now. I thought maybe it would prove that I had nothing to do with it.'

He lets a breath out slowly.

'Some ex-students recognised me at the pub. They didn't bring it up, but I could tell they were thinking it.'

The local girls, the hen's party. They would all be about Elizabeth's age. He didn't want to come in at Koenig's house, which now makes sense. He might have been recognised. Dean goes to the driver's door of the car, opens it.

'I didn't mean to scare you. You scratched me and you had this look on your face.' He puts one foot inside, he reaches in, pulls his hand out holding my phone.

'Just do me a favour,' he says. 'Let me finish reading it.'

I nod. 'I will. That's fair. But, Dean, I'm reading it first. If what you say is true, and you never did anything to Elizabeth, then you've got nothing to worry about. I'll send the photos of the pages to you afterwards. I promise.'

He stands there in the dark for a few awkward moments, his eyes on the phone. Then he hands it to me. 'Okay,' he says. 'I trust you.'

'It's the least you can do, considering you just scared me half to death,' I say.

'Oh yeah, I'm sorry about that, really,' he says. 'Come on then. I'll drop you back.'

I'm still shaking but I don't really have a choice. Dean du Plessis was the name on the card he gave me. He didn't try to hide his identity at all. He's not the real Tate. He's not the man who killed that family. I go to the passenger door and get in the car. Dean's face is contorted in a grimace and his arms are out straight before him on the wheel.

'Shit, I'm sorry,' he says again. 'I was just desperate to see what was in the journal.'

'It's okay,' I say. 'I was scared, and I jumped to a conclusion I shouldn't have. Now I'm just embarrassed.'

Fucking TK, I think, *planting that seed.* Jesus.

'There's nothing to be embarrassed about. Even I was scared. I wanted to tell you who I was and what I knew. I just *needed* to see what Elle wrote.'

I see mud on his elbow, look down and see it on the knees of my jeans; my back is still wet with sweat and probably the dew from the ground.

'I understand,' I say. And I do. 'For the record, I think you would have been a great teacher.'

He gives a tired smile, then we head off.

TK

THE TRIGGER SHIFTS. I brace for the blast . . . but there's nothing. No sound, just laughter. With a falling sense of shock, I realise the gun is not loaded. Michael is standing there. He kneels down, brings his face inches from the barrel of the gun. I pull the trigger once more. Nothing. I feel weak. I glance to Fleur.

'I didn't think you had it in you,' he says, laughter still in his voice. 'It's not so easy to kill, but you . . . you really would have done it.' He shows his canines with the last syllable. Then he reaches for the gun.

I pull it back, swing it like a club. An arm flies up to block it. Too late. It strikes the side of his skull with a sickly crack. My grip loosens at contact, the gun drops. I barge through him, knocking him down. Fleur goes to him. *The gun.* I turn back and reach for the barrel, it's safer in my hands, but Michael is on his knees, gripping it to his chest.

Fleur leans forward, her teeth cutting into my fingers. I cry out, feel something pop in my knuckle and fall back. He has the gun but it's not loaded . . . yet. He says something in French. I scramble back, my feet failing to gain purchase. Eventually I right myself.

Go. An imperative, louder than my heart, louder than the bang of the door as I slam it behind me. *Go.* The dark night opens out ahead of me as my feet slap the earth. I sprint hard until I hit a fence and tumble over it. I get up and keep going. The road is not so far. Turning back, I see a shadow pass before the rectangle of bright light from the door. Then another. They're both coming out now, hunting me.

I keep going, sprinting in the direction of the road, passing through a thin copse of trees. Cows clear a path, shifting listlessly away from me.

'Stop,' his booming voice echoes over the farm.

Movement in my peripheral. My heart leaps. More cows. I keep running. Then I hit another fence, this one wooden. A split-rail gate near the road's edge. I think about the gun and the simple fact that bullets travel faster than sound. *I'll feel it before I hear it.* It's not a comforting thought but I know if they shoot, I won't have any time to duck or get down. I throw myself up over the top rail and roll when I land, falling into the ditch. Springing back to my feet, I get up onto the gravel and continue sprinting. An old, tree-lined carriageway runs in both directions; it won't take long to get to the main road. It can't have been more than a few hundred metres. I hear an engine, my heart is electric. Someone is coming. Help is on the way.

Headlights swing out over the paddock – I see that it's a truck, but it's coming up behind me, where I've just run from. It's them. Fleur, Tate. No, not Tate, Michael. They killed the family and they know I know.

The car turns onto the road behind me. I'm almost there. Traffic won't be far – I'll wave down a passing car. I'll climb in, insist they call the police. I'll escape.

They're closing in. The truck's engine roars. I dive from the road. They fly pass and gravel flings as the truck slides to a halt. I can't run back and they've blocked the path to the main road. I look out into the paddocks; there's no hope for me there. The light has all but drained from the sky.

But . . . headlights coming the other way now. Someone has turned off the main road. I jump up, wave my arms.

Michael is out of the cabin, no rifle in hand. Fleur climbs out next.

The car slows. I run to the passenger side, knock on the glass. The window comes down.

Michael and Fleur crunch toward us along the gravel.

'Police,' I say. 'I need police right now.'

A blank expression on the old man's face.

'Please!' I yell. I point back at Fleur and Michael, who approach, both smiling, hands raised in a conciliatory pose.

'Bonsoir,' Fleur says.

The man behind the wheel leans over out the window, to hear her better, eyeing me with suspicion. I recognise a word. *Gendarme.* Police.

Fleur shakes her head, makes a mock exhausted face and continues speaking. Michael chips in now, bringing his finger up near his temple. There's dried blood beneath his nose.

'Gendarme!' I say. 'Gendarme!'

Now the man smiles and my heart freezes. He turns back to Fleur and Michael, says a few more words before pushing his car into gear.

'No,' I say, running beside it, hands beating against the roof. 'No, wait! Help me! Help me!'

'Police,' Fleur says. Then she speaks to Michael in French. He marches toward the truck. I turn and start to run again.

The engine starts once more. I sprint, my feet slipping on the gravel. I imagine a bullet tearing through my spine, exploding out of my chest. I imagine my body crushed under the weight of the truck.

The headlights find me. I hit a bend where the road cuts through a hill. I cross, racing to the other side, sliding on the stones. The truck is there, a flash of light. There's a screech and a thump. My torso instantly numbs. The ground, the sky, whirling. I'm weightless until the earth comes at me, slams hard into my shoulder. I bounce, tumbling down into a ditch. When I look up, I see the truck, the door open.

Fleur is screaming, Michael responds. They're arguing.

I drag my numb, hopeless body away. This is it. I can't run anymore. I will die here in this ditch.

Amelia.

I think of my daughter. I see her face, the way she beams when she sees me. *Get up.* But I can't, my body won't respond to my brain. I left Amelia for Bill and lost everything. The press of hot tears at the back of my eyes, a knot in my throat.

They walk toward me.

SLOANE

AFTER HALF AN hour of near silence, Dean pulls in at the motel and brings me right up to the door.

'Thanks,' I say to him.

'Do you still need me?' he says. 'I mean, after tonight . . .'

'Go get some sleep. I'll let you know in the morning.'

I let myself into my room and collapse onto the bed. I think about Chet. I realise why he hid the journal. He got rid of it, burying all the family's secrets, perhaps naïvely thinking it might make them disappear. He put it somewhere no one would find it but not somewhere it would be gone forever. He buried the journal because he thought it would protect his mother from whatever had happened between Fleur and Simon. He buried it so Simon wouldn't find out about his sister's crush on Bill. What else is hidden in those journal pages?

I pull my phone out of my pocket and read the next entry.

Daddy doesn't know what I know. That Fleur has been sneaking off with someone. I see her some nights, leaving the cottage, walking down to the front gate then disappearing with someone in a car. In the middle of the night, I heard the cottage door open. I rushed down the stairs to the front of the house, I looked through the window down toward the gate and saw him standing there. Tate. I thought I saw him before but now I know, I'm certain it's him. I know what Daddy said about him having left the country, but he hasn't. He's not in the UK. He never left. He was always close by. And Fleur is sneaking out to see him. What are they doing together ... what are they going to do?

I flip to the next image, the ink is dark and angry, the handwriting messy.

It was raining and Fleur was running late so MK offered me a ride home and I said yes. I texted Mum and told her, she said it would be fine. Then he stopped on a quiet road, he reached over and touched me in his car. He said the most awful things to me and kissed me on the lips. I was frozen. I didn't know what to do, I couldn't move or speak. My breath was so loud. He has been in our house, he knows it well. He knows which room is mine. He's been leaving me the notes. It's been him. This is our secret, he said, you understand? When he dropped me home, I leapt out and ran up the driveway. I didn't know what to do, who to tell. I'm terrified. I don't want to go to school. I don't want to be near him.

Oh Elizabeth, I think. I feel breathless with second-hand anxiety and anger at MK. Another entry.

Mummy and Daddy are making me go back to school. They think I'm just homesick, depressed, hormonal.

And with only half a year left at school, it's the best place to be. So I went back and I knew it was a bad idea. I can barely leave my room, barely get out of bed, barely get dressed. I hate him and I feel so scared, so useless. Why did he do it to me? What did I do to bring this attention? He told me I am his now, that I can trust him. Now I hide in class, too scared to leave. Why me? Why me? Why me? Why me? I want to talk to someone, maybe Bill would know what to do. Maybe Bill could help?

That's it. The last entry. No one can see this except those who *need* to see it. I shouldn't see it and I hate the fact I've trespassed into this girl's mind, this young woman's nightmare. But there is a clue here, something that will definitely help to clear Dean's name . . . something that might even point to the truth of what happened that night. I think about it until, eventually, in the wee hours, I sleep.

It's after eleven when I wake. I'm still tired and shaken from last night but there's renewed vigour too. I could take a day off, catch up on my notes, my interviews – but then again, I have that taste in my mouth, a hound with the scent of blood. This is why I do what I do. The notes are a new mystery, one that was supposed to be solved long ago.

I roll out of bed, shower, dress. I make a quick video call to Esteban and Tara, fill them in. We all agree, we are going to proceed. It's time for them to join me here in New Zealand. We've locked in the case for the next series of the podcast.

Then I call the only contact I have who was a student at St Luke's: the daughter of Andrew Mears, the gas technician, my fangirl. I keep thinking. *MK.* I rack my brains.

'Hello?' she answers after one ring.

'Hi Bec,' I say. 'It's Sloane Abbott here.'

A long pause. 'Sloane Abbott. Oh my God, really?'

'I spoke with your da—'

'I know who you are. I *love* your podcasts.'

'Really?'

'Oh, I'm such a big fan. Dad said you might call but I thought he was pulling my leg.'

'No,' I say. 'Not pulling your leg. I hope I'm not imposing but your dad mentioned you might be happy to chat with me about your time at St Luke's.'

'Of course, yes.'

I find myself smiling. 'Great, when are you free?'

'Now. Or . . . whenever. Whatever works. I just have to fit it around work. I can come to you.'

'No, I'll come to you. I just need to pick up a car,' I say. 'Otherwise, my day's clear. What about, say, twelve noon?'

'That'd be great. I'm so excited to meet you.'

I check out – today I move to a much nicer hotel in Cambridge. I farewell Dean as he drops me off at the airport and I promise to clear his name, and he promises to give me an interview when that happens.

It takes fifteen minutes of paperwork to get the new vehicle then I drive it back to town. Tara arrives tonight and the real work will begin. This, I assume, will be my final solo interview.

It turns out Bec lives walking distance from town in a small flat with her husband, her six-year-old daughter, two cats and a German shepherd that definitely does not respect personal boundaries. Bec is also just as starstruck and lovely as she seemed on the phone.

'Can I hug you?' she says when I arrive. Her dog sniffs at me constantly.

'Sure,' I say, smiling.

We hug. It's long and warm and when she lets go, she says, 'Can I take a selfie?'

'Yeah, okay.' This is uncommon but not unwelcome. I try to keep a neutral expression as she holds her phone out and snaps a pic.

'Alright, where do you want to sit?'

'Here's fine,' I say, nodding at the couches in the loungeroom. I open my recorder app as the German shepherd sniffs my heels and knees, and licks my hands.

'Sarg!' she growls. 'Sorry, he likes you. I'll put him outside.'

We get the preliminaries out of the way. On record, she's more nervous, but I get her talking. She introduces herself, tells me about the school before and after the murders.

'It's all so clear in my head, you know? I just see the hearse passing through the school gates, the silence over the grounds. Some of the boys performed a haka. Nothing much was the same at school after that.'

'A dark cloud was hanging over everything, I imagine.'

'Yeah, that's what it was like. I was a few years younger than Elle but I always liked her. We didn't talk or anything but she just had good energy. She was really pretty; boys liked her, you could tell. And then, well . . .' she exhales, 'just like that, she lost her family. I can't even imagine. Sorry.' She wipes her eyes, takes a big breath. 'It was just hard. Things changed. Dad didn't let me go to parties, everyone was like that after. Even though Bill Kareama was arrested, everyone was just spooked.'

I look around the room, see the pictures of Bec's young family. Her daughter through the years – first a baby with a gummy smile, then a toddler, then suddenly the girl in a school uniform, showing her baby-toothed grin.

'We kind of grew closer as a community but also more distant. Like, we formed our own clusters as families, the only people we could trust. I don't know . . . does that make sense? Sorry.'

'No, that makes sense,' I say, nodding. 'I want to ask about something that happened in the lead-up to the stabbings. Someone was leaving notes. Explicit notes in—'

'Oh, no, that was after,' she says, frowning. 'Long after the murders. I think it was one of the boys.'

'The boys?'

'Yeah, I can't remember what happened. All I know is there's no way anyone would get away with it in this day and age. But the notes thing happened long after the murders, from memory. It was someone in my year.'

'After? Wait, what are you talking about?'

'I mean, it happened for a year or two, until maybe Year 11 or 12. Then I think it stopped. I didn't really know the girls well.'

'The girls?' I say. This isn't making any sense.

'Two exchange students and a boarder at the school. They were receiving these horrible notes. One of the girls, she was from Korea. She left and there was an investigation.'

Of course. There's always a pattern of behaviour. If predators get away with it, they'll keep doing. 'When did it stop, did you say?'

'Year 11 or 12.'

'What year, though? 2011?'

She looks up, her head oscillates side to side as if counting.

'Yeah,' she says, one side of her mouth rising. 'It would have been around then.'

The room seems to shift around me. It wasn't Dean du Plessis, I already sensed that, but he could easily prove he wasn't even in town when this was happening.

'Sorry,' she says. 'Are you okay?'

2011. A conversation comes back to me. *I finished up in 2011.* Mooks – his last name is the same as Bill's: Kareama. *MK.* It was someone who knew the house. He never said why he left his job at the school but he did. He was there when Elizabeth was there.

As groundskeeper, he had access to buildings, the change rooms. He was there at all hours. And he knew Elizabeth, he was probably friendly with her when he worked at the house. She would have accepted a ride home from him. *Mooks.* Could he have framed his nephew? Maybe even got him the job at the house to set him up?

I clear my throat and I finish the interview as best I can, asking questions about the school, Bec's life since then and how the murders affected her. We talk about the town too but my mind is elsewhere. I'm going through the motions, already planning the next steps.

Afterward, I drive to the only place I can think of for answers. What if they discovered it was Mooks and he was pushed out just how Dean had been? Terrence Koenig seemed hellbent on protecting the school's reputation, catching and killing scandals.

'Sloane?' he says through the intercom.

'Hi,' I say. 'If you've got a minute, I wanted to talk to you about the old groundskeeper at the school. Mooks.'

'Sure. I guess we can chat. I've got to head out shortly but come on up.'

The gate groans open and I pull the car in, park on a verge. I hope he doesn't mind, but I am not taking any chances.

The door opens and, despite the warmth of the sun on my back, I'm chilled once more by the house and what I know happened here. I see the crime-scene photos overlaying the beautiful home before me.

'Come, come, grab a seat,' he says. I see a plate with half a sandwich, a cup of tea and the newspaper open at the quick crossword. More or less my dad's daily ritual. 'Remember these?' he says, patting the newspaper. 'A relic from the pre-internet age.'

'I'm probably not as young as you seem to think,' I say with a smile.

'Anyway, how is it all coming along?' he says as I sit down.

'Good, actually. Good. I know you don't want to record but I'll ask again.'

He smiles, shakes his head. 'So you want to talk about the school and this groundskeeper?'

'I do,' I say.

'Well, you've got me for five minutes before I have to head out and meet Karen.'

'Let me get to the point then. Mooks, the groundskeeper. I believe he was the one sending notes to Elizabeth. I think he was upset about being fired by her father and set out to terrorise her.'

His face doesn't change. 'Right, you think we got it wrong with the PE teacher?'

'We found her journal and I spoke to another ex-student. The notes continued after the PE teacher, Dean du Plessis, left. I'm told a girl actually left the school as a result of notes she was receiving.'

'And have you spoken to this girl?'

'Not yet but I plan to.'

He clears his throat. 'I suppose it's possible, but unlikely. I didn't receive any further complaints from any students.'

'Not one?'

He shakes his head. 'Not one, no complaints. Nothing.'

'They started soon after Mooks joined the school and ended when he left.'

'If you're certain,' he says. 'And who told you this?'

'I can't reveal my source but I can say it was a former student.'

'Ah.'

'What does that mean?'

'Well, maybe this former student wants to be part of your podcast and came up with this story. I took the care of our students seriously. I don't know if I believe there was harassment happening under my nose—'

'No, but not everyone is going to talk about it.'

His vintage is showing now. Victims of abuse seldom come forward; he should know this, but then again, I'm unsurprised he doesn't.

'You don't recall Mooks being untoward, creepy or displaying any unusual behaviour?'

He looks down at the crossword – there's one word missing. Now he takes a bite of his sandwich. He chews and swallows. He holds the pen, fills in the letters. Then closes the paper. 'Mooks was a strange man and I think if this girl is telling the truth, he's probably your guy. But it's all ancient history now.'

I'm still staring at his hand, holding the pen. My heart is pounding.

'You visited this house, when they lived here?' I say.

He nods. 'I did. Look, we can chat again another day.' He turns his wrist, checks his watch. 'But it's a serious accusation and I don't think sullying the school's reputation over rumours is fair. Sometimes,' he continues, 'nuance is lost with exchange students, a difference in culture, and English often being their second language, well, that doesn't help.'

I'm fixated on his lips, the tiny bit of spittle on the edge. *Exchange students?* He's still talking.

'A boy might have a crush and pass a note and it comes across as inappropriate.'

Again, I look at his hand. The pen is in his left hand. He worked at the school, he had access to all of the rooms, the students. A stone lodges in my throat.

'Exchange students,' I say. 'I didn't mention any of the girls were exchange students.'

Everything slows down, seems to hang motionless, weightless, suspended in this room as if in space. I understand, without the need for a single thought, that I am in danger. That I need to get out. We know, both of us, what is about to happen. I feel the balls of my feet pressing against the floor. I press my hands flat to the table.

A burgundy hue comes out in his cheeks. 'Oh, I thought you said . . .' he trails off. 'Well, maybe I do remember there was something. Yes, that's right.' He stands. My body is tense, like a spring that might fly away. I stand.

'You knew about the heating from Andrew, your wife's second cousin,' I say. 'You'd been to the house before. Your old property, you said it wasn't far.'

He gives a huff of laughter. 'What are you saying?'

MK, I say to myself. *Mr Koenig.* It's him. I shake my head. He knows.

'I better go—'

His hands fly up. An iron grip on my throat, forcing me back, blocking the air. The table tips, everything falls. The chair clatters against the floor. The scream doesn't escape. I see red, feel my throat closing under his strong grip. I kick out. We both tumble to the ground. Tinsel spreads in my vision. My eyes blur. I try to scream again but he squeezes tighter, and only a hiss comes out. Black spots in my vision.

I raise my knee into his groin but it does nothing to loosen his hold; he just presses himself harder. I kick and claw but he's stronger than me. I feel dizzy. My hands fly out desperately and I scratch at his face. I'm fading. *Leave a mark, scrape some DNA.* No, no, this isn't how it ends. I'm not going to die. *You're not dead. Fight.* I reach for his eyes with my thumbs but he just pushes harder, his fingers digging into my throat. I can't quite reach. The room dims. Darkness closes over. I reach back blindly. Feel something hard, his teacup. I grip it and swing. It strikes the side of his head, shattering in my hand. Blood starts. His grip loosens. I roll over, drag myself up, gasping. His hand reaches, catches my ankle. I kick, feel my heel crunch his nose. Then I find my feet. I run. The stairs are ahead. My heart racing. *Where can I go? Shit.* I'm going up the steps, toward the bedrooms. *Why did I come up here?* I'm trapped. I hear him coming. I run down the hall and slip into a room. Elizabeth's room. His footsteps slow at the top of the stairs.

'Sloane,' I hear him say. 'Look, it's a misunderstanding.'

I stay silent, creeping toward the window. I could open it and jump. Or scream. If I scream, he finds me instantly. *He will find you eventually.* I hear a door open out in the hallway.

'Not in here,' he says, closing the door. 'I used to play hide-and-seek with my boys. Our old house was much smaller – still, they could find places to tuck themselves into. It's amazing how small they could get when they wanted to squeeze into a cupboard or behind a piece of furniture. I'd always find them, though.'

His demeanour is unchanged, as if he is used to this. My phone – it's downstairs. *Shit.* I could run for the stairs. He's coming closer.

'Sloane, where are you?'

He got away with the Primrose stabbings. Does he believe he will get away with this? My phone has me located here, my DNA is in the house, he is cut, scratched. He has the house, the book about the murder. He relives it in his mind, proud of getting away with it. This old mansion is his trophy. And Karen, she didn't want me here. She must know.

My heart is pounding as he comes along the hallway. Another door thrown open. As if reading my mind, Koenig starts talking again. 'Karen is a good, steady woman. She does what she's told. We're traditional. We do what needs to be done for the family, for my sons. She didn't know exactly what happened but she probably suspected something. The good thing is the police never checked my alibi, they never needed to. No one ever thinks to look at the trusted school principal.'

I reach for the window now. Begin easing it up slowly. The door rattles with the change in air pressure.

He's heard. He's coming. I push the window open now. Turn and slide out, gripping the edge. The door flings open, he sprints forward, knife in hand.

I look down, it's three metres at least. No choice. I let go.

TK

'WHAT ARE YOU going to do to me?'

'Fleur wants to take you to the police station, to press charges.'

'What?' I say, too confused to feel any relief. 'Me? Charges for what?'

'You attacked me,' he says. 'You turned up at our house under false pretences. You aimed a gun at me and pulled the trigger. You slammed it into my head.'

'What about the false imprisonment? What about the threats?'

'What threats?' he says. Is he messing with me? 'I am taking you to a hospital, not the police. Fleur has your phone, which we will give you. We will drop your car off and your bag, and you will never contact us again.'

This is a trick, it has to be. Fleur is in the back seat beside me. The parts of my body that are not completely numb are aching; I think my arm is probably broken.

'Don't even think about trying anything,' Michael says. 'You may be big and strong but it won't end well for you.'

'You're taking me to the hospital?'

'Yes.'

'But you hit me?'

'You ran onto the road – what did you expect?' There's anger in his voice again. A long pause. 'We were trying to stop you from running off, doing something stupid. Plus you had just attacked me.'

'And you tried to shoot him,' Fleur adds. 'You never told the truth, why you came.'

'I just wanted to know about your time in the house. I wanted you to verify a few details about Bill and I wanted to tell you. I was going to tell you.'

'You didn't know we were together?' Fleur says. 'Michael and me?'

'No,' I say.

'But you knew he used a false name – we are obviously worried about the repercussions of that. Even now. People are crazy, they search for me, they think I did it – and you sneak into our home like this.'

'I'm sorry,' I say. The tide feels like it has turned, but I don't trust them. How could I after everything?

'I had no idea the family were dead until he dropped me back that night. Yes, he tracked them down in New Zealand. Yes, he used a fake name to get close; maybe he planned to hurt Simon. But he didn't do it,' she says. 'It's not so easy to just hurt someone.'

'I lost my hate when I met Fleur,' Michael says. 'I fell for her pretty quickly. I knew if I hurt Simon, I could lose her. Because of Fleur, I saw a future where I could be happy again.'

'You didn't know each other before?'

'No,' Fleur says. 'We met at the house. We had common ground instantly, a disdain for the family. I learned he was not really who he claimed he was. He is younger, of course, but he had an old soul. He had lived a hard life. Like me.'

'Right,' I say, my head still spinning.

'The police were not so good maybe in this case, but they were good enough to check my alibi,' she says. 'CCTV at the hotel too. One entrance – there was no way for us to leave and get back.

Michael moved to Hamilton but he would come to Cambridge to pick me up.'

The police ruled her out early, of course they checked. It wasn't just Michael's word. They would have spoken to the hotel staff too.

'And the heating?'

I watch Fleur's face in the near dark of the car. She doesn't give anything away. A completely neutral expression.

'Heating?'

'At the house – it was tampered with. It was sending carbon monoxide into the bedrooms.'

Fleur is either an Oscar-worthy actress or really doesn't know anything about it. I finally feel like I can breathe again as the car pulls up outside of the hospital.

'Go on,' she says. 'Get out. We will be back with your things.'

I do as they say. My leg barely bends and my hip explodes with pain after every step, but despite our chat, they're not about to help me any more than they need to.

SLOANE

SEARING PAIN IN my left ankle and left elbow. There's no feeling in my hip. My head pulses, vision blurred. The drop turned the grass into concrete. Looking up, I see him in the window, craning out. I squint. Then he's gone. He's coming. I'm dead. No. *Run, Sloane. Get up and run.*

This man is a killer. *Just get through the pain. Go.* The car keys are in my pocket. He's behind me, running on the back lawn. I hobble, dragging my damaged ankle toward the front of the house. I reach for the keys, press the button to unlock the car.

I hear him coming. I get the door opened. Slip in. Slam it closed. He flies at me. I hit the locks as he pulls the door handle. I start the car. He strikes the window, once, twice. The third time he hits it, the window smashes. His fist flies through, in front of my face. I push the car into gear and press the accelerator as hard as I can, his hand gripping my shirt front. I see a knife then . . . the shirt tightens, tears. He releases, falls, a thump. I swing the car around down toward the gate. It won't open. It should open automatically. Maybe he's locked it. I scream for help. Someone must have heard me. In the rear-view mirror, I see him lying there. He starts to roll over. My phone. I swing the car back around now, drive toward the house. He's still on the ground. I fly past him in the car, driving over garden beds, slamming the brakes on near the door. Inside, I limp through the loungeroom to the dining room. My phone is there, on the floor near the table. I take it and dial emergency services.

'Hi,' I say down the phone. 'Please, he's trying to kill me. I'm at the Primrose murder house.'

'Slow down,' the voice says. 'Where are you exactly?'

Ah, what's the street address?

'You've got to hurry. I don't know the road. It's the Primrose house in Cambridge,' I say, talking as I move toward the back door and onto the lawn. My ankle crunches with each step. 'He has a knife.'

'Okay,' she says. 'Who has a knife?'

'Terrence Koenig. Please, hurry.'

'Are you safe now?'

'No,' I say. 'He's here. He's chasing me.'

'I need you to find a safe place. Stay on the line if you can.'

'Okay,' I say, breathless.

I don't look back. I leave through the back doors, hopping on one leg over the patch of land that was once the pool. I continue to the back of the block.

'Police are on their way.'

'I'm just passing through a back gate.' I say down the phone. It's a building site on the other side. I turn back. He's there, coming across the lawn.

'Help!' I scream. 'Help!' I move through the property, stumbling. Doing everything I can to keep going.

'I'm here,' the operator says.

'There are houses. I'm on another street.'

Turning back again, I see him coming through the gate.

I get to the road, my body torn with pain.

Sirens in the distance. They're coming closer. I don't look back again, I just keep going. The sirens are getting louder and louder. Feet clapping on the road behind me. I take one glance. He's gaining.

An engine revving, the sirens are close. Then I see them. A cop car. It flies around the corner, sliding to a stop beside me. Doors swing outward.

'Please,' I say. 'Please stop him.'

They draw their Tasers and I get into the police car behind them. He can't get me here. *I'm safe.* I repeat this mantra over and over as the armed offenders squad arrive. Someone tells me I'm safe. They repeat it, they hold me. More cop cars.

From the back of the police car, through the steel grille and the glass of the windscreen, I can see him, Terrence Koenig, on the road, his hands on his head. The police swarm him.

TK

AMELIA RUSHES INTO my arms at arrivals. I squeeze her with my one good arm – my other is cast in plaster, held in a sling. I push my nose into her hair and breathe her in. Mum hugs me next and Dad joins in, his hand rubbing the back of my head like I'm just a boy again.

'Flight okay?' Dad says.

I nod, smile – properly, involuntarily, for the first time in what feels like years – and laugh. He does too. 'It was alright, Dad.'

'What?' Amelia says. 'Why are they laughing?'

'They're mad,' Mum says. 'Both of them.'

Dad takes my duffel bag and I lift Amelia up despite the pain of it and hold her tight.

Over the next hour, I hear from Sloane, and read my emails. I catch up on everything I've missed. The journal, Terrence Koenig. Sloane saving herself. Terrence's wife admitting her husband disappeared from their home on the night of the murders.

Amelia keeps asking questions about my trip. I leave out the details that might scare her most. My mind jags on certain moments, like skin on barbed wire. The moment the car hit me – when I was certain I was dead and my mind went to her.

It was a protective instinct that drove Michael and Fleur to lock me in that room – they just wanted to protect what they have, their privacy, a normal life in spite of everything. They wanted to scare me, to keep me from coming back.

The following evening, I meet Sloane for dinner. She's outside the restaurant, her mobile phone wedged between her ear and her shoulder. She's wearing a moonboot on her left leg but, other than that, she looks adequately glamorous for this part of the city. I wait for her to notice me before approaching.

'It's just the *right* thing to do,' I hear her say.

She turns and sees me, waves. Despite the make-up, I can still see a ring of bruise on her neck.

'Alright, I'll record it in the morning. We can schedule socials to go out tomorrow night.'

She hangs up and shoves her phone deep into her bag and hobbles toward me.

'You look a bit worse for wear,' she says. Her eyes go to my arm then back to my face.

'Likewise.'

'The walking wounded. Come on, let's go inside.'

'I wasn't eavesdropping.'

'But you heard everything I said? It was my producer,' she says.

'You're still doing the podcast, right?' I say.

'Definitely,' she says. 'But we can get to that. Why don't we chat about something other than the case?'

I reach for the door and open it for her. 'What use am I to you if I'm not talking about the case?'

When she smiles, it hits her eyes. She clicks her tongue. 'I'm sure we can find something else to chat about, TK,' she says, stepping into the restaurant.

SLOANE

Legacy: 17 Years Later with Tara Hiku.

'Episode Zero – An important message from your former host'

In 2017, while working for *The Age* newspaper in Melbourne, Australia, on the tenth anniversary of the McDuffy murders in Melbourne's inner east, I was tasked with writing 300 words on the crimes. A former police officer had murdered three young women and, for two years, the city was on edge. Then came a tip-off, and Ed McDuffy was investigated, and consequently arrested and charged. When I filed my copy, I was asked to make some edits. My editor wanted me to focus more on the *legacy* of the murderer and less on the victims. In my own investigations, I'd discovered new information about the women who died. I learnt how their families had changed over the years. And the real legacy of the crime was not only the Royal Commission into police conduct. It was not only the Safer Streets initiative, the things my editor wanted me to write about. The real legacy is both societal *and* personal. The legacy we never seemed to focus on was the lives shattered by these crimes. We neglected the holes left behind where Jane Moore, Davina Turner and Anna Tivoli would have otherwise been. I decided there was too much here that was left unsaid. So, with a voice recorder and some blind ambition, I set out to record the first season of *Legacy*.

For the next six years, I would investigate four further crimes, two of which were unsolved cold cases. During this time, we brought about additional charges to a convicted rapist and murderer, along with bringing to trial a case against Dan Mayer, former rugby league star whose wife's disappearance had gone unsolved.

It wasn't until recently that I began to think about my own legacy, my own achievements. I discovered a blind spot and so my team and I decided it was time to investigate a case that had been on our radar for some years.

By now, you may have discovered in the news and social media my own personal entanglement with this case, and the consequent arrest and charges of the alleged murderer. However, you may not have the full story – all the facts and moving parts that make this case both so unique and so common for people like Bill Kareama. This season has many surprises, twists and turns. This case is about the victims, the Primrose family, but also another victim, Bill Kareama, the man who, despite seventeen years of insisting his innocence, was left to rot in prison. Bill was arrested and charged with little investigation into other potential suspects, his appeal was denied and the inconsistencies in his case were overlooked. The entire apparatus of the justice system failed at every step to ensure that Bill had the things we expect from a fair and just society: the presumption of innocence until proven guilty, a fair trial with competent legal representation and an unbiased police investigation.

I believe sunlight is the best disinfectant. I believe justice should be blind. I thought, by investigating this case, I could be part of the solution, but soon realised I was coming in as a saviour and not an ally. As I investigated, there were things I couldn't understand, context I neglected. I realised I wasn't the right person to tell this story.

Someone else saw this world with so much more clarity than I ever could. That's why it is with a tinge of sadness but endless optimism and pride that I am announcing I will be stepping down from my role as your host for *Legacy* season five. Your new host, my former assistant, Tara Hiku, is a wahine Māori who now resides in Melbourne. Tara's brilliant insights singlehandedly unlocked this case, and she was the one who made it all make sense. I couldn't think of a more competent and qualified replacement. She studied journalism, she has a deep interest in the Primrose murders, and she will be using some of my recordings but also making many of her own as she continues her investigation. I will be continuing on as a co-producer behind the scenes, helping Tara adapt to her new role. We can't wait to share with you what we have in store for season five coming very soon.

I pause the recording and check my phone. TK will be here any minute. I put on my coat, grab the swipe card for my hotel room and head downstairs, hobbling along in my moonboot.

Koenig has been charged with attempted murder and assault. He is also being investigated for an historical sex offence. I couldn't quite believe he had exposed himself to the degree that he had – in some ways, he'd led me straight to the smoking gun. But TK explained that it wasn't uncommon for the worst kind of felonious criminals to revisit the scenes of their crimes to relive the experience. TK had a theory about Koenig: he'd wanted to show me the gas heater so that I – and my audience – could see how clever the killer had been, even if we didn't make the connection that it was Koenig. He needed this, because he'd never gotten credit for how calculating he had been. The carbon monoxide almost killed the Primroses, but when that failed, he went a more reliable route. A knife he found in the kitchen, and that knife just so happened to belong to Bill Kareama. I'm told prosecutors will likely commence proceedings against Terrence Koenig for the Primrose stabbings once Bill's release is finalised.

Bill's lawyer, James, TK and I walk into the prison. TK and I take our time getting through security with his cast and my moonboot, but eventually we are on the other side.

We take our seats at a table and, a few moments later, the door opens. Bill appears. He's startled, in his prison uniform and hair clipped short. I imagine him out in the world, the life yet to come for this man who lost everything.

'Bill,' TK says.

'Why am I here?' he says, looking around the room. Then back to TK. 'What happened to your arm?'

I can't help grinning.

'What?' he says. 'What is it?'

'We've got news.'

Bill's eyes dart between us. He lowers himself onto a seat. 'Tell me, James. Just say it.'

'There's no retrial,' the lawyer says.

Bill's eyes fall. He clasps his hands together. He exhales.

'There's no need for one,' TK says in a rush. 'You're coming out, Bill. You're leaving as soon as the paperwork is cleared, which should be any moment now.'

Bill looks to TK first, then to me. 'What do you mean? I'm *leaving*?'

'You're going home. Your conviction has been overturned. If it wasn't for these two, it wouldn't be happening,' James adds.

'What . . . what happened?' he says, his head coming up.

'There's time for that later,' TK says. 'For now, let's get your release processed and get you home. It's only just beginning. You've got your life back.'

TK reaches out to shake Bill's hand, but Bill is still uncertain. Then he stands up, tears in his eyes, and rips TK closer, across the table, in a bear hug. TK's jacket rises up awkwardly around his shoulders. Next, Bill reaches for me, then James, and suddenly we're in a sort of scrum, all leaning over the table while Bill shudders and weeps.

'Sloane recovered something else, Bill. Something I think you should see,' TK says. I feel a sudden heat at the back of my eyes. I know what's coming. 'I'll get you a copy. The original I posted directly to Elizabeth.'

'What is it?'

'It's a letter,' TK says.

'A letter? A letter from who?'

EPILOGUE

Dear future Chester,

You are a man now. I guess you live with flying cars and
robots. You probably forgot all about the time you spent at a
little school in Cambridge, New Zealand. Who knows where you
are and what you are doing? I hope you're the new Tony Hawk
but let's face it, it probably hasn't happened that way. Maybe
you're playing for Blackburn in the premier league? Or maybe
you stuck at chess, became a grandmaster? I just hope that
you're happy. I hope you figured out what you want to do because
I have no idea. Maybe a lawyer?

I should tell you about me in case you've forgotten and left
the twelve-year-old version of yourself in the past. I watch
Yu-Gi-Oh! in the afternoons after school before Daddy gets
home, then I do my homework. Elle and I fight over little things
but she's alright I guess. She's going through a hard time.
I found her journal and that's how I found out about Fleur and
Daddy. I don't know what will happen but I know I will always have

Elle and she will always have me. She cares. She's mean sometimes but she cares about everyone and everything and I hope
she doesn't ever change. It makes me so angry that she's had a
hard year. It makes me even angrier knowing what that man did
to her, how he made her feel. That's why I did it. Last night, I
rode my bike over there, to Mr Koenig's, or MK as Elle calls him.
The man who gave her a ride home that day. He lives near us, not
too far. Daddy had pointed his house out once. I went up and
knocked on the door. I was so scared I was practically shaking.
I told him to leave my sister alone. I told him that I would go to
my Daddy and he would be fired. Then he got this look and I had
to go. I just jumped back on my bike and sped home.

Elle has a crush on Bill, our chef here. Which I guess is
fine. She really likes him, he's a cool guy. Maybe you stayed in
touch with him? I can imagine him running his own restaurant,
something posh or trendy in Soho. I hope you're like him. I hope
you're friendly to everyone, even kids like me. I hope you make an
effort and do what you love. Who knows, maybe he and Elle got
married? Daddy would go mental about that.

I hope you stayed friends with Chris, Sam and Tim from
school. I hope you figured out how to do a Rubik's cube. I wish
I had more to say. I wish I had something really clever or funny.
Mrs Edwards says we should be completely honest. She says it's
important because one day you will look back and be grateful
that you wrote this. She's a nag but maybe she's right. I hope you
are proud of who you became. I hope you made it. I know you did.

See you soon,
Chester.

ACKNOWLEDGEMENTS

AS ALWAYS, MANY thanks to Pippa Masson, Gordon Wise and the team of film and foreign language agents working to get my books into the hands of readers not only in Australia and New Zealand, but around the world.

Thanks also to Rebecca Saunders, Tania Mackenzie-Cooke, Mel Winder, Kate Stephenson, Jackie Tracy, Emily Lighezzolo, Emma Rafferty, Melissa Wilson and to Lyn Yeowart and Doctor Marion Barton. Thanks also to editors Deonie Fiford, Jeremy Sherlock and Rebecca Hamilton.

Thanks to my wife, Paige Pomare, for the endless love and support. Thanks Dad and the rest of my family.

When I write a novel, I tend to write it first, then go back and figure out all the things I got wrong. This book involved trips to London and Edinburgh – I had to go back to Scotland a second time, which (if my wife or the ATO ask) had nothing to do with whisky and everything to do with my dedication to my craft.

On a trip to Cambridge, New Zealand, I discovered how much the place had changed since I was a teenager. I attempted to visit the prison in which Bill is housed and I almost made it to the main building, tailgating my way onto the grounds before I was turned back at a checkpoint. I was rebuffed many times by corrections staff in person, over the phone and via email. Fortunately, I could rely on the firsthand account of Caitlan Kilgour. Without her insights, this book wouldn't be the same.

Doctor Adrian Minson was also a vital resource. Routinely beating me at board games isn't enough for Adi, he also had to point out the myriad ways I was wrong about both stabbing victims and carbon monoxide poisoning. It's always nice to find out where you've misstepped *before* publication as opposed to after.

Finally, thank you to Amanda Knox who pointed me to some extremely useful resources. Her experience within a highly flawed criminal justice system was one of the cases I researched when I set out to write this book. I also studied the wrongful convictions of David Bain, Teina Pora and Alan Hall.

Over a ten-year period, almost 900 cases have been either quashed or sent back to court in New Zealand. Alan Hall received a $4,993,000 payout from the New Zealand government when his conviction was overturned after nineteen years. Many others have received sizable payouts. All of these cases have at least one, but often many, of the following: eyewitness misidentification, false evidence, evidence withheld, coerced or false confession, forensic errors and police misconduct. It has become increasingly clear, to me anyway, that there are serious issues at the heart of the New Zealand criminal justice system and that continuing reform is paramount.

THE WRONG WOMAN

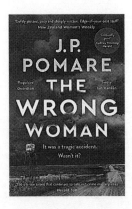

It was a tragic accident, wasn't it?

Reid left the small town of Manson a decade ago after a very public career-ending incident, promising his former Chief of Police boss he'd never return. He made a new life in the city, became a PI and turned his back on the past.

Now, sent by an insurance firm to look into a suspicious car crash, he finds himself back in the place he grew up. As Reid's investigation unfolds, nothing is as it seems and rumours are swirling about the young woman who crashed the car, killing her professor husband, and their connection to a missing student.

Soon Reid finds himself veering away from the job he has been paid to do. Will he jeopardise his new life to take on the town he ran from?

'Keeps readers on their toes from the opening page. His is a rare talent that continues to turn out crime masterpieces' *Herald Sun*

'A twisty small-town PI mystery with a protagonist I didn't want to let go' IAN RANKIN

'Undeniably propulsive. Clever. Satisfying' *The Guardian*

hachette
AUSTRALIA

If you would like to find out more about Hachette Australia,
our authors, upcoming events and new releases, you can visit
our website or our social media channels:

hachette.com.au

HachetteAustralia

HachetteAus